RAVAGED

VAMPIRE AWAKENINGS
BOOK 7

BRENDA K DAVIES

CHAPTER ONE

THE ENDS of the black trench coat brushed his ankles when Aiden shrugged into it. He felt like a walking vampire cliché every time he put the thing on, but it had a lot of places to stash his weapons. It also covered the blood seeping from the gashes on his back and staining his shirt.

The lacerations would heal soon enough. When he pulled the shirt off later, he knew from past experiences some of the material would stick to his wounds. It would take time, and more pain, for the material to work its way out of his flesh, but that fresh pain would help to once again re-center him, for a time at least.

"I can do more for you tonight," Carha purred and fondled his ear.

Aiden recoiled from her touch. She repulsed him almost as much as he repulsed himself these days. "No."

He didn't know why she'd bothered to offer. Every time he came to her, she did the same, and every time he turned her down. He'd already acquired what he wanted from her tonight. Dipping into his pocket, he pulled out a roll of hundreds and threw them on the table. Sex with her would be free, but *no* one would inflict the amount of torture on him Carha did, and for that, she charged a lot.

The money was worth the release she gave him. Or at least it used to be worth it. That release had once lasted a month, then a couple of weeks. Then a week. Now, an hour hadn't passed, and he could already feel the tension creeping back into him. He'd have to find a different way to get some release soon, but it would *not* be with her. Not even he had sunk that low yet.

No. Never so low as to be with Carha. He knew if he did, he wouldn't be himself anymore. He would be a far more twisted version of himself, one he could never come back from.

He'd love nothing more than to walk out of here and never see Carha again, but every time he tried to keep away, he found himself irresistibly drawn back to this place, and Carha. He'd started losing the battle to stay away at an accelerated rate.

"You don't have to pay." She rubbed his ear again.

"I said get off!" he snarled and bared his fangs at her.

She smiled back at him, unfazed by his fangs as she leaned close to offer him a view of her cleavage. Despite his revulsion of her, he found himself growing aroused before he tore his eyes away. He didn't desire her, but he craved sex as much as pain, and he hadn't fucked anyone today. Unlike some of her other clients, he received no sexual release while in this room. This place was strictly about the pain for him.

"I already got off," Carha replied and slid her hands between the legs of what he knew were crotch-less black pants. She'd flashed him more than a few times while she'd been cutting him. Pulling her hand away from herself, she flicked her whip against the ground. Drops of his blood splattered across the floor when they flew off the tip of the whip. "Now I'm offering to get you off too."

Within her green cat-like eyes, he could see the sick twist-edness of her soul. She was not a killer of innocents, he would smell it on her if she were, but she couldn't hide the evil nature within her. If she started killing innocents and turned Savage, he wouldn't be surprised. It shocked him more she hadn't already done exactly that.

Carha's black hair hung in a thick braid over her shoulder. She was one of the most stunning women he'd ever seen with her Jessica Rabbit body and refined features, yet his arousal faded while he gazed at her.

Perhaps she had such an adverse effect on him because, in her eyes, he saw where he was heading. Carha was beautiful, yet twisted. And he came to her once a week to ease his needs. No, now he sought her out more than once a week.

After only making it six days last week, he'd been deter-mined to make it seven days before turning to Carha; he hadn't held out past day five. With the way he'd been descending this past year, and his increased spiral into his viler inclinations since Christmas, he would find himself coming here every day within three months.

But maybe, even if he did have to come here every day, have sex once and sometimes twice a day, as well as feed more than an average vampire, and if he continued to kill Savages, he could keep himself in control. Maybe he wouldn't spiral into the thing he hated the most: the killer vamps who stalked the innocents of this world.

He told himself this and tried to hope it would be true, but he knew eventually he would need more. He *always* needed more. This insatiable, empty pit inside him couldn't be filled no matter how hard he tried.

He should go to Ronan and ask Ronan to kill him now, before he lost complete control and turned into a bloodthirsty monster.

His fingers tore into the flesh of his palms as he turned away from Carha. No, no matter how empty he felt, he would hold out. He may be cracking, but he would *not* break. Not yet anyway. He still had time to find a way to get a handle on this before it became too late for him.

Inhaling a deep breath, his gaze fell on the metal poles sticking up from the concrete ground in the center of the room. A dim red bulb, hanging directly over the poles and the heavy chains attached to them, was the only illumination in the chamber. The thick cuffs dangling from the ends of the chains had never bound his wrists. If they did, he would be able to break free from them, but he would never allow Carha to chain him.

Between those poles, puddles of his blood glistened in the light as it had countless times over the past year and a half he'd been coming to Carha. Near one of the puddles was a drain. The body fluids spilled here were hosed into the drain before the next client entered.

The room sickened him. Two years ago, he never could have pictured himself walking into such a place. Then, he'd stopped aging and everything changed. Now, he couldn't picture how he would survive without the relief Carha's whip gave him.

He wasn't Carha's only client, but she'd once revealed to him that he was the only one she flayed open until even she flinched. He hadn't believed Carha could flinch for any other living creature, but he'd seen her do it for him. It didn't stop her from pulling her hand back and slicing him open as it had the other women he'd gone to before her.

Carha expertly sliced him until his ribs showed through and the blood loss made him unsteady. Earlier, he'd only remained upright by holding the chains while she delivered blow after flesh-rending blow. Only when his legs were about to buckle, and he was dizzy from blood loss, did he ask her to stop. That had been less than half an hour ago, but he already felt stronger. It would be a couple of hours before the world stopped spinning whenever he turned his head too fast.

"I've never seen anyone who can withstand my whip like you," she murmured.

Carha had no idea he was a purebred vampire, and she never would. He wouldn't put it past her to try to use the knowledge to her advantage. The underground ring of vampires Drake had run to capture purebreds—like his sister, Vicky—and feed on them, was mostly eradicated. There were a few stragglers who had helped Drake, but they'd scattered when Drake died. However, there were those out there who would use a pureblooded vampire to their advantage, if they could find a way to do so, and Carha was one of them.

"Soon," she purred when he turned away from his blood and the posts. "You'll be begging to have me."

"That will be the last time I come here," he assured her. Or it would mean he'd lost control and someone like Carha was who he would prefer having sex with. The possibility made him shudder.

"Oh, I doubt that will be the last time," she murmured.

He didn't look back at her as he opened the thick metal door of the soundproof room. He didn't need the door to hide his cries. No matter how deeply Carha cut him, or how often she did it, he'd never screamed. Stepping into the hall, lit by the flame-shaped candles casting shadows over the red carpet, Aiden closed the door behind him.

CHAPTER TWO

HE PULLED his coat tighter around his throat as the blood oozing from his gashes slowed to a trickle. He'd have to change before he met Saxon for their hunt tonight. Otherwise, he would be ringing the dinner bell for the increasing number of killer vamps roaming the streets of Boston. A new threat had started to rise from the Savages, one Ronan and his men were working to take down.

Striding forward, the carpet muffled his steps as he passed the closed doors lining the corridor. Not even his enhanced vampire hearing could detect any sound from the rooms. This hall was a place of hedonism for those who could afford to pay for it.

He'd been in a few of the other rooms, with other women, before moving onto Carha's area. Carha's was the biggest out of all the rooms, but they all had a similar setup. However, each vampire who ruled behind these closed doors did something different with their space.

At the end of the hall, he pulled open another heavy, metal door and stepped into the main club area. Unlike many of the other clubs in Boston, this one didn't pulse with rapid dance music and flashing lights. Bodies didn't pack the dance floor because there was no dance floor. The humans came here to pretend they were vampires; the vamps came to feed on the fools and to indulge their debauchery in the back rooms.

Numerous booths, mostly hidden in shadow, encompassed the club. The only light in the place hung over the bar. It illuminated the bottles lining the twenty-foot-long, glass mirror. Most of the bottles were only liquor, but at either end of the bar were massive jugs that held special, bloody concoctions. Those exclusive mixes sold with far more speed than the regular alcohol did.

A few of the jugs were nothing but straight blood, kept at 98.6 degrees. Usually, no one bothered with the blood; it was mostly for the ambiance, but occasionally a famished vampire would drink some while stalking their prey.

People gulped down their fake bloody mixes, while the vampires sipped at theirs and pursued what they'd come here for, humans. Aiden scented the air as he watched the occupants, but he didn't detect the scent of refuse wafting from the inhabitants.

The sun had just set, so he hadn't been expecting to find any killer vampires here, but he had to be certain before he left. Carha made sure this club remained exclusive, but turned vamps couldn't scent the killers of their kind like a purebred could so she wouldn't know if one walked through the door. He'd encountered a few killers in here before. Carha prohibited killing in her club, but they still came for some of the other decadences she offered.

On the rare occasions he'd scented the killers in here, he'd waited outside to destroy them when they left.

Ronan and his men called the killer vampires amongst them Savages, Aiden had mostly adapted to that, but he and his family had always called them killer vamps, and occasionally he slipped back into that.

He'd better start adapting faster if he was going to be one of Ronan's group, the Defenders. Every day he was getting closer to making it through his training and joining Ronan. It might still be a couple of years before they fully welcomed him into their group, but Lucien had told him he was progressing faster than most and was already way ahead of the curve.

He suspected he'd done so well because he'd gone at his training with a single-minded determination and a sick joy at being able to bestow death on those vampires who deserved it. He needed that outlet to kill. Otherwise, he would go for an innocent.

At one time, joining Ronan's group had been a dream he'd worked tirelessly to achieve. Now, the goal felt as empty and hopeless as the rest of his existence. He'd been confident that training, fighting, and killing would ease this *nothingness* in him, but it was becoming as unfulfilling as everything else that once eased him. All the fighting, bruises, and broken bones endured while training with Ronan and his men had done nothing to curb his hunger for *more*.

He'd tried meditating for a while, but a couple of months ago he'd found himself fantasizing more about tearing a person's throat out and drinking all their blood than focusing on his breathing. He'd stopped afterward.

As time progressed, staying still became the worst thing he could do, so he moved constantly. He hadn't gotten more than a few hours of sleep a night in the past six months because he hated closing his eyes.

He slept only when exhaustion took over.

The smoke of the room stung his eyes, and he blinked against it. Some of the smoke was from cigarettes, as no one in this place obeyed any law set forth by humans. The people here believed the flaunting of rules and health codes was another sign they skirted the edge of danger; the vampires did it because some of them liked to smoke.

The rest of the smoke in the room came from the fog machines in the corner, discreetly hidden within decorative coffins. The music speakers were also concealed in those coffins. The woeful music made him snicker, but the humans ate it up, and they were the main menu for the vampire clientele Carha wanted to attract.

Studying the room, Aiden picked out each of the separate heartbeats and the blood pulsing through the occupants' veins. His fangs pricked, his mouth watered, and his cock stirred as he pictured sinking his fangs into the throats of some of the women here.

Sometimes, after a session with Carha, he would find a woman to take into the second hallway leading away from the main barroom. More soundproof rooms lined that corridor, and each of those rooms held only a bed. The staff changed the sheets every time a couple exited one of the rooms, but he never used the beds.

For him, sex wasn't about touching or love. Like the whip, it was a way to find an escape from himself, if only for a short time. He preferred as little contact with his partners as possible and found standing made that goal easier to achieve.

He became semi-erect as he watched the couples fondling each other, but he would deny himself sex today. He hadn't been able to deny himself the gratification of Carha's whip for a week; he would forgo sex for one *fucking* day.

It would be his penance for the weakness that had propelled him to seek the brutal slices of Carha's whip. He'd lost count of the lashings after twenty-five tonight, but she'd beaten him more than usual before he'd stopped her.

Bowing his head, he ran a hand through his short hair and

tugged at the ends of it. He recalled Ronan's words from almost six years ago now...

"*The beast, the demon, whatever it is you call what lurks within all vampires. In purebreds, it's stronger and more incessant. Upon reaching maturation, it becomes this insatiable, clawing thing inside of us that is only eased by finding our mates or by losing ourselves to the pleasure of the kill. In each of us, this insatiable hunger shows itself in different ways.*

"*Some of us seek out pain, others of us covet copious amounts of blood. Some cannot have enough sex, some lock themselves away from humans, and others give in and kill in order to make it stop. In all purebred males, maturity means three things, they stop aging, their power increases and continues to do so as they age, and they hunger for things so endlessly it nearly drives them mad.*

"*What you will yearn for most after maturity is in you now. You already know you have a penchant for one thing over another, and it doesn't have to be only one thing. Many experience a combination of heightened urges, but there will be one that is more dominant than the others.*"

Aiden hadn't stopped aging at the time Ronan revealed this, yet the words were emblazoned on his mind. Until then, he'd been looking forward to reaching maturity, gaining power like his older brothers had, and finally being able to fight with them again. They'd still wrestled and thrown each other around after Ethan and Ian stopped aging, but he'd known they were holding back with him in a way they never had before. It had *pissed* him off.

After Ronan told them this information, Aiden had spoken with his brothers about their experiences when they stopped aging. Ethan admitted he'd started seeking out pain and blood more. He'd also locked himself away from humans because he'd feared hurting them. Ian occupied his time with an endless array of women. They both agreed they'd sought those things out more *before* they'd matured into purebred, vampire adulthood, but it became far more intense afterward.

After hearing Ronan's words and speaking with his brothers, Aiden found himself no longer looking forward to maturity. He *dreaded* it. Not because he didn't think he could handle craving something more, but because he didn't have a penchant for one thing over another.

Even then, he'd wanted all those things in equal measure. However, his desires then had been nothing compared to the day when he'd opened his eyes and realized he'd become an adult vampire.

From that day forward, he'd craved sex, blood, pain, and death more than he'd ever believed possible. He hadn't locked himself away because he'd known that by joining Ronan's men, he'd have an outlet for his incessant need to see the life fading from another's eyes. If he didn't have the outlet of destroying killer vamps, it would only be a matter of time before he turned on innocent vampires and humans.

A couple of weeks ago, he'd asked Declan, one of Ronan's men, if there had ever been a purebred vampire who wanted everything with equal measure once they stopped aging. Declan had stared back at him with sad, knowing eyes.

"You're one," Declan stated.

Aiden hadn't been astonished when Declan grasped this insight into him. He'd come to realize Declan saw and understood far more than any normal vampire should. It was why Aiden had taken his question to Declan instead of any of the others.

"Have there been any others like me?" Aiden had inquired.

"There have been a rare few."

"What became of them?"

Declan folded his hands behind his head as he leaned back

in his chair. "What they chose to become. Some turned Savage, another continues, and others died."

Aiden hadn't bothered to ask who the one was that continued. Declan would never tell him.

"There have been a rare few."

Those words had looped through his mind over the past two weeks. *I guess I'm one of the lucky few,* he thought with a bitter laugh.

There was always the chance he could find his mate, as so many others in his family had. His *younger* sister Abby had already found hers. He didn't hold out much hope for himself though as he doubted he'd stumble across his mate in time to save himself.

And if he did find her, did he want to saddle her with someone like him and this bloody, brutal life he led? Whether she was a vampire or human, would she stay with him, or would she run screaming when she realized how messed up he was?

He certainly wouldn't blame her if she ran. He was a perfect storm of mayhem swirling altogether, one that probably didn't deserve saving anyway.

CHAPTER THREE

Stepping outside Carha's club, Aiden inhaled the crisp, March air. Spring hovered on the horizon, but this March had come roaring in with a three-foot blizzard, followed by a week of rain, and today the sun had made its first appearance. What remained of the dirty snow was piled up against the brick alley walls or in dwindling snow banks along the street.

He glanced back at the black, metal door of the club as it clicked shut behind him. The locks clicked as they were turned into place by Brutus, the vampire on the other side. No sign marked the entrance to Carha's club; he wasn't sure the place had a name, which was all part of its allure. Only those in "the know" within the subculture of humans who liked to play at being vampires could find the place. They kept its existence hidden from others who might ruin it for them.

Idiots.

Turning away, he pulled his collar closer to his neck to ward off some of the icy wind as he started down the alley. Before he'd come to Boston tonight, he'd suspected he would cave and see Carha, so he'd brought an extra pair of clothes with him to the city and rented a hotel room down the street.

He was supposed to meet Saxon at nine to start hunting killer vamps—Savages, he reminded himself—but that was a few hours away. Before coming here, he'd made sure to leave himself enough time to shower, change, and heal enough to not be a risk to Saxon later by being weakened from his blood loss. Because he occasionally fed on and gained power from the Savages he killed, he was far stronger than a vampire his age should be, even a purebred one, and he healed fast.

The rancid stench of garbage suddenly filled his nostrils. His steps slowed, and his hand slid inside his coat to grip the stake tucked within one of the pockets. There were only two dumpsters in this alley, but the scent filling it made a landfill smell delicious.

There's more than one Savage.

His gaze darted to the slice of darkening sky he could see between the two buildings beside him. It was too early for the Savage's regular hunting time, but something had lured them here. He suspected that something was *him.*

How had they known he was here? He never kept a regular schedule here to avoid having this very thing happen.

He didn't have time to figure it out as five Savages turned the corner of the alleyway. Aiden grinned at them as he removed the stake before reaching in with his other hand to remove another one. Five against one weren't the best odds, but he'd faced worse before. Granted, his back hadn't been freshly sliced open during those times.

"It's a little sooner than I'd anticipated, but I'm always up for some killing," Aiden said to the man moving toward the front of the group.

The man's smile revealed his fangs. "So are we."

Behind Aiden, a foot crunched on one of the icy puddles.

He glanced over his shoulder to find five more vamps approaching from the street behind him. They'd blocked him in.

Ten on one. Despite the steep odds, Aiden smiled as the first one raced toward him. He'd denied himself sex tonight, but they'd brought him the blood and death he craved.

Spinning to the side, Aiden swung one of the stakes out and plunged it into the first vampire's heart. The vamp's mouth formed an O of death before Aiden yanked the stake free at the same time he drove his other stake into the chest of the next one lunging for him. This time he missed the heart, but before he could correct his mistake, the other eight jumped him.

After years of wrestling with his siblings, he could withstand the weight of numerous bodies piling on him, but they staggered him to the side. Bracing his feet apart, he balanced himself beneath the increasing burden. His torn back screamed in protest; his newly healing skin split apart to pour fresh blood down his back. Excited by the scent of his blood, the killers all hissed and clawed more eagerly at him.

Their increased frenzy and the loss of more of his blood caused Aiden to lurch to the side, but he managed to keep from going down beneath them. If he fell now, he'd die. There would be no getting up, no getting away; this would be the end for him. He suspected he would have to be put down one day, but he didn't want it to be by one of these hideous freaks.

One of the vamps hung over his head, blocking his view of the alley. Swinging his stake forward, Aiden sank it into its belly and sliced downward. The vampire howled as his intestines splashed onto the asphalt below.

Recoiling, the Savage he'd sliced fell away from him, opening some of Aiden's vision. One of his eyes remained blocked by a different vamp, but he could at least see some of the alley again. The Savages tore his coat down the back as he drove his fist into the ribs of the other vamp hanging over him. Bone crunched and gave way beneath his hand as he dug his way deeper into its chest.

Fingers shredded his shirt, fangs snapped at his neck, but he batted them away with his free hand. The Savages dug into his sliced skin. He felt their fingers gripping the edges of his flesh before peeling it further apart.

Aiden grunted as white-hot pokers of agony speared through his brutalized back. When an uncontrollable spasm racked him, he suspected that one of the Savages had touched his spine. He became certain of it when one of his legs went numb.

"Fuck you!" Buried wrist-deep in the Savage's chest, Aiden gripped his heart and tore it out.

Aiden's right knee buckled, and he shifted his weight onto his left leg to remain standing. What he could see of the alley blurred before spinning like the Gravitron ride at a fair. Lurching to the side, he smashed another vamp off the brick wall beside him. The vamp grunted but held onto him. Somehow drawing on enough strength to step away from the wall, Aiden battered the vamp against it again. Bone crunched, and this time, the Savage released him.

Somewhere in the distance, screams pierced the air. The garbled, high-pitched shrieks barely cut through the excited chatter of the Savages. Already weaker from the blood loss he'd sustained in Carha's club, Aiden's left knee wobbled.

He would *not* go out without giving these bastards the fight of their lives. Even if they won this, they would never forget him.

"No!" He reeled backward to crunch another vampire against the wall of the other building.

The vamp whimpered, and when Aiden battered him off the brick again, another weight fell away from him. The screaming continued, but it sounded as if it were coming from further away.

His other leg gave out, and his knees smacked against the pavement. Shouts resonated off the brick walls, something cracked, and blue light flashed across his eyes. He couldn't tell what the light was as his senses became hazier by the second.

When he fell forward onto the pavement, he knew there would be no more insatiable cravings for more. It was over for him.

CHAPTER FOUR

"What's it going to be, Mags?" Roger asked as he looked at her, to the drive-thru menu, and back again.

"I'll take two hamburgers and a small fry," Magdalene replied.

She really would have loved to order those burgers rare, but she knew fast-food restaurants, even the ones who proclaimed to cater to your wishes, didn't do rare. They spouted nonsense about laws and health risks, but she'd been eating her food as raw as possible since she was a kid, and she'd managed to survive it.

A squelching noise came over the airwaves of their radio as Roger started yelling their order at the speaker. The poor drive-thru guy would be lucky to have eardrums left by the time Roger finished. No matter how many times she tried to explain he didn't have to shout at the speaker to be heard, Roger insisted on doing it.

Roger had been the type of guy she hated when she worked the drive-thru as a teenager. It had been the shortest job she ever had, and the only one she'd walked out on. Some asshole had shouted his order at her before pulling forward to discover his fries weren't quite ready yet. She'd forced her politest smile while she asked him to please wait in the parking lot and informed him someone would run his fries out to him as soon as they were ready.

He'd replied by calling her a stupid bitch. Still smiling, she'd squeezed his strawberry shake until it exploded in his face and tossed the empty cup into his lap. He'd still been sputtering and shouting obscenities at her as she calmly untied her apron, pulled off her hat, and walked out the door. She could have desperately used the money back then, but she hadn't bothered to collect her last paycheck.

"You don't have to shout," she said again as Roger sat back in his seat.

"I wasn't shouting," he replied, and she shook her head.

She kept telling him to get his hearing checked. Too much time listening to sirens had probably damaged his hearing, or maybe his ears required a good cleaning. Either way, he refused to have them checked, and she wouldn't nag him about it.

Roger had been her mentor since before she'd become an EMT. He'd been her savior through paramedic school and developed into the father figure she'd never had during the four years they'd worked together. With his graying brown hair and the lines etching his face from years of stress and too many years smoking before he'd kicked the habit, Roger looked his fifty-two years.

Over the past year, his fondness for fried food had caused his lean body to take on a bit more paunch in the belly. However, for the amount of crap he ate, he remained surprisingly on the thin side. Despite the years catching up to him, when Roger smiled, it lit his face and made him appear twenty years younger. Maggie loved that rare smile.

The radio made a loud squelching sound again as they pulled up to the first window. The pimple-faced teen leaning out to collect their money winced at the noise and instinctively jerked back. He stayed a safe distance away and stuck out his hand for Roger to pay him. The kid took the money and turned to push the buttons on the register.

Since they were on their dinner shift, Maggie leaned over to turn the radio down a little, but a frantic burst of words spattered the airwaves like gunfire before she could touch it. She froze as she listened to the rushed words of multiple victims and ambulances needed. Her stomach rumbled in protest, but before the next words came out, she already knew her over-cooked burgers were going to have to wait.

"It's too early in the night for this shit," Roger muttered as he turned on the lights and siren. The kid snatched his hand back so fast the money tumbled to the ground. "We'll be back!" Roger shouted out the window as he expertly whipped the ambulance around the car idling at the window in front of them.

Once on the road, vehicles moved out of their way the best they could on the crowded Boston streets. Maggie kept alert for anyone who might think it would be fun to race an ambulance or run a red light, but thankfully, the other drivers decided to obey the laws. Their luck of not having to dodge any wayward cars didn't stop her growing certainty this was going to be a bad night.

The first star wasn't out yet, and already they were getting a call for multiple victims. Roger was right; it was far too early in the night for this.

Roger turned a corner, and numerous police cars parked at the mouth of an alley came into view. Yellow tape hung across the entrance to the alley, officers gathered at the end of it. They looked unusually subdued as none of them spoke to each other.

They were the first ambulance to arrive. Roger pulled to the curb and parked it in front of a nondescript, brick building. Plywood covered the windows on the first and second floors of this building and the one next to it. Wooden boards were nailed across the front entrance, blocking the metal door behind it.

Why would multiple people gather between abandoned buildings? Even as she questioned it, she knew the answer. Whatever lay beyond that tape was probably the result of a drug deal gone way wrong.

Maggie opened her door and hopped out. Usually, her adrenaline would be pumping to get to their victim and possibly save a life. She felt none of that normal rush though. Instead, her dread only grew as the officers looked over at them. Their faces were abnormally pale in the flashing lights, and no one called or waved a greeting to them.

An intuitive sense they were walking into something that might make the Wolfman run grew within her. Instead of rushing to gather their supplies, her legs locked into place.

"You'll need the stretcher," one of the officers called to her after a minute.

His voice snapped her out of the strange paralysis holding her. She nodded to him before hurrying around to open the back doors. Roger met her on the other side, and together they removed the stretcher and medical bag. They carried their equipment over to one of the police officers guarding the alleyway. Maggie recognized Officer Harding immediately.

Harding pulled aside the yellow crime scene tape before they reached it. She and Roger ran into Harding often, and Roger's bowling team competed against Harding's. Never had the officer's pudgy face been flushed or had she seen him sweat, not even in August. Now, Harding's brown eyes held a note of distress she'd never seen in the middle-aged man before.

She'd assumed Harding had seen it all after nearly thirty

years on the force, but whatever he'd seen here tonight bothered him enough that his normally perfect uniform was marred by the hat sitting crookedly on his head. Beneath the hat, his usually neatly combed salt-and-pepper hair stuck out on the sides.

"Roger, Mags," Harding greeted in a voice hoarser than normal. His breath came out in puffs of air as he spoke. "I'm not sure what happened here, but it's bad."

"Survivors?" Roger asked.

"Yes, but don't ask me how."

Maggie frowned at that response and glanced toward the alleyway. Blood didn't bother her; in fact, it had always held a strange fascination for her, and she'd never been squeamish. Both of those things had led her to this career. She also liked helping people.

She'd probably still be bouncing from one hated job to the next if she hadn't witnessed a car hit a woman one day while walking home. The scene repulsed the other witnesses, but Maggie ignored the blood and the jutting leg bones to care for the woman until an ambulance arrived.

Roger had been working that ambulance. Impressed with her ability to handle what she'd seen, and to tie a tourniquet the best she could based on what she'd watched on TV, he'd given her his number. Roger told her to call him if she ever decided she might like to try her hand at being an EMT.

She'd called him the next day and enrolled in an EMT program the following month. She'd hated school while growing up and vowed never to return after she graduated, but she'd plunged into EMT training. Roger helped her get a job with this company when she finished. He trained her, and when she'd applied to paramedic school after a year of being on the ambulance with him, he'd tutored her through it. Never once had she regretted her decision or been spooked while on a call. She had the unreasonable feeling that might end tonight.

Glancing nervously at the alleyway, her nose twitched when she detected the coppery tang of blood and the faint hint of garbage on the air. A *lot* of blood odor wafted out of that alley.

CHAPTER FIVE

MAGGIE STEPPED FORWARD. Multiple someones required their help, and no matter how crazy the scene might be, she and Roger would do what they'd been trained to do. Harding's voice halted her before she could go any further.

"I saw the end of what happened in there, and I still don't believe it. It... it couldn't have been real," he muttered.

He removed his hat to run a hand through his hair. It startled her to see the shine on the top of Harding's head; she'd never seen him without a hat before. The few times she'd gone to watch Roger and some of her other coworkers bowl, Harding had always worn a Red Sox hat. Somehow, seeing him without one made him seem vulnerable in an odd way, and made what waited for them more unnerving.

Harding shoved his hat back on and assumed his usual brusque attitude of business. It helped to embolden her.

"This way," Harding said in the crisp voice she recognized well. "There's one or two still alive."

She exchanged a look with Roger, who shrugged and followed Harding into the alley. Maggie spotted two bodies on the ground, with police officers standing beside them and more yellow tape marking off the area. Maggie tried to ascertain if the victims were alive or not as Harding led them past.

"They're dead," Harding said, as if he'd been reading her thoughts.

"Are you sure?" Roger asked.

"One was stabbed in the heart, and the other had his heart torn out, so yes, I'm sure," Harding retorted.

"Did you say he had his heart *torn out?*" Maggie blurted.

"Yes."

"As in *out* of his *chest?*"

"Yes."

"What happened here?" Roger asked as Maggie's skin crawled.

"I don't know," Harding replied.

Maggie gazed around the macabre scene. The blue strobes of the police vehicles flashing over the blood-splattered walls and the river of red beneath her feet reminded her of a grisly Pollock painting.

Nothing could have survived what happened here, yet Harding continued leading them toward a body lying prone on the ground. As they neared, she realized the victim was a man from his short black hair and the width of his broad shoulders and the size of his large body. His arms, still inside a black trench coat, were spread over his head.

Two police officers stood guard beside him, and on the other side of the alley, two more officers knelt beside another victim. Maggie blinked and stumbled when she spotted the slimy trail of intestines poking out from under that victim.

"We don't think that one has a chance," Harding muttered and waved at the eviscerated man. "This one might have a chance, but...." His voice trailed off.

Despite the icy air, a fresh sheen of sweat beaded Harding's face. He pulled a white, handkerchief from his front pocket and wiped the sweat away before shoving the cloth back inside. Maggie's sick feeling grew when half the handkerchief remained dangling from Harding's pocket. He'd always been fastidious about his appearance, and a ball buster to any of the officers who slacked in that department.

"Are they all stabbing victims?" Roger asked, trying to learn what they were dealing with here.

"No knives present," Harding said in a clipped tone, and Maggie suspected he was trying not to vomit.

Not much in life unnerved her, but she felt like she was having some strange out-of-body experience as she surveyed the surreal scene. Drying blood streaked sections of bricks, and it had slid down to puddle on the asphalt. She searched for any weapon or drugs left behind, but she didn't see any.

"Gunshot wounds?" Roger asked incredulously as he gazed at the intestines lying on the ground.

"I haven't seen any bullet wounds in any of the bodies, but I haven't done a close inspection of them. We've found no weapons at all, but there were others here when we arrived. They grabbed some things before fleeing."

"There were other people here?" Maggie asked.

"Yes, seven of them. We shot at them. I know I hit at least one, and I saw a few others get hit, but they all ran off."

Maggie's head rose at Harding's reply. "They ran off after being *shot?*"

"They did. I don't know what kind of drugs they're on, but being shot didn't slow them down." Harding stopped beside the prone man in the trench coat. "I don't think he has much of a chance, but his vitals were stronger than the other victim."

It didn't matter which one of the live victims were more likely to survive anymore as her coworkers, Glenn and Walt, had also arrived. They were making their way toward the eviscerated man.

When they stopped next to him, Maggie focused her attention on the man lying before her. Her heart leapt into her throat when she saw the flesh of the man's back had been peeled back like some fucked-up banana.

"Is that his spine?" Roger demanded.

Harding gulped and lifted his hat to wipe the sweat from his brow. "You would know better than me."

They all knew what it was; it was impossible not to know. A kid could recognize the white, curving bone of someone's spine. What had been able to do that, *who* had done it, and *why*?

Maggie shuddered. The only thing that ever bothered her about this job were the calls involving children, but this... well, this was pure *torture*.

A pool of blood spread out from beneath the man. Within the coppery tang of his blood, she detected a hint of clove too. It made her stomach turn that she found the aroma almost pleasant when any rational human would find everything about this repulsive. Yet, she couldn't deny she wanted to get closer to the man. Her fingers tingled with the urge to brush his hair back so she could see his face.

The face of a dead man, she realized.

Harding or one of the other officers had to have made a mistake about this guy being alive. She didn't fault them for their error, didn't care she'd missed dinner because of it. This whole scene was disturbing, and for the first time in her life, she was grateful she hadn't had a chance to eat.

Harding settled his hat back into place. "I took his pulse myself. He's alive, or he was alive before you arrived."

"Fine." Roger nodded to her, and together they set their equipment down, careful to keep it out of the blood.

She knew Roger was placating Harding; this victim had to be dead. Not even Superman could lose that much blood and survive. Roger knelt beside the body and took hold of the man's wrist.

When fingers gripped his wrist, Aiden's bones felt as if they were fracturing into pieces. He gritted his teeth as he tried to recall what had happened to him and what was going on now. Was someone taking his pulse?

Lights flashed across his closed lids, voices sounded around him, but he couldn't separate one from the other.

Maggie studied the alley as Roger continued to check for a pulse. The officers stood further than normal away from the two dead victims. Three feet away from her, and near the hand of one of the dead, Maggie spotted what looked like a smooshed tomato. It took her a second to realize it was the brutalized remains of a human heart.

She was never eating again after this, and she may never come out of the shower she planned to take as soon as her shift ended. She would give anything to be somewhere else.

In the side of the brick building to her right was a metal door. Blood streaked the door, there was no knob, and nothing indicated what lay beyond. Near the door, Walt and Glenn were talking to each other as they set to work on their victim.

"Shit," Roger breathed beside her. "He *is* alive."

CHAPTER SIX

MAGGIE BARELY MANAGED to keep herself from gawking at Roger as he leaned back and rested his hands on his knees. His skin had become a pasty color she'd never seen on him before, and his brown eyes were troubled when they met hers.

It didn't make it any easier that Roger and Harding were as unsettled by this as she was; it made it worse. That meant she didn't imagine this was all wrong; it meant it *was* all wrong.

For a second, they stared at each other, and then their training kicked into place. They'd been riding together for so long they didn't have to speak as they went to work on their patient. In the victim's condition, the best thing they could do was get him loaded up and to the hospital as fast as possible.

Kneeling at the man's side, Maggie got a closer look at his back. The skin had been pulled back about three inches on each side from the center of his spine. The wound ran from beneath his shoulder blades to the middle of his lower back. Through the blood, glistening pieces of his spine were visible. The flow of his blood seemed to have ceased as none pooled within the wound and the puddle beneath him wasn't spreading.

No one can survive this. The pain, the shock to his system, the blood loss. This is impossible. Then, she saw the small rise and fall of his back.

She had the unsettling notion she'd tripped headfirst into a Pink Floyd song and someone was about to start screaming at her that she couldn't have her pudding until she ate her meat. She then cursed Roger for making her listen to Pink Floyd.

Maggie's head twisted to the side as she inspected beyond the wreckage of the man's back. Through the blood and the tattered remains of his shirt and coat, she noted raw slices arcing across the man's flesh. Beneath those reddened slices she saw the faint white lines of what appeared to be scars.

It looked as if he'd been... whipped?

"What is going on here?" she whispered.

The man's bloody fingertips twitched on the ground when she spoke. Maggie gazed at his hand, waiting for further movement, but it remained still.

"Drug deal gone wrong would be my guess," Harding said. "I think they were teaching this guy a lesson before they decided to kill him. They picked the wrong place as a group of young bar hoppers stumbled across them and called it in. I was right down the street and the first to arrive."

"Wrong place for them, good for him," Maggie said, and the man's fingers twitched again.

Harding grunted. "I picked the wrong decade to quit smoking."

"You and me both," Roger muttered as he worked. "Let's get him loaded, Mags."

"On his back?" she asked as she gazed at his spine, and the man's fingers jerked toward her.

"Yes," Roger said. "We need access to his chest in case he

codes, which with the amount of blood he's lost, is a very good possibility. He's barely bleeding anymore, so I don't think he'll bleed out if we put him on his back."

"I don't think there's any blood left in him," Harding muttered, and as improbable as it was, Maggie silently agreed.

Maggie gazed from the open wound to Roger and back again. "If we put him on his back, it's really going to hurt him."

"He's probably so far into shock, he's not feeling much pain anymore," Roger replied.

"If it helps, I plan on cuffing him," Harding interjected.

"Are you kidding me?" Maggie blurted.

"No."

"So we won't be able to roll him. He has to go on his back, and if we have any chance of saving him, we have to get him out of here, now," Roger said.

"Shouldn't we bandage him or pack the wound or something?" she asked.

"With his spine the way it is, I'm not risking putting anything in there and causing more damage. Besides, I think it's best if we just get him out of here, instead of taking the time to bandage him."

"I agree with getting him out of here," Harding said.

Maggie sighed in resignation; Roger was right. The longer they stood here and debated a situation they'd never been trained for—because no one ever could have prepared them, or thought to prepare them, for *this*—the more likely it was they would never get this guy to the hospital alive.

Together, she and Roger lifted the man and placed him onto the stretcher. She winced for him as his weight settled on his back. If he had enough sense left to register pain, this had to be agonizing for him.

She nearly shrieked when the man groaned. If she'd been a gambler, she would have bet money on this guy never making it to the hospital, never mind making a sound again. Her eyes shot to Roger, who gazed back at her with a dumbfounded expression she was sure matched hers.

She couldn't stop her hands from shaking as she strapped the man down. Harding stepped forward, captured the man's wrist, and handcuffed it to the stretcher.

A vaguely familiar, sweet odor pushed aside the stench of garbage and blood clogging Aiden's nostrils. It took him a moment to place the scent as butterscotch. There had been a girl in his high school who sucked endlessly on butterscotch candies. The scent made him recall how sweet butterscotch tasted on his tongue.

That high school girl had been the first one he kissed and felt up. She might have become his first everything if her family hadn't moved to England. She existed back in the days when he'd dreamed of living a relatively normal life for a vampire residing amongst humans. He'd gone to college for a time, back in the day when sports and video games had still been fun and important to him. However, he soon realized he'd been a fool for believing he could fit in as his father and the Stooges had in college.

His father and the Stooges were turned vamps. He loved them all, but they didn't have a clue what purebred, male vampires endured when they stopped aging. He hadn't had a clue either.

But none of that mattered right now. That was the past. Something was happening in the present he had to focus on.

Why was his mind so jumbled? Why was he thinking of a girl he'd completely forgotten until now and college days he'd given up?

If he was in this much pain, he was in danger. Hands gripped him, lifting him and rolling him onto something. He was jostled again, and then someone grabbed his wrist. Cold metal enclosed his wrists; he tried to jerk away, but he didn't have the strength.

His body felt like he'd been stretched on a rack before being repeatedly sliced open by Carha's whip. Why was he so weak?

Bits and pieces filtered through his mind. Had Carha just chained him? He'd kill the bitch if she had. It didn't matter if she was the only one willing to flay him open as he needed, he'd warned her not to play games with him.

Then he heard the butterscotch woman speak again. Her voice dragged him back toward full consciousness. Despite the tremor he detected in it, strength resonated in her tone. His hand jerked against the metal before someone clasped his other wrist. He turned his head toward the voice and tried to open his eyes. He didn't like the fear he sensed in her, and if he could look at her, if he could see where he was, then maybe he could *remember*.

"I really don't think he needs to be cuffed," Maggie said to Harding. The metal handcuff rattled when the man's hand jerked against his restraint.

"Until we know what happened here, this man is also a prisoner," Harding said briskly as he walked around the stretcher to cuff the man's other wrist too.

"In case you haven't noticed, he's not exactly in the condition to jump up and run off on us," she retorted.

"Don't care."

"Officer Harding—"

Her words broke off when Harding's eyes met hers, and she saw the wariness in them. It hit her that Harding wasn't handcuffing their patient out of concern the man might make a miraculous escape; Harding was doing it because he worried for *them*.

What have we walked into here? She wondered for the hundredth time since entering this alley.

"Let's go, Mags," Roger said.

Without speaking, the two of them lifted the stretcher and started to carry it out of the alley. There was too much blood to wheel it out of here. She and Roger would be scrubbing the ambulance for hours afterward if they attempted to wheel it, and she wanted as little to do with this whole mess as possible.

When she got the chance, she was going to scrub her skin raw. Until then, she would have to be content with getting out of here, getting this guy to the hospital, filing their report, and forgetting any of this happened. Tomorrow, she and probably all the others who'd been here would feel foolish for being so creeped out, but right now all she felt was the impulse to bolt like a rabbit.

She met Glenn's eyes when she walked by him. His black skin glistened with sweat as he gave her a nod of greeting. Glenn had been on this job for longer than Roger, yet she saw the alarm in his brown eyes before they shifted to Roger.

"It's insane here," Glenn said to him.

Glenn and Roger had been partners for nearly a decade. Before Maggie started working for the company, Glenn was offered the opportunity to move to an earlier shift, and he'd taken it. Glenn and Walt had probably been preparing to return to the station for the end of their shift when this call came in. The timing for them had been worse than the timing for her and Roger.

"Stay safe," Roger replied.

The ground beneath Aiden's back swayed as he was carried somewhere. Male voices spoke with each other. He didn't hear the woman again, but her scent remained strong. Doors opened, and whatever he was on was pushed forward. He gritted his teeth when he was set down somewhere.

"I'll ride with him," Roger said.

"You're better at getting through traffic than I am," Maggie replied. "You'll get us to the hospital faster."

Before Roger could protest, she climbed into the back with their patient. Roger stared at her for a second before closing the doors. Taking a deep breath, Maggie pulled off her winter uniform coat and placed it on the bench before setting to work on gathering the equipment needed to check their patient's vitals and keep him alive long enough to get him out of their lives.

A small jolt of electricity shot from him to her when she grasped his wrist to check his pulse. Unlike static electricity, this current generated from some inner, instead of outer, force. It hadn't been an unpleasant sensation, but her skin prickled with an awareness she hadn't anticipated.

Glancing at the man, she almost recoiled when his eyes fluttered back and forth behind his closed lids. She had no idea how this guy was still alive, but he showed more signs of it than some of her patients who had sustained a *lot* less in the way of injuries.

CHAPTER SEVEN

THE DRIVER'S DOOR CLOSED, and the ambulance roared to life. "You okay back there?" Roger demanded.

"Yes."

Roger grunted before shifting into drive and pulling away from the scene. The man's fingers twitched again when she spoke. "We're going to get you to the hospital," she assured him.

The brush of her fingers on his flesh caused Aiden's skin to come alive in a way it never had before. So startled by the sensation, it took a few seconds for her words to penetrate. The hospital? A *human* hospital?

He had to focus, had to recall what happened. It took far more strength than he ever would have believed possible to crack his eyes open. A blurry glow met him, and he spotted the edge of a khaki shirt before his eyes closed again. Shuffling sounded and cool metal pressed against his stomach.

Then, memory flooded back to him, and his eyes flew open. A gasp sounded. Metal clattered as the khaki blur recoiled.

"You okay?" A brusque male voice demanded from somewhere in front of him.

"Fine," the butterscotch-smelling woman replied, but Aiden couldn't see her anymore.

All around him were shelves, white walls, and medical supplies. Beneath him, he felt the rumble of tires on the road, and he realized he was in an ambulance. He should be dead. How was he still alive?

Maggie inhaled a calming breath and steadied her hands before she bent to retrieve the scissors she'd dropped. The back of her patient's shirt and coat may have been torn open, but the front was not. She'd been preparing to cut his clothing off so she could hook up the EKG machine when he'd *opened* his eyes! The scissors wobbled in her grip as she recalled those eyes on her.

It shouldn't have been possible for him to wake up, but he had. Over her time working on the ambulance, she'd had her fair share of men and women groping her, as well as spitting on her, and cursing her. She'd take a spitter and biter any day over this guy.

Gripping the scissors more firmly, she rose and held them before her. For the first time, she knew she'd stab one of her patients if it became necessary.

When her eyes met his, her heart hit her ribs so violently she thought she might have to hook herself up to the EKG machine to make sure she wasn't having a heart attack. His eyes reminded her of spring as they were the green of oak leaves in May when they were first unfurling and vibrant with new life.

She felt like she was tumbling further away from reality when, beneath the blood streaking his face and caking his short black hair, she realized he was a handsome man. His lips parted, and a breath rattled out of him. He seemed to be trying to speak, but she wasn't getting any closer to hear what he might say. Handsome or not, the guy freaked her out.

"We're going to get you to the hospital," she assured him

again, and suddenly she *had* to make sure he made it there. Over the years, there were so many she'd wanted to save and been unable to; it wouldn't be her fault if this guy died, but she couldn't shake the belief she *had* to save him. The need to make sure he survived hit her so hard that she was amazed her hand didn't shake when she started cutting his shirt up the front with clinical precision.

Aiden watched her capable hands slicing through his clothes before he lifted his gaze to the curve of her cheekbone. He didn't think he'd ever seen skin so fair or unblemished before. It reminded him of the porcelain dolls his sisters Abby and Vicky collected as children. Twisted into a knot against the back of her delicate, swan neck, her auburn hair shone in the light of the ambulance.

She remained focused on her task as she cut his sleeves next. Air rushed over his already chilled skin when she pulled the remaining shreds of his shirt and coat away.

My weapons!

The thought blazed through his mind as she hefted the coat a little higher. She dipped a hand into one of his pockets and pulled out a small crossbow. He saw one auburn eyebrow rise before she carefully set the crossbow aside and lowered his coat with the caution one would take with a poisonous snake.

The woman didn't look at him again as the sound of something peeling drifted to him. Then, she leaned forward to stick things on his chest before moving out of sight again. He heard shuffling noises and a small clatter before a steady beeping started.

"Is that *his* heart?" Roger demanded.

Maggie swallowed to get some saliva into her parched throat before replying, "Yes."

"Jesus Christ," Roger muttered.

Maggie resisted making the sign of the cross. She couldn't

recall the last time she'd crossed herself. It had probably been when she'd fostered with that ultra-religious family who had dragged all the kids to church three times a week. Maggie had only spent a month with them before proudly declaring her love for Satan and all things demonic while dressed as a Goth. She'd never been sent packing so fast in her life. Right now, though, the sign of the cross felt like the appropriate thing to do.

What was this guy?

She could feel him watching every move she made, but she couldn't bring herself to look at him again.

I am not a coward. I have endured too damn much to be rattled by some weirdo with a freakishly high tolerance for everything.

However, she was beginning to question if he *was* a man. What man could endure the amount of damage this one had and not only survive it, but be awake so soon afterward?

At least half his blood remained in that alley, and his *spine* was visible.

She was half-tempted to crawl into the front with Roger, but she'd never backed down from anything before and she wasn't about to start now. She glanced toward Roger as they raced through side streets and past warehouses with sirens blaring. She didn't have to see the speedometer, she could feel the tires spinning faster than normal, yet she yearned for Roger to *go faster.*

"Uncuff me," Aiden rasped out.

A pair of charcoal-colored eyes shot toward him and widened fearfully. The beeping from some machine increased as he got his first full-on view of the woman. He'd never seen anyone like her before. She wasn't what he would call sexy or stunning. He didn't know how to describe exactly what she was, but he couldn't tear his gaze away from her.

Then, he recalled his mother holding one of Abby's porcelain dolls and turning it in her hand as she inspected it. Unlike this woman, the toy had possessed blonde hair and blue eyes, but something about this woman brought the memory back to him.

"She's lovely, Abby," his mother had said and handed the doll back to his then seven-year-old sister.

Lovely, that's what this woman was, but none of those dolls could compare to her.

The woman's rosebud lips quivered. Those dark gray eyes stared at him before rising to the front of the ambulance. "Roger," she whispered.

"Going as fast as I can, Mags," Roger replied brusquely.

Aiden seized her hand as something crashed into the side of the ambulance with enough force to dent the wall and send the ass end of the vehicle careening sideways.

CHAPTER EIGHT

THE SICKENING CRUNCH of metal filled the air as the back of the ambulance skidded out. Maggie screamed, but she didn't know if it was because of the dizzying sensation of the ambulance veering off its course, or from the hand gripping hers tight enough to the stretcher that it kept her from being thrown into the wall.

Oh, God. Oh, God.

The ambulance came to a halt with its engine running and its headlights pointing toward a large warehouse. Completely thrown off by what happened, Maggie couldn't figure out where they were, but it looked abnormally subdued outside the windshield. Most of the warehouse workers had gone home for the night, but she saw people running from the shadows toward them.

"Roger, you okay?" she demanded.

"What was that?" he replied.

Maggie gazed at the dented wall across from her. It was too high up for it to be caused by another vehicle, but what else could have hit them with that kind of force?

"There were no cross streets," Roger said. "No stop lights. It couldn't have been another car. It came out of nowhere."

"Drive," her patient spoke with far more strength than he had before.

"What?" she asked, not because she hadn't heard him, but because she couldn't *believe* she had.

"Drive!" the man shouted at her.

"Roger..."

He was already hitting the gas. The ambulance creaked in protest, but they still had all their tires as it burst into movement. The man released her hand and jerked against the cuffs. She caught Roger's wild-eyed glance back at them before he pressed harder on the accelerator.

"Fahk this fahken night!" Roger declared, his Boston accent becoming far more pronounced. Maggie had only ever heard his accent slip through so strongly once before, the night she'd graduated paramedic school. They'd each been about twelve beers deep when Roger reverted to his Southie roots.

"Maggie, get up 'ere!" Roger barked at her.

Maggie glanced down at the man. A vein in his forehead throbbed to life as he pulled his wrists forward to strain against the cuffs. He bared his teeth at her. Lions were less intimidating than this guy.

"Go!" he snarled at her.

The woman, Maggie, Aiden recalled, leaned away from him and started to rise when something hit the side of the ambulance again. Maggie staggered backward and hit the wall. When she cried out in pain and her hand flew to the back of her head, his vision became clouded by a red haze of fury.

The ambulance screamed a protest when Roger pushed on the gas harder.

"Maggie!" Aiden shouted, and her eyes flew to his.

She gawked at him until another wrenching sound filled

the air and the back door of the ambulance flew away. One of the Savages who had attacked him leapt into the ambulance. The vamp's eyes were bright red when they focused on Maggie. She screamed and lurched forward. Aiden assumed she'd been diving for the front and Roger, but then he heard a strange noise.

Aiden jerked more forcefully against his restraints as the Savage lunged for her. He had to protect her. Maggie spun and, holding out two paddles, hit the Savage in the middle of the chest with them. Another sound filled the air, and the vampire squealed as he staggered back.

"Bastard!" Maggie shouted, and lifting her leg, she drove her foot into his stomach to shove him out the door. The man bounced across the pavement before spinning away. Maggie leaned against the wall, panting for air as she watched the guy miraculously jump back to his feet and race toward them again. "What is wrong with him?"

"Drugs!" Roger declared.

"No, his face...." Her words trailed off. Aiden met her confused stare when she turned to look at him again. He couldn't help but be impressed by her ability to fight off a Savage, but she wouldn't be able to fend off more than one of them.

"What is going on?" she demanded, holding the paddles as if she were going to use them on him next.

"Uncuff me. I can protect you," he replied, aggravated he couldn't break the flimsy restraints yet.

Her eyes narrowed on him. "I can't uncuff you."

"I can keep you safe," he said slowly as she didn't seem to understand what he was saying to her. Perhaps she was in shock; he wouldn't blame her if she were.

She glared at him. "I don't have the key," she replied in the same tone and pace of voice he'd used with her.

He turned his attention to the back of the ambulance and the Savage running down the sidewalk after them, but the vamp was losing ground. It didn't matter, Aiden decided, they'd moved past the threat, for now. He was already getting stronger as his sudden need to keep her safe fueled his adrenaline. He would get out of these cuffs before they arrived at the hospital.

A loud crack filled the air, and when the back of the ambulance tilted to the right, Maggie realized the axle, weakened by whatever hit the ambulance, had snapped. A tire bounced down the street toward the Savage veering off the sidewalk toward them. With an ear-splitting, awful grating sound, the rotor dug into the asphalt, chewing up chunks that banged against the undercarriage of the ambulance. The sparks flying into the air showered the back of the vehicle with bursts of golden light.

Maggie stumbled and tried to catch her balance, but she couldn't fight the downward slant of the ambulance. She was going to plunge straight out those back doors as that twisted freak had. Releasing the paddles, she scrambled to grab something solid.

Strong fingers encircled her wrist, dragging her back. The EKG machine rolled forward, still beeping the impossibly steady rhythm of her patient's heart. She expected to go flying out the door with the stretcher and the machine, but the man jerked himself to the side so forcefully he flipped the stretcher over. Metal bent with a screech as the stretcher twisted to follow her patient's movement. The leads of the EKG machine snapped, and the cart rolled out the back door while her patient remained inside.

Maggie shrank back when he landed before her, the mangled stretcher spreading over the top of them. With his position, he blocked most of the aisle of the ambulance. Less than ten minutes ago, she'd been staring at this man's exposed spine, and now he was *kneeling* on the ground, staring at her.

Have I gone as nutty as my mother? Is this some sort of psychotic break, and I'm imagining it all? Am I going to wake to find myself in a straight jacket? Her mind raced with those questions as his eyes burned into hers and the ambulance came to a grinding halt in the middle of the road.

Despite his earlier, near-dead status, healthy color flushed her patient's chiseled cheekbones. The black stubble lining his jaw made him appear more menacing, something he didn't need as the man had practically pulled a Lazarus.

"Maggie May, you okay?" Roger asked.

She had to think about the answer to his question. "Fine," she finally croaked, having decided that if she'd fallen down the rabbit hole, she might as well ride out the insanity and have some tea with the Hatter. "You?"

"Few more gray hairs, but still kicking. How's the patient?"

"He's ahh..." She gulped. "He's kneeling before me right now."

She heard the creak of Roger's seat as he leaned over to look in the back and then his sharp inhalation. "Well, of course, he is," Roger murmured, and the seat creaked as he sat back again. "I think it's time for you to come up front, Mags."

"On my way," she replied.

The squelch of airwaves filled the ambulance, and then Roger requested help with a calm that didn't fit this situation. The man's eyes burned into hers as, with the care she would take to back away from a rabid animal, she edged away from him.

The others would never believe her and Roger when they told their coworkers about this at the end of their shift. Scratch that, she would *never* tell anyone about this. She'd be locked up right beside her mother if she did.

The man's chest heaved, and his arms were spread out to the sides by the cuffs hooking him to the stretcher. The posture reminded her of an avenging angel. Except, she suspected this man was anything but angelic.

"Go," he commanded, and then something collided with the back of the stretcher.

Knocked forward by the weight of whatever hit him, Aiden almost fell flat onto the ground. If he went down, the Savages would be all over him, and *her*. He would *not* allow the monstrous, twisted malignancies that were the worst of his kind anywhere near her.

When he was shoved forward again, grasping hands reached over his back toward Maggie as excited chatter filled the ambulance. He'd been the one to draw them here, but they'd scented her, they wanted her, and they would destroy her.

Fury pulsed through his veins as he launched himself up off the ground. The Savage on the back of the stretcher screamed, his bones shattered when Aiden smashed him between the stretcher and the roof of the ambulance. While standing, another one tried to sneak between his legs. Plunging downward, he drove his knee into the vamp's back, shattering his spine at the same time he finally succeeded in breaking the links of the cuffs.

Maggie scrambled back when her patient surged up and bashed one of the things trying to get in the ambulance off the ceiling. A putrid aroma drifted to her, reminding her of garbage as another creature tried to crawl between her patient's legs. She froze when he came down, and his knee broke the other monster almost in half. Years of training to save others and compassion warred with her flight instinct as the man's hands beat against the ground and cries of anguish issued from him.

The man's whimpers pierced through her indecision. She

helped others; she didn't run from them, even if they were some kind of twisted freak on super speed. She went to grab the man's wrist when metal snapped and a hand seized hers. Her patient's leaf-colored eyes flickered with red when she met his gaze. Terror crept through her as she realized he'd broken the handcuffs.

"What are you?" she breathed as something else hit the stretcher, shoving him toward her and knocking him off the man beneath him. Her nose wrinkled when the faint stench of garbage grew stronger on the air.

Aiden didn't answer her as the stench of rotting vampire filled his nose. There were more Savages out there, probably the rest of the ones who attacked him, Aiden realized. The one whose back he'd snapped was yanked away as his brethren pulled him to safety. Aiden glanced between his legs to see the Savage he'd battered against the ceiling crawling out the back of the vehicle.

Roger shouted something, and jagged lines fissured across the windshield. Leaning over, Roger grasped the small fire extinguisher and yanked it free. His eyes met Aiden's and widened before he spun around. He smashed the butt of the extinguisher against the hand shoving its way through the glass.

A current of air brushed against his spine, but Aiden felt his veins and muscles knitting together to repair the damage. He was healing fast, but he was nowhere near strong enough to take these things on right now. Not without blood.

His gaze fell on Maggie's neck and the pulse beating through the vein there. His fangs tingled; his mouth watered. Even if he hadn't been weakened, he'd still crave her blood as the scent of it was more alluring than anything he'd encountered before, but now he *needed* it if they were to have any chance of surviving this.

"I'm sorry," he murmured.

"For what?" she demanded.

Maggie didn't have time to move before his hand wrapped around the back of her head and he drew her toward him. She placed her palms against his chest to shove him away, but she'd have better luck moving a mountain as he didn't budge.

"It's the only way I can save you." His warm breath tickled her ear. "Forgive me."

Then, he was sinking his teeth—no, his *fangs* into her throat.

CHAPTER NINE

SHE WENT COMPLETELY STILL against him when those fangs pierced her. She felt them slip inside her vein to draw her blood, but she remained immobile as disbelief caused her mind to spin.

What is going on? How is this possible? What? How? What? My mother's not crazy!

She almost sobbed aloud as that realization hit her, but sobbing would require action, and she couldn't move. He pulled her blood from her in gulps that should have terrified her. Instead, her body went limp as pleasure slid out from where he'd pierced to wind through her body. An indescribable feeling of rightness crept through her bloodstream with every beat of her heart.

She'd placed her hands on him to push him away, yet she found her fingers curling into the solid wall of his chest to draw him closer. His other hand snaked around her waist as he pulled her flush against him. Instead of terror, her body reacted with lust as her breasts felt heavier and her hips thrust toward him.

He growled against her throat, the sensual, possessive sound arousing her more. This man was sucking the blood out of her body, he may kill her, and she was acting like a horny teenager in the back seat of their parents' car.

She wanted to smack herself for it, but she also desired *more*. Never had she experienced something as wondrous and right as this. Maybe she'd hit her head harder than she'd believed against the side of the ambulance, but something within her recognized this man was the piece of her life she hadn't known was missing. Without understanding it, she welcomed it.

The second her blood hit his tongue, a sense of calm slid through Aiden. It was a calm he hadn't experienced in two years, not since he'd stopped aging at twenty-three, and he'd never expected to feel it again. He'd believed dying was the only way he'd find freedom from his twisted compulsions again.

No, he was wrong, he realized as her sweet blood filled his mouth and slid down his throat. He'd *never* experienced a tranquility like this before. Even when he'd been younger, there was a restless emptiness within him that had driven him to constantly go from one sport to another, one party to another, one girl to another.

For the first time in his life, he didn't want to go anywhere. He'd found what he'd always been searching for, found where he belonged. The overwhelming sensation of finally being able to inhale a full, easy breath caused his throat to burn as he latched his arm around Maggie's waist and drew her closer. He'd consumed copious amounts of blood over the years, but none of it had ever strengthened him the way hers did, and it was the most potent he'd ever tasted from a human.

His muscles closed over his spine at a faster rate. His veins reconnected until fresh blood flowed through them once more. Maggie's fingers dug into his chest as her body melded to his and her breasts rubbed against him. When he scented her arousal, he resisted the impulse to lay her down and take her.

Without intending for it to happen, his mind started probing against hers so he could learn what she was feeling too. He reeled it back before he could open that channel. If he got lost in her mind now, they would both die tonight.

Must keep her safe! The reminder blazed across his mind as she went limp in his embrace. *Taking too much!*

His fangs retracted before he could weaken her. She remained leaning against him, her sweet scent stronger. He licked away the trickle of blood seeping from the punctures he'd left on her, but he didn't close the bite. Lifting his head, he gazed into the dumbfounded, charcoal-colored eyes of his mate as she stared back at him from under a thick fringe of dark red eyelashes.

My mate.

He didn't try to deny what she was to him. From the second her blood hit his tongue, he knew she belonged to him. She could save him from his looming madness if he could save *her* tonight.

"I'll keep you safe," he vowed. *And with me.*

Maggie blinked at him as she came out of whatever stupor he'd put her under. Her hand flew to the punctures he'd inflicted on her throat.

What are you? She almost blurted the question again, but it seemed pointless.

A burst of white filled the cab of the ambulance before the cloud floated into the back. Maggie coughed and recoiled as the contents of the fire extinguisher filled the air. She tried to stagger to her feet, but a hand enveloped her wrist and pulled her down. Green eyes filled her vision before his body fell on top of hers. The stretcher crashed forward, half falling on top of them both.

Aiden's thigh spread her legs apart as he pinned her beneath him. Something flew over the top of the stretcher, and Aiden lunged forward. He captured the Savage's ankle and jerked the vamp down before he could make it to the front of the ambulance.

"Don't look!" he yelled at Maggie as he twisted the Savage's head until it turned 180 degrees around.

Roger's shout drew Maggie's attention to the front as something leapt through the broken windshield at him.

"Roger!" she yelled and shoved against the man on top of her. "Let me up!"

Maggie wiggled to try to get free when the man didn't move off her. Instead, he dragged the thrashing monster toward them. Without a doubt, that creature should be dead as *no* one's neck was designed to turn that far, but apparently, these things and the guy on top of her had all forgotten *how* to die.

"I have to help Roger! Get off!" she shouted as her patient tore the head off the monster.

Not the strangest thing tonight, she thought with a laugh bordering on hysterical when her patient tossed the head aside.

"Get *off!*" Lifting her left leg, she hammered her knee into his nuts. All her training and compassion had vanished. Now, all that mattered was making sure she and Roger survived this night.

Aiden's breath rushed out of him; he recoiled as pain speared through his groin. Maggie shoved angrily against his chest, and her hand balled into a fist. He recalled redheaded women were supposed to have a temper before she landed a solid punch to his cheek. The force of the blow startled him and swayed him to the side. His sisters could pack a punch, but this was a *human* woman.

Before he could recover, Maggie clasped both her hands together and bashed them against his cheek. It didn't matter he'd said he would keep her safe, didn't matter she was impossibly attracted to this man, creature, thing—*vampire* who had taken her blood! He was keeping her from *Roger*.

She drove upward with her knee again and elbowed him in the cheek. Finally, she'd knocked him loose enough that she wiggled her way out from under him and scrambled toward the cab in a crouch. The stretcher mostly blocked the back doors of the ambulance, but something else was coming over the top of it.

She spun toward the newest creature when it scrambled toward her, but before it could hit her, her patient surged to his feet. Bone crunched, blood sprayed from the monster's mouth as the man sank his hand into the creature's back.

"Holy shit," she murmured as he tore the thing's heart free. She suddenly understood more of what had happened in the alley as her patient dropped the mangled heart on the floor.

Maggie didn't stick around to see any more of the carnage. She turned and threw herself into the front passenger seat. One of the vampires was perched on Roger's chest; its mouth pressed to Roger's neck. The extinguisher fell from Roger's limp fingers, clattering against the floor as it rolled toward the back.

Roger's eyes spun toward her. "Run!" he gasped.

Maggie hadn't tried to run when four girls jumped her in high school for wearing the same shirt as one of them, and she wasn't about to run now. Then, she'd been unprepared, but she hadn't spent her life in foster and group homes without learning how to fight dirty. She'd made those girls regret their decision, and she would do the same with this *thing*.

Turning to the back of the ambulance, she barely glanced at her patient as he fought with another one of the monsters. She snatched up the fire extinguisher and spun back to Roger.

Roger's eyes were drifting closed when she smashed the extinguisher into the vampire's face.

The vamp's cheek gave way with a sickening crunch. It yelped as it released its hold on Roger. "No!" she cried when Roger slumped against the steering wheel and stayed there.

When the vampire twisted toward her, she pulled back the extinguisher and hammered it into his face. Her hands went numb from the blow, but she managed to keep her hold on the handle. The vampire's lips peeled back to reveal its reddened teeth. Blood streaked from its broken nose and the gash she'd left on its cheek.

It lunged at her, knocking her back in the seat. Swinging the extinguisher up, she bashed the side of the monster's face again and kicked out. The vampire fell back and onto Roger as the glass behind her shattered. Fingers entangled in her hair; pain exploded through her scalp when her head was yanked back.

She tried to swing the extinguisher behind her to batter her new attacker, but it caught the top of the window and toppled from her hands. She reached behind her to beat at the hands twisting in her hair, but the monster didn't ease its hold on her. She was beginning to worry her neck would break when red eyes filled her vision and fangs punctured her shoulder. The pain of the vamp pulling her blood from her ripped a scream from her.

Her patient's bite had brought her rapture; this bite caused an agony the likes of which she'd never known could exist. She tried to kick out, but a strange sort of rigor mortis had set in as her limbs became rigid. Stars burst before her eyes, and it felt as if the blood vessels in her brain were swelling and exploding.

Not like this! Her mind screamed at her. *I will not die like this!*

A roaring noise filled her ears; then something warm splattered her face. The bite retracted, leaving her limp as she struggled to get air into her constricted lungs.

When her eyes cracked open, she discovered her patient looming over her, his broad shoulders heaving. His elongated fangs had sliced into his bottom lip, and she swore his skin held a reddish black hue to it.

Impossible!

Yeah because the rest of this night has been entirely possible. She released a laugh that sounded more like a cackle.

I'm going insane. It runs in the family!

She laughed again and tried to roll away from the window, but she barely twisted to the side before falling back and crying out.

CHAPTER TEN

"You're safe," he murmured to her.

Aiden steadied himself as rage continued to thrum through his body. He'd caved in the face of the vampire feeding from her with one swipe of his hand, but he hadn't killed him. It took everything he had not to leap out the window and finish him, but he couldn't leave her unprotected. When he found the asshole who'd done this to her, he'd flay the skin from the Savage one slow centimeter at a time.

"I've got you," Aiden told Maggie as her gray eyes rolled toward him.

Unable to resist him, Maggie fell against his chest as he eased her into his arms. Flashing red and blue strobes filled the cab when he lifted her. Figures scurried into the shadows as brakes squealed. Some of those figures had bodies draped over their shoulders, and she realized the vamps were carting away their wounded and dead.

She had enough reason left to understand the monsters weren't removing the bodies for nostalgic reasons, but because they were covering their tracks. No one was supposed to know vampires existed, not for sure, but she did.

She'd stumbled into a massive pile of crap here.

Aiden watched the Savages slip away. Two of them carried the bodies of the two he'd killed in the ambulance. The third limped badly as he ran, and Aiden guessed it was the Savage whose back he'd broken. He knew he'd killed at least two in the alley, so where were the other three?

"Roger," Maggie whispered.

Aiden turned toward Roger sitting in the driver's seat. Despite his blood loss and the erratic beat of his heart, Roger's brown eyes locked on them, and Aiden could see the anger shimmering in them.

"Let her go," Roger croaked.

That was not going to happen. Taking the man's chin, Aiden knelt before him and focused all his concentration on those eyes as he wove his way into Roger's mind.

"You have no idea what happened here tonight. You remember nothing of the alley or anything afterward." Aiden glanced at the windshield, as outside doors slammed and shouts filled the air. He had to get them out of here. "You do not know what became of Maggie," he continued. "You do not know anything, understand?"

Roger gave the smallest of nods. Aiden released his chin and glanced at Roger's torn neck. The Savage had ripped his throat open enough to hide all evidence of what had happened to him. Turning, glass crunched under his feet as Aiden slipped into the back of the ambulance.

He lifted the stretcher and tossed it out of his way. Blood from the two Savages he'd killed coated the floor, but their bodies were gone. The Savages may be assholes, but they also didn't want the human race to know of their existence. It could spell the death of all vampires if people ever learned the truth.

Vampires were stronger and immortal, but they were also greatly outnumbered by a species known to distrust and fear anything different than them.

There was nothing he could do about the blood or the destruction wrought here, but he knew humans had a way of explaining away the unexplainable. He had to trust in them to do that here.

"Someone's in the back!" a woman shouted from outside.

Footsteps raced toward them as Aiden leapt out of the ambulance and fled into the night with Maggie cradled against his chest.

W HEN HE WAS certain they were far enough away from the ambulance, and he didn't smell any Savages pursuing them, Aiden risked stopping. Slipping into an unlit side street between two warehouses, he leaned back to gaze down at Maggie. He brushed aside the loose strands of hair clinging to her face. Soft as silk, her hair shone red in the glow of the distant street lamps.

She's mine.

He almost laughed out loud with the knowledge. He'd been so certain he'd never find his mate, that he would die or turn Savage before he encountered her, but now he held her in his arms. And she was amazing.

Not only was she beautiful, but she had the spirit of a hellion, one that more than matched his own. She could pack a punch, didn't back down, and her blood was pure ambrosia. She may be as lovely as the porcelain dolls his sisters had collected, but she was far from delicate; his still aching nuts were proof of that.

She was his, and he had no idea what to do to get her to stay with him. Right now, all that mattered was keeping her safe. Glancing over his shoulder, he studied the shifting shadows, but he didn't detect the stench of garbage.

His gaze returned to Maggie as her fluttering eyelids caused her lashes to tickle his bare chest. He'd stopped the Savage before it could take much blood from her. However, he'd heard it was excruciating for someone to have their blood taken from them against their will, and judging by the rigidness of Maggie's body when he'd discovered the Savage feeding on her, she'd been in a lot of pain.

She hadn't responded to him like that when he'd taken her blood. No, she'd melted against him as if she enjoyed it as much as him. To her, there had been a difference between him and the Savage. He didn't know what that meant, but he hoped it indicated she might develop an attachment to him in the future.

Studying her, he noted the paler shade of her skin and the fine blue veins running through her closed eyelids. Her heart still beat steadily. The bleeding from his marks had stopped, but the Savage had torn her shoulder open, and blood continued to trickle from the wound.

The Savages were still out there, most likely hunting him. Her blood would be an irresistible beacon to them, and he needed her stronger. Shifting his hold on her, he lifted his wrist to his mouth and bit into it. She might be mad at him for this, but it was necessary, and after watching her tonight, he knew this woman did what it took to survive.

He rested his wrist against her parted lips and allowed his blood to flow into her. He wouldn't give her much, and she hadn't lost enough blood for this to start the change in her. His blood would only close her wounds while strengthening her.

Maggie sighed when the delicious liquid hit her tongue. She'd never drunk anything like it, yet she felt as if she'd spent her whole life searching for it. The taste and the sensation of it sliding down her throat made her feel as if she'd suddenly found the answer to a question she hadn't known she'd been asking. The warm, clove-spiced liquid pooled in the back of her throat before she swallowed it.

As if she'd taken five shots of espresso, energy infused her body. Her muscles, which had been rigid and sore, relaxed. Her tongue flickered out and tasted something warm, solid, and salty. When she recognized it as flesh, she couldn't suppress a mewl of need as instinctively she realized who she tasted. Like in the ambulance, her body reacted to his with desire.

Feeling stronger, her fingers curled around his thickly muscled wrist as she consumed more of what he offered her. Wait...

Something wasn't right. Her eyes flew open when she realized she wasn't drinking from a cup but straight from his wrist. She was consuming his *blood*.

Holy shit!

As if his flesh scorched her lips, she threw his wrist aside and bolted upright. Aiden caught her before she could fling herself out of his arms.

"It's okay," he soothed as he set her on her feet. Disappointment filled him when she gazed distrustfully at him while backing away.

"You were giving me your blood!" she accused.

"It was necessary to stop your bleeding."

The calmness of his reply set her teeth on edge. "Bandage the wound then!"

He smiled at her. "That's your area of expertise."

"And yours is blood?"

"One of them."

Maggie glanced around as she tried to figure out where they were and which was the best way for her to bolt.

"I'm not going to let you go," he said.

Her head snapped back around to him as indignation filled her. "You're kidnapping me?"

"No. I'm keeping you safe. The Savages have smelled your blood, one of them has tasted you, and they'll want you as much as me now. They're out there hunting for us right now. I won't let you go while they remain free and alive."

"I didn't do anything to them!" Maggie protested.

"They don't care about that."

She took a calming breath before she started screaming over the injustice of it all or kicked him in the nuts again. She'd simply done her job, and now she was being hunted by some weird-ass vampires, and this crazy-ass vamp was telling her he wasn't going to let her go.

Yep, life sucks, so get a helmet, Maggie. There's a lot worse happening to someone else in the world right now; suck it up.

That reminder helped to embolden her a little. Hitting and yelling might make her feel better, but it would accomplish nothing other than tiring her out. She suspected she would need all her energy to survive this night and escape this guy. She had to remain calm and learn as much as she could, knowledge was power.

CHAPTER ELEVEN

"What are Savages?" she asked.

"Killers."

"I'm pretty sure you did your fair share of killing back there!"

Bricks pressed against her when she backed herself into a wall. She immediately sprang away from it and started edging away again. He followed her with measured steps while he idly pulled off the electrodes from the EKG machine still attached to his chest and tossed them aside.

She couldn't stop herself from drinking in the sight of his bare chest and chiseled abdomen. Black hair ran across his chest and encircled his nipples, but he wasn't overly hairy and his stomach was mostly bare of it. She nearly licked her lips when her eyes fell to the ridges carving the ten pack of his stomach before dropping lower.

The jeans he wore hung low on his hips to reveal the solid V of muscle there and the black trail of hair leading from his belly button to his waistband. Every inch of him was as finely honed as a knight's sword. She'd never seen a man as large or solidly built, at least not in real life.

"I should have said that, unlike me, the Savages are killers of innocents," Aiden said. "They slaughter humans or other vampires who live in peace. They're monsters who must be hunted and destroyed. That's what I do."

And you can keep me from becoming one of them. Aiden kept that thought to himself. She looked panicked enough right now without him throwing more wood on the fire.

His words tore her away from her intense and ridiculous perusal of his body. She should be plotting her escape and staying as far from this creature as she could. She should *not* be wondering what it would feel like to have that body pressed against hers as he thrust into her.

"Well, good for you," Maggie replied. "Is that why they're after you?"

Aiden ran a hand through his hair. He didn't see how the Savages could have known he was a purebred or working with Ronan, but maybe they'd somehow discovered that. They'd come after him with enough numbers to make him suspect they knew who and what he was.

"I'm not sure why they're after me," he admitted.

This was all *way* too much to deal with right now, Maggie decided as she stared at the man before her. All she wanted was a long, hot soak in her tub, a giant glass of whiskey, and to forget any of this had happened.

She'd especially prefer to forget the delicious taste of his blood on her tongue. She couldn't stop herself from licking her lips before she jerked her gaze away from the frozen trickle of blood on his wrist.

What is wrong with me?

Her heart beat faster in her chest, and her knees quaked. She'd only ever backed away from one other, and she'd vowed never to do so again, yet she continued to edge away from him. She didn't think he'd kill her. His bite had only been a pinprick of pain compared to what that other bastard had done to her. This man could have drained her dry by now if he intended to kill her.

She was fast, tough, and fully prepared to claw the eyes out of someone if necessary for survival, but she'd never encountered an aura of power like the one emanating from him. If this man chose to be the windshield, she would be the splattered bug.

No, she didn't continue to back away from him because she feared he would attack her, but because of the way he made her feel all disconcerted yet strangely whole in a way she'd never known she could be. She'd never been normal, but until this man rode her ambulance, she hadn't realized she'd been missing something.

"Roger!" she blurted as the reminder he'd been in her ambulance made her recall the events of earlier. Forgetting her uneasiness of this man, she rushed toward him. "We have to go back to Roger! We have to help him! Those *things* were everywhere!"

Aiden caught her around her waist before she could bolt past him. "He's fine," he assured her as he pulled her back. "The arrival of the police and more ambulances chased off the Savages."

She flailed in his grasp for a minute before going still. "Then I have to go to the hospital to see him."

"Not tonight. The Savages are hunting us."

"How do I know you're telling the truth?"

"You'll have to trust me."

"Trust you!" She snorted. "I don't even know your name!"

"I wouldn't lie about Roger's safety; you would only learn the truth eventually. If you'd like, you can call whatever hospital they took him to and find out how he is. My name is Aiden Byrne, and you are... Maggie May?" he asked, uncertain if that was her name or a nickname.

"Maggie May is a song. Roger calls me that sometimes." Lifting her hand, she rubbed it over her heart as she recalled that thing sitting on Roger's chest, feeding on him. "Are you sure he's okay?"

"He was still conscious when I last saw him, and the humans were with him when we left. I think he'll survive what happened to him."

She glanced longingly at the end of the road. "Let me go."

Knowing that it would be a small step toward gaining her trust, Aiden reluctantly released her. "If you're not Maggie May then you are?" he prodded when her attention remained elsewhere.

"Magdalene Doe," she murmured absently, more focused on her concern for Roger than Aiden.

"As in Mary Magdalene?" he asked as he pulled the last electrode off his chest and tossed it aside.

Her eyes shot toward him. "It was never proven she was a prostitute. Just because someone writes it down or states it at some point in history doesn't make it true!"

It surprised her how easily she slipped back into a defensive stance about her name. Some of the numerous schools she'd attended had been far less fun once the kids learned who Mary Magdalene was in history. Many of those kids chose to forget Mary Magdalene was also a saint and focused on her possible sordid past when it came time to tormenting Maggie.

She'd spent most of middle school denying she was a prostitute, and part of high school throwing dollar bills back at asshole teen boys who asked her for lap dances. Then, during her junior year and at her final school, she'd realized she was throwing back perfectly good money and pocketed it.

They'd stopped throwing the bills afterward and started waving them in her face. One day, having had enough, she'd knocked Ray Jessup on his ass with a roundhouse punch to the face. She'd bashed out two of his teeth and taken the ten he'd been waving at her.

Afterward, there had been no more catcalls, and the boys in that school had given her a wide berth when they saw her in the halls. She'd never had a lot of friends, but after that incident, almost everyone avoided her. She may have been a sickly baby and child, but she'd outgrown that period of her life to become strong and unruly enough, so the kids in most of the schools she attended became scared of her.

Aiden grinned at her, pleased to see the fire back in her eyes instead of uneasiness as Magdalene glowered at him. "I never said anything about her being a prostitute, and I like the name Magdalene," he told her.

"I don't care," she retorted.

His eyes shot beyond her when something cracked behind them. He stepped forward to clasp her elbow and draw her closer. "We have to keep moving," he said briskly.

Maggie tugged at her arm, and he released her as he stalked deeper into the shadows. He searched around them as he scented the air, but all he detected was the briny smell of the ocean and the feral aroma of nearby rats.

"Are you a vampire?" Maggie blurted as she walked beside him.

"What do you think?"

"I think you bit me! And it was a dickhead move!"

Aiden winced. That never should have been the way he first tasted her blood. He could take the memory from her, but the idea of messing with her mind in such a way made his gut clench. He would have to make it up to her, somehow, once he got them out of this mess.

"I'm sorry," he said. "But I was weakened by their first attack on me, and I needed blood to fight them again. Without it, we'd be dead."

Maggie frowned at him before leaning back on her heels to inspect his injury. Her breath hissed in through her teeth. His flesh was still raw and bloody, but where a human would have been on the ground, unable to move, and crying, he strode relentlessly forward. Not only would a human be in the fetal position, but their spine would also still be visible. However, Aiden's muscle had already knitted closed to cover the bone.

"How is that possible?" she whispered.

Aiden didn't have to ask what she was talking about; he knew what she meant. "I heal fast, and your blood helped speed up the process."

Maggie tore her gaze away from his back. The hair on her neck rose as some of her mother's rambling words floated back across her mind. *Monsters. Red eyes. Vampires. Monsters! Monsters! Monsters! Take your blood, take your body! VAMPIRE!!!!*

Maggie gulped as she recalled that last word being screamed at her while she'd hurried from the institute where her mother resided.

CHAPTER TWELVE

"VAMPIRE," she whispered.

Aiden became alarmed by the sudden pallor of her skin. She'd been apprehensive earlier, but she looked ready to pass out now. "Are you okay?" he inquired.

Shaking her head, Maggie took a deep breath and focused on the now. She could sort out the mess with her mother later. She was walking with a vampire while being stalked by other, killer vampires. Those things took precedence over her mother's insanity... or lack thereof.

"I'm all right," she said.

"Can you tell me what happened before I woke in the ambulance?" he asked Maggie. "I thought they were going to kill me; how did I survive?"

She gave him a brief rundown on what she'd seen and what Harding had told her about his arrival at the alley.

"Do you have a phone?" Aiden asked when she finished.

"Why?"

"I don't know where mine is, and I have to call a friend. This mess has to be cleaned up. The humans saw too much tonight, and they can't know about our existence. Those were dead Savages there with me; their bodies need to be removed from wherever they were taken. Probably the morgue."

"Hate to tell you this, but there's countless books, movies, and legends about vampires and their existence. The word is out."

"The legend is out, the truth is not, and it has to remain that way."

"Oh!" Maggie's hand flew to her mouth as she recalled that she hadn't told him everything. "One of those Savages was still alive! Walt and Glenn were working on him! They took him in their ambulance!"

"Fuck, that's not good. Can I use your phone?"

"It's in the ambulance. I put it in the glovebox at the start of every shift, with my wallet."

Aiden's teeth grated together as the splash of headlights illuminated the end of the road. "Maybe we can find a pay phone."

"Did you just crawl out of the coffin?" Maggie snorted.

"What?"

She rolled her eyes. "What century do you think this is? When was the last time you saw a pay phone?"

"They're still around, occasionally, and vampires don't use coffins."

"We'd have a better chance of stumbling across gold on the street than a pay phone. And I'm glad coffins aren't an option for the undead."

"I'm not undead. I have a heartbeat—"

"I'm aware."

"I breathe," he continued, "and I was born."

"You were *born?*" she asked incredulously and shut out her mother's screaming words when they tried to squirm their way back into her brain.

"Yes. Both my parents are turned vampires; those are vampires who were once human but were changed by another vamp. I'm a purebred vampire as I was born to two vampire parents, and so were my nine siblings."

"*Nine* siblings?"

"Yes."

"Your poor mother."

His mouth quirked in a small smile. "We do torment her."

Maggie's mind felt sluggish as she struggled to process the things he was telling her, but the harder she tried, the more lost she felt and the more her mother's screams resonated in her head.

"We'll buy a cell phone," Aiden stated.

The phone situation was an easier problem to deal with, so she decided to focus on it. "With what money?"

"I don't need money."

"And why not?" she demanded.

"Because I can get into their minds and make people do what I command."

She gawked at him and stuttered out some words before finally forming a sentence. "Well, isn't that the cherry on top of this twisted sundae."

"I won't do it to you, and I only do it when it's necessary."

"Well, ah... yippee for me and the rest of humanity, I guess."

Unable to resist touching her again, he pushed back a loose strand of auburn hair and tucked it behind her ear. She watched him with fascinated eyes but didn't try to pull away.

Maggie had been contemplating running away as fast as she could before he touched her. After training for over a year to run the Boston Marathon with some of her coworkers next month, she'd gotten herself down to a sub six-minute mile. She could go faster for sprint distances. He may be an immortal, healing machine, but she could haul ass, and she could run for miles.

That simple touch dissolved her impulse to flee. She didn't know what it was about this blood-sucking creature, but she couldn't resist him. Maybe it had something to do with the need she saw in his eyes. She sensed it was for *her*, but she didn't understand why. Maybe it was the tender way he caressed her when she'd seen how vicious he could be. Or maybe it was because it had been so long since anyone touched her with any kindness, she couldn't resist it now.

You better start resisting, she told herself.

"Even if you don't need money," she said, and stepped back so his hand slid away from her, "no one is going to let you enter their store looking like that. If your whole goal is to go incognito for the vampire race, walking around shirtless and with a gaping wound in your back won't help your cause. Do you plan on taking out all the security cameras inside the store and along the way to the store too?"

"You can go into the store and buy a phone."

"Hate to break it to you, Nosferatu, but *I* require money for purchases, or at least a credit card."

Aiden felt the pockets of his jeans, but he knew they would be empty. He'd tossed his cash onto Carha's table. A sick feeling built within him at the reminder of Carha. He suddenly felt filthy standing next to Maggie, as well as ashamed of where he'd been earlier and the reason why he'd been weak enough for the Savages to take him down.

His foul appetites had put him in this position, and because of it, he'd placed Maggie in danger. "I'll keep you safe," he murmured as self-hatred grew within him.

"That means a lot coming from the guy who sucked a pint from me earlier," she retorted. "Without asking me first, by the way. Which I think should be proper etiquette before sinking your fangs into someone's throat, just so you know."

"Noted."

"Hmm," Maggie grunted and sent him a side-eyed glare.

It was going to be difficult to get her to warm up to him, he realized, but he'd work on that later. Now, he had to get a hold of Saxon, let him know what happened, and find somewhere safe for Maggie to stay. Too much had happened, the bodies of the Savages were too scattered, and too many humans were involved for him to be able to clean this mess up by himself.

"Where do you live?" he asked.

"Like I'm going to tell you?"

"Do you have a phone at your place?"

"No."

"Magdalene—"

"No one calls me that," she interrupted. "And I don't have a landline. I'm not eighty, are you?"

Caught off guard by her question, he did a double-take before chuckling. "Maybe one day, but I turned twenty-five on February twenty-seventh. And how old are you?"

"Twenty-four. Are vampires immortal?"

"Yes."

"All right. So anyway, I don't have a phone at my place."

Aiden's hand fell to his empty pockets again. He'd always kept his cell in the front pocket of his jeans. "Did I have my phone with me in the ambulance?" he asked her.

"I didn't go through your coat pockets. Once I discovered a crossbow, I decided it was best not to touch your things."

"I kept my phone in my pants. Did you notice it?"

"I didn't see any phone when we put you in the ambulance."

Aiden stopped at the end of the road. There were a few cars

parked nearby, probably from overnight employees working the warehouses. At the end of the road was a cross street. A few cars idled at a red light there. When they started driving, one of them turned toward them and crept forward. He'd run at least a mile from the ambulance before stopping, not nearly as far as he would have liked, but he'd had to check on Maggie.

He should have gone further.

CHAPTER THIRTEEN

AIDEN'S FANGS throbbed as he watched the vehicle, fully prepared to destroy any threat lurking within it. Most Savages preferred to use their feet as transportation when they hunted. It was a lot easier to jump someone and kill them on foot than it was to park a car and go after them, but he'd come across Savages hunting from cars before.

The streetlights illuminated the couple behind the wheel. From somewhere nearby, music thumped, and he suspected someone was throwing a party in one of the warehouses. They could go to that party in search of a phone; any man would gladly hand his over to Maggie if she asked for it. However, he wasn't about to send her into somewhere with people he didn't know alone, and she was right, in his condition, he would only attract unnecessary attention.

He felt the pockets of his jeans again as he recalled the phone in his hotel room. He'd tucked the key card to his room into his back pocket, but it was gone too. The hotel had been about as nondescript as it got, there weren't any cameras, but there had been a fair amount of foot traffic on the street outside it.

He could change the memories of the clerk, but he'd never go unnoticed by pedestrians in his condition, and he couldn't alter the minds of everyone he encountered. Also, if the police found the key card, they might go to the hotel before he could cover this up.

The phone and key card wouldn't lead back to him in any way. The phone was a burner, the hotel room rented under another name, and the clerk wouldn't be able to recall his appearance. Aiden had twisted that memory in his mind. It wasn't often Ronan's men messed up, but they had strict regulations in place to cover their asses in case it happened.

He wasn't one of Ronan's men yet, he still had more training to go through, but he followed their rules and precautions. After tonight, Ronan might decide to cut him loose and Aiden wouldn't blame him.

He had to return to the alley where he'd been attacked to see if his phone had fallen out somewhere there. If he couldn't find it, he would have to go back to Carha's club. He didn't want Maggie anywhere near Carha. From what he'd seen of Maggie tonight, she could hold her own, but Carha was a malignant, twisted thing.

Carha was also his shameful secret; Maggie could be the redemption his ravaged soul needed.

He could make his way to Saxon instead of returning to the alley or Carha's, but his meeting place with Saxon had been twelve blocks beyond the club. Without Maggie, he could cover the distance in no time, but he couldn't move as fast with her. Trying to reach Saxon would only waste more time and, with the Savages hunting them, put Maggie at unnecessary risk for longer.

He had to take care of this mess if he was going to keep all those he cared about safe. It had been months since he'd seen his young nieces and nephews, but he loved them all and would die for them. Their lives would be in peril if the truth of vampires ever came out to the human world.

As much as he preferred to shelter Maggie from Carha, he might not be able to.

"This way," he said and turned to the right.

"Where are we going?"

"My phone might have fallen out in the alley." He wasn't going to mention Carha's place unless it became necessary.

Some of the color leeched from her face. "We're going back there?"

"Yes."

"There are probably still police all over the scene," she said.

"I'll deal with that when we get there."

"You could let me go. I promise I won't say anything about what I saw tonight or vampires. I prefer not being locked away for the rest of my life because people think I'm crazy."

"I can't let you go until I know you'll be safe." He didn't want to let her go at all, but he might not have a choice if she decided to be free of him.

"I'd go straight to the closest hospital or police station to find out where they took Roger. No one is going to attack me before then."

"Maybe when the sun is out."

"Vampires really can't go out in the sun?" she blurted.

"The killers amongst us can't. I can."

"Why can some of you go out in the sun, but not others?"

"The more a vampire kills, the stronger and weaker their corrupted soul becomes. Their physical strength increases, but they lose the ability to tolerate sunlight, holy water, crucifixes, and they become less able to cross bodies of water. Some of the legends the humans weaved over the years have a basis in fact."

"Fascinating," she murmured.

She walked swiftly beside him, her long legs keeping stride with his. Gauging his height compared to hers, she guessed he was about six inches taller than her five-eight, yet she didn't labor to keep pace with him.

She'd prefer not to go back to that blood-soaked scene, but she didn't resist him either. More than anything, she didn't want to come across one of those Savages on her own. She'd bide her time until she knew she'd be safe, and then she'd run.

Aiden's gaze raked her frame again. Her baggy, khaki shirt hid most of her figure, and so did her black, cargo pants, but he'd felt the lushness of her breasts and the strength in her lean body when she'd worked her way out from under him in the ambulance earlier.

If he got the chance, he would enjoy peeling away her clothes to reveal what lay beneath. It would be better than any present on Christmas morning. The thought of it stirred his cock. He gritted his teeth as he forced aside thoughts of hearing her passionate cries. Now was not the time.

He tilted his head as he studied her more closely. She was taking all of this amazingly well. She could be in a state of shock, but he didn't think so. Maggie struck him as a person who picked herself up and carried on no matter what it took for her to do so. What had her life been like to make her that way? What was it like now?

"Do you have a boyfriend, Magdalene?" he inquired, and she shot him a look.

"No one calls me that," she told him again. "Everyone calls me Maggie or Mags. And why do you want to know?"

"I'm curious."

"Look how well that worked out for the cat."

Before he could reply, a metal trash can lid clattered ahead of them, drawing his attention back to their surroundings.

They'd left the warehouse district behind and entered a street lined with row houses. The scent of human food cooking, the sounds of TVs, laughter, and music drifted from the homes.

Most of the residents of these houses had settled in for the night, but a bald, middle-aged man with a cigarette dangling from his lips emerged from one of the driveways. He cursed as he kicked the lid toward the curb. Aiden relaxed as the man's eyes came toward them. The man nodded a greeting before plopping the trash can he'd been carrying on the curb. He picked up the lid and shoved it onto the bag poking out from the top of the can.

Then, his gaze raked Aiden. "What happened to you?"

"Lost a bet," Aiden replied.

"I guess so," the man muttered and turned to walk back toward his house.

A window slid open, and then a woman shouted, "You better not be smoking out there!"

The man tossed his cigarette down and stomped it out. "Get off my back, woman!"

Maggie chuckled. "I love Boston."

"Were you born here?"

She shot him another look then decided it didn't matter if she told him. "Yes."

"And your boyfriend?" He had to know how difficult it would be to win her. Was she already in love? Was she married? He glanced at her left hand but saw no rings there.

"I'm between boyfriends." She thought he smiled, but it was so fleeting she couldn't be certain. "Were you born here?"

"No. I was born in Oregon."

"You're a long way from home."

"Oregon isn't my home, not anymore."

"So where is your home, Nosferatu? A cave somewhere so you can hang upside down like a bat or in actual bat form?"

She'd asked the question in a teasing tone, but she held her breath, afraid he would say yes.

"I live in a house in Massachusetts, and vampires don't shapeshift," he said.

That was good to know. "What about your girlfriend? Is she a vampire?"

"No girlfriend."

A clammy sweat coated her skin when she realized they were getting closer to the alley where this all started. Some instinct caused her to step closer to him when they turned onto another street.

They strode past the entrance to another alley, and Aiden stiffened beside her. He clasped her elbow and drew her so sharply against him that she staggered to the side. She opened her mouth to yell at him, but when she spotted the ambulance parked against a chain-link fence at the end of the dark alley, her words died off. No lights were on, and no sounds came from the vehicle.

CHAPTER FOURTEEN

MAGGIE FROWNED AT THE AMBULANCE, not sure what was going on. Why was it here? Where was everyone? Then it sank in that she was staring at the ambulance Glenn and Walt had been riding. The ambulance they had stuck one of those *creatures* in.

"Glenn, Walt," she breathed.

She leapt forward so fast she yanked her arm free of Aiden's hold before he could stop her. Her arms pumped as she raced down the alley. Skidding to a halt at the back of the ambulance, she saw the doors were cracked open and flung them wide.

Arriving at her side, Aiden wrapped his arm around her waist and spun her out of the way before something could launch out at her.

"What are you doing?" she demanded, squirming to break free of his hold.

When nothing sprang out of the back, he set her on her feet but grabbed her again when she went to jump inside. Maggie spun on him. "They're my friends!" she snapped. "Let me go!"

"You don't know what happened here," he replied. "There's a reason why the ambulance is here and not at the hospital, and it's not a good one. You have no idea what you could be running into."

Maggie eased her struggle as she gazed into the back of the ambulance. The interior light illuminated the empty stretcher within. Blood coated the stretcher and the floor, but she saw no bodies or signs of a struggle. The stillness mixed with all that blood gave her the strangest sensation of having just stepped into the Twilight Zone.

"He was eviscerated. Look at the blood he lost," she said. "There's no way he would have been capable of attacking Walt and Glenn."

He sensed Maggie wanted him to reassure her that her friends were okay, but he wouldn't give her false hope. "You didn't think I would heal so fast either," he said gently. "And ten Savages jumped me in that alley. I killed two in the alley and injured this one, but only five came after me again in the ambulance. The two others either went back to the alley to clean up the mess they created with the humans, or they followed this ambulance so they could stop the ambulance before it reached a hospital."

He'd been the one to eviscerate the man? She didn't know why that surprised her. She'd seen him tear the heart out of a man, but she hadn't fully put it together that he'd also killed those other two and incapacitated this one. She did now.

She didn't look at Aiden as she gazed at the blood-streaked walls and floor. Her nose wrinkled at the familiar, coppery tang of blood mingled with garbage. "Why does it smell like trash?" she muttered as she pulled herself into the back.

Aiden glanced at the nearby dumpster before focusing on Maggie again. He didn't detect the pungent stench of a Savage nearby, but there was a faint aroma of refuse from the dumpster and the drying blood of the Savage.

Careful to avoid stepping in the blood, Maggie made her way to the front of the ambulance. She was terrified of what she'd find there, but she couldn't stop herself. She glanced behind her and froze when she saw Aiden was gone.

Through the open doors, she watched two cars drive past. She didn't breathe while she searched for Aiden. Had he left her? She should be jumping for joy, but she didn't feel any joy.

When one of the ambulance's front doors opened, she almost shrieked as she spun toward the front. She bit back her cry as the ambulance sagged and Aiden's head appeared between the seats. His blood-streaked face was a welcome relief.

"Stay back there. You don't want to see this," he said to her.

"No, I don't, but I have to."

She covered the remaining distance between her and the cab in one step. Two bodies were in the front seats. Tears burned her eyes, and her hand flew to her throat when she identified them. Walt leaned against the passenger window, his glazed eyes open and his throat torn out.

Her gaze turned to where Glenn lay slumped over the wheel. She couldn't see his face, but gashes sliced his throat and blood stuck his khaki shirt to his neck. Roger would be devastated when he learned of Glenn's death. They may not work together anymore, but Glenn was Roger's best friend. Both divorced, they bowled on Monday nights, went to baseball games every summer, and argued politics.

She'd never seen Roger cry before, but she knew he would cry for Glenn. Roger was the closest she'd ever come to a father figure in her life, and the idea of anyone hurting him made her itch to claw their eyes out. Glenn and Walt had dedicated their lives to helping others and some *monster* had killed them. They'd deserved so much better than this.

Lifting her gaze, she met Aiden's over Glenn's back. "Whoever did this, can't be allowed to live."

"They won't be," he promised, hating the sheen of tears in her eyes.

"I can use the radio, call for help, and wait for it to arrive," she told him. "They'll take me to safety."

"I can't be here when they arrive, and I'm not leaving you."

She had expected as much, and she wasn't up for arguing right now. "The ambulance has a GPS, but I can't leave them here like this until they're noted as missing and located."

"We have to," Aiden replied. "If you use the radio to call someone and aren't here when help arrives, you could become a suspect. It's unlikely that anything will stick to you, but is it a chance you're willing to take?"

Her gaze fell to Walt and Glenn again before she bowed her head. "No," she whispered.

She turned away from him and started back. Dropping down from the driver's side, Aiden rushed around to meet her before she could climb out of the ambulance. Maggie's eyes were dry when they met his.

Aiden wiped off the handles she'd touched when she opened the back doors. Even if they pulled his prints, they weren't on file. Besides, the police would never be able to locate him or keep him imprisoned for long if they were somehow lucky enough to stumble across him.

"Did you touch anything inside?" he asked.

"No," she replied. "We have to let someone know they're here. They *can't* stay in this alley. They deserve better," she said.

He rested his hand on her arm to draw her closer. "We'll call someone as soon as we can, but we have to go."

∽

TRUDGING ALONG BESIDE AIDEN, Maggie kept her head down as she tried to process everything that had happened tonight. Exhaustion tugged at her; her shoulders hunched up as the memory of Glenn and Walt dead in that ambulance flared back to life.

She'd never lived under the delusion life was fair, but she *loathed* that it was sometimes a cruel bitch with razor-sharp claws, who laughed as she sliced you open.

Maggie could hear the cruel laughter of life bouncing around her skull now.

"I'm sorry about your friends," Aiden said.

When he rested his hand on her shoulder, she flinched away from him. Aiden buried the stab of hurt the rejection brought with it. She had every right to hate him. He didn't blame her for it, yet if he let her walk out of his life, he would have to go to Ronan and ask to be destroyed. Yesterday, that prospect hadn't seemed bleak. Now that he'd met her and glimpsed the promise of a life without his constant, insidious cravings, death was the last thing he wanted.

They were only a couple of blocks away from the alley when the putrid stench of garbage hit him. Aiden grabbed Maggie's elbow, halting her as he searched for the enemy he knew was near. He looked to the doorway beside them as Maggie tugged angrily on her arm.

"Let go!" she hissed.

"There are Savages near," he said.

Maggie forgot all about fighting him as she glanced wildly around. Those *things* were close! Where were they supposed to go? Which way was the right way to avoid them?

"Where?" she whispered.

"I don't know."

"Then how do you know they're close?"

"I can smell them. This way."

He pulled her toward an alley tucked between two brownstone houses. Maggie's nose wrinkled as the aroma of the garbage in the dumpsters wafted to her. Aiden's pace increased; he hurried her forward and turned to the right. Before Maggie could stop him, he spun her into his arms, lifted her off the ground, and plunged downward.

Maggie gasped, her hands dug into the solid muscle of his shoulders as he hit the ground. Glancing around her, she realized he hadn't dropped off the face of the earth but into a staircase leading to a basement.

Cradling her closer against him, Aiden cupped her nape as he edged into the shadows until his back came up against a metal door. He shifted Maggie and set her down as he gripped the metal handle behind him. If it became necessary, he would rip the door off and enter into whatever lay beyond, but he wouldn't alert the Savages to their presence or trigger any alarms if he didn't have to.

Maggie's heart beat rapidly against his chest as her short nails bit into his shoulders. The silken strands of her hair tickled his hand. He caressed her neck with his thumb, hoping to calm her. If he didn't have her to worry about, he'd go after the Savages and hunt them down with or without his weapons.

However, if something happened to him, there would be no one to keep her safe from the killers. His family and friends didn't know she existed yet, and she wouldn't know where to turn for help.

Mate or not, her blood was more potent and sweeter than any human blood he'd ever consumed. The Savage who attacked her still lived, the others had to have smelled her, and they would all hunt her for her blood. It wouldn't be difficult for the Savages to find her either. They knew where she worked and could easily track her with that knowledge.

Savages may be ruthless killers, but they weren't mindless. Many times, they were almost too cunning in their hunt, and they often liked to play with their food. They would destroy her.

His gaze fell to her throat and the wound the Savage had left in the hollow of where her neck and shoulder met. His blood had healed the wound, as well as the marks *he'd* left on her. Blood still stained her shirt, but the odors of the alley should cover it.

Aiden's muscles rippled against her cheek when footsteps rang off the buildings surrounding them. Maggie had resolved to distance herself from him as soon as she could, but she found herself pressing closer when the footsteps drew nearer.

She turned her face into his chest, the hair there tickling her nose. His flesh was warm against hers, and she had to resist the urge to nuzzle it, or even worse, lick him. Her skin prickled with awareness, her body came alive in a way that was completely out of place given their current circumstances. His masculine scent filling her nostrils pushed out the lingering odors of blood and trash as whoever was out there ran past where they stood.

Aiden remained unmoving while he strained to hear more. Maggie's breath warmed his chest as the rotten scent of Savage faded away. Briefly, he closed his eyes to relish in the feel of her lush breasts pressing against him.

His driving urge to keep her alive opened his eyes and propelled him back into motion. He didn't release her as he edged toward the bottom of the stairs and craned his head to peer up. "It's gone," he murmured.

Lifting her head, her lips brushed his chest when she turned to look too. She hated the thrill that went through her at the contact. It made her recall when he'd bitten her in the ambulance and the rush of erotic carnality that swept her. She took a deep breath and cursed her sweaty palms.

"If you could smell him, how come he didn't smell you?" she whispered.

"I don't carry the same rancid stench the Savages do."

"But he's a vampire; he couldn't detect your blood or mine?"

"There are thousands of scents in this alley, including blood. And going by the strength of the odor of blood here, someone bled a *lot* in this alley within the past week, possibly to the point of death. There is also the feral aroma of wild animals as well as the stench of garbage that has nothing to do with the Savage who went by," he whispered in her ear. "Those scents masked us from him."

Maggie inhaled deeply, picking out hints of the different things he'd spoken of on the air. "The Savages smell like garbage to you?"

"Like extremely rotten garbage. I don't scent him anymore, but stay here while I take a look."

She started to protest, but she didn't have it in her to deal with any of those monsters again.

Icy air brushed over her skin when he released her, and for the first time, she realized she'd left her coat in the ambulance. They'd been moving so much and so rapidly, she hadn't had a chance to process the cold. Without Aiden's arms around her, and just standing there, the frosty March air cut through her clothes. Her warm exhalations created plumes of smoke in the air as she shifted from foot to foot to get some heat back into her numb toes.

It felt like she'd left her entire life behind in the ambulance, and she couldn't shake the thought she may never get it back.

Of course, I'll get it back, she firmly decided. As soon as

Aiden found a phone and she figured out a way to go home, she'd return to her life.

She had no idea how she would explain all of this to the police, her boss, Roger, and everyone else, but she'd puzzle that out when she wasn't running for her life, cold, starving, and exhausted.

Maggie's gaze fastened on Aiden's back as he walked up the stairs. Not only was his spine no longer visible, but neither was his muscle, and she swore his skin was closing before her eyes. Around the healing flesh, faint white lines spread across his back. She recalled seeing them when he'd been lying in the alley and thinking they looked like whip marks zigzagging out from his wound earlier.

What had he endured to leave scars like that on him?

With the way he healed, she wouldn't have expected him to have any scars, but there they were. Tonight wasn't the first time he'd been severely injured, and with the brutal life he apparently led, she suspected it wouldn't be the last. She sensed a darkness in Aiden that might match or exceed that of the vampires hunting them.

Aiden turned back to gaze down at her. Illuminated in the dim glow of a distant street light, his face was stark, his body streaked with blood and dirt. She should run screaming from the danger he radiated. She should draw the attention of someone who might call 911 or help her. She could flee easily enough, yet when he descended a couple of steps to extend his hand to her, she took it.

CHAPTER FIFTEEN

To avoid the Savages, Aiden traveled a crisscrossing route that eventually led them back to where it all started. Maggie froze when she saw the empty alley and the lack of police cars there. "I don't understand," she whispered. "They should still *be* here."

Aiden glanced over the brick walls and the blood-streaked asphalt. "One of the Savages must have come back here to clean up their mess while the other went for Glenn and Walt. Or both of them came back here, and the Savage in the ambulance worked alone."

Panic clawed at her as she tried to process his words. "But where did all the police go? Did the Savages kill them all?"

"I don't know," Aiden said.

"Some of those officers were my friends, or at least acquaintances. I have to find out what happened to them."

"We'll find out," he promised. "But they're probably not dead. Killing a bunch of police and emergency workers, or turning them, is a lot tougher to cover up than changing their memories and sending them on their way. The Savages would have preferred to kill them, but though they're bloodthirsty, they aren't stupid."

"You really think the Savages didn't kill them?" she croaked.

"Yes."

"But they killed Walt and Glenn?"

"That was different," Aiden said as he carefully picked his way around the blood splattering the alley floor. If the police happened to come back here, they couldn't see his fresh footprints, or Maggie's. He didn't have to tell Maggie that as she also avoided the blood.

"Most likely the two who didn't pursue me came back here to fix the mess they created," Aiden explained. "They must have decided their friend would either awaken and take care of himself, or they would deal with it later, if he did make it to a hospital. The Savage with Walt and Glenn was mutilated, ravenous, and looking to feed so he could heal himself. If the two Savages came back here, it was probably to cover their tracks and not to kill."

"You're not just saying that?"

He heard the note of hope in her voice and turned to look at her. "No, I'm not," he replied. He would have done anything to make her smile, but he wouldn't lie to her. "I don't know for sure, but I would say those who were here are still alive, minus some memories, and probably any cameras or evidence they had."

"Okay, good."

Aiden searched the alley for his phone and the key card to his hotel room. He discovered the phone at the other end of the alley. Lifting it, he examined the broken bits before tossing the useless thing aside. The key card was gone. Either one of the officers had picked it up before the Savages returned, one of the Savages had it, or it had fallen out somewhere else.

Either way, it didn't matter, they couldn't use it to find him.

Aiden's head lifted when the scent of garbage wafted to him; he sniffed at the air as the aroma drew closer. Maggie placed her hand over her nose. Aiden frowned as he studied her, but the growing stench drew his attention away. They had to get out of here, but the only safe place to go was Carha's club.

He despised revealing any glimpse of the depravity of his soul to Maggie, but her safety was far more important than keeping his secrets hidden. Most of the vampires in the club weren't fighters, but they wouldn't tolerate an attack from Savages on anyone, especially since Savages had a habit of turning on and killing their kind for more power.

Placing his hand on the small of Maggie's back, Aiden hurried toward the door. "What are you doing?" she whispered.

"They're coming."

Maggie glanced nervously over her shoulder, but she didn't see or hear anything. She wouldn't argue with his vampy senses. However, she had no idea what he expected to do with a closed metal door that had no handle. She had no doubt he could break it down, but their location wouldn't exactly be unknown if he did.

Stopping before the door, Aiden knocked three times on it. He paused for a few seconds before knocking two more times, then paused again and rapped five times.

A window in the middle of the door suddenly slid open. Maggie would have leapt back if Aiden's hand hadn't been there to stop her. Perfectly hidden, she hadn't seen the outline of the window until it opened. Leaning forward, she tried to peer inside, but there was only darkness on the other side.

Maggie jumped when a set of brown eyes appeared in the window. Those eyes settled on her before going to Aiden. "Back so soon?" a gruff voice said from the other side.

"Let us in," Aiden commanded, and he could sense Brutus's annoyance over the order. He also knew Brutus would do as he said.

After a hesitation, the click of locks turning filled the air, and the door creaked as it swung open. Maggie's heels dug in when Aiden nudged her forward, but unwilling to face those Savages again, she gave in to his prodding and stepped inside.

The door swung shut behind them, and the locks slid back into place. "Reeks of blood out there, and you look like shit. What happened?" Brutus demanded.

The voice coming from her right sent shivers down Maggie's spine as she glanced anxiously around, but with the door closed, a tomblike darkness enveloped them.

"Didn't you look?" Aiden inquired.

"Couldn't risk giving away our location," Brutus replied. "Heard the voices and sirens and figured it was a human situation."

"Not entirely," Aiden replied. "Some killer vamps were involved, and they're coming back."

"Bastards," Brutus hissed. "They may be coming back, but they won't be coming in."

"Good." Aiden turned away from Brutus, and keeping his hand on the small of Maggie's back, he led her onward.

"Carha will be happy to see you again," Brutus said from behind them and gave a small chuckle.

"Who is Carha?" Maggie inquired.

"She owns this place," Aiden replied.

"Where are we?"

"It's a private club."

"As in a private *vampire* club?"

"Yes, but there are humans here too."

Maggie's step faltered before she forced one foot in front of the other again. "Did you bring me here to pass me around to your friends?"

"I would *never* allow such a thing to happen to you. *No* one will touch you here; I'll make sure of it."

"Is this where you were before the Savages jumped you?"

"Yes."

She heard a hint of something she couldn't quite place in his voice; was it reluctance? Annoyance? "You said you didn't have a girlfriend."

"I don't."

The crisp way he said it made her hackles rise. She should be the irritable one. She was the one who'd been bitten by *two* vampires tonight, consumed vampire blood, attacked, and who was now walking into a vampire club with one of her biters. He may say he'd keep these vamps from touching her, but what if he couldn't? She'd seen how brutal he could be, but how many vampires were inside here? And what if he changed his mind and she became the vampire equivalent of movie theatre popcorn in this place?

All she knew about vampires was what she'd seen in movies or read in books; so, he was either a completely misunderstood, brooding guy looking for love, or he was biding his time before turning her into a bloodless husk. Either way, she didn't know vampire culture, and she didn't like uncertainty in her life. She'd had far too much insecurity as a child and teen; she didn't tolerate it as an adult.

"So is Carha an ex-girlfriend who will be happy to see you again so soon?" Maggie retorted and hated the jealousy she couldn't keep from her tone.

"She's not an ex."

Maggie opened her mouth to speak before closing it. She didn't care who Carha was to him. As soon as he got a phone, she could go home.

At the end of the hall, Aiden pulled open another door, and the most cliché, slow, emo music she'd ever heard drifted to her. She rolled her eyes and looked to Aiden. "Really hyping up that whole misunderstood creature of the night vibe in here, aren't they, Nosferatu?"

Aiden's mouth quirked in a smile. "It's not my place."

"Nope, you just support it."

Something flashed through his eyes, but she couldn't make out what it was before he glanced away from her and led her forward. Maggie kept her face impassive as they passed shadowed booths with couples sitting in them. Many of the couples were sipping glasses full of red liquid, but judging by the scent and the viscosity, they weren't drinking blood.

The place was huge and could easily hold at least three hundred people, but there were only fifty or so occupants. Maggie's eyebrows shot up when she spotted the coffins in the corners of the room. When she realized the music came from those coffins, she had another eye-rolling moment. She almost gagged at the coffin-shaped bathroom doors.

"Oh, for fuck's sake," she muttered. "I feel like I stepped into a bad, B horror movie without the campy humor. I don't know who in here is human and who isn't, but they're all eating this up."

"For some, this is a way of life."

"For some, or for you?"

"Not for me."

"Could have fooled me. That guy at the door knows you, and so do they," she said as two men waved to Aiden and he returned the wave with a nod.

His eyes flashed to her. "There's much you don't know about me, Magdalene."

"And I never will."

The tug of sadness accompanying her words startled her.

She wanted free of Aiden, and she'd prefer not to learn anything more about him. So then why was she trying to figure out what he'd been doing in this place earlier? She may not know him well, but she didn't think he'd have to come to a place like this for sex and blood.

Aiden's teeth grated together. He'd finally met his mate, and everything that could have gone wrong with their meeting had. He didn't expect it to get any better while they remained in here, but he couldn't do anything about that.

CHAPTER SIXTEEN

AIDEN STEERED her toward the bar and an empty seat at the end of it. "They're not all real blood," he assured her when he saw her gazing at the red jugs.

"I know," she replied.

"I guess you would know, with your job and all."

She shrugged. "I can also smell the difference."

He opened his mouth to question her further, but the bartender arrived before he could. "Aiden," Zeke greeted and was unable to keep the surprise off his face when he saw Aiden's hand on Maggie's back. Unlike many of the other vamps who frequented Carha's, Aiden had never brought someone with him. "I'm Zeke."

Maggie took the hand Zeke extended toward her. "Maggie."

"You weren't gone long, and you look like shit; what happened to you?" Zeke asked Aiden as he released Maggie's hand.

"Long story," Aiden replied.

"Anything to do with the commotion Brutus reported outside?"

"Yes."

"Glad you're okay." Zeke glanced at Maggie again. "Looks like you two could use a drink."

"Yes," Maggie said. "I'll take a glass of the best whiskey you have that doesn't have food dye or blood mixed in with it." She thrust her thumb at Aiden. "I'm assuming he has a tab, so it's on him, and so is everything else I order."

Zeke chuckled. "And you?" he asked Aiden.

"The same. I also need a phone."

"You got it." Zeke dipped into his shirt pocket and pulled out his phone; he tossed it over to Aiden who caught it. "I'll be back with those drinks."

Aiden pulled up the touchscreen pad for numbers and typed in the one he'd memorized for Saxon earlier in the night.

"What?" an irritated voice inquired after the first ring.

Aiden stepped away from Maggie, who didn't so much as glance at him before snatching up the glass Zeke placed before her and downing its amber contents. She pushed the empty glass toward Zeke, took Aiden's drink, and consumed it too. She held up two fingers to Zeke.

"It's me," he said to Saxon.

"Where are you?" Saxon demanded. "I've been standing on a street corner for half an hour waiting for you, and more than a few women are hoping I'm a male prostitute. I've been propositioned more times than the last woman on earth would be if the entire male population survived. I shit you not."

"And how many have you taken up on their offers?"

Saxon chuckled. "None yet, but there were a few it distressed me to turn down."

Aiden was aware of what inner battle Saxon waged to keep

his demons at bay as Saxon spent much of his free time in a woman's bed.

"I ran into some trouble tonight." Aiden explained what happened while Maggie downed another glass of whiskey and leaned across the bar to speak with Zeke.

Zeke nodded before heading through the door connecting the bar to a back room.

"Where are you now?" Saxon asked.

"I had to come back to Carha's. I was hoping to find my phone, which is garbage."

"I see." Saxon didn't ask what he'd been doing at Carha's to begin with; they all had their ways of dealing with the darkness plaguing them.

"There's more."

"When isn't there?"

"I found *her*," Aiden said.

"You're kidding?"

Saxon knew immediately who he meant as there was only one *her* any of them would mention finding. "No. She's one of the paramedics who picked me up, and she's sitting at the bar in Carha's right now."

"Get her *out* of that place."

"You think I want her here? The Savages are outside. I have no weapons, and I'm weakened. I can't take them on, and I can't put her at risk by taking her out of here. One of them already bit her." Remembering the attack on her caused his fangs to lengthen. "I'd rather have her safe and repulsed by me than have one of those *things* get their hands on her again."

Saxon took a deep breath. "Okay. I'll call Ronan and get some backup. I'll meet you there."

"Be careful. I have no idea if they've brought in more Savages to help them with this or not. They cleaned up most of their mess pretty quick, but there's still more cleaning up to do."

"We'll take care of it. See you soon."

Saxon hung up before Aiden could reply. He walked over to return Zeke's phone to him as Zeke slid a plate of food in front of Maggie. Aiden glanced down at the steak in front of her and the blood oozing from it.

"Is that undercooked?" he asked.

"I hope so," Maggie said as she picked up her knife and fork.

He watched as she sliced into the steak and shoved a piece in her mouth. She rolled her eyes and practically danced in her chair as she gave Zeke an enthusiastic thumbs-up. "Didn't realize you served human food here," Aiden said to Zeke.

"Occasionally we receive an order for it, and you know Carha, she'll take every penny she can," Zeke replied. "Can I get you anything else?"

"I'll take a pint of blood," Aiden said.

He expected Maggie to flinch or give him a disgusted look, but she didn't glance up as she continued to devour her meal. Usually, he wouldn't drink anything that didn't come straight from a vein, but he needed to gain strength, and he required blood for that.

Zeke returned with a pint glass full of blood and placed it in front of him. Aiden drank it as Maggie shoved her empty plate away, patted her belly, and downed another glass of whiskey.

"I have to clean up," she said and hopped off the barstool.

She felt revitalized by the whiskey and food as she strolled across the bar toward the bathrooms. Unlike other clubs or bars where she would have to fight her way through people dancing, most of the crowd here were in the booths. Some of the patrons slipped behind one of the two metal doors on the other end of the room, opposite the bar.

Maggie frowned at those doors as she wondered where they went and what they hid. Then, she realized she was better off not knowing.

She felt Aiden's body heat against her elbow before she made it twenty feet, but she didn't look back at him as she walked toward the bathrooms. Stopping outside the hideous doors, she almost laughed when she saw one marked Dracula and the other as Dracula's Bride.

"Oh, for crying out loud," she muttered and pushed into the Bride's room.

She couldn't hold back her laughter when she spotted the fake garlic hanging from the light fixtures and the cross-shaped soap dispensers before heading into one of the stalls. The corniness of it all made her giggle again when she emerged from the stall to wash her hands.

She barely recognized the pale, dirty woman staring back at her from the mirror above the sink. She washed the grime from her face and scrubbed her hands. Blood stained the collar of her shirt, and the front of it was streaked with dirt and blood, but no wounds marked her neck. She poked at the places where Aiden and that thing had bit her, but not even a tenderness remained. Gulping, she shoved aside her unease and focused on getting herself at least a little cleaned up.

She undid the buttons of her shirt and pulled it open to reveal her black tank beneath. She was half-tempted to take her ruined uniform shirt off and throw it in the trash, but if they went back outside, she would regret her decision to stroll around in a tank top in March. She shouldn't be wearing her uniform in a bar, everything in her protested it. However, she didn't think anyone here would report her, and she doubted anyone she knew was going to enter this place anytime soon.

A knock sounded on the door before it pushed open a little. Aiden stuck his head inside. "You okay?"

She glanced at him as she pulled the elastic from her hair and slipped it onto her wrist. "Fine."

Running her fingers through her hair, she worked the tangles from it the best she could. She jumped when Aiden suddenly appeared behind her in the mirror. She'd assumed he'd gone back out, and she hadn't heard him enter.

She gazed at his reflection in the mirror while he stared at her. Seeming almost transfixed by her hair, he lifted some of it and ran it through his fingers. She went to pull it away from him but stopped when he spoke.

"Beautiful," he whispered. "You are so beautiful, Magdalene."

She didn't know how to reply to that as his scent of cloves and male engulfed her when he leaned closer. He set his hands on her hips and turned her to face him. She'd witnessed his supernatural abilities, yet the vulnerability in his eyes stole her breath.

His eyes fell to her mouth. Before she knew what he intended, he bent to brush his lips over hers. She jumped a little when a jolt of electricity sizzled across her lips and through her body. She should pull away from him. The last thing she needed was to get entangled with a vampire, especially one who had more layers than an onion.

She didn't move.

She'd watched him tear into other vampires like they were gummy bears. He'd bit her and taken her blood. Her mother was in an institute probably screaming about vampires right now, and Maggie had always feared they'd be sharing a bunk one day, but she couldn't pull away from him.

"So beautiful," he murmured against her mouth before nipping her lip.

Her body reacted like he was the artist and she was the clay as she melded against him. His hands slid over her hips and around to cup her ass. He pulled her so close she could feel the rigid length of his cock straining against his jeans as it pressed into her belly. She'd only had one boyfriend who mattered, but even though they'd loved each other deeply, she'd never felt desired before.

That was *all* she felt now.

Unable to stop herself, she rose onto her toes, slid her arms around his neck, and ground against his erection. The motion caused more pleasure to spiral through her as it stoked her passion. He released a sound that had her contemplating tearing off her pants as her nipples hardened and a wetness spread between her legs.

When Aiden slid his tongue over her lips, they parted to let it slip inside. A feeling of calm spread over him again as he ran his tongue over the sweet hollows and contours of her mouth. He'd only meant to check on her, to make sure she was okay, but when he'd seen her, he'd been unable to resist the lure of her.

He'd expected her to push him away, to leave the room or order him out. He hadn't expected her to drape her arms around his neck and draw him closer. He hadn't expected her to respond to him as enthusiastically as he did her, and now he couldn't let her go. Lifting her, he settled her ass onto the restroom sink so he could nestle his rigid cock between her thighs.

Her fingers dug into his nape; she pulled him closer as her body arched toward him. Sliding his hand toward her breasts, he was about to cup one of them when hinges squeaked.

Maggie didn't have time to process what caused the squeak before the kiss ended, she was abruptly lifted off the sink, and set down behind Aiden. She blinked as she tried to figure out what happened. One second, she'd been in a lust-filled haze. The next, she was staring at Aiden's broad, still healing back.

"Oh," a voice squeaked. Maggie peered around Aiden to the woman standing in the doorway. The woman blushed prettily, put her hand over her mouth, and giggled. "There are rooms in the back for that."

"Get. Out," Aiden commanded in a voice that made the hair on Maggie's arms rise.

The woman's smile vanished, and she ducked away. Maggie tugged at her shirt, buttoning it over her tank again as she tried to hide the blush creeping through her cheeks. Never in her life had she considered sex in a public place, especially not the bathroom of a funky vampire club with a virtual stranger, but if that woman hadn't walked in, she didn't know what would have happened between her and Aiden.

Scratch that, she *did* know; that was the problem. This man was a killer, he was a vampire, she didn't know him from Adam, and she'd been about to screw him in this germ-ridden room. *What is wrong with me? Get it together!*

She straightened her shoulders, smoothed back her hair, and stepped out from behind his back. She dodged his hand when he reached for her and hurried toward the door. "Maggie—"

"I want another drink," she interrupted.

"I'd like to clean up. Please wait for me in here."

The please made her stop at the door, but she didn't look at him again. When the water turned on, she glanced back to make sure he was distracted before slipping out the door.

CHAPTER SEVENTEEN

MAGGIE SLID onto the barstool she'd vacated and held up two fingers to Zeke. He brought down two more glasses of whiskey and set one in front of the place where Aiden had stood. Zeke removed Aiden's empty glass with its remnants of blood at the bottom. She drank her whiskey before grabbing Aiden's glass.

"You sure can handle a lot of whiskey," Zeke remarked.

"High tolerance." It was something she'd always had. It would take another five drinks before she'd start to feel the warmth of a buzz and the whole bottle to get her drunk, but even then, she'd still walk and talk mostly normal.

"Hmm." Zeke's eyes roamed over her. When she narrowed her eyes at him and drew her glass forward as if she were going to hit him with it, he chuckled. "You're a beautiful woman, but I much prefer the company you're keeping to you. No offense."

Maggie relaxed and chuckled. "None taken. You can have him."

"If only," Zeke sighed. "I've never seen him come in here with a woman before."

Maggie frowned at him, uncertain of how to reply or why

he'd revealed that to her, but she sensed he was trying to tell her something as his warm, golden-brown eyes held hers.

"Can I get you something else?" he asked after a minute.

"A bottle of Sam, please," she said. She'd love to keep chugging whiskey down, she'd welcome the oblivion being drunk would bring her, but losing her wits would be a horrible idea. "And a water."

"You got it," Zeke tapped the bar with his hand and turned away from her.

At the end of the bar, a woman waved her hand at Zeke and shouted for two red delights. Now that it was getting later, the place was starting to pick up. Zeke walked over to one of the jugs and poured the woman's drink while Maggie sipped at her whiskey.

Turning on her stool, she studied the other occupants in the bar. Two men were slipping past one of the metal doors together. They must be going to the rooms the woman who walked into the bathroom mentioned. Maggie's neck flushed with the reminder of what nearly occurred in the bathroom and what that woman had interrupted.

Taking another sip of whiskey, she pondered if vampires carried diseases. She'd seen the way Aiden healed; would their bodies fight off disease in the same way they fought off death? It would be fascinating to study them to find out.

The more she watched those in the bar, the more she could differentiate between the humans and vampires, or at least she believed she could. The vampires held themselves in a confident way no human, not even the most gorgeous supermodel, could match. The humans fawned like a puppy lapping up the attention of its owner. The people laughed; the vampires placated with smug smiles.

Appearance-wise, the vampires all looked human, but they couldn't completely disguise they were on the hunt. There was something about them that reminded her of a cheetah stalking the hapless gazelle.

Maggie smiled at Zeke when he returned to set her beer and water in front of her. "Thanks."

He hurried away to take care of the growing crowd gathering around the bar. Judging by the fluid way he moved while filling orders, and the speed with which he did it, Zeke was also a vampire.

Tearing her attention away from him, she glanced at her watch. It was almost nine. She felt as exhausted as if it were four in the morning, but it was only the time when many people were getting ready to start their Friday night.

Aiden emerged from the bathroom. Anger glinted in his eyes when they met hers across the crowd. She must have annoyed him by not obeying his order, but then she didn't obey anyone who didn't sign her checks, and sometimes she had a problem with that. She lifted her glass and gave him a small salute with it before finishing off the whiskey and setting the glass aside.

She tried not to, but she couldn't help admiring Aiden as he stalked toward her. Clean of dirt and blood, the skin of his face and chest were unblemished and the golden color of someone who spent a lot of time in the sun. His wet, short black hair had been shoved back from his face as if he'd been running his hands through it.

His pushed back hair emphasized his broad cheekbones and square jaw. The green of his eyes brightened as they remained focused on her. There were actors in Hollywood who didn't look anywhere near as alluring as this man, and she realized he could entice her to sin in ways no other ever had.

Look away! Her mouth went dry as her gaze remained riveted on the etched muscles of his torso, shoulders, and arms.

This was a man who kept himself in shape. Not because he

wanted to show off for his friends, like some of the guys she'd seen at the gym, and not because he was trying to pick up women. No, instinctively she knew Aiden had worked himself into this condition because he was a hunter, a killer; it was what he did, and he did it well. In the process of making himself ever more lethal, he'd carved himself into a six-foot-two mountain of predatory grace.

And right now, that mountain looked like it might turn volcanic.

Maggie lifted her beer and gulped half of it down. Every inch of this vampire exuded wrath and brutality, yet her skin prickled at the memory of the way his kiss warmed her from head to toe, and she found herself craving more of him.

Twenty feet away from her, a voluptuous, black-haired woman stepped in Aiden's way. A thunderous expression crossed his face. Maggie expected the woman to shrink away from that look, most would have, but the woman placed one hand on her rounded hip and stuck it out in a flirtatious way.

"Who is that?" she asked Zeke when he came back to rest his elbow on the bar next to her.

"Carha, my boss."

"Oh."

This was the woman who would be happy to see him again. Maggie's hand clenched on her bottle as she studied the woman with a far more critical eye. She would have pegged Carha as a vampire before she learned Carha owned this place. Carha moved with the same confidence and fluidity they all did.

Carha was shorter than her and voluptuous where training for the marathon had honed Maggie into a runner's lean build. Even before she'd started running, Maggie hadn't possessed the curves this woman did. She forced herself not to glance at her chest. She'd been a C cup since she turned sixteen and was perfectly sized for her body. Easily a double D, Carha's breasts were thrust enticingly high by the form-fitting, red bodice she wore. Carha's black, leather pants hugged an ass that would have cartoon character's tongues rolling out, and her thighs could crack a skull.

When Carha glanced over her shoulder, she discovered Maggie staring at her. Maggie held her gaze; she'd already been caught, glancing away was pointless. Smiling at Carha, Maggie took a swig of her beer. Malice flashed through Carha's green eyes, and her exquisite face scrunched up. Then she smiled, turned back to Aiden, and rested her hand on his bare chest in a gesture that screamed intimacy.

The impulse to tear Carha's fingers off hit Maggie so hard that, for a second, she felt as if someone had taken a sledge-hammer of jealousy and bashed her with it. She looked away from the two of them before she leapt off her barstool and smacked Carha with her bottle.

She'd had some violent encounters in her life, knocked a few people out, but she'd never done it because she was *jealous*. And certainly not because she was jealous over a guy who'd done nothing but put her in jeopardy since she'd had the misfortune of meeting him.

I'm losing my mind, or maybe it's already gone.

She couldn't stop herself from glancing back at Carha and Aiden. He'd told her Carha wasn't his girlfriend or his ex, yet there was obviously something between them. However, he'd just kissed *her* in the bathroom.

Yeah, like you've never been kissed by a guy who was only looking to get laid before.

But Aiden's kiss had felt different. There had been a yearning in it she'd never experienced from another before.

Or did you want it to feel that way because of how badly you desire him?

She couldn't deny that was possible. And maybe Aiden was

only using her to make Carha jealous. Maybe there hadn't been Savages outside and he'd only brought her here to get Carha's attention. Her stomach knotted at the possibility.

Maggie turned back to find Zeke watching her. She didn't see pity in his gaze, but an understanding that made her like him more.

CHAPTER EIGHTEEN

"THOUGHT YOU MIGHT LIKE THIS, HON," Zeke said and nudged a fresh beer toward her.

"Thank you."

"Would you like something else?"

"A foot massage; my feet are killing me."

Zeke smiled at her and patted her hand. "I hear that. Far too much time on my feet tonight, and it's just getting started."

"Those gel inserts for your shoes help," she told him and lifted her foot. He leaned over to look at her black boots. "Seriously, these things killed me before I discovered those inserts."

"I'll have to check them out."

"Well, hello, Red," a voice purred from beside her.

Maggie glanced at the man who had walked over to stand by her left elbow. She wasn't in the mood to be hit on tonight, especially not by a vampire—which, judging by the way he glanced at her throat, he was. She somehow managed to keep her face blank as eyes the color of the sky stared back at her. His blond hair had been styled in the best way to enhance his extremely handsome features. She suspected it had taken him hours to get his hair to look as if he hadn't done anything to it.

This vampire was more handsome than Aiden. He possessed the smooth, polished look of a GQ model, but unlike the way Aiden made her feel, she didn't experience the tiniest flutter in her belly when she looked at him.

Focusing on Zeke again, she ignored the vamp as she continued their conversation. "I get them at Walmart for only five bucks."

Like Aiden, Zeke probably didn't have to stress about paying for things, but he was a bartender, which meant he worked for some reason. And from what she remembered of the income she'd earned while tending bar when going through EMT school, he might be looking for a deal like she always was.

"That's my price range!" Zeke declared.

"Would you like a drink, Red?" the handsome vampire asked.

"Got one," she replied and lifted the fresh beer Zeke had brought her.

"How about something stronger?"

Maggie turned on her stool to stare at him. "No, thank you."

His smile faltered before he showed all his pearly whites again. "Come on, Red, I'm trying to be friendly."

"Seriously, no. I'm not in the mood."

Zeke straightened behind the bar as he glanced between her and the vamp. Then, he looked to where she'd last seen Aiden. Her hackles rose when she saw this. With her back now to him, she couldn't see Aiden anymore, but she was quite capable of taking care of herself.

"Red—"

"Blond guy," she interrupted as she set her beer down. "Let me give you a clue. One"—she lifted her index finger—"men who hit on women by calling them Red or Blondie are annoying. We know the color of our hair; no need to remind us. Do yourself and all women a favor, find a new line.

"Two"—she lifted her middle finger to hold it next to the other one—"when a woman tells you no, she means *no*. Three, I have a drink." She continued to lift her fingers as she counted off her points on them. "Four, when someone is speaking to someone else, that is not an invitation for you to insert yourself into their conversation. It's rude and, once again, annoying."

The smiled faded from handsome's face before she counted to two. Now his eyes glittered with malice. This man was unaccustomed to hearing no, but more than that, he was the type who expected her to be fawning all over him. She'd fended off her share of unwanted male attention over the years. This was the first one who could snap her neck between this breath and the next, and he looked pissed enough to do it.

"Let me tell you something," the vamp said as he leaned so close she could smell the peppermint toothpaste on his breath.

"Back off, Nigel, now," Zeke stated in a steely tone that had replaced his casual air.

"First off, *Red*," the vamp sneered.

Maggie's hand tightened on the neck of her beer bottle in preparation of braining him with it if it became necessary. When his hand wrapped around a chunk of her hair, another hand shot out so fast in front of her that she didn't see it until it enclosed on Nigel's fist gripping her hair.

"Let her go."

The frigid tone of Aiden's words sent a shiver down Maggie's spine even as his body heat warmed her on the side he stood against. Nigel's eyes shot past her. Maggie risked the tug on her hair to turn her head. When Nigel's grip on it caused her hair to pull taut, Aiden's eyes flashed down to it, and a crackle of power radiated off him.

Maggie's breath caught. The wrath emanating from Aiden caused some of the other patrons to slink away from them. She glanced at Nigel to find he'd bared his fangs. Nigel was either extremely brave or a flat-out fucking moron. She was guessing the later.

She was trapped between two immortal, formidable beings, yet she felt no fear as Aiden stepped protectively closer to her. Nigel could snap her neck in a second; Aiden could tear his throat out in less time than that.

"Easy, fellas," Zeke advised. "Nigel, let her go."

Nigel's hand constricted on her hair. Maggie didn't make a sound; she feared if she cried out, Aiden would kill him. Then, Nigel gave a small tug on her hair, pulling her toward him. Crimson bled through the green of Aiden's eyes and the muscles in his forearm bulged until the veins stood out against his skin.

Maggie didn't know what Aiden was doing until she heard bones snap, crackle, and pop like a bowl of cereal. Nigel howled as Aiden's fist continued to compress on Nigel's. She couldn't suppress a gasp when she realized Aiden was crushing Nigel's hand within his grasp.

She didn't have a chance to blink before Nigel released her hair and Aiden swung his other hand up to punch Nigel in the cheek. Blood spurted out of Nigel's mouth, but none of it splattered her as Aiden had somehow already moved around the barstool to stand between her and Nigel.

His hands twisting in Nigel's shirt, Aiden lifted him. Aiden propelled him three feet back into the wall as if Nigel weighed no more than a toddler when he had to be at least two hundred pounds. The wall shook, and plaster cracked and rained down around them.

Releasing his shirt, Aiden thrust his forearm up into Nigel's throat. He lifted Nigel until his toes dangled a good foot off the ground. Wheezing for air, Nigel kicked his heels against the wall; his face turned beet red as his eyes bugged out of his head.

Blood rushed through Aiden's ears as the need to kill pounded inside him and his darker urges rose to the forefront. Death. He *needed* death and blood. Needed to feel the life slipping away from another and the rush of their warm blood filling his mouth. He trembled with the restraint it took to keep from destroying Nigel.

Stay in control. Don't lose it. Not in front of Maggie.

But this man had dared to *touch* her. He'd placed his hands on her, he'd pulled her hair, and he'd been pushing her after she'd told him no.

He never should have left her alone. Her beauty was a homing beacon to every vampire in this place, as was the sweet scent of her blood. But after their encounter in the bathroom, he'd needed to steady himself before seeing her again. When he'd looked up and discovered her gone, he hadn't immediately gone after her because he half feared he wouldn't be able to stop himself from taking her into one of the back rooms to finish what they'd started.

And there was no way his first time with her was going to be in *this* place.

When he'd finally stabilized enough to leave the bathroom, Carha had intervened. He had to tell her what happened outside her club. He would never return to this place for her services again, but he couldn't make an enemy of her either— not while Maggie was in here, vulnerable and exposed. Carha was also a good source of information as she learned a lot of what happened in the vampire world from the many vamps who frequented her club.

Carha's eyes had flashed red when she'd asked him who Maggie was and what she was doing here with him. His constant refusal of Carha had annoyed her; bringing Maggie here infuriated her. It had taken more to placate Carha than he'd liked, and this vampire had mistakenly assumed Maggie was fair game.

Aiden should have been able to control himself enough after the bathroom to keep her safe. He didn't know who he was more furious at, himself or Nigel. Nigel's eyes bugged further out of his head. His good hand tore at Aiden's arm to pull it free, but Aiden only dug his forearm deeper into Nigel's windpipe.

"There is no fighting in *my* bar!" Carha shouted from behind him.

"Nigel crossed the line," Zeke said.

"I don't care!" Carha spat. "I do not tolerate fighting in my place and especially not over a fucking *woman!*"

Maggie bit her lip when Carha sent her a scathing look that also somehow dared her to say something. Maggie hadn't survived this long by running her mouth when she shouldn't, and the whiskey hadn't loosened her tongue enough for her to say something stupid. She sensed their situation was precarious, and she'd prefer to see tomorrow.

"Aiden, let him go!" Carha barked, her attention turning back to the men.

Aiden showed no signs of releasing his hold.

"What's going on here?" a voice demanded.

Maggie turned to find a handsome vampire with blond hair and hazel eyes shoving his way through the crowd. She hadn't realized they'd gathered so many onlookers, but a circle had formed around them. The new arrival stopped short when he reached the front of the group. His eyes flashed over all of them as he took in the situation.

"Stop him, Saxon!" Carha snapped at the new arrival.

"Aiden, let him go," Saxon commanded.

Aiden remained rigid for a minute before his muscles

relaxed and he set Nigel on his feet. Maggie heaved a sigh of relief and glanced at Zeke who gave her a wan smile. Aiden's face was a mask of stone when he stepped to the side to let Nigel pass. His eyes followed Nigel's every move as the wounded vamp kept his good hand on his throat.

"You're going to have to leave, Aiden," Carha ordered. "Don't come back here again for at least a month."

"Whore," Nigel was brave enough to hiss at Maggie while Carha spoke.

Maggie didn't even glance at him. Uncertain of what he would do, she didn't want to give Aiden any indication Nigel had said something more to her. She'd been called worse in her lifetime, and the battered vampire was the least of her concerns. Her main worry was for Aiden as she sensed he teetered on a dangerous precipice. He'd released Nigel, but his eyes still shone the color of lava, and his chest heaved with his breaths.

She didn't think anyone else had heard Nigel, but Saxon's eyes flashed toward Nigel as Aiden charged forward.

"Idiot," Saxon hissed.

CHAPTER NINETEEN

Unwilling to attack Nigel with his back turned, Aiden grabbed his shoulder and spun him around before driving his fist into Nigel's face. The scent and sticky feel of the blood bursting over him provoked his bloodlust, and he gave into the ever-present brutality coursing through his veins.

Nigel wailed and threw up his hands to protect his nose, but all that did was hammer his hands into his face when Aiden punched him again.

"Whoa!" From the corner of his eye, Aiden saw Saxon lunge forward and yank a stool away from someone. "This is between them. You don't want more of *us* involved."

"Enough!" Carha shouted. "Saxon, tell him to stop." Saxon stared wordlessly back at her. Carha glared at him before focusing on Aiden again. "That is enough! If you don't stop, Aiden, I'll ban you for life! And that means from *my* services too!"

Aiden lifted his head to glower at Carha when she revealed this in front of Maggie. His brief distraction allowed Nigel to punch Aiden in the jaw, but he barely felt it as he pummeled Nigel's stomach.

Maggie gawked at Aiden as he battered the vampire and Carha shouted at Aiden to stop before promising to cut him off from her services. Maggie's mouth fell open further, and her stomach rolled. What services? Was Carha a prostitute? She didn't see why Aiden would need to use prostitutes. With his looks, he could get a lot of women, but men were weird, and vampires were stranger.

She forgot all about Carha when Aiden flattened Nigel's nose. Over the years, she'd seen countless violence, been on the receiving end of it more than a few times, but she'd never witnessed anything like the rage driving Aiden. She'd caught glimpses of his control slipping, but it appeared to be completely gone.

The stench of blood permeated the air, and the sounds of punches hitting flesh resonated through the club. Aiden was doing this because of *her*. Nigel was an asshole, but she did *not* want this. However, she had no idea how to stop it. Aiden had become a mindless, killing machine who would only be satisfied with death.

Saxon paced back and forth in front of the fight, keeping back anyone who might try to get involved. The crowd shrank away from him when he smacked his fist into his palm.

"I think he's had enough, Aiden," Saxon said, but whereas his words had stopped Aiden before, he showed no response to them now.

The slightest touch on her hand drew her attention to Zeke. Full of concern, Zeke's eyes held hers as he spoke. "If you tell Aiden to stop, he will."

She glanced at the growing pool of blood spreading beneath Nigel. She had no idea what Zeke was talking about; Aiden wouldn't stop until he'd beat Nigel to death.

"I wouldn't touch her," Saxon said in a low warning.

Zeke yanked his hand from hers before he continued speaking. "He *will* stop if *you* tell him to."

Maggie glanced from Zeke to Saxon who gave her the briefest of nods before he glowered at a vamp who was edging too close. She turned back to the bloody scene before her as Nigel's cheekbone gave way beneath Aiden's next blow.

"Stop." The croaked word barely traveled beyond her. "Aiden, stop. Please, *stop*." The words came out stronger this time.

In the process of drawing his arm back to batter Nigel's already half-smooshed face some more, Aiden froze. Maggie held her breath as she waited for the brutal beating to continue. Instead, Aiden lowered his arm until both his hands rested on the ground beside Nigel's head. His back hunched and his shoulders curved forward like a wolf guarding its prey.

Maggie's eyes widened on his back when she realized his wound had completely closed. The still reddened skin around it made the white scars slashing across his flesh more visible. There was no denying those marks had come from the lashing of a whip or some similar type of weapon.

"Oh," she breathed, her hand flying to her mouth as sorrow mixed with dismay. What had he endured in his life? Who had done this to him and why?

Aiden grappled to get control of himself as Maggie's frightened voice replayed through his head. Nigel had touched her and called her a whore, but he shouldn't have gone after him like that. Not in front of Maggie, not *ever*. He was closer to the edge than he'd realized. Tasting her blood without claiming her had accelerated his need to complete the mating bond as well as started to unravel him faster.

It didn't matter; he could control himself, he *would* control himself, for her.

Slowly, he rose to his feet and braced himself to see her revulsion of him before he turned to face her. He expected her to shrink away when he stepped toward her, but she stared at him with an expression he couldn't quite read. Her eyes ran over the fresh blood coating his chest and face.

"I'm sorry. You shouldn't have seen that." He reached a hand toward her, but when blood dripped from his fingers, he lowered it.

"Here," Zeke said and handed a wet rag over the bar.

Aiden took the rag and wiped most of the blood from him before setting the cloth on the bar. Maggie remained unmoving on the stool when he held his hand out to her. She gazed between him and Nigel for a long minute before she slid her trembling hand into his.

"I'm sorry," he said again.

Maggie tried to tell him not to apologize for who and what he was. She hadn't wanted to witness what she had, but he was a vampire, and as extreme as this had been, he'd done it for her. However, the words froze in her throat when her gaze went behind him to the hostile eyes of the crowd. Some were retreating to their booths, but others remained. The ones who stayed glared from her to Aiden to Nigel and back again.

"Time to go," Saxon said and waved his hands at the crowd. "What? Like you've never seen a man beat another man before? Shoo. Go back to your business. Shoo now."

More of the crowd dispersed, but a few slipped free to kneel at Nigel's side. Nigel groaned when they lifted him to his feet.

"Get out!" Carha spat at them.

Aiden helped Maggie off the stool and clamped his arm around her waist.

"Get out!" Carha nearly shrieked.

"What do you think we're doing?" Saxon demanded of her.

Carha's eyes shot to Maggie when Aiden drew her closer against him. Her lips peeled back to reveal her fangs as her red eyes raked Maggie from head to toe.

"If you touch her," Aiden snarled, "I *will* kill you."

Carha recoiled as if he'd slapped her; hatred simmered in her gaze when it met his. "Don't ever come back here," she grated through her teeth.

"I didn't plan on it," he assured her and kept Maggie well away from Carha as he hurried her forward.

Saxon led the way, waving his hands to gesture the straggling onlookers out of the way as he strode forward. His demeanor remained casual, a smile curving his mouth, but Aiden sensed the tension in him. Carha trailed behind them as the crowd continued to part.

"I mean it. Don't ever step foot in here again," Carha said.

Aiden didn't acknowledge her as he continued forward.

"Do you hear me, Aiden?" Carha demanded and grabbed his arm.

"*Don't* touch me." He yanked his arm away from her. "I have no intention of ever seeing you again, Carha. *Ever.*"

Lifting Maggie off the ground, he switched her in front of him and set her down away from Carha. He slid his hand up to Maggie's nape and cradled her head protectively against his chest. Saxon glanced back at him before slipping into the hallway, and Aiden followed. The door slammed behind them, throwing them into the inky blackness once more.

No one spoke as they walked to the end of the hall where Brutus undid the locks, and they exited into the alley. Aiden glanced around, but he didn't detect any foul aromas. At the end of the alley, a black Ford sat idling. Saxon led them to the car and opened the back door.

"Where are we going?" Maggie asked as she dug her heels in and refused to move forward.

"I'm taking you home," Aiden said.

Her shoulders slumped in relief. She was so exhausted her lumpy bed was a welcome slice of Heaven.

"Go on," Aiden encouraged, and she slid into the back seat.

A man in the front seat turned to face her. She had no doubt the man was a vampire as one fang became visible when he smiled before speaking. "What's up, Red?"

Maggie's heart leapt into her throat when she saw his hair color and gray eyes, but the more she studied him, the more she relaxed. His hair was similar in shade to hers, but it leaned more to the brown of auburn whereas hers leaned more to the red. They both had gray eyes, but hers were so dark they sometimes appeared black, and his were so pure a gray they were nearly silver.

Besides, she'd inherited her coloring from her mother, not the father she'd never known.

"She doesn't like being called that," Aiden said as he sat beside her and closed the door.

He'd been through hell tonight, killed and beaten vampires, yet he still smelled entirely too enticing for her liking. She was acutely aware she didn't smell anywhere near as good. It was completely unfair, yet Aiden seemed not to notice the sweat and alcohol scents clinging to her as he settled close beside her.

Maggie shifted when Aiden's thigh pressed against hers. After everything she'd witnessed from him, after everything she'd learned, she couldn't stop the thrill of excitement that ran through her when they touched. She had to put some distance between them.

"Completely understandable. I'm not all that fond of it either, but it's better than ginger, am I right?" the auburn-haired vamp asked her.

"It is," Maggie agreed.

"It's annoying."

"Not as annoying as when someone tries to pick you up by asking if the carpet matches the drapes."

"I think it's different if a woman asks a man that question. I find myself more than willing to prove it."

Maggie couldn't stop the burst of laughter that escaped her. "It's entirely different then," she agreed.

"Declan," he said before holding his hand out to her.

"Maggie," she said and clasped his hand.

"Pleasure to meet you, Maggie. Where to?" he asked as Saxon opened the passenger door and climbed inside.

Aiden looked expectantly at her, and she gave Declan her address. She held her breath as they drove through the streets of Boston. She was half afraid they would go in the complete opposite direction, but Declan headed toward her apartment on the far outskirts of the city. She lived in a quiet section filled with brick apartment buildings, row houses, and family-owned businesses. Cars lined the streets, but she directed Declan around the back of her building to the small parking lot there.

CHAPTER TWENTY

Before Declan had the car in park, she grasped the door handle and flung it open. Leaping into the night, she inhaled the crisp air before jogging around the building to the front door. She could enter through the back if she had her keys, but she didn't. She punched a code into the keypad beside the outer glass door.

A buzzer sounded, and she pulled the door open as Aiden climbed the stairs toward her. He stepped off the last stair and into the vestibule with her. The door was closing when Declan grabbed it, and he and Saxon stepped inside too. She knew it had been too much to hope they would drop her off and leave her alone.

The three large, male bodies crammed into the vestibule made her feel claustrophobic. She glowered at all of them. "I don't need an escort to my door. I'm perfectly capable of getting there on my own."

All of them conveniently chose to ignore her as she punched numbers into the second keypad. The solid wood, inner door buzzed, and she pushed it open. The familiar aroma of cats, cigarette smoke, and pizza greeted her. Her landlady chain-smoked and had half a dozen cats. The pizza scent came from the Italian restaurant next door.

Maggie was halfway up the gray, carpet-lined stairs, and more than halfway asleep, before she recalled she didn't have her keys. She turned and trudged back down. Saxon and Declan leaned against the outer railing to let her pass, but Aiden followed her.

"Where are you going?" he asked.

"My landlady has my spare key." She stopped outside the first door and knocked on it. "Don't you have somewhere else to be?" she asked when he leaned against the wall next to the door.

She didn't like the idea of him leaving, or the realization she would most likely never see him again when he did leave, but she needed time alone right now. She wished she had a landline so she could call to find out where Roger was and made a mental note to get one as soon as possible. Never again would she rely solely on a cell phone.

"No," Aiden said.

She didn't have time to argue with him before Mrs. Mackey opened her door. Maggie forced herself not to recoil from the cigarette and cat aromas bursting out the door. Mrs. Mackey materialized through a haze of smoke. A shower cap covered her gray curls, the pink bathrobe she wore was threadbare, and a cigarette dangled from the corner of her wrinkled mouth. Mrs. Mackey's watery blue eyes surveyed her before going to Aiden. She smiled and pulled the cigarette from between her lips.

"Magdalene," Mrs. Mackey greeted though she didn't take her eyes from Aiden.

"I'm sorry, but I left my keys at work, Mrs. Mackey," Maggie said. "Could I please have the spare?"

"I hope no one else can find them."

"They're locked safely away," Maggie lied.

"Hmm," Mrs. Mackey grunted and nudged one of her cats back with her foot when it tried to escape the smoke. "Just in case, I'm calling a locksmith to replace your locks and the building's locks, on your dime."

Maggie didn't argue with her. She didn't have much extra money, but she'd prefer her locks and the ones to the building changed anyway as she had no idea where her keys were right now. However, she highly doubted locks and keypads would stop any vampire trying to get into this place. They were good security against humans, not so much against the supernatural.

"Of course," Maggie replied and kept her smile in place. Mrs. Mackey could be difficult, but she also baked a mean chocolate chip cookie, which she handed out to the tenants she favored. Maggie refused to be kicked off the cookie recipient list.

The door closed, and Maggie listened to the drone of the TV in the background as she waited for her landlord to return.

"She's interesting," Aiden said.

"Hmm," Maggie replied and rubbed at her neck.

Aiden's hand covered hers. She should knock his hand away, but when he started kneading her aching muscles, she relaxed into him. Distance was what she needed from this vampire, yet one touch from him had her melting like butter in a hot frying pan.

It's been a rough night, cut yourself some slack, she told herself.

Yes, please cut yourself some slack for lusting after the vampire who might prefer prostitutes and who bit you!

Maggie knocked his hand away as Mrs. Mackey returned with her key. A gleam lit Mrs. Mackey's eyes when she looked at Aiden, and Maggie realized not only had she removed her cap, but she'd also applied a layer of lipstick. Apparently, even senior citizens couldn't help themselves around Aiden.

That didn't make her feel any better about her lack of self-restraint.

Maggie took the key from Mrs. Mackey's outstretched hand as the woman batted her lashes at Aiden. "Have a good night, Mrs. Mackey," Maggie said. "And thank you for the key."

"Of course, dear," she replied.

Mrs. Mackey rested her hand on Maggie's arm and tugged her back when she started to turn away. When the older woman hooked a finger and gestured Maggie toward her, Maggie bent closer. "If I were you, dear, I'd take that man for a ride. Perhaps you'll smile more."

Unprepared for the words, a blush crept up her cheeks as she stepped away. Aiden's smirk didn't help as she turned and shuffled toward the stairs. Feeling more like ninety than twenty-four, Maggie trudged tiredly up the stairs and back past Saxon and Declan.

"I'll help you gather your things," Aiden said as she turned onto the stairwell for the second floor before continuing to the third.

"My things?" she asked, too caught up in her fantasies of food, a hot shower, and pillows to process what he was saying. She'd eaten at Carha's but her stomach was already rumbling again. Apparently, she'd worked up quite the appetite while running for her life.

"Yes. I'll help you pack so we can get out of here sooner."

"Out of here?" she asked stupidly, hating that she parroted him, but she had no idea what he was talking about.

"And somewhere safer."

"I'm not leaving my apartment," she told him. She glanced over her shoulder to find Aiden's eyes narrowed on her. Behind him, Saxon and Declan exchanged a look.

"You can't stay here," Aiden replied.

"I have nowhere else to go."

"You'll come with me."

"No. I won't."

Declan and Saxon slowed their pace; their heads tipped back as if they suddenly found the water stains on the ceiling of the stairwell fascinating.

Aiden didn't break her stare while he spoke. "It's possible the Savages know where you live. They'll come looking for you if they do."

"It's also possible aliens could arrive tomorrow. I'm willing to take my chances."

"I'm not."

"No one asked you!" she snapped and pulled open the door to the third-floor hallway.

She stepped out of the stairwell and stalked toward the door at the end. The same gray carpet lined this floor as all the others. Stopping outside her door, she slid her key into the deadbolt, unlocked it, and swung the door open. She flipped the switch and stepped inside. The glow from a lamp next to her fifth-hand couch illuminated the small living room with its old, hardwood floors and blue throw rug.

The floor had seen better days in the seventies, but she loved the character of every dent and scratch on its golden surface. Sometimes, she would sit and wonder about the families who had lived here before her, the lives they'd led and the love they'd shared. In all her imaginings, no one had lived here alone, as she did.

She may have no one else to share this place with, but it was her home, and she took pride in her ability to keep it. She'd spent the past two years turning it into a place she looked forward to returning to every night.

"I will not leave it," she muttered. "Damn pushy vamps

thinking they—no, *he*..."—over her shoulder, she shot a look at Aiden—"knows what's best for me. You don't."

He didn't speak as he remained standing in her doorway. Maggie bent and unlaced her boots. She tugged them off and set them in the box next to the door before stalking toward her small galley kitchen. She didn't bother with shutting the door behind her; she knew it wouldn't stop Aiden from following her inside.

Opening the fridge, she removed a bottle of Gatorade and the leftover Chinese noodles from the night before. She took a fork out of the drawer as she stared at the open door, but none of the three massive men entered her apartment. Keeping the box of noodles in hand, she slurped some into her mouth as she walked over to the doorway.

Aiden had his hand resting on the doorframe as he leaned against it. He gave her a small smile. "You going to invite me in?"

Maggie froze with a forkful of noodles halfway to her mouth. "That's a *real* thing!" she blurted as she dropped the fork into the box.

"Yes, we have to be invited into homes."

"Does it apply to the Savages too?"

"Yes."

She stood for a minute, torn on what to do. Then she glanced around her home before strolling back toward the door. "In that case...." She shut the door in his face and locked it.

Silence followed. Then she heard Declan and Saxon laughing loudly in the hall. A knock sounded, but Maggie grabbed her remote, turned on the TV, and upped the volume on the news. When she heard another knock, she turned the volume higher.

CHAPTER TWENTY-ONE

MAGGIE LACED up her sneakers and rubbed her hands together as she bounced on her toes for a minute. Her gaze went to the window across from her and the dawn starting to brighten the sky. Dawn had become her favorite time of the day to run, and right now she needed to run as far and fast as she possibly could.

She'd been exhausted when she crawled into bed last night, but her dreams were haunted by a pair of leaf-green eyes and kisses that heated her blood. She'd awoke feeling edgy and aching for more than Aiden's kiss.

She doubted there would be any more of those kisses though, as she'd probably never see him again. He'd knocked twice more before giving up the ghost. She hoped he never came back.

The sad thing was, she didn't buy her own lie.

She wanted her life back, but how could she return to her simple life with everything she'd experienced last night? What would happen when she went to work today? What had become of Harding and the other officers? What did they know? What didn't they know?

Even if they couldn't remember going to the alley, there would be a record of the call, and she hadn't been with Roger when they found him. She had no idea what to tell anyone that wouldn't possibly land her in jail or the nuthouse.

And what of Roger? Where was he? How was he? Then there was Glenn and Walt. How would that be explained? Had it already been explained somehow? Had they even been found yet? They had to have been discovered by now, but with everything that happened last night, she'd completely forgot to call someone about them. She took a deep breath to try to calm the guilt and anxiety building within her.

A good run would clear her mind of vampires and help her sort out the pieces of her life. She also needed a phone. Savages didn't go out in the sun, so she would be safe now if they did discover where she lived, but would she be safe from them if she reported to work later?

They might not know where she lived; they definitely knew where she worked.

The memory of that thing tearing her blood from her sent a shudder down her spine. Her limbs locked again, and it became difficult to breathe. How could Aiden's bite have been almost orgasmic while that thing's bite was excruciating?

Deep breaths. One obstacle at a time, Mags. And you can't conquer any of the obstacles while standing here.

Right. She undid her deadbolt and cracked the door. She heard nothing in the hallway, and when she opened it further to poke her head out, no one stood there. The intensity of the disappointment crashing through her almost caused her legs to give out.

She'd shut the door in Aiden's face, so of course, he would go, but she hadn't expected this loneliness to creep through her at the confirmation of it. Stepping into the hall, Maggie was about to close the door when a step on the stairwell halted her. If one of those crazed vamps came at her, she'd duck back inside.

Instead, Aiden stepped off the last stair and turned toward her. The smile that lit his face caused her pulse to skyrocket. At some point, he'd showered and changed. Bare-chested and wild, he'd been magnificent last night, but now he robbed her of her breath.

The jeans he wore hugged his thighs and legs in all the right ways. She tore her gaze away from the obvious bulge in the front of his pants before running it over the black sweater cleaving to his broad shoulders and chest. The black shirt made the green of his eyes stand out and caused a twinge of yearning in her heart. Free of blood, she saw the hint of a curl at the end of his short black hair. The trench coat he wore was similar to the one she'd cut off him last night, and she suspected there were weapons stashed in these pockets too.

"Good morning," he greeted, and the scent of coffee and food hit her.

For the first time, she noticed the two large coffees stuck into the tray set on top of the pink Dunkin' Donuts box he carried.

"Were you here all night?" she asked.

"Most of it. Declan stayed for a bit while I went to shower and change," he replied. He'd also gathered some weapons and picked up a replacement wallet with ID and money. "I sent him home when I came back from the donut shop."

"*Why* did you stay here?"

"To make sure you remain safe."

"Oh." She had no idea what else to say to that.

He lifted the donut box a little higher. "I wasn't sure which type of donut you liked, so I got you one of each."

"One of each?" There she went parroting him all over again.

He stopped before her. "Yes. Plus some bagels and cream cheese, in case you don't like donuts."

"Oh," she whispered. She hated the tears pricking her eyes, but she'd experienced kindness from only a rare few people in her life, and this was something so simple, yet so sweet.

"I'm also told you humans like this place," he said and tapped the name on the front of the box.

She smiled at him. "Dunkin' is the only way to go, at least for me. Thank you for this, but I was on my way out."

Aiden's heart thundered as he gazed at her. He lowered the box to cover his growing hard-on as he took in the body-hugging yoga pants emphasizing her shapely calves and thighs. She wore a black jacket and had her hair pulled into a knot on her head. Healthy color tinged her cheeks.

"You're a runner," he said, stating the obvious but unsure of what else to say to keep her from stepping inside and closing the door in his face again. He could make her leave here, but she'd hate him for it, and he'd already botched their meeting enough without making it worse.

"I've been training for the Boston Marathon. Some coworkers and I are going to run it this year."

He didn't tell her she probably couldn't return to her old life; she would come to that conclusion in her own time.

"I didn't think I'd like running, but last year, I agreed to try to qualify for the race because our team will be raising money for foster children. It turns out, I actually enjoy running." Maggie couldn't stop herself from blathering out words like an idiot. What did he care why she was running or if she liked it? "Anyway, I have to get a run in today."

"I'll go with you."

"Why? You said the Savages couldn't go out in the day."

"They can't, but their cronies can."

"Their cronies?" *Stop repeating everything he says!*

"Yes." He glanced up and down the hall. "I'd prefer not to discuss this out here."

Maggie examined her neighbor's doors before her gaze fell on the box in his hands. Stepping back, she nudged the door further open with her heel. "You did bring breakfast, so you might as well come in."

Aiden managed to stop himself from crushing the donuts as relief washed over him. This was a big step for her, he knew. One he hadn't expected her to make. He vowed to bring her donuts and coffee every day for the rest of her mortal existence if it meant this much to her.

Entering the apartment, Aiden took in the threadbare furniture, small TV, and hall leading toward what he assumed were the bedroom and bathroom. Plants hung from hooks over the windows, orchids lined the windowsills, and sunflowers were in a vase on the kitchen table. The redolent aroma of the plants, the butterscotch of Maggie, and a soft cinnamon scent filled the air. The place was small, nothing within it new, but it was clean and obvious that she took pride in it.

He followed Maggie as she walked into the kitchen. Small paintings of landscapes hung on the walls, but he saw only one picture of someone else in the place. Setting the box on the counter separating the kitchen from the living room, he lifted the wooden picture frame to inspect the photo within.

In the photo, Maggie looked to be in her late teens. She was laughing and had her arm around the waist of a handsome young man. Love radiated from her eyes as she gazed up at the man. The man stared down at her with that same vibrant love evident in his eyes. He was also laughing at something.

Studying the picture, Aiden got a sense of closeness

between them that made him think whatever they laughed at was a private joke meant only for their world.

He resisted crushing the photo in his hand. "Who's this?"

Maggie nudged the top of the donut box open to peer inside. She didn't glance at the photo as she replied, "A.J."

"You two look very close."

"We were." She already felt herself shying away from this conversation. She poked a Boston crème donut before closing the box. "I should run before stuffing myself."

Aiden continued to stare at the photo. "You *were* close?"

"Yes."

"Was he your boyfriend?"

"What does it matter?" she replied impatiently.

"I'm trying to get to know you better."

"Why?"

"Because I like you."

Maggie blinked at him, unsure of how to respond to those honest words. "Are you willing to discuss all of your exes with me?" she inquired.

"So, he *is* an ex?" Aiden pushed.

"He was much more than that, and you didn't answer my question."

Aiden's teeth ground together, but he knew he wouldn't get any more out of her without giving her something too. "I don't have any exes. I don't date."

"You don't have even *one* ex-girlfriend?"

"No."

Red flags waved all around Maggie's face, but she ignored them all. "So you don't have any exes because you don't date; is that because you prefer to use prostitutes?"

After Carha's words last night about not using her services again, Aiden knew why Maggie had asked that question. He dreaded the one he knew would follow his answer. "No."

"Then what services of Carha's were you using? Do you do drugs?"

"I don't do drugs."

Maggie tapped her fingers on the counter as she waited for him to explain more, but he remained silent. "Not going to tell me what she did for you then?" she inquired.

"There are things I'd prefer you didn't know."

"And there are things I'd prefer you didn't know." Taking A.J.'s photo from him, she traced his beloved face before placing the picture down. "I'm going for a run now."

"There are things about me, Maggie, that I don't want to touch your life."

She'd been making her way between her countertop and the card table that served as the kitchen table she never used. His words stopped her. "Are you going to hurt me?" she demanded.

"No! Never!"

"I've seen and been through a lot in my life. I think I managed last night pretty well. Most probably would have shit themselves or run screaming. Believe me, there's nothing I can't handle."

"You did handle last night well." She'd certainly taken the knowledge of vampires with far more ease than he would have expected from someone who'd been doing her job one minute and plunged into a supernatural war the next.

"But you're still not going to tell me what Carha was talking about?" she asked.

"No. Not now."

"Fair enough." She took another step forward before recalling his earlier words and halting. "What about these cronies you mentioned before?"

"Since they can't tolerate the sun, Savages sometimes use humans to do their bidding during the daytime. If the Savages know where you are, they could send some of those humans after you to either monitor you or to take you to them."

"Why would those people do anything the Savages wanted them to do?"

"There are some who will do anything for a chance at immortality."

"You think the Savages would send those people for me?" she asked.

"Yes. You shouldn't go out alone, at any time."

"I'm not getting my life back, am I?"

"Not anytime soon, and maybe not ever."

"I'm going for a run."

CHAPTER TWENTY-TWO

Maggie's feet slapped against the sidewalk as she ran up the hill with her head bowed and her arms and legs pumping to propel her faster. Sweat dripped off her brow and stuck her clothes to her body. Strands of hair had worked free of her bun to stick to her face. Her lungs burned as she pushed herself onward. He kept pace with her as she ran up one hill and down another. She ran so far they went through neighborhoods she'd only ever traversed in the ambulance before.

She'd never run this far or fast before, but she couldn't stop as her mind spun with Aiden's revelations. They hadn't spoken since she'd walked out of her apartment with him trailing her.

Finally, unable to continue, she came to a gasping halt on a street corner. Her hand went to the stitch in her side as she bent over to catch her breath. Aiden rested his hands on his knees beside her.

"Thank you for stopping," he muttered, and she burst into laughter broken only by her inability to breathe. It felt weird to be laughing when everything was crumbling around her, but she had no idea what else to do, not anymore.

"You're in good shape, Nosferatu." That was the understatement of the century. "You should have no problem keeping up with a mere mortal."

"I'm not much of a marathon runner, and I'm not used to working out in jeans. Which is something I hope never to do again."

He pulled at the denim sticking like glue to his legs, and she bit her lip to keep from laughing again. Rising, Maggie stretched her arms and legs before pulling her bottle of water free from where she'd strapped it to her side. She squirted some liquid into her mouth as she took in their surroundings.

Without realizing it, she'd looped around to within three blocks of her place. Only a few people were venturing out this early on a Saturday morning. Watching them, she couldn't help but wonder if one of them might be working for a Savage and hunting *her*.

"At the club last night, I could differentiate between the vamps and the humans, but would I be able to spot one of the people who work for the Savages?" she asked.

"No. They'll look and act as human as you. How did you tell the difference between us at the club?"

His words chilled her. Did enemies surround her now? Was that woman in the pink jumpsuit really someone looking to take her to something that would tear her throat out, or was that man walking his poodle a threat to her?

"Vamps move differently," she answered as she studied every possible enemy strolling the sidewalks. "And there's something predatory about all of you that's almost undetectable unless someone is looking for it."

"Most people wouldn't bother to look for it."

"Most people wouldn't *know* to look for it," she pointed out. "I did."

"Even if they did know, many wouldn't spot it."

"You don't grow up like I did and not learn to trust your instincts and learn your environment *really* well."

"And how did you grow up?"

"That conversation is way too complicated to have right now."

Aiden took the water bottle from her before she could replace it. She stretched her legs as he squeezed water into his mouth and swallowed it. He'd taken his sweater and coat off before they'd left her apartment. A sheen of sweat covered his chest and abs in an enticing way that had her contemplating licking her lips, or *him*.

"Can all vampires drink stuff other than blood?" she asked to distract herself from the bead of sweat making its way through the trail of hair leading from his belly button to his waistband.

"Yes." He handed the bottle back to her and tucked a strand of loose hair behind her ear. She started but didn't pull away from him when he traced the outer shell of her ear with his finger before lowering his hand. She'd almost killed him with her run, but the sparkle in her eyes was worth it. "We can eat too if it's necessary."

"Fascinating."

"Do you always run so far and fast?" he asked.

She smiled at him and drank some more water before recapping the bottle. "No. I was trying to work things out in my mind, and running helps me do that."

"And did you get things worked out?"

"No."

The smile slid from his face. "I'll keep you safe, Maggie."

"I don't know you, Aiden. And no offense, but my life has gone to shit since you entered it."

He winced at the truth of her words. He was supposed to

bring happiness to his mate's life, not turn it upside down and place her *in* danger.

"What would you like to know about me?" he asked.

She tilted her head to the side. "But you said, 'there are things about me, Maggie, that I don't want to touch your life.' Now you're willing to share with me?"

No. But instead, he found himself saying, "If it helps you to trust me more, I will tell you as much as I can."

"And what do you expect from me in return?"

"Who said I expected anything from you?" he asked.

"Everyone always expects something."

"Not true."

"For a vampire, you're very naïve."

"For a human, you're very jaded," he said with a smile.

Maggie didn't smile back. "Why did you attack Nigel like that?"

Aiden stiffened as he contemplated his answer. "He hurt you, he was harassing you, and I won't tolerate someone treating you that way."

"But it was so... so..."

"Violent," he supplied when she seemed unable to find the word.

"Yes. And an unnecessary overreaction."

"I know," he admitted. He ran a hand through his hair as she studied him warily. "You never should have witnessed it, and I will try to keep you from seeing anything like that again, but I'll do whatever it takes to keep you safe."

"Why?"

"Because I got you into this mess, and I will get you through whatever follows. But no matter what happens, I will never hurt you."

"Hmm," Maggie grunted, not entirely sure she believed him about why he'd reacted that way, but she did believe him when he said he wouldn't hurt her. "Why did you stop hitting Nigel when I asked you to?"

"Because I knew I'd overreacted and you'd already been through and seen too much. I *never* should have attacked him like that, not in front of you."

His earnest words and the plea radiating from his eyes for her to understand tugged at her heart.

"Don't fear me, Maggie," he whispered.

"I don't," she replied honestly.

She turned away from him and started walking down the street. She stopped at the small convenience store on the corner, pushed the glass door open, and waved to the clerk behind the counter. She saw the clerk every day, and they always exchanged casual conversation, but she couldn't remember his name, and he didn't wear a tag.

"Hey, you! No shirt, no service!" the clerk declared when the bell over the door jangled and Aiden stepped into the store behind her.

Maggie glanced over her shoulder and froze when Aiden's gaze locked onto the clerk. "It's fine," Aiden said in a soothing tone. "We'll be out of here soon. Go back to doing what you were doing before we entered."

The clerk became slack-jawed before he went back to flipping through the magazine on the counter. Maggie frowned at Aiden when he walked over to join her. "Have you done that to me?" she demanded.

"No."

"Would you tell me if you had?"

He cupped her cheek with his hand and rubbed his thumb tenderly over her skin. "I will not lie to you, Maggie. And you don't ever have to be concerned about me changing your memories or messing with your mind. I will *never* do that to you."

"And I'm supposed to believe you?"

"You remember everything about last night. It would have made things much easier on me if I erased our first encounter, but I will *not* mess with your mind."

"Hmm." She wasn't entirely sure she believed him, but she did recall everything about last night, or at least she thought she remembered it all.

Turning away from Aiden, she strolled down the cramped aisles until she found the disposable phones hanging from a rack at the end of one. She cringed when she saw the twenty-five-dollar price tag, but there was nothing she could do about that. She removed the phone and a phone card before hurrying to the front with them.

"That it for today, Maggie?" the clerk asked as he flipped his car magazine closed.

"That's it," she replied and pulled her debit card from the pocket of her jacket.

"Sure you don't want some scratchies? You could hit the lotto."

"I'm not that lucky."

"You'll never know if you don't play."

"No thanks," she muttered and tapped her fingers as he ran her card.

Aiden prowled closer until she could feel him against her shoulder. The clerk glanced nervously at him before smiling at her and handing her card back. "You're all set. I'll see you tomorrow."

"See you tomorrow," Maggie replied with a smile and then cringed when she wondered if she *would* see him tomorrow.

Back on the city street, Maggie studied the increasing number of people moving about. "Anyone of them could be an enemy," she murmured.

Aiden clasped her elbow and drew her closer. "Yes."

"What have I gotten into?"

"I have a car at your apartment." He'd packed a bag and placed it in the trunk in the hope he would be able to get her to agree to leave her place. "I think we should go somewhere that the Savages won't be able to locate you."

"Where?"

That was the question. He'd prefer not to take her to where Ronan and the others resided. She'd handled all of this well, but he didn't think she'd appreciate being placed in the middle of so many vampires. He didn't want to take her to his family in Maine, that could be more overwhelming for her, and he wasn't stable enough to trust himself around his family.

"A hotel, for now," he finally said. "Until we can take down the Savages who attacked last night and make sure there aren't more of them involved."

"Are they going to hunt me for the rest of my life?"

"I'll kill them all first," he replied, and Maggie knew he wasn't just saying that; he meant it.

"I don't have the money for a hotel."

"I'll pay for it." He held his hand up to forestall the argument he saw her gearing up to make. "You have to be kept safe, and you can pay me back later." He'd never take her money, but he had a feeling she wouldn't agree to let him pay otherwise.

"I *will* pay you back," she said. "How much time will we have to spend at the hotel?"

"I don't know," he admitted.

Maggie opened her mouth to tell him to forget it; she couldn't risk losing her job. Then, she looked around at the growing swell of people, and a shiver crept down her spine. She had her pride, could take care of herself, and she didn't want to lose everything she had, but she would have a lot less if she died.

"I will do everything I can to eliminate this threat to you soon," Aiden vowed.

Maggie tore her eyes away from a passing man who was staring at her a little too attentively. Perhaps his stare only meant he was a creep, but it might mean he was tracking her to report to his bosses where she was. If she stayed in her apartment, this constant paranoia would drive her crazy.

"There are things I need from my apartment if I'm going to leave it," she murmured.

Aiden hid his relief over her acquiescence as he led her across the street to her building. They climbed swiftly up to her apartment, and he waited while she packed clothes and toiletries into a large duffel bag. She rushed around, watering all the plants and murmuring promises of returning for them. He didn't miss that she placed the picture of A.J. into the duffel bag with tender care.

She stuck both coffees he'd bought her in the microwave and hit a button. Her foot tapped as she waited for the microwave to beep. She removed both cups and stuck one in the tray while she set the other on the counter.

"I have to call out of work," she said as she opened a drawer and removed a pair of scissors. With care, she cut away the packaging encasing her phone. "But I have no idea what to say to them or what they know."

"You don't have to speak with them at all," Aiden said.

"And why not?" Maggie demanded as she yanked at the plastic and cursed loudly when it still didn't open.

Aiden took the packaging from her and tore it open.

"Show off," she muttered as he handed her the phone and he smiled.

"Things with the police and at your work have been taken care of," he said.

"How is that possible?"

"Lucien and Killean went to speak with your coworkers,

and Ronan and Brian went to the police station after I contacted Saxon last night."

"Who are they?" she asked.

"Men I work with."

"And what did they learn?"

"The Savages cleaned their mess up well. The bodies of their friends were removed from the morgue. They did kill the morgue attendant, but there were no other casualties."

"Is that supposed to make it better?" Maggie whispered.

"No."

"What about the police and my coworkers, what do they know?"

"They know they responded to a false call at the alley last night. Ronan had some of the trainees clean up the alley after we left the club last night. So if anyone goes back there, they'll believe the false call report. When you and Roger left the false call, you were in an accident. They believe Glenn and Walt were jumped and killed during a carjacking gone wrong. Their ambulance was found on fire about five miles from where we originally discovered it."

"Walt and Glenn?" she croaked. "What happened to them?"

"Their bodies were untouched by the fire as, whoever killed them, removed them first and placed them in the alley."

"And who really removed them from the ambulance?"

"Ronan and Brian. Ronan then placed an anonymous call as to where to find the bodies."

She rested her hand on the counter as a wave of nausea hit her. "Okay, but the police will be able to tell our ambulance wasn't hit by another vehicle, and there was blood *all* over the back of it."

"The ambulance was destroyed, and the memories of any

blood have been eradicated from the minds of those who saw it."

"How?" she croaked.

"Brian took the ambulance to a junkyard. Your coworkers and the police have a record of an accident, but nothing to investigate. There are probably some loose ends, but not enough to worry about. Most people prefer to live in denial than to pursue the truth. They know others might find them crazy for claiming something unnatural happened."

Just like people found my mom crazy, Maggie thought. Unable to support her weight anymore, she leaned against the counter. "What about Roger, where is he?"

"Mass General. He's going to be fine."

"And where do they think I am?"

"They believe you have a concussion, were disoriented, and walked away from the scene."

"They'll want to see a doctor's note."

"No, they won't. They believe they've already spoken with your doctor. You have at least three days off, and if you need more time, I'll make sure you get it."

The scope of the cover-up they'd perpetrated left her numb. She'd known Aiden was powerful, but she hadn't realized how deep and far the power of him, and those he worked with, ran. "There were so many factors to take care of," she murmured.

"The Savages took care of some for us."

"What have I gotten myself into?"

"Maggie..." When he rested his hand on hers, she pulled it away. "I'm going to keep you safe."

The color had faded from her face; she stared at the far wall as she bit her lower lip. She wanted to run, but she had nowhere to go and no one to turn to. "I'll finish getting my things."

She shoved off the counter and hurried out of the kitchen to her bedroom once more. Aiden prowled after her. Standing in the doorway of her bedroom, he gazed at the paintings of ocean scenes on the walls and the blue comforter on the neatly made bed. He heard her muttering to someone in the bathroom to his right and turned to find her pouring water out of a fishbowl.

"It's okay, Beta Blue. I'll get you some fresh water soon." She came out of the bathroom with the bowl clasped in both hands. She stopped when she saw him and hugged the bowl against her chest as if he were going to take it from her. "I'm not leaving him."

"You don't have to. I'll ask Declan to take care of the plants for you if we can't come back soon."

Maggie's heart melted; her shoulders slumped. "I know it seems stupid, but...." Her words trailed off as she gazed at the plants hanging from their hooks and cluttering her sills. Many of them were orchids, but she had spider plants, an orange tree, two ferns, and three red prayer plants. She'd owned them all since they could fit in her palm.

"I care for them," she admitted. "And Beta Blue, or Blue as he's better known, he's been keeping me company for three years now."

"It's not stupid," he said, "but we have to get out of here."

She followed him back into the living room with Blue.

CHAPTER TWENTY-THREE

MAGGIE WATCHED the city flash by from the passenger seat of the black Toyota. She'd spent her life in and around Boston. Normally it felt like her home; today it felt like enemies lurked in every corner of the vast city.

"I feel like I can't trust anyone," she murmured.

"You can trust me."

"I haven't known you for twenty-four hours yet, so I'm not ready to hop on the trust train with you. I only came with you because I trust you more than a stranger. You ever hear the saying the devil you know is better than the devil you don't?"

"And I'm the devil?"

"I haven't decided."

He smiled at her. "Let me know when you do."

"I will."

"The amount of time you know someone doesn't always matter when it comes to trust. Sometimes you can know a person for years and still never trust them."

"True. We never can know what another person or vampire is thinking."

"But there are some we trust as much as ourselves." *There are some I trust more than myself,* Aiden thought.

"Do you have anyone like that?"

"My parents, my siblings, and the Stooges."

"Who are the Stooges?"

"Mike, David, Doug, and Jack. They all grew up with my dad and were all turned into vampires around the same time as each other. They've been together ever since. The Stooges are like uncles to my siblings and me. Do you have anyone you trust?"

She rested her hand on top of Blue's bowl as she shifted it in her lap. "I have Roger."

"What about your parents?"

Maggie absently traced the opening of Blue's bowl. "I don't know who my father is, and my mom is nuts."

He chuckled. "I think all moms can be a little nuts, but I'm sure it has nothing to do with their children."

"I'm sure it doesn't either," Maggie said with a smile. "But my mother really *is* certifiable. She's also a murderer. She was locked away before I was born. I haven't seen her since the day I turned eighteen. Which is also the only time, other than my birth, I've ever seen her. While I was a ward of the state, I wasn't told anything about her. On my eighteenth birthday, I learned the truth about her, where she was, and I went to see her. I swore I'd never go back."

There were only two people she'd ever told about her mother. One was Roger, and the other was dead. She didn't know why she'd revealed it to Aiden, but she figured he should probably have a heads-up if they were going to spend an unspecified amount of time together. If she were going to go crazy too, it would probably happen before all this was over, so he deserved to be warned she had homicidal lunatic ingrained in her DNA.

However, after last night, she knew her mom wasn't crazy after all, at least not entirely. At the very least, her mother had hit on the truth in her ravings.

Aiden glanced at Maggie's bowed head as her finger trailed over the opening of the bowl while she stared at the fish. He now understood why she'd handled last night as well as she had; she'd endured more than he ever could have imagined in her life. He rested his hand on her knee and braced himself for her to push it away, but she didn't.

"It was a fun eighteenth birthday," she continued. "I became eligible to vote, and my mother revealed she wished she'd succeeded in killing me."

Aiden's hand clenched on her leg. "Your mother tried to kill you?"

Maggie thrust her shoulders back and turned to face him. "Yes, but to be fair, my father wasn't exactly the type of man women are clamoring to have a baby with. The police chased my father off when they stumbled upon him raping her in an alley. Severely beaten, my mother couldn't speak about the trauma she'd endured. The police took her to the hospital where her rape was confirmed, but they couldn't get anything out of her aside from screams and mumblings of red eyes and vampires."

Aiden's head turned toward her but shot back to the road when he drifted into the other lane and a horn blared at him.

"The state and doctors put her under a psych eval for thirty days while the police searched for a family they never discovered. I have no idea if I have any grandparents, aunts, uncles, or cousins. I might, but the police couldn't find anyone, and no one came forward to claim her. During the thirty days she was under evaluation, they learned my mother was pregnant with little ole me."

Brakes squealed and horns blared when Aiden jerked the

wheel. He pulled the car to the side of the road and put it in park. He stared at the car in front of him as he tried to process what she'd revealed.

"What happened after that?" he inquired.

"They kept my mother's story mostly out of the news because of her rape and consequent mental state, but I've read the police, doctor, and social work reports about her. I also gathered some information from her when I saw her. In the reports, I learned that upon hearing she was to be the bearer of vampire spawn, my dear old mom grabbed a scalpel and tried to cut me from her belly. She would have succeeded too if it hadn't been for the doctors, nurses, orderlies, and guards who rushed in to stop her. Of course, this was after she already stabbed one of the other doctors and a nurse. The nurse didn't survive."

"Shit," Aiden breathed.

"Yeah, pretty much. They deemed dear old Mom incapable of standing trial, took me from her as soon as I was born, and locked her away. She still screams of vampires, devil spawn, and Hell. And I... well, I am the source of her madness. I believed she was crazy, but the one thing I did figure out while we were running last night is that she's *not* crazy. You yourself said you were born."

"You smelled the Savages," he murmured. "I noticed a couple of times you covered your nose or picked up a garbage scent, but I assumed it was because there was garbage nearby, but you scented *them*."

"There was no garbage in the ambulance when they first attacked us, and I smelled the faintest hint of it then. I don't think it's anywhere near as strong as what you described, but yes, I think I can smell them."

Aiden felt like someone had punched him in the gut as he gazed at her. He recalled the way she'd reacted to him in the ambulance, then in the bathroom, and realized she might not be feeling the mating instinct as fiercely as he was, but she felt something for him.

"It would be possible for a vampire and human to conceive, or at least I think it would," he said as he tried to puzzle it out. "We're unable to contract or carry diseases, but we do have many human functions, including producing sperm. However, most vampires are careful to keep our existence listed firmly in the mythological, and spreading half-vampire children around could rock that boat, big time, so we take care not to breed with humans."

"Judging from what I read about my mother's condition that night, I don't think she was meant to survive her attack. They reported a knife had slashed her throat, but I realize now it wasn't a knife. The doctors feared she would die from her blood loss."

"Vampires who attack humans never intend for them to survive."

"So, my father is, or most likely was, a Savage." For some reason, Maggie didn't feel as sick as she'd thought she would over that realization. But then, she'd known she was the product of rape for six years. This knowledge was no worse than that.

"It sounds like it."

"Why wouldn't he go after her again to make sure she didn't speak if you're all so concerned about keeping your existence from humans?"

"It's hard to say," Aiden replied. "Maybe he thought she'd died, especially if she was kept out of the news. Maybe he wasn't strong enough to go through all the police, doctors, and everyone else who was involved to change their memories and cover his tracks. I believe that's the most likely scenario if he didn't kill the police, and her, at the scene. It sounds like he was a vampire who had recently given in to his Savage nature."

"I wonder how long the asshole held out before he started killing," Maggie snorted. "Do you think he's still alive?"

"If he got smarter about his attacks, he could be. If he didn't, then no, he didn't survive very long. Any vampire, Savage or not, would have taken him out to stop him from leaving more witnesses behind, as he did with your mother."

"Hmm," Maggie murmured.

Aiden didn't want to say his next words, but he knew he had to offer it to her, especially if she became a member of his family and met his brother-in-law, Brian. "I know someone who might be able to help you find your father if you'd like to try?"

Maggie bit her lip as she pondered this before shaking her head. "No. I got all I ever needed from that asshole."

"Okay," Aiden said. "What about your mother's family?"

She considered it before shaking her head. "No, the past is best left to the past."

"If you change your mind—"

"I won't. What exactly is a vampire?" Maggie asked to switch the subject. "I mean, how is it possible you have so many human traits and tendencies?"

"Vampires are the children of demons who once walked this earth. Those demons mated and had children with people to create vampires. We have human tendencies from our human DNA, but supernatural abilities from our demon DNA."

"I see." Maggie dropped her head into her hands and rubbed at her temples. "This is all so crazy. Ever since I learned the truth of my mother six years ago, I've dreaded becoming like her. I've constantly searched for some sign reality might be slipping away from me. Acknowledging my father was most likely a vampire feels like a step toward the crazy train for me, but I can't deny everything I saw last night or the fact you ran fifteen miles with me today when your spine was exposed yesterday."

Aiden squeezed her knee. She glanced at his hand as if she were contemplating removing it from her leg, but she let it remain. "Vampires are real. Admitting it won't make you crazy."

"Have there been others, who had only one vampire parent, like me?" She wiped away the sweat trickling down her neck as she braced herself for his reply.

"I don't know, but I know someone I can ask if you want me to?"

Maggie bit her lip and turned to gaze out the window. She'd love nothing more than to remain in blissful ignorance of everything, but unless she asked Aiden to wipe her memory, she couldn't stick her head in the sand.

"Yes," she said. "I want to know."

"I'll call as soon as we're settled."

"Okay."

She realized he'd pulled over near Fenway. From where she sat, she could see the Citgo gas sign. The streets here were busier with people wandering the stores and bars.

"Baseball season starts soon," she murmured as she watched a woman hustling her child across the street toward a deli. "A.J. and I came to Fenway every opening day from the time we were twelve on. If we couldn't get tickets for the game, we'd hang out and soak up the atmosphere. There's nothing better than the smell of hot dogs cooking, the crack of a bat on the ball, and the cheers of the crowd. When we got older, we would sit in the bars and celebrate with everyone else. A.J. could always get the best fake ID's."

Maggie dragged a hand through her hair as she pulled herself from her strange reverie. When she focused on Aiden again, she noted the clench of his jaw, but his hand remained gentle on her thigh.

"What happened to A.J.?" he asked.

Maggie glanced at Blue. She hadn't wanted to tell him anything about her when he was so unwilling to talk about himself, but now that she'd opened this box of memories, much like Pandora, she couldn't close it again.

"He made the mistake of getting in his car and driving at the same time a *stupid* kid decided planning his seventeenth birthday, via text, was more important than not killing someone." Maggie had worked through most of her grief, but the lump in her throat made talking difficult. "The kid survived; A.J. died on his way to the hospital. At one time, that knowledge *infuriated* me. I wanted to kill the boy myself, but I've mostly gotten past that."

She said this, but she heard the bitterness in her voice as she revealed this to Aiden. "I've stopped wishing it had been the other way around and A.J. survived, but occasionally I wonder what would have happened if the kid had been smart enough not to use his phone or to at least *look up* a few seconds before the crash." She didn't doubt A.J. would have a child by now, and she would have been a kick-ass aunt.

"However, the lack of skid marks on the teen's side of the road revealed he never realized he'd switched lanes and was driving head-on at someone. A.J. saw because he'd braked and jerked the wheel. The kid didn't know his life was about to change forever; A.J. watched his death coming at him."

"I'm sorry for your loss," Aiden said. Jealousy seethed within him when she spoke of A.J., her love for the man was obvious, and he could never compete with a ghost. However, her sorrow tore at him, and he would give anything to take it from her.

"I once heard someone say, 'Life sucks get a helmet.' It's

something I tell myself every time something bad happens. I strapped my helmet on really young. It's dented, scratched, and it's almost broken a few times, but it's kept me going. Things can always be worse. I know, they've been worse for me. They've also been better, but every day I take a moment to find something good in all the bad."

Of course, she'd never expected to have vamp DNA tossed into her mixing bowl of lemons, but it might also explain some other facets of her life. Facets she'd never realized required explaining.

Aiden released her knee and brushed back a strand of her silken hair. His finger lingered on her cheek until her charcoal eyes lifted to his. He didn't see bitterness in her gaze, only a steely resolve to face every day with a determination many didn't possess.

From what he'd learned about her life, some would have been broken by it, others would have become bitter, but Maggie had chosen to be strengthened by it. Drawing her closer, he kissed her forehead. Now was not the time for anything more than the briefest of kisses, but he needed to connect with her.

"Is what happened to A.J. the reason you became a paramedic?" he inquired when he sat back again. He lowered his hand to cup her nape and leisurely ran his thumb over her silken skin.

"I became a paramedic because I can handle the sight of blood and gore better than most people. I saved a woman's life one day, and Roger happened to be working on the ambulance called to the scene. When Roger saw how I handled the woman, he took me under his wing and helped me get through my EMT and paramedic training. I enjoy helping people, but no, I didn't look to this field because of A.J. I was already four months into my training when A.J. died."

"Were you still dating A.J. when he died?"

"No." Maggie glanced out the window again. "He was my first everything from kiss to sex, but more than that, he was my first best friend. For years, he was my only friend, and I was the same for him. I think we only started dating because we had no one else and because we did love each other so very much."

She focused on Aiden again. "Being together seemed like the next logical step when we were all we had. Growing up, we were both bounced through numerous foster homes, group homes, and anywhere the state could find a place for us. We'd be split up, only to rejoin two weeks or months later. From the time we were sixteen on, we lived in the same group home while we waited to turn eighteen.

"I think we both worried we'd lose the other if we didn't progress into a dating relationship, or at least I know I feared losing him. We started dating when we were seventeen, but by the time we were eighteen, we realized it wasn't *us*. We were better friends than lovers. There was no big breakup, no tears, we simply went back to the way things were supposed to be for us, and we were happy with it.

"After we turned eighteen, we lived together for a while as roomies. When A.J. died, he'd been preparing to ask his girlfriend to marry him. I went with him two days before the accident to pick out the ring, and I hid it away until he was ready to propose. I gave her the ring after his funeral."

A single tear streaked down her cheek, and she wiped it away. "I dated a few guys after we broke up, but nothing serious. I've always been a bit of a loner and fine with being single. Once I started EMT school, I became focused on my studies and getting through my training."

Aiden drew her closer to hold her against his chest. When she turned her face into his neck, her warm breath tickled his throat as she leaned into him. He had no idea what he'd done to be rewarded with a mate like her. It certainly hadn't been anything good as he'd been on a one-way, self-destruct mission for years, but whatever it was, he vowed to become worthy of her if she joined him. There would be no more dented helmets for Maggie; there would only be love and security.

"I will keep you safe," he vowed.

"Why?" she asked, pulling back to look at him. "Why do you care what happens to me? Why don't you change my memories and move on from me? You said you're going to protect me because you got me into this, but I'm sure you could figure out some way to make me forget everything I've learned and still protect me. You and your friends managed a pretty big cover-up last night."

He didn't know how to answer her. He had a feeling she'd bolt if he started talking about eternity and vampirism, but he couldn't lie to her either. A hand thumped down on the hood of the car, causing Maggie to jump.

Aiden turned to find a young man standing in front of the car with his hand resting on the hood. The man grinned and waved to Maggie. "Heeeyyy beautiful," the kid slurred and flexed his biceps.

When Aiden glowered at him, the kid was sober enough his smile faded, and he stepped away from the car. A few of the kid's friends ran up, laughing as they rushed past the front of the car. They all wore the same emblem on their sweaters.

"College kids," Maggie muttered and shook her head. "Probably still drunk from last night and continuing the party. You'd think they'd be smarter and do some sobering up before going out in public."

Aiden's gaze followed them as they jumped on each other and high-fived. Theirs was a life he'd once enjoyed with his high school friends and during his brief college time. It felt like it had been years ago and the life of a different man.

Shifting the car into drive, he pulled away from the curb

and onto the busy street. Thankfully, Maggie seemed to have forgotten her question as she gazed out the window.

CHAPTER TWENTY-FOUR

AIDEN HUNG up the phone and looked over to where Maggie was carefully pouring some bottled water into the fishbowl. The blue fish flitted happily to the top before settling against the white rocks at the bottom with a swish of his tail.

Maggie recapped the bottle and set it on the hotel dresser. He'd taken her to a hotel in Quincy near the ocean. They were far enough away from Maggie's apartment and Carha's place, no one would think to look for them here. But they weren't so far he couldn't return to help the others if it became necessary.

Taking a deep breath, Maggie turned to face him. She didn't speak as she waited for him to tell her what else he'd learned during his call to Ronan.

"I didn't reveal it was about you when I asked him, but Ronan confirmed there have been children of vampires and humans before," he told her.

"I'm sure he's already figured out why you asked him," she murmured.

"Most likely."

"What were those children like?"

"According to Ronan, the combination of a human and a vampire doesn't happen often. Most of these children live normal, human lives while others differ in certain ways. They may be stronger and faster, or healthier than other people. I can testify you're damn fast."

Her mouth pursed, and Aiden sensed his words had struck a nerve, but when she didn't speak, he continued. "Ronan also said some of those children choose to be turned later in life. I'm assuming the ones who decided to change were aware of their heritage. Once turned, those half children can be stronger than an average turned vamp, but not as strong as a purebred vampire."

"I see," she murmured, and her gaze went past him to the curtained window. He didn't understand the pensive expression on her face, but he had a feeling she was sorting through something in her mind.

His gaze fell on the slender column of her throat before darting away. His fingers dug into his thighs as he fought the impulse to take her and claim her as his mate, but he remained where he was. She'd been through enough without him heaping the mate thing on her today. He would tell her eventually, but he would wait until she was ready.

He dug his fingers deeper into his flesh when his skin prickled with the compulsion to feel pain and his fangs throbbed for blood. Whereas before these impulses had nearly sent him over the edge, now they were mild cravings he could handle with Maggie near him.

You will control this! She is more important than you.

He'd seen his parents' relationship, his siblings with their mates, and David with his. He'd always known what a mate did for and to a vampire, but now, experiencing it, he'd never truly realized how much his mate would mean to him. It was more than Maggie being able to calm him in ways pain, blood, death, and sex never had; it was also that he liked and admired her. She'd weathered much in her life, and in the past day, but she hadn't allowed it to destroy her.

His parents, siblings, and David were all deeply in love with their mates. He'd hoped to find the same, but there was no guarantee love would come with the bond. He didn't love Maggie, but he knew it would be easy to fall in love with her.

"When I was a baby, I was very sickly," she said, and her eyes came back to his. "I was placed with a family as soon as I was born. They were going to adopt me. They were so excited to have a baby they were willing to overlook the possible insanity lurking in my genes."

A sickly child seemed against what Ronan had told him, but no one knew everything for sure, not even Ronan the oldest vampire in existence. "What happened to them?" he inquired.

"I don't know. Their names weren't listed in my records, only the history of my time spent with them. They were willing to overlook the possibility I might one day stab and kill someone, but they hadn't signed up for a sick child. They kept me for three months, but after numerous doctor appointments where no one could figure out what was wrong with me, they wiped their hands of me and gave me back to the state. I do know they named me Coraline while they had me, but when they gave me back, my name reverted to the name my mother gave me, Magdalene."

"Your mother named you?"

"Yes. Apparently, she had a few minutes of lucidity after my birth. She told the social worker to call me Magdalene because I was a blessing who came from the worst of sins. She also hoped one day my soul could be redeemed instead of remaining pure evil. You know, because being a baby and all, I was more evil than a killer clown on acid playing the bagpipes."

"That is pretty evil."

"It's worse than the devil. Anyway, my mother didn't want to name me Mary Magdalene because Jesus's mother was Mary and she was pure while I was evil incarnate, but Magdalene was good enough for her daughter. The social worker documented this conversation in detail. I don't know why; maybe they were trying to understand her or something."

"Your mother was wrong. No child has to be redeemed, and no baby is evil."

"I know, but vampire or not, my father was a vicious rapist. *That* DNA is in me. If I could cut it out of me, I would, but it's as much a tapestry of my life as all those foster homes, A.J., Roger, and my mother."

Aiden didn't know what to say. He'd never been good with words. Maybe Ian, with all his smooth ways, would know how to respond. Jack would sniff and say *fuck that*, Vicky would get her drunk, and his mother, Isabelle, and Abby would offer comfort, but he had nothing to give her other than the truth.

"From what I've seen of you, Magdalene, your father is a tiny piece of the tapestry. His actions helped to create you, but you've forged yourself into someone who doesn't take joy in being cruel to others. You've used the circumstances of your life to make you stronger rather than weaker. Many wouldn't have done the same. Your father gave you the beginnings of life, but nothing else of himself."

Tears pricked her eyes at his words. After a few deep breaths, she felt capable of speaking again.

"Since my mother has never revealed her name, she's always been known as Jane Doe. I became Magdalene Doe when I returned to the state. Over the years, I saw numerous doctors, but none of them could pinpoint why I had such a difficult time gaining weight, growing, cried often, was extremely pale, and anemic. I think they believed I would die, but I've never seen any documentation of that.

"When I was three, I started getting a little better. The state tried adopting me out again when I was four, but I wasn't healthy enough. There were still too many doctors involved, so they sent me back. I went through some foster homes, but most foster parents don't want to deal with a sick kid either. When I was nine, I started feeling a lot better."

"What caused the change?"

Maggie fiddled with the edge of her shirt as she recalled events she'd always preferred to forget. "I went to a foster home with a woman who was incredibly sweet, but she had this nasty, drunk bastard for a husband. I know some people have these atrocious stories of foster homes, but out of the many I lived in, this was my only *really* awful experience with one."

Aiden's teeth ground together. "What happened?"

"His favorite pastime was using her as a punching bag when he was drunk. He never touched the kids in their care, that could lead to a mess he was too cowardly to wade into, and he needed the money we brought, but he would beat her until she couldn't scream for him to stop. I think her screams were what excited him.

"Often, I would hide under my bed with some of the other foster kids. I was the eldest out of them, the one they looked to for protection. I had no idea what I would do if he ever came at one of us. He was two hundred fifty pounds of pissed off, alcohol-fueled rage, but I vowed I'd do whatever it took to keep him from hitting one of them."

"Did he come after you?" He didn't kill humans. It would start the stench of rot on him as it did with the Savages, but he'd make an exception if this man were still alive.

"No, not really," Maggie said. "He beat her so bad once she couldn't get out of bed for a week. During that time, he informed me I would be making the meals. I'd never cooked a day in my life, but I'd watched others do it enough to know at least a little. I made simple meals, sandwiches, cereal, spaghetti, mac and cheese before he demanded steak. So, I cooked us all steak. Except, I didn't cook it enough.

"Infuriated with my inability to cook it properly, and screaming about wasting his money, he forced me to eat one of the raw steaks with all the blood seeping out of it. The steaks weren't ruined, I could have cooked them longer, but without his wife to abuse, he started to turn on me."

Aiden sat up straighter on the bed as he recalled the steak she'd devoured last night. He'd never seen a human eat a steak so rare before.

"What happened?" he asked.

"At first, I cried. I couldn't help it. It was so gross with all the blood and *so* red. I didn't know how to cook steak, but I knew it shouldn't look like *that*. I was afraid I'd get some parasite or disease or something; I was more terrified of him and what he would do to me if I didn't eat it. With him standing over my shoulder, breathing down my neck and grinning at me while he smoked a cigarette and chugged his vodka, I started eating.

"I choked down the first five bites before realizing I *liked* it. My reaction wasn't normal, but I didn't care. Before I was halfway through the steak, I tossed aside my silverware and started using my hands. When I finished, I began to eat one of the other steaks with the same enthusiasm. I felt consumed by this insatiable, animalistic hunger for *more*.

"My foster siblings looked on in revulsion, as did the man. When I lifted the plate to my mouth to drink the blood off it, he tore it away from me, slapped me across the face, and sent me to my room with the perfect imprint of his hand already bruising my cheek."

Red shaded Aiden's vision.

"The next day, I woke to find the mark from his slap gone, I felt *healthy* for the first time in my life, and I was sent back to live in a group home once more. After that, I started eating raw meat as often as I could get my hands on it, and the only time I saw a doctor was for my yearly physical. None of them could believe my turnaround, and I haven't had so much as a cold since."

"The blood made you stronger."

It hadn't been a question, but she answered anyway. "Yes. After that day, I also vowed that never again would I allow someone to abuse me. Like I said, most foster homes weren't bad, but I was tired of being a pawn in this never-ending game of new homes, new people, and new possibilities that always fell through, so *I* became difficult to handle. Then, when I was twelve, I met A.J. His mother had overdosed the year before, and his father was never in the picture. The two of us bonded fast, and whenever we were sent out to live somewhere else, we did whatever we could to get back to each other."

Aiden ran a hand through his hair as he contemplated everything she'd revealed. "It seems there is no denying your heritage."

"I have to see my mother."

She'd never expected to say those words again in her lifetime. The first time she'd uttered them had been to A.J. who told her sometimes it was better not knowing. He'd been right, but he'd also known she had to satisfy her curiosity, and he'd gone with her to the institute.

Now, she had to let her mother know she understood everything and believed her. Maybe her mother wouldn't care, but Maggie felt compelled to tell her.

"I don't know what all of this means for me. The only thing it changes in my life is that I now better understand things I didn't understand before and have answers for things I never expected answers for, but I have to prepare myself to see her again," Maggie said.

"When you're ready, I'll take you to her."

Maggie nodded and turned to stare at the curtain once more. She had to see the woman who had given birth to her again, but when would she ever be ready for that?

CHAPTER TWENTY-FIVE

AIDEN HAD RENTED ADJOINING rooms for them, paying with cash and a fake ID. Soon after Maggie revealed parts of her childhood to him, she retreated to her room. She hadn't bothered to lock the door between them. This wasn't a home, he could come and go freely, but he wouldn't walk in on her without knocking first.

After taking a shower, and a little bit of time to get her tumult of emotions under control, Maggie pulled her new phone out of her duffel bag. She called the hospital and waited while they transferred her to Roger's room.

"Roger," she breathed when she heard his brusque hello.

"Maggie May, it's so good to hear from you! How are you?"

"I'm okay. How are *you*?"

"Too much blood loss and a concussion have left me not quite as bright right now, but I'm still sexy as ever, and that's all that counts, right?"

"I'm sure you're still sexy, but you were never very bright," Maggie teased.

Roger released one of his guffawing laughs. Her heart

warmed, and her tensed muscles eased. He had to be okay if he could still laugh like that.

"I don't remember anything that happened," Roger said. "It must have been a pretty bad wreck."

"Yeah, I think so. I don't remember much either." Maggie despised lying to him, but she couldn't tell him the truth.

"They said the ambulance was pretty banged up. Where *are* you? Where did you go?"

She rose when a knock sounded on the door between their rooms. Walking over, she opened it to find Aiden standing on the other side. He frowned at the phone but didn't comment as he leaned against the doorframe to watch her.

"I, uh... I'm home. I must have wandered away," she said to Roger. "I barely remember getting to my apartment."

"Did you get yourself checked out?" Roger demanded.

"Yes, I'm all right."

"Are you going in to work tonight?"

"No. Doctor's orders are to rest for a bit. How long is the hospital keeping you?"

"I think another night."

She didn't ask him if anyone had told him about Glenn and Walt. They were probably waiting until he was out of the hospital or at least well enough to handle it. If he didn't mention their deaths, then she wouldn't either.

"I'm going to come see you," she said.

"No," Roger said. "I'd prefer you didn't. Not in this place. I'll see you at work."

"It might be a few days before we both get back to work." She had no idea if she would ever make it back. Maggie sat on the edge of the bed and propped her elbows on her knees. "I'd like to see you before then."

"Nothing's going to keep me down, Maggie May. You can

come see me at home if we're not back to work soon, but not here, okay?"

"Okay," she whispered.

"You sure you're all right?"

"I'm fine," she assured him.

"Good. I gotta go, my nurse is here, and I see meds. This woman enjoys stabbing me."

"I'm sure she's not the first," Maggie quipped, and Roger laughed.

"And she won't be the last! Take care of yourself; I need my partner in tiptop shape. I'll talk to you soon, love ya, kid," he said gruffly.

Before she could reply, he hung up. "Love you too," she said anyway.

Maggie closed the phone and set it on the stand next to her bed. She swallowed the lump in her throat as Roger's last words ran through her head. It had been years since someone told her they loved her, not since A.J. And A.J. only said it once, after they broke up. It seemed he'd felt compelled to make it clear there was no change in his feelings for her, but she'd known that without words. She'd awkwardly said it back to him. Now, Roger was the second person, and only the second time she'd heard those words from another. She hadn't gotten the chance to say them back to him, but he knew she loved him.

"How is he?" Aiden inquired.

"He has a concussion and doesn't remember anything, but he thinks they're sending him home tomorrow."

"It's not just a concussion," Aiden said. "I took the memory from him."

"I see. Will the Savages go after him again?"

"There are already some trainees from Ronan's men keeping watch over him."

"Is Ronan your vampire leader or boss or something?"

"I guess you could call him my boss." He couldn't get into details with her about Ronan, not while she remained human and they were unmated.

"How long will they watch over Roger?"

"For a few weeks after he's released. If any Savages go after him, they'll be taken down. However, they'll know we also won't leave any loose ends and would have changed his memories. They won't see him as a threat, and unlike you, his blood is not a *big* temptation."

He'd known the second her blood hit his tongue she was his mate, and he'd believed that was the reason her blood was potent. Now, he knew the truth. "You're a powerful human with blood that any vampire who tastes it would crave more. The Savage who bit you won't stop until he's destroyed."

"You drank from me too. Will you be stopped? Will you take more; do you *expect* more? Is that why I'm here?"

Aiden's gut clenched. "No. I won't take from you again without your permission. I have control over my baser instincts." *Barely.*

"And if I give permission?" Maggie didn't miss the flash of red in his eyes or his glance at her neck. Her nipples puckered as anticipation clamored through her body. It hurt so bad when the Savage bit her, but it had been one of the greatest pleasures of her life when Aiden fed on her. God help her, she knew she shouldn't, but she wanted to experience that again, with him.

"Then I would taste you over and over again."

Maggie's breath caught as she struggled to suppress the rush of lust his words evoked in her. She had no idea what it was about him, but he could arouse her faster than any man she'd ever encountered.

Get your libido in check. Getting involved with this vamp would be one of the worst decisions you ever made.

"I'll keep that in mind. I, uh... I need a shower," she muttered and rose.

She probably should have mentioned something that didn't involve nudity, but it was the only thing she could think of for a quick escape. She didn't look back at him as she stepped into the bathroom and closed the door. Leaning against the door, she took a deep breath and listened as he left the room.

MAGGIE DIDN'T SEE Aiden again until later that night when he knocked on the door. Taking a deep breath, she braced herself to face him before pulling it open to reveal him looking like a walking, talking temptation on the other side. He wore a pair of loose-fitting jeans; his forest green sweater brought out his eyes and enhanced the golden color of his skin.

He could attract every woman in a hundred-mile radius, yet his eyes filled with yearning when they ran over her body. He didn't look at her like he was stripping her bare as so many other men had over the years. No, he looked at her as if she were the most exquisite woman he'd ever seen.

There was nothing special about the sweater and yoga pants she wore, but she suddenly felt like the sexiest woman in the world.

"I thought you might be hungry," he said.

She was starved, but she didn't know if it was for food or him. When her stomach rumbled, she had her answer. "I am."

"There's a restaurant downstairs. We could go there for dinner."

"Sounds good. I'll get changed."

Again, she had to mention nudity in front of him. When she felt a blush creeping up her neck, she closed the door. Hurrying to the dresser, she pulled out a black sweater and tugged a pair of jeans from a hanger in the closet. She dressed, ran a brush through her hair, and gave herself a critical inspection.

She couldn't recall the last time she'd cared about her looks, but now she found herself fluffing her hair. She picked at the small defect in the stitching of her sweater that enabled her to buy it at 60 percent off the regular price. The odd stitch was almost unnoticeable, but it became all she could see.

Stop it!

She released the sweater, slipped her feet into her sneakers, and hurried to the door. She knocked before stepping into Aiden's room. He sat on the edge of the bed, his hands clasped before him and his head bowed as if he were in pain or deep contemplation. When she entered, he looked up at her and froze.

Aiden swore his heart stopped when Maggie stepped through the door. Her thick, auburn hair flowing around her face and down to the middle of her back emphasized the loveliness of her features. Her sweater and jeans hugged her slender waist, round hips, and full breasts. Feeling like an awkward teen again, he couldn't stop staring at her while he rose.

"You look beautiful," he murmured.

She glanced nervously away before meeting his eyes again. "You're not so bad yourself, Nosferatu."

He smiled at her as he walked over and held his arm out to her. "I think that's a high compliment coming from you."

"It is."

Leading her out of his room, he closed the door behind them and walked with her down the hall to the elevator. Maggie fixated on the numbers as they descended to the lobby and stepped out. Aiden escorted her into the dimly lit restaurant with a large, square-shaped, mahogany bar in the center. Glasses hung from racks above the bar. They had a good crowd for a weekday in March; she suspected many of those gathered within were locals and not guests.

A young, pretty woman led them to a booth in the back and set their menus on the table. "Enjoy," she said before walking away.

Maggie lifted the menu, flipped through it, and set it down again. She already knew what she wanted. When the waiter came, she ordered her steak as rare as they would cook it and a whiskey on the rocks. Aiden also ordered a steak and whiskey.

The waiter collected their menus and left them to sit, staring awkwardly at each other. Maggie swore her mind had abandoned her as she fumbled for something to say to him. "You told me you're one of ten," she finally said and sipped her water. "Where do you fall into the ten? Are you the oldest, youngest, middle?"

"I'm the fourth, so I guess I'm toward the middle," Aiden replied.

"What is it like to have so many siblings?"

"Our house can get pretty hectic."

"It was probably more chaotic than some of the group homes I stayed in, and you couldn't get away from your family. At least when someone pissed me off, I knew there was a chance one of us would be leaving soon."

"And they pissed me off often," Aiden said with a chuckle.

"I bet."

When the waiter came back with her whiskey, she gripped the glass but didn't drink it. "Do you have any nieces and nephews?"

"Six," he replied, "and I'm sure my siblings will make more."

"Wow."

She had no idea what else to say, so she lifted her whiskey

188 BRENDA K DAVIES

and downed it. "You have a high tolerance," Aiden remarked when she set her glass down.

"It's something I've always had."

"So do I, so do all vampires." He'd leaned across the table as he said the last word, but there was no one within earshot of them.

"Another little piece of the Magdalene puzzle I didn't know was missing," she said.

The waiter returned to ask if she would like a refill.

"No need to ask, just keep them coming," Maggie said with a smile as Aiden drank his whiskey and slid his empty glass next to hers.

The waiter smiled at her as he collected the glasses. He didn't acknowledge Aiden who scowled at his back when he turned away.

"He's very nice," Maggie said with a teasing grin.

Aiden leaned away from her and draped his arm across the back of the booth. "I think you might have a little bit of the devil in you after all, Magdalene."

She laughed. "I definitely do."

CHAPTER TWENTY-SIX

AFTER THE WAITER LEFT, they fell into an easy conversation about their completely different lives. Aiden regaled her with stories about how he and his siblings would all torture each other, the Stooges, and their parents. She told him about knocking out Ray Jessup and the couple of foster homes she'd actually liked, but she'd still acted horribly in them until they sent her back.

"Looking back, I think I was scared I'd become attached to the people and get hurt by them," she said as she cut up her bloody steak. Aiden sliced the meat in front of him too, but whereas she dug eagerly in, he picked at his and spent more time pushing it around his plate. "Sure, I wanted to get back to A.J. too, but now I realize there was more to it. I never would have admitted it to anyone else or even myself then. It totally would have ruined my wicked badass reputation."

"Totally," Aiden agreed, and she laughed.

"What about you? What did you do after high school? Did you go to college?"

"I did, for a few semesters, but I left soon after."

"How come?"

"It wasn't for me." He couldn't tell her that even before he stopped aging, the urges he started having didn't fit in well with the human world.

"Didn't know what you wanted to be when you grew up?"

"I wanted to get into sports medicine or become a coach, something along those lines. I enjoyed sports, even if I had to keep myself in check around humans when I played and couldn't go to a school where they did drug testing for athletes."

"Take a lot of drugs, did you?" she asked, her hands freezing on her utensils.

"No drugs. Like alcohol, it would take a lot to affect me, and I don't like being out of control." For him, such a thing could prove lethal to anyone near him. "But my blood isn't exactly human DNA compatible, and trying to keep up a front and change memories all the time wasn't worth it."

"Oh, yeah." Maggie wiped her mouth and placed the napkin on her plate. "They took a lot of my blood when I was a kid, and they never found anything unusual."

"Your human side must be stronger in that aspect," he replied.

"Interesting."

The waiter returned to remove their plates. "Would you like dessert?"

"No, thank you," Maggie replied, and Aiden shook his head. From somewhere out back, music started playing. "What's that?"

"The hotel also has a club; the doors open at eight," the waiter replied.

"Oh."

"Would you like to check it out?" Aiden asked when the waiter left again.

"I've never been one for clubbing or that kind of music."

"And what kind of music are you into, Maggie May?" Aiden asked.

"I'm a straight-up alternative, hard rock kind of girl," she said with a smile. "I like my music angry."

"I see."

She wasn't sure if it was the atmosphere, her increased energy from dinner, the whiskey, or Aiden, but she felt almost flirtatious as she leaned across the table toward him. "I'll tell you a secret."

His eyebrow lifted as he sat forward. This close, she could see the emerald and forest flecks of green in his amazing eyes. A five o'clock shadow lined his jaw, and the clove scent of him enveloped her.

"And I'll keep it," he replied.

"Sometimes, when no one else is around, I secretly listen to eighties music. And I don't mean like Megadeath or Slayer; I mean Tiffany and The Bangles."

"That's not what I'd typically consider angry music." Aiden held himself back from clasping her face and lifting her lips to his as her eyes twinkled with irresistible amusement.

"It's not," she agreed, her voice breathier as her eyes dipped to his mouth. "Especially not Cyndi Lauper."

"That's about as far from angry as you can get."

"What can I say? Girls really do just want to have fun," she told him with a wink and sat back when the waiter arrived with their check.

Maggie felt more alive than she had in years as she watched Aiden pull out his wallet and place some cash on the table. She'd never been a boy-crazy teen, but she suddenly felt young and carefree in a way she'd never experienced before.

When Aiden held his hand out to her, she knew she shouldn't take it, but she did. He helped her out of the booth and drew her closer when she rose beside him. Her skin came alive until she felt their contact over all her nerve endings.

"Is there something you'd like to do now?" Aiden asked. He ran his hands over Maggie's arm when she tilted her head to look up at him.

A smile played across her lips. "The beach."

"The beach it is then."

Maggie resisted laying her head on his chest as he walked with her across the restaurant. She glared at a couple of women eyeing Aiden with a look that made it clear they'd happily shove her out of the way to pounce on him. One of them smiled smugly back at her and fluffed her blonde hair. Aiden didn't look at them as he pushed open one of the glass doors in the lobby of the hotel and held it open for her.

The March air caused goose bumps to break out on her arms, but the briny scent of the ocean drew her across the street and toward the beach. Aiden helped her over a guardrail and down a hill toward the ocean below. The wind whipped her hair away from her; she licked the salt from her lips as the air froze her cheeks and her breaths plumed before her.

The dim light from the hotel illuminated some of the shadows, but the beach was more in the dark than out of it. With the stars twinkling against the black night and the sliver of moon hanging low over the bare trees, she could almost pretend everything was normal and she was simply on a date with a man she liked. When they reached the shoreline, she closed her eyes as she listened to the ebb and flow of the waves rolling onto the shore.

Aiden stopped at the edge of the water with Maggie's arm locked securely in his. The awe on her face captivated him. Then she tugged her arm free of his, bent, pulled off her sneakers, and set them down. She removed her socks next and stuffed them into her shoes before digging her toes in the sand.

The wet sand froze her feet, but she burrowed her toes in deeper as the icy water swirled around her ankles and between her toes. Removing her arm from his, she picked up a pink shell, twisted it in her fingers, then slipped it into her pocket and bent to pick up a rock. Pulling her arm back, she skipped the rock across the surface of the sea.

Aiden couldn't recall the last time he'd found joy in anything, but his heart swelled as he absorbed her delight. He was tempted to draw her close, to kiss her again, but he couldn't interrupt this for her. She walked closer to the ocean then laughed and danced back when the cresting waves chased after her.

"It's cold," she said when he approached. She bent to roll the bottom of her jeans up and snugged them into place above her knees.

"So that means you're going further in?" he asked.

"Of course, Nosferatu. Don't go getting all broody on me tonight. Relax and have some fun. Tomorrow we can go back to worrying about being jumped by a bunch of Savages, my mother's insanity, and world peace, but tonight...." She sighed and gazed at the crescent moon reflected on the surface of the vast sea.

"We think we're so big, so important, but we're this infinitesimal speck in the grand scheme of things," she said as she glanced at him. "Tonight, I want to *be* that speck."

Maggie didn't look back at Aiden as she walked into the water. Icy waves crept up her legs, but she continued until she stood midway up her calves in the ocean. When the waves rolled in, they brushed against her knees, dampened the bottoms of her jeans, and occasionally grazed her fingers. The flow of her blood seemed to match the rhythm of the waves.

She didn't hear Aiden approaching, but his arm warmed hers when he stopped beside her. She looked up at him, and her breath caught at the expression on his face. She'd never seen such raw hunger from another before, and it was focused on *her*.

Is it my blood he hungers?

A strand of her auburn hair blew forward, and Aiden clasped it in his hand. The moonlight brought out the deeper shades of red in it as he slid his fingers over the silken lock. Her mouth parted while she watched him.

Ignoring the chill of the waves, he stepped closer until they stood chest to chest. She nibbled her bottom lip as he wrapped her hair around his wrist and cinched it in his fist. Gently tugging her head further back, he bent until her breath whispered over his mouth.

For years, he'd craved pain, blood, sex, and death; now all he craved was *her*. Keeping her hair in his grasp, he slid his hand up until he cradled the back of her head. Her hands fell on his chest; he waited for her to push him away. When she didn't, he stopped denying himself and claimed her mouth.

Maggie's knees almost gave out when his tongue caressed her lips before she parted them and he entered her mouth. She felt drugged by the heady sensation as he kissed her like he was making love to her. Her fingers curled into his shirt; the muscle of his chest felt carved from stone as she pulled him closer.

Everything about him was hard, yet when he tugged her hair further back to deepen his kiss, his touch was tender. Maggie gasped when he slipped his other arm around her waist and, lifting her onto her toes, drew her hips flush against his. When the evidence of his arousal pressed against her, she flattened her hands on his chest to push him away.

This was all going far faster than what she was used to, but when his hand stroked her side, her hips thrust forward and she ground against his erection. All thoughts of shoving him away vanished. She melted against him as his tongue and hands wove a spell around her that had everything in her begging for more of him.

Then, something slimy brushed against her calf before wrapping around it like an octopus embracing its prey. With a squeak, Maggie jerked back and his arm slid away from her waist. Her eyes flew to the sea, she half expected to see a tentacle clinging to her as whatever it was tickled her leg again. Then, she started to laugh.

"Seaweed," she said between chuckles.

Aiden's hand remained enclosed on her hair; his eyes burned in the night. A flash of trepidation shot through her when red shimmered through his gaze. He'd never touched her in anger, but she'd seen what he could do to others, and there was something wild about him right now.

When she took a step back, his grip on her hair eased. "Aiden?"

Aiden fought to keep himself from pulling her against him once more. He needed to run his hands over her bare flesh and taste her again, but he'd seen the apprehension in her eyes before she stepped further away from him, and he'd heard the tremor in her voice. His hand tightened on her hair before he released her.

Maggie backed away from him before turning and making her way to the shore. Eager to get away, she was heedless of the water splashing around her legs. "I'm cold," she tossed over her shoulder as an excuse to put some distance between them.

When she glanced back, Aiden remained in the water with his head turned toward her. The ravenous gleam in his eyes sent her primitive instincts into flight mode. She'd never seen a look like that on anyone before. Then, his expression cleared, and he smiled at her.

"It is cold," he said as he walked from the sea to join her.

CHAPTER TWENTY-SEVEN

MAGGIE TOSSED and turned in bed as she replayed everything that had passed between her and Aiden tonight. Her body ached for him, but her mind retained enough sanity to know having sex with a vampire might be the biggest mistake she'd ever made, and she'd made some whoppers in her life.

Like stealing that car at fifteen. She still swore the tree jumped into the middle of the road that day. The police hadn't caught her after the accident, but she could have been killed, and she could have killed A.J. who was riding shotgun when the tree pulled up its roots, strolled on into the middle of the road, and committed suicide. Miraculously, she and A.J. had been uninjured enough to run from the scene, but the car was totaled.

Then there'd been the time she'd gotten herself expelled from school after setting the trash can on fire. She'd done it so she could be sent back to the group home where A.J. was staying, but it had been the first school where some of the teachers had taken an interest in her. She'd enjoyed attending there, she'd started to like learning, and she'd purposely blown it.

She didn't regret her choices, she wouldn't be where she was if she hadn't made them, but she could come to regret sleeping with Aiden. She suspected he might break her heart if she got too close to him and it all blew up in her face.

And she couldn't see it doing anything other than blowing up. He was a vampire, and she was... Well, she didn't know what she was anymore.

My mother was telling the truth.

That realization bolted her out of bed at two in the morning. She paced restlessly over to the heavy drapes covering the window and pulled one back. Across the roadway, the crescent moon created a small path across the waves.

My father is a vicious rapist. And a vampire.

Shivering, she dropped the curtain back in place. Stalking over to Blue, she watched as he happily flitted around his bowl, completely unaware of the turbulent state of her mind. When she put her finger on the outside of the bowl, he went to it and nudged it with his nose. She ran her finger over the plastic side, and Blue followed her motion as if he were receiving a pet. She'd discovered a couple of years ago it was something Blue liked to do. It always made her smile.

Done with his petting, Blue swam away with a flick of his tail. Maggie's heart sank as she lifted her head to take in the room. She'd never felt so alone in her life. Could she return to her old life with everything she'd seen and now knew about this world? About herself? What would her mother say when she got up the courage to see her again? And what of Aiden?

Screwing a vampire was a Bad idea with a capital B, but she'd never felt as alive as she did when she was in his arms. He may be a bloodsucker, but she also liked him. He made her smile, made her laugh, and he'd saved her ass a few times last night. But then, she'd also been put in danger because of him.

No, not because of him. He'd been attacked, and she'd done her job.

But even if everything that happened last night wasn't his fault, she sensed there was a lot more to him, his life, and his relationship with Carha than he was telling her. She believed him when he said he didn't use prostitutes or do drugs, but whatever that *more* was, she didn't want to be part of it. And she definitely didn't want to be anywhere near Carha again.

Aiden may be drop-dead gorgeous, but his life was perilous. Her life had been too uncertain for too many years to risk losing the stability she'd worked relentlessly to achieve by getting more entangled with him. She would never have millions of dollars, but she had what she'd always dreamed of: a place to call home, a career she enjoyed, and control of *her* life.

And she could lose it all if she couldn't return to her job soon. She hadn't been this scared since she'd been a sickly child who had no idea what was wrong with her or where she would be sleeping the next night.

Maggie ran her finger over the rim of the bowl as she thought about the blood that made her healthier as a child, her mother's ramblings, and the reports she'd read. How had she not put what she was together sooner?

Because who in their right mind would think they could be the offspring of a vampire or that vampires were *real*?

Maggie prowled to the window before going to the bathroom then crawling back in bed. She turned on the TV and flipped idly through the channels. What she needed was a run, but even before her knowledge of vampires, she wouldn't have been foolish enough to go for a run by herself at two in the morning.

There was a gym in this hotel; she'd seen signs for it when they checked in. She hated running on treadmills, but she figured it was the treadmill or she knock on Aiden's door and jump him when he opened it. One of those two things would get this restless energy out of her. Running may not be the more fun option, but it was the far saner one.

Tossing the covers aside again, she turned off the TV, changed, threw her sneakers on, grabbed a towel, and checked the peephole before cracking the door open. It didn't matter if she stayed here or in the gym, one of those Savages could get her in either place. Aiden had explained no invite was necessary to enter a hotel room because it wasn't someone's home. The only thing safer about her room than the gym was having Aiden next door. In her current mood, that seemed more hazardous to her.

Leaving her room, she crept past the closed doors to the stairwell. The hush of the hotel at this hour was more than a little unnerving, and she kept expecting a Savage, or even a poltergeist, to attack her. Refusing to live in fear, she continued down the red-carpeted hall.

When she arrived at the door to the concrete stairs, she hurried down. Her sneakers squeaked on the steps, making her location obvious to any would-be attacker, but nothing leapt out to suck her blood or slime her before she reached the lobby.

Located on the first floor, the gym was in a side hallway beyond the check-in desk. She hesitated outside the restaurant when she heard music coming from the club. The club would be closed to the public at this time of night, but Maggie suspected the employees were hanging out, listening to music, and probably having a couple of drinks as they cleaned the place. She almost went to see if she could join them but decided against it.

She left the restaurant and empty front desk behind as she followed signs to the gym. The lights were off when she located it, but when she stepped inside, they flickered to life overhead. Maggie glanced over the equipment stashed in the rectangular room. The concrete walls made it feel more like a prison than a gym, but at least there was a treadmill.

Maggie found the remote for the TV, turned it on, and searched for a music station. She settled on a nineties alternative station, did a quick stretch, and hopped on the treadmill. Working her way through a warm-up, her feet thudded with increasing speed as Nirvana followed Green Day.

A sense of calm descended as her feet settled into a comfortable rhythm, and she found herself starting to work through everything that had happened in the past two days. Much of it was beyond her control, but some of it wasn't. She focused on the things she could change, or do, as she worked out a plan in her mind. The one thing she had to do was the one thing she dreaded the most, but she couldn't put off seeing her mother for a week or two, not even a day or two. She would get it over with tomorrow.

When Aiden appeared in the doorway, she wasn't surprised to see him, but she didn't acknowledge him either. He didn't say anything before ducking out of the room again. She couldn't see him anymore, but she knew he stood outside, watching over her. She wasn't sure if she found it charming or annoying, but she didn't stop running until her legs turned to rubber, sweat coated her, and her lungs burned.

She moved through a cooldown and wiped herself with the towel when the machine came to a stop. Draping the towel over her shoulder, she strolled over to the water bubbler, pulled a paper cup from the dispenser, and filled it.

"Are you going to be my new shadow?" she inquired when Aiden returned to the doorway.

"You should have let me know you were leaving."

"I thought you were sleeping."

"I wasn't. It's not safe—"

"Maybe not, but you said a Savage could enter my room

too, so it's no safer there than it is here. Besides, I won't be caged. For years, everyone else dictated my life, where I would be, what I would do. I won't allow that to happen again."

"I'm not trying to cage you."

"No?" she inquired and tossed the cup into the trash can next to the bubbler.

Aiden rested his hand against the doorframe as he sought to maintain his composure. Being near her helped to steady him, but it also made him more uncertain. When he'd heard her leave her room, he'd believed she was fleeing *him*. The crushing sense of relief he'd felt when she came here, and the anger that followed when he realized she'd risked herself for a run, nearly unraveled him.

This woman held his future in her hands, and she didn't know it. Only part vampire, she had no idea what was happening inside him or what she meant to him. She may decide to reject him, but he had to make sure she remained safe.

"I should have taken you to Ronan's estate. He owns a large property, with a big gym, and you can move about freely there. It has a lot of security." He didn't like the idea of having her close to so many vampires, but he trusted enough of them to keep her protected if something went wrong with a fellow vamp. "We'll get our things and go there now."

"First off, that sounds like it's a *big* cage to me. Second, no one is taking me anywhere I don't agree to go. Third, I have no idea who Ronan is, where his place is, or anything about it, and I was taught young to avoid going anywhere with strangers."

"Not with strangers, you would be going with me."

"You're not much more than a stranger to me," she replied.

Aiden shoved down the twinge that statement caused to his heart. "You'll be safer there, and they have a much better gym."

"Treadmills aren't much of a bribe."

"Maggie—"

"I have a *life*. I know it's in danger, I got that memo when that *thing* bit me. But I have friends, an apartment, a career. I worked hard for all of it, and I refuse to let it go without a fight. This problem will be fixed so I can go home. I'm not going to hide out with a bunch of vampires I don't know. Which sounds about as fun to me as a tween concert where I'm the only adult and they don't serve alcohol."

His fangs pricked in his mouth, and his hand on the doorframe—the one she couldn't see—dug in so deep the metal bent beneath his fingers. She had to realize she couldn't return to that life, that she belonged to him.

If I change her, maybe she'll feel the bond, maybe—

No! He angrily broke the thought off. *She'll have the life she chooses, even if it's not with me.*

But that didn't mean he couldn't try to win her. He just wasn't sure how to go about doing that, and with the way he felt, he might only push her away from him.

"I can take you somewhere else," he offered. "Anywhere."

"You said you wanted to stay close to the city."

"The Savages have to be taken care of, but I will take care of *you* first."

"I have a *job*. That might not be much of a concern in your world, but I can't warp Mrs. Mackey's mind into believing I paid my rent, and air doesn't fill my belly. I have to return to work."

"You can't return without putting yourself at risk."

Maggie slung the towel over her shoulder. "Can I ever go back?"

He stared at her, his eyes hooded and his body tensed. The crunch of metal drew her attention to where he'd placed his hand on the other side of the doorframe, but she couldn't see what had caused the noise.

"I will do everything I can to give you the life you deserve," he said.

"Why?"

"Because you deserve it."

"You don't know that; you don't know me."

"No, but you didn't know me either when you tried to save my life."

"It's my job to help others."

"Yes, and mine is to protect the innocent from those of my kind who would destroy them. Where would you like to go, Maggie?" he asked to distract her from questions that were edging perilously close to his connection with her.

"If I can't go home, then I would prefer to stay here. I won't be locked up in some vampire compound. I also want to see my mother. Today if possible. I have to get it over with."

"We will do that then. The next time you decide to go for a run, or leave your room, will you let me know you're going?"

The look of concern in his eyes buried the resentment swelling within her. He was only trying to protect her, and no matter how much she disliked it, for the time being, she might need his protection.

"Yes," she said.

Aiden lowered his hand and stepped away from the door when she approached him. As she left the gym, she looked up, and her eyes widened on the dents his fingers had left in the metal trim around the door. She gazed questioningly at him, but he didn't say anything as he turned and strode down the hallway.

CHAPTER TWENTY-EIGHT

MAGGIE HADN'T BELIEVED she would get any sleep, but after returning to her room and showering, she fell onto the bed and passed out. Dreams of Aiden haunted her again, and she woke feeling achy with desire for him. If he'd been in the room with her, she would have screwed him, bad decision or not.

Her tongue poked at her canines as she recalled her last dream of him. A dream in which she'd sank *her* fangs into *his* throat. The memory was so real; she could almost taste the rush of his blood against her tongue.

Maggie moaned and shoved the pillow over her face when she recalled they'd been having sex while she drank from him. She bit her lip to hold back anymore sound as she threw the pillow aside and shoved herself out of bed. She didn't glance at the doorway separating their rooms; she might make a beeline for him if she did.

What a strange, sensual dream to have, and what a weird thing to have turn her on. But then, she supposed it wasn't all that bizarre to have the idea of feeding on Aiden stimulate her. She did have vampire DNA after all.

She'd known for years raw meat and the blood from it invigorated her, but was she starting to need more than that? Would she have to start drinking *human* blood too?

The idea of consuming a stranger's blood repulsed her; the idea of feeding on Aiden had her running her hands over her bare breasts as she imagined it was him stroking her in such a way.

Maggie flipped the switch in the bathroom and stood before the mirror to inspect her reflection. Small shadows circled her eyes, but the rest of her looked the same. Opening her mouth, she examined her teeth in the mirror. They didn't lengthen into fangs when she poked them with her tongue.

"Am I becoming a vampire?" she asked her reflection, but it had as many answers as she did.

She'd have to ask Aiden.

When she stepped into the shower, she continued to imagine Aiden's hands running over her body as she stroked herself to an orgasm that somehow left her unsatisfied. She turned the water colder than normal and stood beneath it as she tried to rid herself of the horrible, unfulfilled desire plaguing her.

Hopping out, she hurried to get ready. She fed Blue and glanced at the clock on the bedside table. It was almost one. She'd slept longer than she'd expected, but she would be able to get in to see her mother until five.

She could pretend it was a wasted day and push the visit off until tomorrow. If she had any chance of spending more than an hour with her mother, she would have done that. However, if this visit were anything like her last one, she'd be there for less than half an hour. She'd rather get it over with today and maybe, during this visit, she would at least get some closure.

The idea of closure made her chuckle. How could she get

closure from a woman who screamed for garlic when she learned her daughter had come to visit?

Taking a deep breath, Maggie tugged at the end of her sweater and knocked on the door dividing their rooms. After a few seconds, it opened to reveal Aiden on the other side. She'd tried to prepare herself, but the sight of him still sent her heart into her throat. All her dreams came back to her in a flood of erotic memory.

Aiden's nostrils flared when the scent of her arousal hit him, and color crept into her cheeks. His hand clenched on the doorknob as his dick hardened in response to her need. Her eyes fluttered away before coming back to him.

"I overslept," she murmured.

"You needed it."

"Yes, I... ah... yes."

Maggie glanced at him from under the long fringe of her thick, red-tipped lashes. Without thinking, he released the knob and clasped her chin to stroke her cheek with his thumb. Tranquility descended over him as her mouth parted and he heard the increased beat of her heart.

Unable to stop himself, his eyes drifted to the slender column of her throat and the vein running through there. Before he could slide his hand to her nape to draw her closer, she stepped away from him. His hand fell to his side, and he gripped the knob again.

"I want to see my mother," she stated. "I should get it over with."

The rush of her words and the frantic uncertainty he heard within them buried his disappointment over her avoidance of him. For Maggie, this visit was a thing of intense dread. Aiden stepped back, and with a wave of his hand, he gestured her into the room.

When she entered, her gaze fell on his unmade bed, and

the erotic sights and sounds of her dream flitted across her mind again. She tore her eyes away from the bed, but then her attention returned to *him*. And he was far more alluring than any dream.

The sweatpants he wore hung low on his hips, revealing the trail of hair from his belly button to the waistband as well as the V shape of his muscles pointing her directly where to go. Shirtless, sweat glistened on his chest as he closed the door. His arm brushed hers when he strode past her to grab the towel hanging over the chair in the corner. He wiped off his hair and chest before draping the towel over his shoulder.

"Did I interrupt something?" she asked.

"I was just working out, doing some push-ups and sit-ups."

"Oh. I can wait until later. The place doesn't close until five."

"I'm done."

He didn't tell her he'd been doing them to keep from going for her. She'd filled his dreams, and his persistent erection made sleeping difficult. No matter how many times he jerked off, his shaft still roused when his mind wandered to her. He'd never believed it would be possible for someone to have him so wound up yet so at ease, but Maggie did both those things to him.

"I'll take a shower, and we'll go," he told her.

Maggie watched as he walked into the bathroom. Clasping her hands together, she tried not to think about him standing naked beneath the water when it turned on, but the more she tried not to picture it, the more she imagined the water sluicing off his body.

Dangerous or not, bad decision or not, she didn't know how much longer she'd be able to resist this vampire.

∾

"Can I turn into a vampire?" Maggie asked as she watched the cars rushing through the intersection.

Aiden hit the gas when their light turned green. "If you lose enough blood and are given the blood of a vampire, yes, you can become one."

"No, I mean, if I'm a half-vampire, can I start to turn into one at will or something?"

"No. You would have to go through the transformation, the same as everyone else does."

"Are you sure?"

"Yes." He glanced over at her, sensing more behind her question. "Why do you ask?"

"I had the strangest dream last night," she murmured. "And I didn't know if it would be possible for me to transition into a vampire at will or something. Blood has helped to strengthen me for years without me knowing why, so if I drank enough of it, would it turn me?"

"According to Ronan, you still need to be changed from mortal to immortal by a vampire. You can't spontaneously make the transition. What was your dream about?"

"I dreamt I bit something, and I had fangs when I did it. It felt very real."

She didn't look at him when she revealed this, and a flush of rosy color bloomed on her cheeks. He'd give anything to know what she'd dreamt.

"Does garlic work to keep vampires away?" she asked.

He chuckled and shook his head. "About the same as a person who eats excessive amounts of it would deter you."

"Got it. What about crucifixes and stuff?"

"Why do you ask?"

Maggie fiddled with the edge of her sweater as she focused on the traffic. "There are things out there possibly hunting me. I should know what can hurt them. Plus..."

"Plus what?" he prompted when her voice trailed off.

"The last time I saw my mother, she started screaming for garlic when she realized who I was. So, I was wondering, if it did work against vampires, would it also work against me somehow? I mean, I've eaten garlic before and held a cross, of course, but maybe if a person *believes* it will ward off a vamp, it really will. I think I read or saw somewhere that it's more the person's faith in the object working than the actual object, so is that true?"

His fangs pricked at this revelation. Maggie's mother had endured a trauma many wouldn't have survived. It wasn't her fault she was so messed up, but he would gladly kill the woman if she upset her daughter again today.

"No, that's not true. There's nothing she could use against you. You are still more human than vampire, and if you were a vampire, only an invite would hold you back unless you were a Savage, and then as I explained before, sunlight and the other things would affect you more."

"Good."

CHAPTER TWENTY-NINE

MAGGIE FELT like a dead woman walking as she stared at the brick building before her. *You don't have to do this!*

Yes, you do.

She knew she did. She had to face her mother again, her past, her heritage, everything she'd written off years ago. Opening the car door, she didn't pause to think before shoving herself out of the vehicle. Her shuffling gait took her from the car and to the bluestone walkway of the building. She didn't look at Aiden when he fell into step beside her.

"Shortly after my mother killed the nurse, she was deemed incapable of standing trial due to insanity. They placed her here, in this high-security mental facility, which is essentially a fancier prison. If she'd gotten better, they might have freed her, but I don't think she'll ever leave this place."

Aiden's gaze traveled over the brick building with its brown vines creeping up the walls. They were most likely ivy vines, but their leaves had yet to bloom so he couldn't tell for sure. Neatly trimmed boxwoods lined the walkway as they approached the glass front door. When they stopped before the door, the brass plaque on the wall beside it revealed the building was completed in 1852, but he saw nothing marking the name of the place or its purpose.

"It's nice, for a state-run facility," Maggie said.

She chewed on her bottom lip as she fiddled with her sweater again. He'd seen her jump-start a Savage with paddles in the ambulance and tell a vampire to pretty much fuck off without so much as breaking a sweat. Now, her skin was ashen and she looked petrified as she rambled.

"I was impressed with it when I came before," Maggie continued. "Don't get me wrong, most of the group homes I stayed in were okay, but you know, this is a place for those with mental illness. The people here are the ones the rest of the world prefers to forget. Everyone loves and feels sorry for kids who have nothing; they're terrified of the mentally ill.

"So, when I first came here, I was expecting, you know, broken windows, dirty floors, and people leaning out the windows screaming. It's not like that. It's.... Oh, it doesn't matter what it's like. I should go in now. I probably won't be long."

"I'm coming with you."

"You don't have to do that. I'm glad you brought me here, but you don't have to deal with this."

Steely resolve filled Aiden's gaze. "I *am* coming with you."

"I doubt there's a threat in there."

"I do too, but I'm not going with you because of that. You shouldn't be alone for this."

Maggie opened her mouth to protest further. She didn't want him to see her mother, or hear the things the woman might say, but more than that, she didn't want to be alone for this. It could be humiliating to have Aiden with her, yet she'd get through it better with him by her side.

"Okay. Thank you."

"Don't thank me," he said. "Don't ever thank me for caring about you, Maggie, or being here for you."

She was about to ask him why he would do this for her or care about her when the door opened and a young man stepped out.

"Oh, hello," he said as he held the door open for her. Maggie recognized the subdued tone of his voice as someone who had been to hell and back. He probably had a loved one inside, and not a loved one who worked here.

When she remained unmoving, unable to take the door from the man, Aiden gripped it. "Thank you," Aiden said.

The man didn't respond as he shoved his hands in his pockets and shuffled away with his shoulders hunched up to his ears. That's exactly how she'd walked the last time she left here.

"Maggie?" Aiden inquired.

Tearing her attention away from the man, she stepped inside the vestibule before continuing to the door across the way. Before she could reach the door, a buzzer sounded, and a man wearing white scrubs opened it for her. Maggie entered the front reception area and walked toward the desk. So polished, the white tile floor was nearly blinding in the overhead fluorescents glaring down on it.

"Can I help you?" the cute blonde woman sitting behind the desk asked her.

"Yes, I'm here to see Jane Doe," Maggie replied in a steadier voice than she'd anticipated.

If the woman was at all astounded her mother had a visitor, she hid it well. She focused on her computer while her fingers flew across her keyboard. "And you are?"

"Her..." Maggie paused to pull at the collar of her sweater. "I'm her daughter."

This time, the woman couldn't hide her surprise as her eyes flew back up to Maggie. She didn't doubt that most, if not all the people working here, knew her mother's story and, therefore, part of hers. It wasn't this woman's fault, of course, but Maggie resented the woman's knowledge she was the child Jane tried to cut from her belly.

"Can I see some ID?" the woman asked as she worked to cover her shock.

Maggie's heart sank. She'd completely forgotten she'd required ID to get in here before. She wanted to kick herself in the ass. It wasn't exactly a tiny detail she'd overlooked, and she had no idea when she'd get her license back.

Aiden rested his hand on the small of her back and stepped closer to the desk. The woman's eyes widened on him and she smiled sweetly.

"I have our ID right here," Aiden said. Reaching into his pocket, he removed his wallet and pulled out a license and credit card. "Here is mine," he pointed to the license with his picture and a fake name. "And here is Magdalene Doe's." He indicated the credit card.

Maggie hadn't heard the tone of his voice change, but there was a subtle shifting in *him* and a flow of power rippled across her skin. The woman gazed at the cards he held before her. Maggie realized he was holding them so the security cameras couldn't see them

The woman's brow furrowed in confusion. "I'm not sure where the license number is on Magdalene's."

"It's right here," Aiden said and pointed to the credit number. As he pointed, he read off a set of numbers and letters that weren't on the card at all.

"Oh, yes. I see it now," the woman murmured, and her fingers flew over the keyboard once more.

Maggie didn't realize she'd stopped breathing until her lungs started burning. Aiden's hand pressed more firmly into her back when her breath exploded out of her. She'd never tried LSD, but she had the unsettling feeling she was taking a strange trip.

Aiden turned toward the orderly who had buzzed them in when the man was drawn forward by his exchange with the receptionist. "Everything is fine," Aiden said to him. "Return to the doorway."

Maggie's skin crawled when the man retreated. A muscle in Aiden's jaw twitched as he met her gaze. He seemed to be bracing himself for condemnation from her. What she'd seen unnerved her, but he'd done it for her, and he hadn't hurt anyone.

She gave him a wan smile; it was all she could muster in this place.

"I have to contact Jane's doctor to let her know Jane has visitors," the woman said. "Jane may not be up for seeing anyone today."

Maggie knew this was the woman's polite way of saying, *Jane may be completely off her rocker today and might try to kill you again; we'd prefer not to deal with the paperwork.*

But none of that mattered because Aiden would stroll through all of them with a smile and a few words. Maggie swallowed to wet her suddenly parched throat.

"Understandable," Maggie said as the woman lifted the phone.

THE PETITE WOMAN, who was her mother's doctor, gestured to where Jane sat in a chair in the corner of the large rec room. From her position, her mother could see out the bar-covered window to the parking lot below. If she'd been there when they arrived, then Jane might already be aware Maggie was in the building.

The doctor hurried over to some of the nearby orderlies who doubled as security in this place. She spoke in hushed whispers with them. The staff would be extra careful while she was here.

Maggie's gaze traveled over the other patients in the room. Heavily medicated, most of them weren't aware of their surroundings, but some were coloring, and one was reading. A handful had gathered on or near the TV to watch a rerun of the *Family Feud*, and a few of them were playing Scrabble.

It was impossible to judge their ages as they all had a haunted, knowing look that should only come from a vast number of years, yet many of their faces were unlined. One of the patients, a young man of maybe twenty, clapped his hands and gave an excited whoop over something on the Scrabble board.

The last time she'd been here, she'd met her mother in her bedroom. That small, concrete cubicle had been awful enough; this was so much worse. Like some of the foster and group homes she'd been through, the broken air here made it seem as if they'd all given up. Aiden stepped closer and settled his hand on her back.

"Take your time," he whispered before brushing a kiss over her temple.

Maggie glanced up at him. She'd only known him for such a short time, yet the kiss felt natural, and his presence here strengthened her in ways she never would have believed possible. He hadn't needed to use his abilities again after the front desk, but she knew he would have done everything he could to get her here. She gave him a brisk nod before striding through the chairs toward her mother with him at her side.

Aiden studied Jane as they approached her. Her auburn hair hung to just below her ears. Some white hair streaked the dark tresses, but what he could see of her face remained remarkably untouched by age. Her hands were on her lap, and she had a blanket draped across her knees. Like the other patients in this room, she wore blue scrubs.

The woman didn't look at them when Maggie stopped before her. "Jane," Maggie said. "Jane Doe."

Maggie's voice had a small tremor in it, but he felt the strength forging the rigid length of her spine against his hand. He lost contact with her when Maggie knelt before the woman. She reached out to rest a hand on her mother's knee but pulled it away before they touched.

"Jane, I'm not sure if you remember me. I came to visit you six years ago."

The woman's head turned slowly toward her. Aiden braced himself to intervene if Jane tried to attack Maggie. He may not be able to stop the emotional damage this woman might inflict on her, but he would *not* allow her to hurt Maggie physically.

Able to see Jane's face, Aiden took note of the strong resemblance between mother and daughter. Jane's eyes were a paler shade of gray than Maggie's, but they were the same shape, and their hair was the same shade. Both of their mouths were full and their cheekbones high. Maggie had a smaller nose and a more feminine chin than Jane's square jaw, but there was no doubt Jane had once been almost as beautiful as her daughter.

"Mom," Maggie breathed, then winced at the word. Jane had given birth to her, reluctantly, but she'd never been a *mom* to her.

Maggie's fingers dug into her palms as she glanced nervously toward the doctor. The doctor had told them not to do or speak of anything that might upset Jane, but what she had to say to her mother was far from comforting.

Aiden rested his hand on Maggie's shoulder as he surveyed the other patients gathered within. A few of them turned to watch Maggie and Jane, but most seemed unaware of their interaction. He doubted the Savages had a spy in this place, but he wouldn't take any chances.

"Jane," Maggie said, drawing his attention back to them. "Do you remember me?"

Jane scanned Maggie's face before her head tilted to the side. The vacancy in her eyes cleared a little, and a smile curved her mouth. "You look like me."

"I do," Maggie agreed.

Jane's hand fluttered up to her hair. "They cut it all off," she murmured sadly. "Took it all away."

Maggie had never seen her mother with long hair, but Jane said this to her during her last visit too. "It looks pretty."

Jane's hand fell away; her eyes went back to the window. "Watched you coming."

Maggie glanced out the window and spotted Aiden's car in the lot below. "Do you remember me?"

Jane remained focused on the window. Maggie didn't know why she'd come here. What had she hoped to accomplish? What did she expect from her mother? Answers?

No, she wouldn't get those. Jane knew less of what had happened to her than Maggie did now. Had she come to say she was sorry? Because she was so very sorry for what happened to this woman and for believing she was completely insane when she was unbearably traumatized. She wanted to apologize for being the reason this woman was so broken, but that wasn't her fault.

Then, she knew why she'd come. Jane had to know she understood. That one person, out of Jane's entire wretched life, saw her for who and what she was: a young woman who'd been traumatized beyond the limits of what anyone should have to endure.

Experiencing a rape was devastating enough, but to be

raped by a monster and to have no one else believe you about it was something else entirely.

"I used to be so beautiful," Jane murmured and touched her cheek. "Too pretty. It's why..."

Jane's mouth pursed, and Maggie couldn't stop herself from resting her fingers on her mother's knee to offer some comfort. "No matter how pretty you are, what happened to you wasn't your fault."

She probably shouldn't be talking about this. She was certain the doctor wouldn't tolerate it, but Maggie couldn't allow Jane to blame herself.

Jane's eyes were more aware when they returned to her. "You came to visit me before."

"Yes, years ago," Maggie replied.

"I remember. You are... You are—" Jane suddenly recoiled. "Magdalene."

"Jane—"

"No! Monster! Vampire! *Get away!*"

Maggie winced and leaned back as her mother used her fingers to make a cross. She thrust the cross into Maggie's face. "Get back vampire spawn!"

Aiden's hand tightened on Maggie's shoulder; he stepped closer when Jane leaned further away. From the corner of his eye, he saw the orderlies and doctor coming toward them, but Maggie was already rising.

"I know you're telling the truth about what happened to you," Maggie stated in a flat tone of voice.

Jane stopped shouting at her to get back when Maggie spoke these words.

"I won't come back here, I won't bother you again, but I needed to tell you that. I'm sorry for what happened to you, and I believe you."

Jane's hands fell into her lap; her mouth parted. "You believe me?"

Aiden intervened with the doctor and orderlies before they could pull Maggie away. "It's fine," he said to them as he pushed his power out to ensnare their minds in a trap. "Give them a few more minutes."

The three of them stayed where they were, their faces slack as he kept hold of their minds. Aware of the cameras in the room, Aiden commanded them to talk to each other like they normally would.

"I believe you," Maggie said again.

Tears spilled from Jane's eyes with such intensity Maggie swore someone *did* turn on a faucet behind them. Her shoulders heaved until Maggie worried she'd harm herself.

"Oh, don't cry," she whispered and rested her hand on Jane's shoulder. The bone protruding against Jane's flesh dug into Maggie's palm. "Please, don't cry."

Jane jerked her shoulder away from her, and Maggie's hand fell helplessly to her side.

"You and your father destroyed me!" Jane wailed.

A sword to the heart might have hurt less than those words. They'd never had a relationship where love could develop between them, but it was heart-wrenching to be blamed as the source of a ruined life. No, she was not the source, that had been her father, but she was a byproduct of the miserable bastard's destruction.

"I'm sorry," Maggie said again.

Aiden clasped her hand and pulled her back as her mother threw up another cross and started screaming as if she were on fire.

"We should go," Maggie whispered.

"Calm down, Jane," Aiden commanded, and her screams became shrill bird-like cries. "You don't remember us being here," Aiden said to the other people still within his control. He couldn't do anything about the numerous cameras in this place, but at least no one would stop Maggie from returning here if she should decide to try again. "Now, help Jane."

When the doctor and orderlies rushed toward Jane, Aiden pulled a shaking Maggie against his side and hurried her toward the doorway. Once they were out of the room, Jane's shrieks escalated until they followed them down the hall to the elevator.

"I wish I'd killed you!" Jane screeched as the elevator doors slid open with a ding.

Aiden released Maggie as she stepped into the elevator, threw back her shoulders, and lifted her chin. Images of tearing Jane's head from her body flashed through Aiden's mind when he saw the anguish in Maggie's eyes. Jane had done nothing to deserve what was done to her, but no one should be allowed to hurt Maggie in such a way and live.

"I want to go," Maggie stated.

Reluctantly, he entered the elevator and pushed the button for the ground floor. The doors closed on Jane's continued screams for Maggie to die.

CHAPTER THIRTY

SITTING BESIDE AIDEN, Maggie sipped her whiskey as she gazed across the bar. The only words she'd spoken to him since leaving the institute were to tell him she was taking a shower before going to the bar. Aiden didn't try to comfort her, didn't tell her that her mother was crazy and therefore hadn't meant what she said. None of it would do any good.

They both knew her mother wasn't completely crazy and she had meant it.

Maggie had to work through what was going on in her head on her own, and he knew there had to be plenty going on up there after everything she'd been through recently.

While Maggie had been in the shower, he'd decided to call home. Over the past couple of years, he'd avoided going home with increasing frequency. It wasn't that he didn't love his family and miss his home, he did, but he couldn't sit there and laugh and smile with them while feeling like a ticking time bomb. It became harder to pretend he was normal while knowing the things he did to resist his appetite for blood, death, and pain.

And more recently, he didn't trust himself to be around his family. He loved them, he would die for them, but he didn't know if he could keep himself from unraveling and slipping into the darkness while at home. He didn't have access to the outlets he needed there.

He'd chanced going home for Christmas because it had been a couple of months since he'd returned. He'd played the role, but the whole time he'd been terrified this would be the time he snapped. Never had he been so happy to get out of a place as he was to leave his home. That was the moment when he realized he was slipping beyond the point of salvation.

He hadn't been home since Christmas, and his phone conversations with his family had become increasingly brief and rare.

Running a hand through his short hair, he tugged at the end of it. He considered shaving it off again; he hadn't felt bothered to do it in a couple of months, but then he realized he was only debating it to stall making the call.

He didn't know what he would say to his mom. After what he'd witnessed with Maggie's mother, there were so many things he wanted to say, mostly thank you. Inwardly, he was a chaotic mess, but he'd been blessed to have his family, and he'd been nothing but loved by them.

Finally, he'd dialed the house phone, and when his mom answered, he settled on small talk. He couldn't bring himself to tell her about Maggie, not yet, not when he didn't know how things would work out between them. His mother would only worry about him more than she already did if she learned he'd found his mate but hadn't completed the bond.

After a few minutes, his mom handed the phone over to his dad, then Mike, and finally his older brother Ethan. He could have told Ethan everything, he'd always confided in his older brothers, but Ethan and Ian had families now. Ethan didn't need Aiden dumping more on him, and neither did Ian. So, he'd laughed and chatted and pretended everything was fine while he listened to the shower turning off in the room next to his.

He'd hung up afterward and waited for Maggie to come to him before going to the bar. Now, she drank her fifth whiskey before chasing it with a beer. A man with a guitar walked into the bar and settled in the corner of the restaurant. Apparently, they also offered live entertainment in here as well as the club.

Maggie watched the man setting up his music stand. She felt numb. No, *more* than numb, she was hollow in a way she'd never been before. Aiden's quiet presence was the only thing keeping her from breaking down. She appreciated he didn't think he had to fill the silence with idle chatter. If she started talking, she knew he would listen, but she didn't know what to say to him.

The man with the guitar finished setting up, asked for some water from one of the bartenders, and opened with a Lynyrd Skynyrd song. Maggie smiled, finished her whiskey, and pushed it across the bar. One of the bartenders refilled it.

Another hour passed, and Maggie found herself swaying to the music as a pleasant warmth spread through her body. When the singer switched to "Unchained Melody," a few people got up to dance.

"I love this song," she murmured. They were the first words she'd spoken all night.

"Would you like to dance with me?" Aiden asked.

Most guys she knew wouldn't be caught dead on a dance floor. She couldn't picture Aiden, a vampire who tore the throats out of his enemies, willingly doing so. "You dance?"

"Yes, and I do it well. Come."

His hand slid into hers, and he rose from his stool with effortless grace. He helped her off her stool and led her past the other couples and onto the small, makeshift floor. He spun her around before drawing her effortlessly into his arms and clasping her against his chest. Their bodies melding together caused her breath to catch.

She lifted her head to look at him as he draped his arms around her waist. Maggie rested her hands on his hips and moved awkwardly through the first steps with him. Then, as the heat of his body warmed her and her muscles relaxed, she fell into a comfortable rhythm with him. Maybe it was the alcohol, maybe it was the events of this day, but his arms felt right.

She slipped her hands over his hips and pressed them into his back as she settled her head on his chest. His head dropped down. His mouth moved over her forehead, and he nuzzled her hair. She desperately wanted to get closer, but she was petrified of what would happen if she did.

Maggie shuddered, but she didn't pull away when his hands slid up her back and he held her closer. His heartbeat sounded beneath her ear, and her pulse increased to match the rapid pace of his.

The evidence of his desire swelled against her stomach as he continued to sway with her around the dance floor in a slow, sensual pace. At any other time, a man's arousal during a dance would have caused her to pull away. Now, her fingers curled into his back, and she inhaled his enticing scent. She could dance with him forever, she decided.

Aiden's head came up when a shout sounded from the club. The distant beat of the dance music barely penetrated this room, but the yelling grew louder, and then someone screamed. His hands tightened on Maggie when she lifted her head from his chest.

More shouts followed another scream that was punctuated by the smashing of furniture. Aiden's lips skimmed back when the scent of fresh blood drifted from the other room. Hunger tore through him, and he realized it had been a while since he'd fed. So focused on protecting Maggie, he hadn't thought of it.

Now, he started to unravel as the scent of more blood filled the air and someone shrieked. He'd been feeding every day for the past two years to keep the demon within him at bay. It had been almost three days since he'd last had blood.

The realization that whatever was going on in the club could put Maggie at risk heightened his growing bloodlust.

Maggie tried to step out of his arms, but he wouldn't release her. "I have to go look," she protested and tried to pull away again. "Someone could need medical attention."

More screams filled the air and furniture splintered apart. A man staggered through the doorway separating the restaurant from the club. The couple seated in the booth closest to the man leaned forward as another man barreled through and tackled the first.

A dozen more fighters spilled through the doorway. A man lifted a stool over his head and brought it down on the back of another. One of the bartenders spoke into the phone as Maggie lunged against Aiden's hold. Before the fight could get much further into the room, shouts of the police resonated through the club and restaurant.

"Assholes," the guitar player muttered from behind them and started putting his things away.

"We have to go," Aiden said to Maggie.

"But I can help!" she protested.

"Is there a chance someone who comes here could recognize you?"

"Yes," she reluctantly admitted.

"Then we have to go. Right now, your job thinks you have a concussion. If they find out you were here—"

"I can't lose my job."

Aiden hoped she wouldn't return to her old life, but if the

possibility of losing her job got her moving, he would use it to his advantage. "No, you can't."

Not to mention, if he stayed here much longer, he might feed off one of the injured. His fangs pricked, and his mouth watered at the prospect. His eyes latched onto the blood trickling from a cut on a man's forehead. He struggled to keep himself under control as he nudged Maggie toward the door.

The police started filing into the restaurant as the two of them crossed the lobby to the elevators. Aiden steered her away from the police and toward the stairwell. Maggie kept her head down as more shouts sounded from behind them. He hurried her up the stairs.

Opening the door for her on the third floor, Aiden held it as Maggie stepped out of the stairwell and into the hallway. Fire licked over his veins, and his thirst grew with every step he took toward their rooms. He sniffed at the air while listening to the beat of hearts behind the closed doors lining the hall. The idea of hunting so close to their rooms wasn't one he liked, but he couldn't go far from Maggie, and he had to feed soon.

He didn't care if he snapped and killed a human; they meant nothing to him. He would live with the rotten stench until it faded from him, but he couldn't take the chance he might go for Maggie. He should have known this was coming and prepared for someone to watch over her while he hunted, but it was too late for that.

Stopping outside his room, he slid the key card into the lock and pushed open the door for her. Instead of following her into the room, he backed away to put more distance between them. He had to leave her before he couldn't.

Maggie frowned when she glanced over her shoulder at Aiden standing in the hall. His fisted hands caused the muscles in his forearms to bulge. He looked as predatory as the night when the Savages attacked them, but she had no idea what had put him into this state.

"What's wrong?" she asked.

He rested his hand on the doorframe but didn't go any closer to her. "The blood, downstairs. It's been a while since I fed." He could barely get the words out as the prospect of blood caused saliva to fill his mouth. "I have to. Now. I need you to stay here. I won't leave this floor."

Maggie glanced at the hallway behind him. "You plan to feed on some of the people in those rooms?"

"Yes."

"You can't."

"I have to."

"But there are families—"

"I'll stay away from the families. I don't feed on children."

"They might panic."

"They'll never know what I'm doing. I'll take the memory from them."

She knew he had to feed to survive, and looking at him, he had to do it soon, but to do it to unsuspecting people felt wrong. "It will hurt them," she said.

"No, it won't. I promise you, they'll never know what's going on. They'll never remember it, and there won't be any pain."

"But—"

"Maggie, if I don't feed now, I could lose control and attack someone, or worse, I could hurt *you*. Do you understand?"

"Yes, but—"

"No buts. This is how I survive. I must feed if I'm going to keep you safe, and that is the most important thing to me."

"Why?"

"Because I care about you."

The blunt way he stated it robbed her of all further

protests. That sentence wasn't a line coming from Aiden. She believed him when he said it, just as she believed he wouldn't cause any suffering to anyone he drank from tonight. If they experienced a fraction of the pleasure she'd received from his bite, then they would know only bliss.

Her pulse quickened as she recalled the ecstasy that flooded her when his fangs sank into her throat. She yearned to feel that again, but more, she didn't want anyone else sharing the experience with him. She gulped when his eyes fell to the vein in her throat and red flashed through their green depths.

"What of me?" she whispered, unaware she was going to ask the question before she did. "What about my blood?"

His head bowed, his shoulders heaved as his fangs extended. He craved her blood more than a dying man sought Heaven. "You don't know what you're asking."

"Don't you want it?" She should be jumping for joy he'd prefer not to use her as a human blood bag, not feeling dismayed that he may go elsewhere.

When his head lifted again, Maggie couldn't stop herself from taking an abrupt step back. No green remained in his eyes, only a vivid ruby red blazed out at her. She edged further away when he bared his fangs. The razor-sharp points glistened in the hallway light. Her heart was going fast enough to win a race against a horse, but instead of turning and fleeing into her room, she stopped backing away.

Aiden had been there for her today, and she would be here for him now. She had no idea what this was between them, but she wouldn't turn him away, and she wouldn't let him seek from another something she could give him.

"Aiden—"

"I thirst for your blood so badly I can barely think, but you don't know what you're asking. It won't be enough; I'll want to feed from you again."

"Will you hurt me?"

"Never."

"Then I'm offering my blood to you."

"You don't know what you're saying."

"There are many things in this world I'll never be able to understand or help with, but I know a small fraction of your need for blood, and I can help. When you bit me..." She paused as she tried to think of the right words. "When you bit me, it was a rush of pleasure, unlike anything I've ever known. I *want* to be the one who nourishes you. Don't go to someone else; come to me."

Aiden's hand dug into the doorway as he realized jealousy tinged her words. Perhaps she had come to care for him too, or at least she cared for him enough to offer him this.

"I'll want *more*, Maggie," he said again. She had to understand that.

"I'll give you what I can, when I can, for as long as we're in this."

He should walk away from her. She didn't know what she was getting into with this, but he couldn't resist her, and if she was willing to give him her blood, she might eventually be willing to stay with him forever.

Releasing the doorframe, he entered the room and closed the door.

CHAPTER THIRTY-ONE

SHE WIPED her sweaty palms on her jeans when the door closed with an audible click. The hallway light cut off, and with the drapes pulled over the windows, she couldn't see him.

She was in this room with a predator who required her blood and would take it from her. Any sane person would flee; she didn't move as she listened to Aiden prowling closer. If she escaped into her room, she believed he would let her go, but her feet remained planted on the ground. She couldn't deny she was terrified, but she also couldn't deny she'd been desperate to experience this with him again.

When he stopped before her, he stood so close his body warmed hers and his breath whispered against her face. His hand encircling her nape caused her to gasp. She hadn't heard him move.

"You can change your mind," he said.

The husky tone of his voice sent a shiver down her back. "I won't."

He pulled her gently forward, and she braced herself as she waited for him to strike as he had in the ambulance. Instead, his lips moved over her forehead in a tender caress. The rigidity of her muscles eased as he kissed her cheek before his lips settled on hers. Standing in the hallway, he'd appeared starved, yet now he seemed more concerned with putting her at ease.

She opened her mouth to his tongue and sighed when it slid inside. He kissed her with the leisure of a man who had all the time in the world. He tasted of whiskey, but beneath that, she detected the faint hint of clove. When his hands slid around to grip her ass and he lifted her, she wrapped her legs around his waist. The rigid evidence of his erection sent delicious shivers down her spine when it rubbed between her thighs.

I didn't expect this to happen. But as she thought it, she knew she lied. She'd known when she offered her blood this is where the night would lead them.

Aiden groaned when Maggie's legs locked around him and she rubbed against the head of his swelling cock. He continued to kiss her, delving deeper into her mouth as she rose above him before sliding back down his erection. His kiss muffled her sensual cry. When she repeated the motion, her nails bit into his nape.

In two strides, Aiden carried her over to the dresser and set her on it with the mirror at her back. Breaking the kiss, he pulled back to take in her flushed face and swollen lips. She stared breathlessly up at him, looking so enticing it took everything he had not to tear her clothes from her.

Take it slow; savor her.

He traced her bottom lip with the tip of his finger before bending to nip at it. She didn't flinch when a bead of blood formed there. He slowly licked her blood away. That small influx of blood calmed him more than all the beatings, sex, and death he'd received and given over the years.

Minutes ago, his body had been waging war with itself, but

she gave him peace. Having done nothing to deserve her, he would do everything he could to keep her.

He nipped at her lip again and swallowed another drop of her blood. Releasing her bottom lip, he kissed his way over her skin and down to her throat. Maggie braced herself for the brief pinprick his bite brought with it, but he still didn't strike. Instead, he ran his tongue over her vein before gripping the bottom edge of her sweater and lifting it to reveal her stomach.

He stroked her flesh in a slow, teasing manner from the bottom of her bra to her jeans and back again. Her skin came alive where he caressed, and every part of her screamed for him to ease her torment as he sucked on her throat, but still didn't bite.

When Aiden pushed her sweater higher, she lifted her arms for him, and he pulled it over her head. Her lacy black bra revealed more of her flesh than it hid as her nipples were visible through the material. He circled one of his fingers around her dusky areola and growled when her nipple stiffened beneath his ministrations. Her breast was slightly larger than his hand when he cupped it and bent to flick his tongue over her hardened nipple.

Maggie's eyes had adjusted enough to the muted light filtering around the drapes for her to watch him as he teased her. One of his fangs scraped her breast before he lifted his head to gaze down at her. She could see the outline of his fangs against his lips as he undid the clasp at the front of her bra.

He inhaled sharply when her breasts spilled free. His fingers skimmed her shoulders when he pulled the straps of her bra back and slid it off her. She had no doubt he'd slept with many women over the years, yet he gazed at her as if she were Aphrodite come to life. Maybe he made every woman feel like that, but she didn't think so. Whatever this was between them, she sensed it was unusual.

"So lovely," he murmured before cupping her breasts in his hands and bending to kiss one nipple before turning to the other.

A growing wetness spread between Maggie's thighs; her head fell back as he ran his tongue over her breast. His fangs scratched her skin before he sank them into her, just above her nipple. Arching her back, she thrust her breast deeper into his mouth as the brief pain of his bite faded and ecstasy rose to replace it.

Releasing his bite on her, Aiden rose, yanked his sweater off, and tossed it aside. Her heavy-lidded eyes opened to watch as he stroked her belly before lowering his hand to the button of her jeans. He slid the button free and pulled the zipper down.

Maggie traced the dips and ridges of his abdomen. His skin rippled beneath her touch as she learned his body, memorizing every detail of him. When she cupped his erection through his jeans, he pushed his hips into her grasp and planted his hands on the dresser next to her as she stroked him.

Releasing him, she undid the button and zipper of his jeans and slid them down his hips a little. Without any underwear to hold it back, his erection sprang free to stand proudly out from his body. Unable to resist, she took it into her hand. Hard and hot, she marveled at the size of him and grew wetter with her need to have him inside her. She stroked his shaft before tracing the supple skin on the head of his cock and the thick vein running up the side of it.

He seized her wrist, halting her movements. Maggie froze, she didn't know if she'd somehow pushed this supernatural being too far. Tension radiated from him, his vast aura of power rippled across her skin. Then, he closed her fingers more firmly around his shaft and guided her hand over him.

"Fuck," he groaned.

After another stroke, Aiden pulled her hand away from

him before he came in her palm. He bent to lift one of her feet and pulled her sneaker off. He let it fall before removing the other one. Her hips rose off the dresser when he tugged her jeans and underwear down her thighs.

The excitement building within Maggie became a tumult she could barely contain as he tossed aside her jeans and stepped closer again. His body warmed hers as he trailed his fingers up her inner thighs, his eyes following every move he made.

Aiden discovered two freckles marring the creamy perfection of the skin on her inner thigh. Those freckles looked to be spaced about fang width apart, beckoning him to bite her there. Between her legs, her neatly trimmed auburn hair did nothing to hide the fact she was already wet with her want for him.

Lowering himself between her legs, he placed a kiss against the two freckles before sinking his fangs into them. Maggie's legs slid over his shoulders and drew him closer.

"Aiden," she breathed as he drank deeper from her thigh than he had from her breast.

Releasing his bite, he kissed and licked his way up her thigh to the juncture between her legs. Maggie's head fell back when his tongue flicking over her clit sent a current of ecstasy through her. She gripped the edge of the bureau as he slid a finger in to stroke her in an unrelenting motion that matched the demands of his tongue.

Her hips rose and fell, matching his pace as every nerve ending in her body came alive. Then, her body came apart, and she cried out as an orgasm rocked her. She'd experienced orgasms before, but she'd never *truly* experienced one that made her toes curl, her nerve endings sing with pleasure, and her entire body bow before going limp.

Aiden rose over Maggie, his control fraying as he tugged impatiently at his jeans. She'd calmed him before, but now the taste of her blood and her release on his tongue were pushing him to the brink of madness. He had to be inside her, possessing her.

He kicked his sneakers off, yanked his jeans down his legs, and threw them aside before stepping between her legs again. She smiled lazily as she reached for him. Aiden captured her wrists before she could touch him and pinned them to the mirror behind her head. Maggie's eyes widened, but she didn't thrash against him or tell him to stop.

She couldn't touch him; touching was not for him, not during sex. It didn't matter this was Maggie, that she was far different and more important than anyone else he'd been with, he'd waited too long. His darker inclinations had clamored to life within him and were moving beyond his control.

He kept her wrists pinned as he held her gaze and pressed the head of his shaft against her wet center. Then, he drove forward until her wet heat enveloped him. Sheathed deep inside her, all his malevolent impulses vanished as he experienced the tranquility she gave him.

"You feel so good," he said and lowered his head to rest it on her breast. She was incredibly wet and ready for him, but the tightness of her muscles gripping his cock made him realize, if he moved too fast with her, he would hurt her.

A feeling of completion stole through Maggie as she adjusted to the size of him inside her. Needing to touch him, she jerked against his restraining hold.

His hands briefly clamped on her wrists as old habits surged to the forefront. However, this was not some stranger he didn't want to touch or be touched by. This was *Magdalene.* When he released her, she lowered her hands to cup his face. He turned his lips into one of her palms and she cupped his cheek.

"My Magdalene," he murmured as she ran her fingers over his cheekbones.

It had been years since he'd been touched with care during sex. Even before his maturation he'd stopped wanting affection from his partners. When he'd been in high school, he hadn't offered promises of future calls to the girls he slept with. Once he started having sex, he'd avoided dating anyone from his school because there would be too many complications, and he'd known none of them was his mate.

As he'd gotten older, there had been less contact between him and his partners. Some women touched him to hold onto him, and he'd handled them when he had to, but there had been no caring in those caresses, only necessity. Over the past six months, the contact had become rarer.

Their touch had disgusted him.

No, he realized, *he'd* been disgusting. He'd been as unworthy of any kindness from them as he was of his family's understanding and support for him. If those women knew the things running through his mind while he'd been with them, they'd have run screaming. Often, he'd considered giving in and tearing their throats out so he could bathe in their blood.

He didn't deserve for anyone to care for him, especially not Maggie, but her hands on him soothed his ravaged soul in ways he'd never known possible. No thoughts of killing or inflicting pain went through his mind; he only experienced the wonder of her. She made him crave more of her caresses as her fingers moved over his shoulders and down his back. Unable to stop himself, he withdrew his cock partially from her before sinking inside again.

Maggie hadn't expected her recently quenched passion for him to return so fast, but it sparked to life until it became a wildfire. One of his arms locked around her waist, and his other hand cupped her nape as he took possession of her. Despite his total control of her body, and the strength of this supernatural being, she felt like *she* held *him* in the palm of her hand, as if he was somehow more vulnerable than her right now.

His face turned into her neck, he inhaled her sweet scent and shuddered when her hands ran over him again. "More," he breathed. "Touch me *more*."

Unexpected tears bloomed in Maggie's eyes at the hoarseness of his voice. She sensed he was showing a side of himself he never revealed to anyone and that he needed her more than she'd ever realized.

With her hands, she learned every flex of the muscles in his back and felt the faint scars crisscrossing his flesh. She sensed those scars were part of what drove him, part of why he craved her touch more than her blood right now. His ragged breath warmed her flesh, his fangs abraded her neck, but he didn't bite. She kissed his throat and ran her hands down to grip his firm ass as a growing sense of possessiveness for him built within her.

"Aiden," she breathed, and his fangs pierced her neck.

Maggie cried out as her nails raked his flesh. Everything in her became centered on him as endless waves of pleasure crashed over her.

Aiden drew her blood until it coursed through his body and doused his hunger as she climaxed again. The muscles of her sheath gripped him, milking his seed from him. Thrusting into her again, he growled against her throat as he came inside her, something he'd never done with a woman before. His orgasm went on with every pull of her blood until he had to withdraw his fangs or risk hurting her.

Never in his life had he come as hard as he had inside of Maggie, and he wanted more of her.

Maggie smiled lazily at him before closing her eyes. "I don't think I'll have to go for a run tonight to sleep."

Aiden laughed and held her closer.

CHAPTER THIRTY-TWO

MAGGIE WOKE the next morning to Aiden's lips moving over her neck. She sighed, stretching as he rolled her onto her stomach. His hands and mouth moved over her flesh, kneading her muscles before nudging her legs further apart. Maggie was more than ready for him when he entered her.

Rising over her, Aiden's chest brushed her back as he clasped her hands and held them while he moved within her. He didn't keep her hands because he didn't want her to touch him, but because he needed the contact with her. She cried out, her fingers clenched on his when he brought her to release. Plunging into her once more, Aiden shuddered as he came with the same intensity he had the three times he'd taken her last night.

Lowering his head, he kissed his marks on her shoulder. It was too soon to take her blood again, but the pulse of it called to him. Rolling to the side, he drew her into his arms. Her lush breasts pressed against his flesh as he settled her on his chest.

When he glanced at the clock, he realized last night was the first time he'd slept more than a few hours at once in a couple of years. With Maggie by his side, he'd slept for nearly eight hours, a feat he would have believed impossible yesterday.

She lifted her head to gaze down at him. Against the white sheets, her hair was a vibrant red curtain. Her charcoal eyes shone with amusement, and the flush in her cheeks was irresistible. He found his finger tracing the contours of her nose before dipping down to the curve of her upper lip.

His finger had a mind of its own as he couldn't stop touching her, and he knew he'd never get enough of this woman. He just had to convince her he was worth becoming a vampire for.

"Good morning," he said and lifted his head to nibble on her lip.

"Good morning." She smiled at him when he kissed the tip of her nose. "That was a better wake-up than coffee, but don't think that means you're getting out of buying me coffee. I can be a little unbearable in the morning without caffeine."

He chuckled as he cupped her nape and caressed her cheek with his thumb. "I don't believe it."

"Oh, believe it," she replied. "I got by on this hotel stuff yesterday, but I need some Dunkin' if I'm going to continue to stay with you, Nosferatu. Plus, I'll be much more energized for the rest of the day." She winked at him as she ran her hand over his chest.

"Then I will buy you a coffee factory."

She laughed. "I should probably go for a run too if I'm going to be ready for the marathon next month."

"I will take you for a run and get you some coffee."

"Good man."

She kissed his nose and threw back the covers as she sat up on the bed. She felt like leaping to her feet and laughing while spinning in circles. It took her a minute to find the right word to describe her emotions, as they were all inadequate. Then, she realized exactly what she was, *elated*.

She'd never been this happy before, which made no sense to her. Her entire life was in upheaval, yet she understood what people meant when they said they were walking on clouds. And her cloud walking was from more than having had the best sex of her life last night and today; it was also Aiden.

She liked him. She shouldn't, but she did. She might be the insect strolling into the trapdoor of the spider's den, but she didn't think so. He was a vampire, he fed on her, yet he also acted as if he cared for her. In the short time she'd known him, she'd come to care for him too. She cared for him more than she would have believed possible so soon after meeting someone.

She shouldn't be falling this fast, she'd learned caution early in her life, but trying to stop her emotions seemed as possible as trying to stop a runaway train. She'd always rolled with the flow in her life; she never would have survived it with her sanity intact if she hadn't, so she decided to keep rolling.

No matter what happened, even if she could never fully regain her old life, she would always be glad she'd met Aiden.

She turned toward him when he sat up. The sheets fell around his waist when he swung his legs to the floor, and Maggie plummeted from the clouds. Sorrow choked her as she gazed at his back. The lines running across his flesh formed a starburst pattern where they all met in the center. A few dozen scars ran in different directions and wrapped around his ribcage to end beneath his arms. She'd seen the rate with which he healed; she couldn't imagine what he must have endured to bare these scars still.

"What happened?" She traced one of the faint lines, but when Aiden flinched away, her hand fell onto the sheets.

Aiden turned to look at her as he recalled the marks on his back. In her arms, he'd forgotten about them and the compul-

246 BRENDA K DAVIES

sion that had propelled him to such repeated degradation at the hands of another.

"This is from a whip, isn't it?" she asked.

Grasping her fingers, he brought them to his lips and kissed them. "It's the past."

"I've seen how fast you heal. There's no evidence of the injury you had when we first met, but I saw these scars around that wound. Why do the scars remain?"

"They'll eventually fade too."

Especially now that he wouldn't require someone to beat him to near unconsciousness anymore. Not while he had Maggie to keep him grounded. Now that they'd slept together, his need to change her would accelerate, but for now he was happy just to have her near him.

"But *why* are they still there?" she demanded. "That other wound was horrific. Were these injuries even worse?"

"No."

"Then why do you have scars?"

He knew this was a topic she wouldn't let go, and if he had any hope of getting her to trust him enough to turn for him, he would have to reveal some of the things he'd prefer to keep from her. "Because sometimes, after repeated, sustained injury, our wounds and scars take longer to heal and fade away."

"Repeated, sustained injury?"

"Yes."

"*Who* did this to you often enough to leave you scarred?" The color drained from her face as her gaze shot up to his. "Was it your family?"

"No!" he yelled far louder than he'd intended. "No," he said more calmly and squeezed her fingers. "My siblings and I may have tried to kill each other a time or two. We may have dared each other to do some stupid things, but none of us would have done this to another."

"Your parents?"

"My parents never raised a hand against us. They had far more creative ways of punishment. Some of which involved allowing our siblings to decide our fate. Isabelle got to choose my punishment once for hanging her favorite doll from a tree after cutting off its hair, dipping it in paint, and tossing it in the lake. In retaliation, she tied me and that stupid doll to a tree together and kept hitting the button to make it pee. Every time she hit the button, the doll also declared it was hungry or called me mama in this horrible robotic voice made only worse by its swim in the lake."

He'd told the story in the hopes of coaxing a smile from her, but Maggie remained straight-faced while she stared at his back. "I never touched one of her dolls again afterward," he finished.

"Maybe your parents didn't raise a hand against you, but a whip isn't a hand," she said.

"A whip isn't a hand, but my parents never hurt me, and neither did the Stooges. Let it go, Maggie. The marks will fade."

"I've seen what you can do, Aiden. If you weren't a child when this happened, then who was strong enough to do this to you as an adult and why? Was it Ronan?" She didn't know the guy, but she'd kick his ass if he'd done this. "Was this a job requirement or something?"

"No."

"Then what happened?"

Frustration filled her when his lips clamped together and he didn't speak. He knew so much about her, yet she knew so little about him, and he refused to let her in. She wanted to kick her cloud-walking self in the ass. She knew better than to get her hopes up about anything. She wasn't pessimistic or optimistic; she put herself strictly in the pragmatic category, and that was where she liked to stay. She'd forgotten that this morning; she would not forget it again.

"You continue to ask about me and demand answers, you expect me to trust you, yet you won't open up to me at all," she stated.

Aiden heard the anger in her voice and sensed the distance opening between them when she leaned away from him. He'd prefer not to tell her where the scars had come from, or why, but if he didn't give her something, she would walk away from him.

"Nothing happened that I didn't allow to happen," he said.

"You *let* someone do this to you?"

"Maggie—"

"Why would you *allow* this to happen to you? Why would you stand there and take *this*?"

"Maggie—"

"Who did this to you?"

"That doesn't matter."

She gawked at him before tugging on her fingers. He held onto her. "It will never happen again," he promised.

Maggie glared at him, almost as infuriated by his unwillingness to share with her as she was by the knowledge someone had done this to him and he'd willingly allowed it! Why? What kind of twisted individual would stand there and take this from another? What had she gotten herself into with him?

Then, Carha's words from the club came back to her and she froze. *"That is enough!" Carha had hissed. "If you don't stop, Aiden, I'll ban you for life! And that means from my services too."*

"Carha," Maggie breathed. "*Carha* did this. *This* is the service she was talking about."

CHAPTER THIRTY-THREE

AIDEN'S HEAD BOWED, and his shoulders hunched up as if she were going to strike him. Part of her *did* want to hit him for allowing Carha to do this to him, for turning to that insidious woman in the first place. She'd only met Carha briefly, but she hadn't survived numerous foster and group homes without becoming a good judge of character. Carha would make Jeffrey Dahmer smile and give her a thumbs-up.

The way Aiden looked as if he expected her to hurt him far worse than Carha ever had deflated some of her anger with him. It didn't lessen her rage at Carha. Vampire or not, if Maggie ever saw that bitch again, they wouldn't have a catfight. No, it would be a full-on tiger brawl, and Maggie knew more than a few moves that would have Carha begging for mercy.

"What is going on? Why would you let her do this to you?" she asked.

Aiden braced himself before meeting her gaze again. "When a male purebred vampire reaches maturity and stops aging, they experience an increase in other needs," he said. "The women can feel it too, but not as badly. Most matured males experience an increase in one thing. Some want to kill more, others have a heightened appetite for blood, some need more sex, and others crave pain. Those incessant desires can sometimes push a vampire over the edge, turning them Savage. I stopped aging two years ago and have spent that time struggling to maintain control of my darker impulses."

"And those darker impulses made you seek out pain?"

"Not just pain. I started seeking *all* those things in equal measure. Declan told me it happens to a few rare purebreds."

Maggie gulped; she didn't know how to feel about any of this. "So, to maintain control, you paid Carha to whip you?"

"Not in the beginning. At first, I went to some of the other women in her club, but after a while, they became unwilling to inflict the amount of pain on me I started to require. Only Carha was willing to slice me as badly as I demanded to be cut."

Maggie's lips thinned out. "Of course that bitch was willing to do this."

Aiden lifted an eyebrow at the vehemence in her voice. It seemed some of Maggie's vampire blood was emerging within her. It might be easier to get her to agree to become his mate than he'd thought; a part of her might already be experiencing the bond too.

"And did you have sex with Carha when she was done or before she got started?" Maggie demanded, nausea twisting in her stomach at the thought of him with *that* woman.

Aiden almost smiled over the jealousy in her voice, but she wouldn't find it at all amusing if he did. "I've never had sex with Carha." She gave him a doubtful look. "Never. I used her service for pain only."

"I saw her in that club; it's obvious she wanted you, and you said you wanted it all in equal measure, so that would include sex too, right?"

"Right."

"So why wouldn't you sleep with her? She's beautiful."

"Maybe on the outside, but she's got the soul of a shark."

"She does," Maggie agreed, glad he saw it too. "Okay, so you allowed Carha to beat you to fulfill your need for pain, and she whipped you often enough that your body stopped healing as it should, but what about your need for sex, blood, and death? How did you satisfy those urges?"

"I started working with Ronan to focus my compulsion to kill on something good by destroying Savages. Whereas most vampires usually drink blood every other day, and some can go as often as three or four days in between feedings, I consumed blood every day. Sometimes I fed two or three times a day to keep myself in control, but I've never harmed those I fed on."

"Do you always feed on women?"

"I've fed from a man when necessary, but mostly women."

"Did you have sex with all those women?"

"Not all of them."

"But most of them?" she pressed.

This was a conversation they should have had before she slept with him, but Aiden was like a tornado, once she got caught up with him, she couldn't get free. She'd gone on the pill when she started having sex with A.J. and never stopped as it helped with her PMS. Aiden had said vampires couldn't carry diseases, but she should have been safer, and she should have guarded her heart better against him.

"Many of them, yes," he admitted.

"How many women have you been with?"

"It might be better to let this go."

An icy chill raced down her spine. "Do you know how many?"

"No."

This time when she pulled on her fingers, he released her.
"Could you guess?"

"Do you want me to?"

What good would it do either of them for him to guess at that? "No."

She scooted to the edge of the bed. Minutes ago, she'd been elated. Now she knew she was only one of hundreds of women, maybe *thousands* of them.

"I've never forced another," he said. "And I've never gone to a prostitute."

"It's always good to have standards."

She had no idea what else to say to that.

She gathered the sheet against her chest and wrapped it around her waist. It was ridiculous to cover herself now when he'd already seen it all, but she suddenly felt vulnerable around him in a way she hadn't earlier.

She was about to rise from the bed when he seized her wrist. She jerked on it, but when he didn't release her, she spun back to him. The anguish etching his features froze her furious words on her tongue.

"It's the past," he said in a gravelly tone she barely recognized. "It's an existence I *loathed* and will never return to. You are my present, Maggie, and I hope you'll agree to be my future too."

Her mouth fell open as he clasped her cheek with his other hand. She should pull away from him, but she found herself entranced by his words and his touch. Here came the damn tornado again, and he could sweep her away as quickly as Dorothy had been taken to Oz. She needed to get her hands on some ruby slippers; maybe they would help fortify her against him.

"It's all over now," he said. "*All* of it."

"But I won't do to you what you asked Carha to do. I will

not injure you in such a way, even if you ask me to do it, even if you *need* me to do it. And you can't feed on me multiple times during the day, and you'll—" She swallowed before continuing. "—you'll turn to other women to satisfy your craving for sex."

"No, I won't. I don't require those things now that I have you. You're all I need, if you'll have me."

"How can you say that?" she demanded as her anger returned. "You've spent years engrossed in your hungers and trying to maintain control. You've spent *three days* with me!"

"Since the second I heard your voice and inhaled your scent in that alley where we first met, you're all I've wanted."

"Your fingers twitched toward me when I spoke," she recalled.

"Yes."

Maggie shook her head; her hand tightened on the sheet. "So, you've replaced all your other obsessions with me? It makes no sense. Why me?"

He couldn't keep the truth from her anymore. "Because you are my mate."

"I'm your what?"

"Some vampires have mates, and you are mine. I didn't think I would ever find you. I believed I would lose control long before I discovered you and that I would have to be destroyed. However, the second I tasted your blood, I knew what you were to me. For the first time in years, maybe the first time in my *life*, I experienced peace."

His words robbed her of her breath as she gazed at him.

"I'm not saying you have to feel it too. I'm not saying you have to stay with me; I'm simply informing you that you are it for me, Magdalene Doe. There will never be another," he murmured as he rested his forehead against hers.

He couldn't tell her he wanted her for eternity, not yet,

she'd had so much thrown at her these past few days. He'd let her adjust to everything else before piling on more.

"But I *can't* do for you what Carha did. And I can't feed you multiple times a day, and if you're used to numerous partners—"

"I'd never ask you to beat me or to nourish me so often," he interjected. "I may still have to feed on others, but I can also use blood bags. Now that you've calmed me, I won't have to feed as often, I won't need pain and death, and I will *never* have sex with anyone else, ever again."

"Aiden—"

"You're the first one I've allowed to touch me during sex in years, Maggie."

"It's impossible not to touch someone when you're having sex with them."

"Perhaps, but it's not impossible to minimize that contact."

Maggie recalled the way he'd grabbed her hands and pinned them to the mirror before releasing her. Recalled the way he'd turned into her hand as if he were a beaten dog absorbing its first kind caress. The way he'd asked her for more of her touch. A sob lodged in her throat when she realized how starved he'd been for affection. Releasing the sheet, she tugged her wrist free of his hold and slid her arms around his neck.

He was so much more messed up than she'd realized, but she understood the vulnerability she'd sensed in him last night. He'd seemed vulnerable because he *had* been vulnerable.

"Aiden."

She kissed the corner of his mouth before sitting back to run her hands over his chest. He closed his eyes as she explored his body, tenderly touching him everywhere. She had no idea what all of this meant for them or where it would lead, but she didn't care as she pushed him back on the bed and climbed on top of him.

CHAPTER THIRTY-FOUR

"I'LL TAKE A JELLY, a Boston crème, a coffee roll, and two of the brown sugar muffins," Maggie said as she hungrily examined the contents lining the shelves behind the counter. The sweet scent of baking pastries and coffee entangled her in a ravenous trap that had her licking her lips in anticipation of stuffing herself.

Tapping her foot, she was debating a bagel and cream cheese when Aiden placed his hands on the counter on either side of her. He pinned her in as he rested his chin on her shoulder. "Hungry?" he inquired, the amusement evident in his voice.

"Starved!" Not only had they spent another hour in bed, but she'd insisted on getting a five-mile run in afterward. She was fairly certain she could eat every one of the donuts and muffins remaining after the morning rush.

He chuckled as he kissed her neck. Behind the counter, the young woman making her coffee almost dropped it when she saw Aiden. Someone behind them muttered something about getting a room, and Maggie laughed. She wasn't walking on clouds anymore; she was too famished for that. Besides, it was a long fall from the clouds, and she enjoyed her view from Earth.

Nope, she wasn't walking on clouds, but she felt deliriously happy as she took the box of goodies from the young man who handed them over. Aiden stepped back and claimed her coffee before walking with her to the register. He dipped into his pocket and paid the woman behind the cash register.

Unwilling to take the time to walk back to the hotel before eating, Maggie settled at a corner table and dug into her box of treats. Aiden sat with his back to the wall, his eyes surveying everyone who entered.

"I called Roger earlier," she said in the hopes of getting Aiden to relax a little. He'd been tense ever since they'd left the hotel room, and he studied every person they came across like a possible enemy. He was giving her a complex.

"How is he?" Aiden asked without looking at her.

"They're sending him home today, and someone told him about Walt and Glenn. He said he was okay, but he was lying."

"And how do you know that?"

She shrugged as she pulled the top off one of the muffins and started eating it. "He gets all impatient and manly when he's emotional."

"Manly?"

"You know what I mean."

He finally looked at her and gave her a small smile. "I do."

"Anyway, Walt's funeral was this morning and Glenn's funeral is tomorrow. I don't expect to be able to go; the doctors think Roger should rest and stay away too, but—"

"It's a bad idea, Maggie. The funeral will be the prime place for the Savages to stick a human to watch for you. They'll expect you to show up there."

She sighed and rolled a piece of muffin between her fingers, creating a ball with it. "I understand, but I have to get back to work soon. I have bills to pay, and I can't keep expecting my coworkers to cover my shifts. It's not fair to them, especially since I'm healthy."

"It's not safe."

"I don't have a choice."

"I'll help with your bills."

"No."

"Maggie—"

"No. I won't allow it. I take care of myself."

"But you don't have to anymore."

"I'm not sure what this is between us. I like you, a lot, but I haven't known you long, and I'm not going to rely on you to support me. It's bad enough you're buying my food and paying for my hotel room. I'm not used to this; I don't like it. Even if we were married, I wouldn't like it, and we're not married. I can only do one small step at a time, and you supporting me is *not* a small step."

"Fair enough," he relented.

"Besides, we can't continue to keep hiding out in the hotel. Are we supposed to spend days, weeks, months there?"

The way his eyes raked her body made her pulse race. "Would that be so bad?"

"For my job and the rest of my life, yes. For us, no," she replied honestly, and he smiled. "But that's not the way the human world works."

"No, it's not."

He didn't tell her the mate bond was a far more binding connection than marriage. If she agreed to complete it, she would realize that on her own.

"I've always taken care of myself or pulled my share of the weight," she stated.

"I'm not supporting you," he said. "I'm helping you as you've helped me."

She stopped eating, but her fingers continued to pick at her muffin. "How have I helped you?"

"By bringing tranquility to my life."

"Oh."

"Not all support is money."

"True." She popped a ball of muffin in her mouth.

Aiden's eyes were drawn to the door when a young couple entered, laughing as they made their way to the counter. He watched them until he was certain they weren't a threat.

"Okay, so we're helping each other," Maggie said. "But we can't remain locked away forever, no matter how much we both want to."

"No, we can't," he reluctantly agreed.

"So, what do we do next?"

"Why don't we take the rest of today to enjoy each other and figure that out tomorrow?"

Maggie lifted her coffee and sipped at it as she contemplated this. "I like the way you think, Aiden Byrne."

He grinned at her and rose to take her hand after she finished the last of her food. Leading her out of the donut shop, he walked with her down to the beach. Maggie laughed when he spun her across the sand as if they were dancing.

When they returned to his room, his phone rang. He pulled it out of his pocket and glanced at the screen. He recognized his sister Abby's number. Turning his phone off, he tossed it onto the bureau. It could all wait until tomorrow, he decided as he pulled Maggie into his arms.

THE NEXT MORNING, a knock on the hotel door drew Aiden's attention to it. His eyes narrowed as he listened for any indication of who stood on the other side. They'd ordered

room service last night, but this morning they'd gone out so
Maggie could get coffee and donuts. The housekeepers had
come through, cleaned the room, and made the bed while
they were out. Rising, he walked over to the door, put his eye
to the peephole, and spotted his sister Vicky on the other
side.

Vicky placed her middle finger against the eyehole. "Open
up, asshole."

"Shit," he grumbled before turning the locks and pulling
the door open. "It's good to see you too, Victoria."

"It always is," she replied as she pushed past him and
strolled into the room.

"What are you doing here?" he asked when Vicky plopped
herself onto the chair in the corner.

"I couldn't resist your jovial company anymore," she
retorted as she bounced on the cushion. "Comfy."

"How did you find me and why?"

He hadn't told anyone where they would be staying. It
wasn't that he didn't trust them, it was that he'd been hoping to
avoid *this*. He wanted time alone with Maggie, and he'd
checked in often enough to keep them from searching him out,
or so he'd assumed.

"When you shut your phone off, you know it's only a
matter of time before someone in this family hunts you down.
We do have the vampire equivalent of a GPS as a brother-in-
law, so hunting someone down isn't difficult."

"Brian," he muttered. Brian was the other reason he hadn't
told anyone where he was. If he stopped checking in, Brian
would be able to locate him. However, it had been less than
twenty-four hours since he'd spoken with Declan. There was
no reason for them to come looking for him.

"Oh, don't be angry with the oaf," Vicky said with a wave of
her hand.

Aiden scowled and closed the door. "Where are Abby and Brian?"

If Vicky was here, then Abby was too.

"Downstairs. Brian's making sure it's safe before coming up. I, on the other hand, was far too eager to meet our newest family member to wait. Where is my future sister-in-law? Are you hiding her somewhere?" Vicky asked as she glanced around the room. "Did you scare her off already?"

"In her room taking a shower," he replied. When they'd returned to find housekeeping in his room, Maggie had gone to hers to shower and call Roger again. "And don't scare her."

Vicky's green eyes widened innocently, and she rested her hand against her chest. "Me?" she asked with a flutter of her lashes. "I would never!"

"I told her she's my mate, but not that she has to turn to complete the bond."

"Big detail to omit."

"She's had enough to deal with recently. We'll get to that when it's necessary."

"From what I've seen of you recently, it's necessary."

"What do you mean?"

"Oh, come on, Aiden. I'm not blind or stupid. You've been walking a fine line for a while. It's why you joined up with Ronan, after all."

He'd believed he'd kept his deterioration into madness a secret, but if Vicky noticed, then he'd done a piss-poor job of hiding it. He loved her as much as the rest of his brothers and sisters, but Vicky was probably the most self-centered one in the family. She rarely considered the consequences of her actions.

Unfortunately, she'd almost been killed because of that recently, and it had gotten her abused in a way she never should have been. Self-absorbed she may be, but she was also incredibly loving, and that part of her had taken a beating while she'd been imprisoned by vampires who fed on her.

Just thinking about finding her in that warehouse, chained to a wall with numerous bite marks on her made Aiden want to kill those vampires all over again.

"I didn't realize you and the others had noticed," he said. He saw no reason to deny her words. All his siblings may have spent a good portion of their childhoods torturing each other, but they were also each other's best friends.

"The others have been so wrapped up in their mates and growing families they haven't detected your increasing withdrawal from us. And the rest of the brood is too young to be a part of this or to understand. As the only unmated vampire left amongst our matured siblings, I did notice."

Last year, Vicky never would have perceived anything off with him as she would have been too busy hopping from one party and boyfriend to the next. Her imprisonment had changed her more than he'd realized.

Leaning back in the chair, she crossed her legs and kicked one in the air as she grinned at him, but there was something strained about her smile. "Guess I'm the lone holdout, but I'm okay with that. The single life is how I like to roll."

"You're lying."

"Perhaps, but what difference does being mated make for me? Unlike you, I'm not about to plunge over the deep end and into a murderous rampage. I'll be fine, and Willow will soon be joining me in the ranks of the gloriously single and matured."

He couldn't picture Willow, the most tomboyish one of his sisters, reveling in her freedom and maturity as Vicky had.

"You'll find someone," he said.

"No, I won't," she said with more vehemence than he'd expected. Then, she smiled again and slapped her hands on the arms of the chair. "What is my future sister-in-law like? Declan and Saxon have been pretty mum on the details."

"Have you met someone?" he inquired, not at all fooled by her abrupt change in conversation.

"No."

She'd said no, but he sensed she lied.

"Vicky—"

"I bet she's beautiful," Vicky gushed, and for a minute he caught a glimpse of the girl she'd once been, pouring over fashion magazines, prattling on about clothes, and dreaming about one day visiting Paris. He hadn't heard her mention traveling in months.

He'd become the most self-centered of his siblings, he realized with a start. He'd been so obsessed with not falling over the edge, he'd failed to notice Vicky walking a path that might end up as destructive as his.

"She is beautiful," he said, sensing Vicky needed a distraction of some sort. "And she's a paramedic."

"She's caring too then!"

"I'm here for you, you know. I've been a bit lost, but I've always been and always will be here for you."

Vicky stared at him as if she were trying to find words. Finally, she swallowed and nodded. "You came for me in that warehouse. I know you're here for me. And I'm happy for you, but I'd be happier if you spilled some details on this girl! The others won't shut up about how amazing their mates are, and I feel like I'm pulling fangs out over here!"

Aiden walked over and bent down. He slid his hands under Vicky's arms to lift her. She froze, and for a second, he sensed the same thing in her that had been inside him, a revulsion to touch because she didn't feel worthy of it. Then, she eased against him and draped her arms around his neck.

The clean scent of her filled his nose. He was relieved to

note the faint stench of rot clinging to her since her captivity had faded. During her imprisonment, Vicky was starved to the point where she lost control and killed a human. Because of that, she'd born the stain of death on her, but Vicky wasn't a vampire who killed regularly or took pleasure in it, and time had mostly washed the aroma from her.

"Welcome back, Aiden," she whispered. "I missed you."

"One day, you'll come back too."

"Oh, I'm like a cockroach, not even a nuclear bomb can keep me down," she said in a voice that no longer held a teasing tone.

Behind him, he heard a door open. He turned as Maggie stepped into the room. The smile slid from her face, and her expression became murderous. If she'd held a crossbow, he knew she would have shot him.

"I like her already," Vicky declared and slapped him on his shoulders.

CHAPTER THIRTY-FIVE

RAGE ALMOST CHOKED Maggie when she spotted the pretty blonde in Aiden's arms. She was ready to strangle them both. No! She'd find herself a stake and stab him in *every* one of his extremities, starting with the wandering one between his legs!

Idiot! Moron for believing anything a vampire says! It was a good thing she didn't walk on those clouds anymore because this fall would have broken every bone in her body. Aiden set the small blonde down and stepped toward her.

"Maggie, this is my sister, Vicky."

Maggie blinked at him as his words gradually penetrated the haze of red shading her vision and the fury buzzing like bees in her ears. Then, her gaze returned to the woman who tilted her head to the side while she studied Maggie.

Maggie hadn't calmed enough to deal with this change of events. She'd experienced and felt many things in her life, but seeing Aiden hugging another woman had readied her to kill in an instant. Her hand trembled when she pushed aside the strand of wet hair falling across her eye.

"Maggie, is it?" Vicky elbowed Aiden in the ribs. He

grunted and rubbed his chest as she stepped forward. "I was trying to get Aiden to tell me all about you; however, he takes that whole Hollywood brooding vampire thing to a ridiculous level. But then, I'm sure you've already figured that out."

Aiden glowered at his sister. Less than a minute ago, he'd been hugging her. Now, he contemplated choking her as she strolled toward Maggie with her hand extended. Maggie blinked again, seeming to come out of some reverie.

There had been no denying the wrath darkening her features before, and she appeared to be having a difficult time pulling herself out of it as her jaw remained clenched. He couldn't stop himself from smiling over how irate seeing him with Vicky had made her. Yes, convincing her to become a vampire might not be so difficult after all.

"I'm Vicky."

Maggie gazed down at the hand Vicky extended to her before taking it. Vicky was about two inches shorter than her, but strength reverberated from the small vampire. Though Vicky's eyes were an emerald green instead of Aiden's spring green, Maggie saw a similarity in their shape. There were few other similarities between the siblings.

"It's nice to meet you," Maggie said.

Vicky enclosed both her hands around Maggie's and squeezed. "It's wonderful to meet you, Maggie. You're a life-saver, and I don't mean just because you're a paramedic. Kudos for that, by the way. I could handle the blood, of course, but the guts and bones? Ugh," Vicky grimaced. "Keep that stuff where it belongs, am I right?"

"Ah, yeah," Maggie replied, still too thrown off by her violent reaction to seeing Aiden with another woman to register everything Vicky said.

"You'll save my brother's life; I'm certain of it," Vicky declared.

Maggie's breath caught at those words and the depth of emotion radiating from Vicky's gaze.

"Enough, Vicky," Aiden said as he stalked across the room toward them. "You'll scare her off."

"If your menacing exterior hasn't frightened her off yet, I sure won't," Vicky replied with a laugh.

"You're an ass," Aiden muttered.

"I am," Vicky agreed blithely and released Maggie's hand. "I'm also adorable, unforgettable, and magnificent."

"Your ego could fill the Grand Canyon."

"That hole has nothing on me," Vicky said to him and winked at Maggie.

Vicky was a whirlwind, but Maggie found herself liking the outgoing woman.

"I'm the black sheep of the siblings. Has Aiden told you how many of us there are?" Vicky asked.

"He has," Maggie said as her eyes bounced between the two of them.

They may not look much alike, but they had the easygoing banter of those who knew and loved each other well. She and A.J. had often flowed like this together. Sometimes they forgot anyone else was with them as they traded insults and quips.

An unexpected stab of longing speared her. What would it have been like to grow up secure in the knowledge of unconditional love? To know that no matter how badly you screwed up, there would be someone to help you through it?

Sensing her sudden melancholy, Aiden stepped forward and slid his arm around her waist. "I'd consider myself more of the black sheep," he said to Vicky.

Vicky's mouth pursed and twisted to the side as she studied him. "Yeah, you might be the closest to me. You call home about as often as I do."

"I talked to Mom yesterday."

"Oh, you call more than I do then!" Vicky's smile slid away; she fidgeted with the edge of her shirt before grinning again. "How are things at the zoo?"

"Good. They're enjoying their grandchildren, and Willow is preparing for college."

"Hopefully she does better with it than I did."

"And me."

Vicky's attention shifted back to Maggie, but before she could say anything more, a knock on the door distracted her. "That must be our sister Abby. She might be the whitest sheep of us all, but we still love her," Vicky said to Maggie.

"I'd give the title of whitest sheep to Isabelle," Aiden said.

"Or Cassidy," Vicky shot over her shoulder as she hurried toward the door.

"Actually, you might be the only female problem child," Aiden remarked.

"And I rock it." Vicky lifted her hand and formed the rock sign over her head as she pulled the door open. "Welcome to the den of iniquity," she greeted.

"Do I want to know?" Abby inquired.

"Nah, you white sheep wouldn't get it."

"You're an ass."

"You know Aiden just said the same *exact* thing to me. If you two aren't careful, I might develop a complex."

"Then stop being an ass," Abby retorted.

Maggie's eyes widened when another blonde woman entered the room. Unlike Aiden and Vicky, where she saw few similarities in their appearance, there was no telling Vicky and Abby apart. Except one had shorter hair than the other. Because she hadn't been expecting twins, she hadn't been tracking Vicky once Abby entered the room, so she couldn't tell if it was Vicky or Abby who had shorter hair.

She'd known a few identical twins over the years, and she'd

always been able to find some tiny difference between them. Other than their hair, she couldn't see any difference between these two. She was about to ask who was who when the one with the longer hair walked toward her.

"I'm Abigail," she said. "Everyone calls me Abby."

Abby took hold of Maggie's hand and clasped it in both of hers as Vicky had done. "I'm so happy to meet you. We've been hoping for you."

Maggie blinked at her and then glanced at Aiden. For the first time, she started to really grasp what she meant to him and his family. He'd told her she was important to him, but now she saw it instead of only *hearing* it.

"It's bad enough I have to deal with this shit from Vicky, but I wasn't expecting it from you too," Aiden said.

Abby laughed as she released Maggie's hand. "You know we sometimes like ganging up to humiliate you all."

"Hmm." Aiden released Maggie and lifted Abby to give her a bear hug.

"It's payback for all the things you older ones put us through when we were younger," Vicky said as she leaned against the wall. "You know we were never as good at those prank wars as the rest of you."

"But we are good at irritating and embarrassing when we get the chance," Abby said.

"You are," Aiden agreed and set her down. "Where's Brian?"

"Here," Brian said.

Vicky glanced over her shoulder as a man stepped into the room. Maggie's mouth almost fell open when she spotted the stunning man with platinum blond hair and ice blue eyes. Abby released Aiden and walked over to slide her hand into Brian's. The iciness of Brian's eyes melted when he smiled down at her.

Mated. Maggie didn't know how she knew it, but she had no doubt Abby and Brian were mates.

Brian tore his attention away from Abby to focus on Maggie. In his eyes, she saw the same curiosity she'd seen in the others. She suspected she would endure this from all of Aiden's family when she first met them.

A small shock went through her when she realized she was thinking long term for them if she was considering meeting his family.

Brian released Abby and walked over to shake her hand before turning to clasp Aiden's shoulder. "Sorry I had to track you down," Brian apologized as he returned to Abby.

"Why did you track me down?" Aiden inquired.

"If you'd answered your phone, you'd know," Abby admonished.

Vicky placed her hand against the corner of her mouth and hid her finger behind it as she pointed at Abby and mouthed to Maggie, *"White sheep."* Maggie stifled a laugh while Abby glared at her sister.

"Know what?" Aiden demanded.

"Using the ruined shirt left in the ambulance with the two dead drivers, I located one of the Savages who attacked you," Brian said.

Aiden drew Maggie closer when she winced at Brian's blunt words. Brian looked guiltily at her, and Abby elbowed him in the gut.

"You can track others like that?" Maggie asked Aiden.

"Brian can, I can't, and I know of no one else who can," he replied. "And?" Aiden prodded Brian.

"Ronan has the Savage imprisoned now. They're going to work on getting information from him, and Ronan thought you might like to be involved," Brian said.

CHAPTER THIRTY-SIX

MAGGIE LEANED back on the barstool and shook her head. The Red Sox were getting their asses handed to them. Granted, it was only spring training, but she still wanted a win, especially against the Yankees.

"Damn it," she muttered and finished off her whiskey.

"I don't get this game at all," Vicky said from beside her.

"I was alive when the first major league game played, and I still don't get it," Brian said. The bartender gave him a startled look. "What?" Brian demanded of the young man.

Vicky laughed, and Abby rested her hand on Brian's forearm as the bartender backed away. "He's kidding," Abby said and smiled at the bartender, who made the mistake of smiling back at her. The scowl on Brian's face sent the man scurrying away.

"Way to go, Grumpy. Now he's never going to come back." Vicky looked morosely into her nearly empty margarita glass.

"That would be awful," Maggie agreed.

She'd need a lot of whiskey to get through this ball game if it continued this way. Not to mention, she'd had this awful empty pit inside her since Aiden left shortly after Brian made his revelation. He'd been gone all day.

At first, Aiden stated he would stay with her, but she knew he wanted to be involved in destroying the Savages who attacked him, so she'd told him to leave. Then, he'd insisted on taking her with him. However, she was still adjusting to meeting these three and being the focus of speculation; she was not in the mood to have a whole lot more vampires scrutinizing her.

When Brian offered to stay and watch over her, Maggie vehemently refused a babysitter, but eventually, she'd conceded to staying with the three of them, for Aiden. As soon as the bar opened, Vicky dragged them all down here. She'd immediately started plying Maggie with alcohol and questions about her life.

Normally, Maggie would have felt resentful of the near inquisition, but Vicky's affable nature made it easier to handle. As did the fact the twins were excited about getting to know her better because they loved Aiden and expected Maggie to remain in his life.

Vicky finished her drink and lifted the glass in the air before beckoning the cute bartender toward her with a crook of her finger. "Ignore the grumpy Gus!"

The bartender glanced warily at Brian before returning. Maggie finished her drink and slid the glass next to Vicky's as she returned her attention to the TV.

"You know," Vicky said when their drinks were refilled and the bartender left again, "for a human, you sure can handle your alcohol."

Maggie looked at her in surprise. "Didn't Aiden tell you?"

"All I got out of him before you arrived was you're a para-medic." Vicky propped her chin on her hand and fluttered her lashes. "So, tell me, what did my brother leave out?"

Abby leaned forward to look around her sister at Maggie. After a few seconds, Brian leaned forward to stare at her too.

Maggie fiddled with her glass as she contemplated the question. Was she ready to share her past with them? But then, what difference did it make? It's not like they were going to run around blabbing the information to everyone they encountered, they couldn't use the knowledge against her, and she wasn't ashamed of her history. She despised how she'd come into existence, but it was part of her, and she liked who she was.

"My father was a vampire," Maggie stated.

Four eyebrows shot up in an identical look of astonishment before Vicky and Abby glanced at each other. "Interesting," Brian murmured.

"Who was he?" Abby asked.

"I don't know," Maggie replied more crisply than she'd intended. She sensed their rabid curiosity, but none of them questioned her further. "I have to go to the bathroom."

Rising from her stool, she walked across the restaurant to the bathrooms. The doors faced the bar, so it would be easy to spot someone if they tried to follow her in and there was only one exit.

Maggie went into the stall and re-emerged to wash her hands and face. She stared at her reflection in the mirror over the sink, noting the strain in the corners of her eyes and around her mouth. Pulling her phone out of her pocket, she checked it to make sure she hadn't somehow missed something from Aiden. Still nothing. She returned the phone to her pocket.

Her heart twisted as fresh concern for him coursed through her. Aiden had assured her he'd be safe, but she couldn't stop worrying about him when she knew what those Savages were capable of doing. Absently, she scratched at her arms as her skin seemed to stretch too thin over her bones.

"Get it together," she muttered at her reflection. "He's okay and you will *not* be this dependent on someone else."

Taking a deep breath, she threw her shoulders back and strolled out of the bathroom. Vicky had her hands in the air as she cheered loudly. The dozen or so people gathered around the bar were all giving her the death stare.

Vicky went from happy to confused as she gazed at the irritated patrons. Maggie craned her head to see the TV before scowling at Vicky too.

"What?" Vicky demanded of her. "They hit the ball over the wall, and the men are running around the, ah... the square thingies."

Maggie gawked at Vicky as she glanced at the TV to confirm all the men were indeed running around the square thingies because the Yankees' batter had hit a grand slam. Then, she hated herself for calling them square thingies even if it had only been mentally.

"Have you never seen a baseball game before?" Maggie asked.

"Not willingly, and I certainly didn't pay attention to it," Vicky replied as she lowered the arms she'd raised while cheering.

Abby nodded, and Brian snorted as he folded his arms over his chest.

"I swear you vamps really do live in caves," Maggie muttered. "You're cheering for the wrong team. We don't want those men to hit it over the wall." She felt like an idiot for describing a home run in such a way, but it was easier.

"Oh," Vicky said.

"Also, they're not square thingies, they're bases, and if I see you cheering for the Yankees again, I'll stake you myself."

Vicky blinked at her before laughing. "Alrighty then, no rooting for the guys with the stripes."

"We'll stick to the drinks," Abby said and nudged Vicky's glass with her finger.

"Good plan," Vicky declared and cheerfully lifted her margarita. "So, Maggie, while you were gone, we got to wondering what your views on weddings are? Yay or nay on a ceremony? Our family is a little unconventional after all, so we're perfectly okay with a nay, but we do all enjoy a good party."

Maggie had been swinging onto her barstool as Vicky spoke. She nearly fell off before she could sit on it. She gawked at Vicky as she settled herself unsteadily on the seat. "I'm not going to the bathroom again."

"That's a good idea," Brian told her. "Next time, you'll be engaged before you return."

"CARHA," Aiden greeted as he stepped into the room where he'd spent a fair amount of time and shed a lot of his blood.

Chained to the posts, a naked man stood before him with his head tipped back to gaze at the ceiling. Red marks marred his back, but they were already fading. The man moaned as the other woman in the room, who was kneeling before him, gripped his ass and drew his cock deeper into her mouth. Neither of them acknowledged his arrival.

Standing behind the man, Carha's arm fell before she could strike him again. "How did you get in here?" she demanded.

"I have my ways," Aiden replied.

"Brutus was instructed to keep you *out*."

"He was, but he didn't obey."

"Get out!" Carha commanded and lifted her hand to bounce the end of the crop against her palm.

In the beginning, a crop had been enough to keep his baser

impulses under control, but that hadn't lasted long. However, Aiden was unable to stop his visceral reaction to the sight of that crop as the flesh on his back tingled and his balls tightened.

Away from Maggie, he found himself thirsting for the pain again. He should have gone to her or at least called her before coming here. However, he didn't want Maggie tainted by this, and unreasonably he'd felt that talking to her on the phone while coming here, would somehow stain her. Now, the demon part of his DNA was rolling toward the forefront once more as it sought to be released.

Carha spun and swung toward the man with her crop. When it whacked his back, the man shouted and jerked against his chains. Judging by the other marks on him and his reaction to this blow, it was far harder than he was accustomed to being struck.

"What the fuck?" the man shouted, and his head turned toward Carha. He froze when he spotted Aiden standing in the doorway. "I didn't sign up for any weird voyeur shit!"

"You're getting sucked off while I watch," Carha retorted.

"I'm not paying for a man to watch."

Carha hit him with the crop again, and the man jerked against his chains. "Enough, Carha," Aiden commanded.

"I bet you wish this was you," she purred to Aiden as she stroked the man's flesh with the crop before hitting him harder.

The crack of the crop mingled with the man's cry. Aiden kept his face impassive, refusing to give Carha the satisfaction of seeing his craving for pain, but need churned within him.

Carha circled to the front of the man. She placed her foot on the side of the kneeling woman and shoved her out of the way. The woman cried out and scampered into a corner. Her gaze darted to Aiden before she rose and started gathering her things.

"Are you already done with that piece of ass you brought in

here the other night?" Carha inquired as she trailed the whip over the man's cheek.

Drawing on the lingering taste of Maggie's blood on his tongue, Aiden kept himself restrained from attacking. He intended to take Carha alive.

"Look, Carha—"

Whatever the man had been about to say was silenced by the blow Carha delivered to his face. His head snapped to the side, and his legs gave out. The blood spurting from his mouth sprayed the floor. Shouting obscenities, the man struggled to regain his feet, but Carha's next blow dropped him to his knees.

"Enough!" Aiden commanded.

The woman gave up on trying to dress and fled the room. The startled squeak she released in the hallway drew Carha's attention. Red blazed through Carha's eyes as she gazed behind him to where Saxon and Declan stood in the hall. Ronan, Killean, and Lucien were in the club, working their way through the patrons and employees to see what they might know about Carha's extracurricular activities.

Carha hit the man again before turning and fleeing toward the back of the room. "She's running!" Aiden shouted before chasing after her, though he had no idea where she hoped to go as she barreled straight at the wall.

A foot from the wall, she stopped and stomped her foot on something. Hinges squeaked and then Carha fell through the floor. Aiden skidded to a stop next to the trapdoor Carha had vanished through.

"Shit," Aiden muttered as he gazed into the black pit.

The dim, reddish glow of the room did little to illuminate what lay below. It could be a deathtrap waiting to spring on him. He never would have hesitated to follow Carha to his possible death before, but he remained standing over the hole. *Maggie.*

He had her to live for now, but they weren't bonded yet. She cared for him, he knew, but she could move on from this, and if he didn't stop Carha, then the hunt for him and Maggie might never end. He couldn't let Declan and Saxon do this on their own either, and if he didn't move now, Carha would get away.

Wind buffeted his hair and clothes as he plunged into the hole behind Carha.

CHAPTER THIRTY-SEVEN

AIDEN LANDED in a crouch with his fist on the dirt floor as he surveyed the darkness. Some instinct told him to roll a second before he heard a crossbow release. He bit his lip to keep from making any sound when his back came up against a wall. Dirt rained down on him, and he realized the bolt had embedded in the wall above him.

Twenty feet over his head, he saw the opening of Carha's trapdoor. Behind him, soft footsteps crunching on dirt drew his attention away from the door and to the woman fleeing him. Aiden launched to his feet and raced after Carha. He had no idea where he was going, couldn't see his hand in front of his face, but her footsteps drew him onward.

The thrill of the hunt pumped his adrenaline faster, and his fangs lengthened. Instead of trying to bury his more malevolent nature, he let it have free reign. He'd intended to take Carha alive, but he would do whatever it took to keep Maggie safe; Carha's existence was a threat to her he wouldn't tolerate.

The footsteps moved toward the left. He turned to follow them, but not in time to prevent his shoulder from colliding with a wall. The impact staggered him briefly to the side; debris clattered to the ground. Recovering his balance, he honed in on Carha as she continued with barely a sound. She'd traveled this escape route often to remain so silent down here and to progress so fast.

Hearing a creaking sounded ahead, he poured on the speed as he realized a door was opening. He ran headlong into what he initially thought was another wall. The impact rocked him backward, but not as hard as it should have if he'd hit something completely unmoving.

Whatever he hit, swung away from him, and instinctively he reached out to grab it before he fell over. His hand curved around the edge of a door. Jerking it toward him, he wrenched it off its hinges. Chunks of debris crashed onto the floor when the door smashed into the wall.

As if a dozen tanks were being driven through it, the tunnel shook from the impact of the door. A thundering crash rocked the tunnel behind him, and when a shout sounded, he suspected part of the ceiling had collapsed near Declan and Saxon, if they'd both followed him.

Carha released a startled cry and Aiden continued his pursuit of her. Judging by the increased sounds of her breathing and the closeness of her steps, he was almost on her. Then, something creaked again, and the light suddenly flooding the dark space nearly blinded him.

"They're after me!" Carha shrieked.

Aiden blinked as he tried to acclimate to the influx of light. He skidded to a halt in the doorway, and five heads turned toward him; he recognized the faces of each one. The Savages' red eyes blazed in the fluorescents hanging above.

One glance at the cavernous space told him Carha's escape route had led into a warehouse with the remaining Savages who had jumped him. The concrete floor was barren and night pressed against the rectangle windows set high up in the walls.

Smiling smugly, Carha slipped behind two of the Savages and rested her hands on their shoulders. He had no idea why she didn't stink as badly as they did, but it was clear she was in league with them. The Savage Ronan captured had ultimately given Carha up as their ringleader before Aiden destroyed him.

"You should have taken me up on my offer," Carha taunted as the Savages surrounded him.

"And what offer was that?" Aiden growled.

"The one for the best fuck of your life."

Aiden's mind flashed back to their last conversation in her room. *"Soon,"* she'd said. *"You'll be begging to have me."*

"That will be the last time I come here," he'd told her.

"Oh, I doubt that will be the last time," she'd replied.

Then, he'd assumed she meant he would only come back for more sex with her afterward, but what she'd truly meant was she expected that night to be the last time he entered her club. He'd refused her advances too many times, and the miserable bitch had taken the saying "Hell hath no fury like a woman scorned" to a whole new level.

He'd make her pay, not for what she'd done to him, but because Maggie had been caught up in Carha's spitefulness too.

"And when they're done with you, they're going to kill that little human bitch you brought into *my* club," Carha said.

Aiden's hands fisted, but he kept himself from lunging at her. "You'll be dead before that can ever happen," Aiden vowed.

Fear flickered in Carha's eyes, but his attention was drawn from her and to the vampire beside her, the one who had hurt Maggie. "She tasted delicious," the Savage murmured and licked his lips.

Aiden smiled at the Savage as his fangs lengthened. "I'm going to enjoy killing you the most."

Aiden widened his stance as he beckoned the Savages forward with a wave of his hands.

∽

MAGGIE GLANCED AT HER PHONE, worried she'd somehow turned it off or accidentally placed it on silent. It wasn't her normal phone, after all; it was possible she'd done something to it. Or at least that's what she kept telling herself.

It was still on, the screen obnoxiously blank. She'd tried calling and texting Aiden, but it had gone straight to a computerized voice mail, and there had been no reply to her messages. Maggie drummed her fingers on the bar as she gazed at the occupants.

Sitting here was driving her nuts, but she had no idea what else to do. Usually, she'd go for a run, but she had at least a bottle of Crown Royal in her, and she didn't think a whiskey-fueled run was the best idea. Absently, she scratched at her arm before rechecking her phone.

She hated this almost clinginess feeling and sense of loss enveloping her. This wasn't who she was. Yes, she cared for Aiden, but her whole world couldn't revolve around a man; she refused to let it.

"He's fine," Vicky said, but she didn't sound as confident as she had earlier.

Maggie glanced at the TV. The game had ended over an hour ago. She rose and stood on the backside of her stool. She gripped the seat. "Then why do I have such a bad feeling?" she muttered.

Vicky and Abby exchanged a nervous look. "Why don't you

call Ronan?" Abby suggested to Brian, who already had his phone to his ear.

"Ronan's phone is off," Brian replied, "but that's normal if they're working on something. Also, now that Ronan's mated, his phone's off more often too."

"Those damn mated vamps," Vicky quipped and winked at her sister before smiling at Maggie. "See, there's nothing to worry about."

"You don't believe that either," Maggie said to her. "Can we go to where they are?" she asked Brian.

"No. I'm not taking you three anywhere near what is going on. No," he said more firmly to Abby when she opened her mouth to protest. He placed his hand over hers as if to temper his next words. "You won't win this one. Besides, Maggie is mortal."

Abby stared at him for a minute. "He's right. Aiden will have our asses if we risk yours."

"Maybe he's decided not to return," Maggie said.

"That will *never* happen," Abby said. "I know you don't get the bond of mates, but believe me, Hell itself wouldn't keep him away from you."

Brian nodded his agreement. Maggie downed the rest of her glass and pushed it toward the bartender. The heat of someone's body warmed her elbow. She glanced at the man who had walked up to stand beside her. "Can I buy you a drink?" he inquired.

"No." She turned dismissively away from him.

"Come on, just one. It looks like you enjoy your whiskey."

Brian started to rise from his seat as she turned back to the man. "Creepy stalker guy is *not* attractive, and if you know my drink, then that makes you creepy stalker guy."

The man's forehead furrowed as he seemed not to process her words. Given the glassiness of his eyes, Maggie suspected he'd had more to drink than she had. "Only one," he said and placed his hand over hers.

Maggie snatched her hand away and turned it over to seize his palm. Pressing down between his thumb and index finger, she gave a firm squeeze. "Back off."

The man's knees buckled, and he nearly went to the ground. "Let go!" he wailed.

Maggie released him. He gazed at her as if she were the antichrist before shaking out his hand and hurrying to a booth crowded with other young guys. They were all laughing at him.

She focused on the others once more.

"I don't know why I'm here," Brian said as he sat back on his stool.

Vicky and Abby both grinned at her. "Where did you learn to do that?" Abby asked.

"You grow up as a foster kid, and you learn how to defend yourself," Maggie replied.

"You grew up in foster care?"

"I did."

"Come, sit, tell us more about yourself," Vicky said and slapped the stool. "It will help take all our minds off things."

With no idea what else to do, Maggie sat, but she kept her phone in front of her as her uneasiness grew.

CHAPTER THIRTY-EIGHT

AIDEN DUCKED low and swung his fist out, driving it through the chest of the first Savage to come at him. His heart beat once in Aiden's grip before he yanked it out and threw it aside. Reaching into his coat, he pulled a stake free and thrust upward at the next vamp to lunge at him.

Unable to get in a killing blow against the Savage, Aiden propelled the stake straight up through the bottom of the vamp's chin. The Savage stumbled back; his hands clawed at the stake in an attempt to pull it out, but Aiden had pushed it deep enough the vamp wouldn't be able to remove it on his own.

The vampire who had attacked Maggie moved further back to stand protectively in front of Carha. Carha crossed her arms over her chest as the other two Savages charged him from the sides, coming at him low and hard. Snarls of excitement radiated from them as the one with the stake embedded in its jaw recovered enough to run at him from behind. The one blocking Carha moved a little closer.

Carha edged away, creeping toward the door on the other

side of the warehouse. Aiden tracked her every move; she would not get away. When the two vampires charging him from the side were nearly on top of him, he jumped back. The buffoons crashed headfirst into each other. Blood burst from the head of one, while the other fell back, his broken neck causing him to twitch on the ground.

Carha's smile vanished when he lifted his head to meet her eyes. Aiden started toward her when the Savage with the stake embedded in his jaw leapt onto his back. Aiden threw his hands up to pull the vamp away, but before Aiden could grab him, the Savage's weight was yanked away from him.

Aiden spun to find Declan tearing the heart from the Savage's chest. Behind him, Saxon ripped the head from the idiot who had split open his skull. The one with the broken neck made a gurgled sound when Declan knelt over him with a stake in hand.

The Savage who attacked Maggie turned and fled to follow Carha toward the door. When she didn't move fast enough for him, he shoved Carha out of his way. Saliva filled Aiden's mouth as the thrill of the hunt took over. Bursting into motion, he chased after the Savage. The vamp was almost to the door when Aiden pounced on his back, seized his head and yanked it to the side.

The cracking of bone reverberated off the cavernous walls and high ceiling of the warehouse. The Savage wailed, his hands beat against Aiden's head. When Aiden gave another twist of his neck, severing his spinal cord, the Savage fell out from under him.

He'd envisioned torturing this bastard for a long time after what he'd done to Maggie, but Carha was still fleeing toward the door. This piece of shit had hurt Maggie, but Carha had been the cause of it.

Aiden bellowed in fury as he wrenched the Savage's head

off and tossed it aside before jumping to his feet. The need to kill thrummed through him as he raced after Carha. When she reached the door, he drew on the strength of Maggie's blood flowing through his veins and poured on the speed.

Carha was pulling the door open when he caught up to her. Slamming his hand against the metal door, he tore it from her hands and shoved it closed. He wrapped his arm around her waist and lifted her off the ground. She kicked her heels against his shins as she spat like a cat. Her fingernails, filed into lethal points, peeled back the flesh on his hands, spilling his blood.

Aiden ignored her thrashing as he turned and stalked back toward the others. He dropped her into the center of the Savage bodies littering the floor. Unprepared for her abrupt release, Carha landed on her ass with a loud *oomph*. The end of her black braid slapped her in the face; blood splashed onto her black leather pants and red corset.

Shoving her braid aside, she lifted her chin to glare at him. Kneeling in front of her, Aiden rested his fingers in the blood coating the floor as he met her fiery gaze. Smirking, Carha seemed to decide to try something new as she propped her hands behind her, leaned back in the blood, and spread her legs. Aiden recoiled when she revealed her crotch-less pants.

Keeping her legs open, she focused on Saxon. Sweat beaded Saxon's brow as he stared between Carha's legs. After a few seconds, he looked to the wall.

"Saxon wouldn't have turned me down," Carha purred.

Unable to tolerate standing so close to her anymore, Aiden rose and stepped away. "This really is all because I wouldn't fuck you?"

She shrugged again. "I get what I want, and when I don't, my friends take care of the problem."

"What is that supposed to mean?"

"It means Carha's been working with the Savages for a

while. She hires them to do her dirty work, such as eliminating her competition, taking care of those she has a problem with, and those who owe her," Ronan said.

Aiden turned to find Ronan standing in the open doorway of the tunnel. Ronan's reddish-brown eyes were more red than brown as he gazed at Carha. Aiden saw no sign of Killean and Lucien and assumed they'd stayed in the club to make sure everything stayed safe there. Paler than normal, Zeke stood at Ronan's side. Carha's legs closed; her eyes narrowed on Ronan and Zeke.

"Tell them what you revealed to me," Ronan said to Zeke.

"He's a bartender. He doesn't know anything beyond how to make a drink!" Carha snapped.

"He knows more than enough to condemn you," Ronan replied. "Go on, Zeke."

"Over the past year, I've noticed if a new vampire bar crops up somewhere, the owners often meet with an untimely and often violent demise," Zeke said. "There has also been a growing number of vampires with less-than-legal occupations disappearing recently. We may not have the vampire equivalent of Facebook, but word spreads fast through our community. Those deaths sparked a lot of gossip."

"Pushing drugs too, Carha?" Ronan inquired.

"I wouldn't dare, Ronan," she replied with a false innocence. She opened her legs before leisurely crossing them once more.

Aiden's skin crawled; he couldn't stop himself from stepping further away from her. He'd allowed this woman to do things to him that would make some of the most toughened vampires cringe. All he'd wanted was to return to Maggie, but he wouldn't go anywhere near her while feeling as tainted as he did by his urges. As soon as he left here, he planned to scrub his skin bloody.

"You know drugs are *not* allowed to be sold to vampires," Ronan growled. "I will keep the vampires who follow me and who are innocents in all this safe; you are a threat to them."

"Prove it," Carha taunted.

"You proved it by running to these pricks when you fled the club," Aiden stated.

"I simply hired them to keep me safe. They're my body-guards," Carha replied with a flutter of her lashes.

"You hired them to keep you safe from me?" Aiden inquired. "I never hurt you, but these were the remaining vampires who jumped me outside your club."

She assumed a demure air. "I've seen how unstable you've become. I was afraid that the next time you came to me, you would snap and kill me. I've seen how much pain you can withstand, so I knew I had to hire a lot of help to protect me from you."

"You're lying," Declan said flatly.

"Yes, she is," Ronan agreed. "Continue, Zeke."

"A couple of weeks ago, I was taking out the trash and overheard Carha in the alley with that one," he pointed to one of the dead Savages. "They were talking about some clients who owed her money."

Carha's demure air faded, and she sat upright. "You didn't hear anything!"

"She gave him the names and addresses of those clients. I assumed those customers would receive a beating, but figured it was best I stayed out of it."

"But?" Ronan prodded.

"Last night I overheard a few patrons talking and caught one of the names they were discussing. It was one of the names Carha had given to that guy. He's been missing since Carha handed him over."

Carha looked about ready to leap up and attack Zeke.

"Is the missing vamp a purebred?" Declan asked.

A chill ran across Aiden's skin at the possibility there was another vampire out there, kidnapping and imprisoning purebreds to sell their blood to the highest bidder. Vicky had already been exposed to that vile degradation; he couldn't stand the idea it might happen to another member of his family.

"No," Ronan said. "I think she handed those clients over to be turned into Savages."

"*Fuck*," Aiden spat when he understood what Carha might have truly planned for him.

Before Aiden joined Ronan's men, Joseph, the vampire who had run the training facility previous to Lucien, turned Savage. Recently, Ronan had discovered Joseph was forcing vampires to become Savages by keeping them imprisoned. Joseph starved those vamps until they were so ravenous they killed whatever food he offered them. With each kill it became easier to continue killing until those vamps no longer cared about trying to control themselves.

Ronan had been hunting Joseph for a while, but after discovering what Joseph was doing, Ronan closed the training compound. He'd moved everyone to a mansion he'd purchased so they would be at a location Joseph didn't know about.

"Did you plan to have them turn me into one of them?" Aiden snarled at Carha.

"No. They were supposed to kill you. It's why they attacked you as soon as you left me."

"Because I was weakened."

"If you'd stayed with me longer and done what I wanted you to do, you wouldn't have been so weak. I might have even called them off if you pleased me well enough," she replied.

"You're a sick bitch."

"What can I say? I don't like the word no."

"How did you know where and how to locate a vampire willing to kill our kind?" Declan inquired.

"I know far more than you, and *you*," she said with a pointed glance at Ronan. "You don't work in my business and not learn things. I know how to get what I want and where to go to get what I need."

With the grace of a cat, Carha launched to her feet and spun away from him. Expecting her to go for the door, Aiden was unprepared when she bent to rip a stake from one of the corpses. She lunged at Declan when he tried to grab her. Declan jumped back as the stake sliced open his shirt.

Running toward her, Aiden smacked her arm aside when she lifted the stake to drive it through his heart. Spinning her around, Aiden tackled her face-first onto the ground. Carha's back bowed against his chest as she made an odd gurgling noise.

Grabbing her shoulders, he turned Carha over to find her mouth open in a gaping *oh* of horror while her fingers clawed at the stake protruding from her chest. When he'd taken her down, she'd fallen on top of the stake and driven it straight through her heart. She tried to yank it out, but it was already too late.

"Shit!" He slammed his hands onto the ground. Blood splattered around him as Carha convulsed beneath him. "Shit!"

"It doesn't matter," Ronan said as Carha released a final breath and went still beneath Aiden. "She told us all she knew."

He'd stayed away from Maggie for too long, and he could feel himself teetering toward the treacherous edge of savagery. Aiden inhaled a shuddering breath as he struggled to get himself under control. For the first time, he wanted nothing to do with this life he'd chosen.

CHAPTER THIRTY-NINE

MAGGIE DESPISED the blank screen of her phone. A few times she'd picked it up with the intention of breaking it so she wouldn't have to look at it anymore, but she'd managed to restrain herself. Now, she set it back on the bar, scratched her arm, and fiddled with the edges of the coaster she'd set on top of her empty glass. It was pointless to keep drinking when the whiskey wasn't doing anything to calm her nerves.

A ripple of motion in the restaurant and a shift in the air caused her head to lift. A prickle of awareness ran over her skin and the sensation of her flesh being stretched too thin over her bones eased. She didn't have to see Aiden to know he'd returned.

"Oh, shit," Brian said.

Maggie turned on her barstool. Her heart lodged in her throat before plunging into her stomach when she spotted Aiden in the doorway of the restaurant. His green eyes were locked on her; his black hair was wet and disheveled. He'd been wearing different clothes when he left, but she saw no marks on him, and he appeared uninjured.

He did appear murderous though.

She had no idea what it was about him, but he exuded a lethal aura that had the people closest to him scampering away while he stalked across the restaurant toward her. Brian rose and stepped forward to block his way. Aiden's eyes slid toward him, and a flash of red swirled through their leaf-green depths.

"You'll frighten her," Brian said in a low voice when Aiden was close enough to him.

Maggie realized Brian would protect her if he believed it necessary. The resulting fight would make the fight Aiden had in the ambulance look like a schoolyard scuffle.

Besides, Brian was wrong; she wasn't frightened of Aiden. She'd seen him like this before, maybe not quite *this* wound up, but she'd seen him on the verge of losing control, and he would never harm her.

Leaping off her stool, Maggie hurried forward as Aiden stopped in front of Brian. "Get out of my way," Aiden growled at Brian.

"Aiden—"

"It's fine," Maggie interrupted Abby. She strode around Abby and Brian to place her hand on Aiden's chest. When his hand enclosed on her wrist, some of the tension eased from his body and he pulled her against him.

"Maggie," he breathed.

Awe swept through her as she realized how *much* she affected this powerful being. He'd entered here primed to kill, but now he appeared only half murderous.

Neither of them looked back at the others as he turned and hurried her out of the room. Maggie ignored the startled receptionists at the front desk when Aiden lifted her into his arms and stalked toward the stairwell. To avoid tripping him or kicking him in the shins, Maggie wrapped her legs around his waist.

"What happened?" she asked as he pushed through the swinging doors and into the stairwell.

Instead of replying, he clasped the back of her head and kissed her. Though his kiss was harsh and demanding, Maggie went limp against him and slid her arms around his neck. His erection rubbed tantalizingly against the junction of her thighs with every step he took up the stairs. She had no idea how he concentrated on climbing when all she could think about was getting him naked, but he never missed a step.

Holding Maggie again calmed him more than the numerous blood bags he'd consumed before coming here. It had taken more blood than he typically required, but eventually he'd felt in control enough to shower and return to her.

Part of his lack of control was because of Maggie. They weren't bonded yet. If they were, he could have connected mentally with her and her presence would have soothed him before he returned to her. If they were mated, he wouldn't have to fear her fragile mortality.

Aiden shook as the reminder of her humanity caused the unraveling within him to start again. Breaking the kiss, he turned to press her against the wall at the second-floor stair landing. Kissing her neck, he pulled her hair back and sank his fangs into the delicate column of her throat. Maggie gasped and rubbed his cock in a way that had him on the verge of taking her there.

He'd made sure to learn the location of every camera in this hotel. The stairwells didn't have any, and neither did the hall-ways. All the cameras were on the first floor. He could bury himself inside her here, no one would see, and she wouldn't stop him.

His hands fell to the button on her jeans before he realized there might not be cameras, but anyone could stumble across them at any time. And *no* one would see Maggie exposed in such a way.

Retracting his fangs, he pulled her away from the wall and opened the door to the second-floor hall. Their rooms weren't on this floor, but he didn't care.

Maggie nuzzled his neck as he listened to the heartbeats behind each door they passed until he didn't detect any behind one of the doors. Aiden grabbed the handle, jerked it down, and shoved against the door. It gave way with an audible crack, and he had the laughable notion that they'd probably install hallway cameras after tonight.

"Aiden, this isn't one of our rooms," Maggie whispered.

"It is now," he said as he kicked the door shut with his heel.

Setting his hands on her waist, he lifted her off him and placed her on the bed. Undoing the button on her jeans, he pulled them down her creamy thighs before tugging off her sneakers and tossing them aside. He removed his boots and jeans next.

She glanced nervously at the closed door. "What if they find us?"

"They won't." He placed his hands on her knees, spreading them apart as he climbed onto the bed with her. She leaned back as he knelt between her legs. Grasping his shaft, he rubbed the head of it against her entrance and groaned. "You're so wet for me."

When he thrust forward, Maggie forgot all about her nervousness over being discovered. All she could think about was the sensation of him sliding in and out of her as he planted his hands beside her head. In the muted light filtering through the window, his eyes shone red.

"Must see you."

She didn't know what he meant until he grasped her shirt and tore it open. He gripped the front of her bra and twisted it until the material gave way. Cool air rushed over her heated skin when he bared her to him. His lips skimmed back to reveal his glistening fangs as his gaze ran over her. A thrill of apprehension went through her. He was more out of control than she'd realized.

"*My* Maggie," he breathed, his eyes fastening on her breasts. She grasped the bottom of his shirt and tugged it impatiently up; suddenly, she had to see him as badly as he'd needed to see her.

He pulled his shirt the rest of the way off and tossed it aside before lowering himself to take one of her nipples into his mouth. He worked his tongue over the hardened bud as he sank his fangs into her. Her hands entwined in his hair, drawing him closer while he consumed her blood.

A sense of loss filled her when he retracted his fangs and leaned back to gaze down at her. A bead of her blood glistened on his lips. Sliding her hand up, she gripped the back of his head and dragged him toward her.

She licked the blood away before sliding her tongue into his mouth. His arms cinched around her as he lifted her. Kneeling on the mattress, he braced his legs apart while he plunged her onto his shaft. Maggie's legs locked around his waist, and she clung to him.

He nipped her ear and circled his hips in a way that had his body rubbing her clit in all the right ways. She cried out and her body bucked against his. "Do you like that?" he murmured, and his fangs scraped her neck.

"Yes." Her belly clenched as their sweat-slicked bodies moved against each other.

"Would you like to taste my blood again?" he asked.

A need unlike anything she'd ever known speared her. "Yes."

Her charcoal eyes were filled with longing when she leaned

back to look at him. Releasing her hair, he lifted his wrist to his mouth and bit deep. Maggie licked her lips when she saw his blood trickling from the two punctures.

When he brought his wrist to her mouth, she seized it and drank deeply from him. She moaned as his blood filled her mouth. It was more delicious than the finest chocolate, she decided as it slid down her throat.

"My Maggie," he breathed as she drank from him.

Her tongue licked over his flesh. When she started riding him again, her body grinding hard against his, he couldn't deny he was lost to her. Love swelled within him as he nourished her. There was nothing he wouldn't do for this woman who had brought peace and happiness to his tumultuous life.

She let go of his wrist and turned her head to kiss him. He tasted his blood on her lips as her butterscotch scent engulfed him. When she cried out against his mouth and the muscles of her sheath clenched around his cock, he gave himself over to the release building within him.

CHAPTER FORTY

THE FIRST RAYS of the sun were warming the earth when Aiden carried her back to his room. She was far too exhausted to walk. Her head slumped against his chest as she yawned. With her bra and shirt ruined, she wore his shirt and her jeans.

Entering his room, Aiden set her on the bed and lay down behind her before pulling her against him. He held her close as she drifted off to sleep.

According to the clock on the stand, it was two in the afternoon when she woke again. Glenn's funeral was over. A twinge of sadness tugged at her heart. She stretched her hand behind her for Aiden, but it fell on an empty bed.

Rising, she searched for him before spotting him sitting on the chair in the corner of the room. He smiled at her, but strain etched the corners of his mouth, and she didn't understand the sadness in his eyes.

"What's wrong?" She drew her knees against her chest and hugged them to her. "Did something go wrong yesterday? Is everyone okay? Are *you* okay? You seemed more stressed than normal last night, Nosferatu," she teased in the hopes of coaxing a real smile from him.

"Everything went as well as expected," he said. "And I'm all right."

"What happened? Did you learn why the Savages attacked you?"

"The Savages attacked me because Carha hired them to do it. She didn't like that I kept turning her down."

Maggie's mouth dropped at this revelation. "This was over sex?"

"Or lack thereof. It was also because of her pride and the fact she was a malicious, sick bitch who thrived on the misery and pain of others."

"I'll kill her."

More of a smile curved Aiden's mouth as he clasped his hands before him and leaned forward. "Too late."

"She's dead?"

"Yes."

"Good. What about the Savages who attacked you?"

"They're dead too, including the one who attacked you. There is no risk to you from them anymore."

"Oh," Maggie breathed as her shoulders sagged in relief. "That's great. Can I go home and back to work?"

Aiden kept himself from wincing as his fingers tore into his palms. "If you choose."

"Was Carha working with them for long?"

"It looks like it. From what we've learned, she was setting up some of her other patrons too. There is a purebred vampire, Joseph, who worked with Ronan before I joined them. Joseph gave in and turned Savage. Now, he's trying to build an army against Ronan. Carha wanted the Savages to kill me, but there is a chance they intended to bring me to Joseph, and we think that's what has happened to at least some of the others she set up."

"Joseph turns other vampires into Savages?"

"Yes. The need to kill rules Savage vampires, but they're not stupid. In fact, they're annoyingly cunning, and Joseph has found a way to create more of them."

"So Savages are like the ingenious criminals who figure out how to break out of prison using a bar of soap and a toothbrush."

"Exactly. We know they're smart, but they seem to lose themselves in the blood, and they also appear to lose all sense of a conscience. If I became one, I could lead them to my family."

Aiden shuddered at the possibility as he stared at his feet. He'd rather die first.

"You could never be like one of those things," Maggie whispered.

"But I could. There have been many times when I was right there on the edge of becoming one, including last night."

Maggie gulped as she recalled how out of control he'd been when she'd first seen him. "You've pulled yourself back every time."

Without her, he didn't know if he could keep pulling himself back anymore. "A mate is very special to a vampire, Maggie."

"Yes, you've told me, and I saw how close Abby and Brian are."

"The mate bond is eternal, and to complete it, both individuals have to be a vampire."

Maggie gripped the comforter closer as his words sank in. "Both?"

"Yes."

"You want to make me a... a vampire?" she croaked.

"Yes."

"And bind me to you forever?"

"Yes."

Maggie's throat went dry. She'd always been in over her head with him, but suddenly she felt like she was sinking faster than the Titanic. She'd seen how wild he could be, how brutal his life was. She didn't know if she could be everything he needed, or if she *wanted* to be bound to him for *eternity*. Moving in together seemed like far too large of a commitment given the amount of time they'd known each other, never mind being bound together forever!

"You already crave blood," he said. "I will feed enough for the both of us, so you'll only ever have to drink from me if you want."

"I see."

"You'll live as an immortal, with me."

"We barely know each other. I like you, a lot, I won't deny it. But you're suggesting binding ourselves to each other for an eternity, and this is only the fifth day we've known one another. What if I drive you nuts in a week? What if in a month or a hundred years from now, you start regretting your decision to make me a vampire? What if you end up hating me?"

"I could never hate you."

"You don't know that!" she insisted. "What if, after fifty years, my snoring makes you wish you could stake me. Or what if *I* start hating *you*? What if I decide the way you put your toothbrush back makes me want to stab you with it?"

He smiled grimly as he leaned back in the chair. "I'm sure you'll want to stab me often over the years, but as long as it's not through the heart, I can take it."

"I'm serious."

"I know you are, but these are all things we will deal with together. When you're a vampire, you'll understand how intense this bond is."

Terror tore through Maggie. She recalled how pathetic she'd felt sitting at the bar last night, waiting for him to come back, and how annoyed with herself she'd been because of it. She'd spent the first twelve years of her life with only herself to rely on. Then, she'd had A.J. for such a brief time, and now she had Roger.

She cared for Aiden, but she didn't know if she could count on him too. She believed she could, but she hadn't known him long enough to be certain. She didn't like uncertainty. And Aiden was talking about eternity, a commitment *much* larger than any she'd ever experienced before, and it didn't sound as if he were giving her much choice on it either.

"*When* I'm a vampire? Have I already agreed to this, or do I simply have no choice?" she asked.

The acid dripping from her voice made him realize he'd said the wrong thing. "Of course, you have a choice."

"What about my life? My career? My friends? What happens to all those things? Am I supposed to toss them aside for a life with no guarantees if it all blows up in my face?"

"Even if this blows up between us, which it won't, I promise you'll be taken care of."

"I don't need you to take care of me!"

Aiden took a deep breath as he tried to figure out how to proceed. Fiercely independent, Maggie wouldn't embrace relying on someone else more often. "We can find a way for you to keep your job if you prefer. You would probably have to take some time off from work in the beginning. Newly turned vampires are often in control of themselves, but with what you do and the blood you'll be around, it could be more difficult."

"Yeah, eating the patients would be bad."

He gave her a wan smile. "Yes."

She stared at him before looking at the window as she contemplated everything he'd said to her. No matter how much she cared for Aiden, she didn't know if she could make this leap. She'd worked too hard to gain the security she had now to risk everything.

"I care about you; I *really* do, more than I ever believed possible in such a short time, but I'd like some time to think about this, Aiden. It's a *big* decision."

"Whatever you need."

"I have to go home, go back to work, go back to the real world. Hiding out in a hotel room with you is more a dream than reality. I need some reality," she said and smiled at him to soften her words.

Aiden's fangs extended. He could turn her and complete the bond so she could never leave him, but not only would she despise him, he'd despise himself. He wouldn't tell her that he could already feel himself unraveling because of their incomplete bond. It might destroy him, but he would abide by whatever she decided, and he would control himself, for her.

"I understand," he said. "I'll take you home today."

"I need to be alone, Aiden."

His teeth clamped together with enough force to crack a few. "I see."

"It's the only way I'll be able to sort this out," Maggie gushed. She felt like she'd stabbed him straight through the heart, and she hated it, but she had to do this. "When I'm with you, I can't think straight. There's so much I have to process, and taking some time to do that is nothing compared to an eternity, right?"

"Right."

"And you said there's no threat to me anymore."

"There's not. The Savage Ronan and the others captured and we questioned revealed they didn't tell anyone else about what happened the night they attacked me."

"Why did they keep it quiet?"

"Because they almost exposed all of our kind that night. Since it appears they were working for Joseph as well as Carha, Joseph would have had them pleading for death by the time he finished with them for making such a blunder of that night."

"So, I'll be safe if I go home alone?"

"Yes."

"Then, I think it's best if I go now."

"Sure." He couldn't think about going to sleep without Maggie tonight or waking to find her gone. He'd tear everything in this room apart if he did.

"I'll meet you here, at the bar, in four days. I don't know if I'll have everything sorted out by then, but give me those four days before we talk again."

"Whatever you need."

"Aiden—"

"Do what you need to do, Maggie. I'll be here for you, always."

Unexpected tears burned her eyes, and a lump formed in her throat. She'd asked for this time away from him, yet it took everything she had to place her feet on the ground and rise from the bed. If she said yes to him, she could stay in this dream world forever, but she would be giving up so much for someone she barely knew.

Her heart ached for him as he kept his gaze focused on his feet. His knuckles turned white from clenching them.

Padding over to him, she bent and kissed the top of his head. "Two o'clock on Friday, we'll meet back here. Four days from now."

"Yes," he agreed. "You can't reveal anything about what you know, Maggie. If you breathe one word about the existence of vampires to anyone, I might not be able to protect you."

"I would never do anything to put you or your family in danger, Aiden. *Never*. Besides, my worst nightmare is ending up in a room next to my mother, and that's where I'd be if I started telling people vampires were real."

Aiden nodded, but he found it impossible to say anymore to her.

Maggie slipped from the room before she threw all precaution to the wind and plunged over the edge with him. However, if she chose to join Aiden, it would be the most permanent decision she'd ever made in her life. She couldn't make that choice without at least thinking it over first.

Her brain repeated this over and over again, but her heart felt like someone had stuck it in a shredder.

CHAPTER FORTY-ONE

AIDEN ARRANGED for her to return to work the next day. She didn't like the idea of him messing with her friends' minds again, but she didn't have much choice on this one. It felt good to be back at work, kidding with her coworkers and taking their ribbing about her concussion. They all agreed she couldn't bruise a brain that wasn't there.

She'd expected their teasing, and she took it in stride, but something about it didn't feel right. None of this felt like her life anymore. Her apartment, a place she'd worked to make a home, was no longer inviting to her.

When she saw Roger, she didn't want to let go of him as she hugged him. "You're gonna break a rib, Mags," he grumbled, and she released him.

"Sorry."

"Hmm," he said as he straightened his shirt and fixed his hair. Then he hugged her so tight her back cracked.

She laughed when he set her down and hugged him again. "Did you go to Glenn's funeral?"

"Yes. Doctor's orders be damned."

"I'm sorry I wasn't there with you."

"It's okay, kid." He turned away from her, but not before she saw the sheen of tears in his eyes. "How you been feeling?"

"Better."

"Good."

"I love you too, Roger." She knew it wasn't exactly the time to tell him, but she'd never gotten the chance to say it back to him during their phone call.

He waved his hand at her as he busied himself with taking inventory of their supplies. They fell into a comfortable silence with each other as they prepped for their shift.

"You remember anything about what happened?" he asked when they were pulling out of the station.

"No," Maggie said and clicked her seat belt into place. She was glad she couldn't see his face as she uttered this lie. "I remember leaving here for the night. I have some flashes of being in an alley, and then I was at home."

She resisted scratching at her arms. She'd found herself scratching often since she'd parted from Aiden, and her skin felt like it had the night he'd gone after Carha. She *hated* the sensation. Without Aiden lying beside her, she'd also been unable to sleep last night. Tossing and turning, she realized she missed his arms around her.

Giving up on sleep, she'd climbed out of bed and gone for a run when the sun came up. The slap of her feet on the sidewalk lulled her, the rush of running propelled her onward, but it had done nothing to ease the pressure building in her chest. She'd run ten miles, gone home, and collapsed onto her bed. Finally, she fell asleep at nine and woke up often before she finally crawled out of bed at two to get ready for her shift.

Maybe she would adjust to a life without him again after a

few days, but she worried she knew too much now to go back to the way things were. Scratching absently at her skin, she stared out the window as they passed the Prudential building.

"You okay, Maggie May?" Roger asked after they'd been on duty for a few hours.

"I'm fine. How are you feeling?"

"Me? I'm fit as a fiddle," he said. "You've been quieter than normal, and I think you're going to scratch your skin off."

Maggie glanced at the backs of her red hands and the scratches on her arms. Her hands had become so raw she'd drawn blood and never even realized it. She folded them in her lap to hide the marks.

"I guess I'm still a little out of it," she said.

"Concussions are a tricky thing."

"Yeah," she muttered. *So are vampires with green eyes who somehow manage to dig their way under your skin.*

"Maybe you should have stayed out of work longer."

"No. I'm fine. If I weren't, I wouldn't be here. I wouldn't risk someone's life that way."

But aren't I? She'd never actually had a concussion, but her mind wasn't in the game right now. She shouldn't be here, but she didn't know where else to be. Back in Aiden's arms? Jumping into a life with no preparation for it falling apart on her?

She'd spent her entire childhood and teen years uncertain of where she'd be the next day. Once she was old enough to be on her own, she swore she'd never again know that kind of uncertainty. One of her biggest dreams had been knowing where she would be sleeping the next night, and she'd achieved it. The idea of letting her security go scared her more than the Savages ever had.

Aiden said mates were eternal, but marriage vows were

until death, and many people walked away from those. She'd understand if she were a vampire, he'd said. *Great, I'll understand once I choose to live forever with a man I've known for five days.*

If someone else had come to her looking for advice on this issue, she would have told them they were a fool for considering it. People lived together and shared their lives for years before getting married and still divorced a year later.

She realized she'd started scratching her hands again. What was wrong with her? Lifting her hands, she examined them, but there was no rash or insect bites to indicate why she'd started this obsessive itching. No, there was only the ever-tightening presence of her skin.

The radio squelched before the dispatcher's voice sounded. Maggie forgot all about her discomfort as she focused on their call.

"Did you tell her that mates can't live without each other? Does she know you could go mad or die without her?" Vicky demanded as she followed Aiden down the stairs of Ronan's mansion to the gym in the basement.

"No," he replied in a clipped tone that should have warned her to back off.

"You should have told her; she wouldn't have left!" Vicky insisted.

"She didn't leave."

"Then *where* is she?"

When he spun around, she lurched back. "She's back in her apartment and her life."

"But she could be dooming you, and she doesn't know it! She has to know!"

"She doesn't have to know anything! You and every other member of our family, including the Stooges, are to stay out of this. None of you are to tell her anything or have *anyone* else approach her. Do you understand me?"

"But, Aiden—"

"No," he snarled, and Vicky took another step away from him. "She has a right to make her own choices about *her* life. She will be allowed to do that."

"And if she decides not to be with you?"

Aiden's fangs slid free; his nails pierced his palms, and blood pooled into his fists. He couldn't think about the possibility Maggie might not choose him. He'd go mad if he thought about it, and then he might go after Maggie, something he was determined not to do. She'd asked for four days, and he would give them to her. If she asked for more time after that, he would give it to her. If she needed him before then, all she had to do was call.

"That will be her choice," he said and turned away.

Stepping into the massive gym, he ignored the handful of other recruits training there. Like an annoying gnat, Vicky followed him as he stalked across the floor to the weapons hanging on the back wall. The gym held every piece of exercise equipment imaginable, and beating the shit out of one of the practice dummies was exactly what he needed.

"I'm worried about you," Vicky said.

"I know."

"I can't lose you."

He couldn't hold onto his annoyance with her when he knew her worry came from a place of love. "You won't."

"There is vampire DNA in Maggie too. Enough for her to smell a little something off about Savages and to require blood to be healthy. There will be enough for her to recognize you as her mate too. Or at the very least, miss you too much to stay away from you."

"Perhaps," he said and removed two swords from the wall.

Vicky removed two smaller swords and hefted them to test their weight. Aiden spun his weapons in his hands as he stepped back to look at his sister. Before her imprisonment, Vicky had been more focused on fashion and parties than anything else. Since being freed, she'd become almost as dedicated to training as him.

Vicky grinned at him as she stepped back. "Want to spar?"

"With the mood I'm in, I'm not sure it's a good idea."

"Are you scared?" she taunted before giving him a small jab with the tip of her blade.

Aiden glanced at his shirt, but she hadn't poked him hard enough to draw blood. "Remember, you asked for it," he said.

Vicky danced back, and they fell into an easy rhythm with each other as they moved around the blue gym mat. As a purebred vampire, Vicky was strong, but she didn't possess his strength. What she lacked in power, she made up for with her quickness. He could move with speed and grace, but Vicky was smaller and more nimble. She deftly avoided many of his jabs as their swords clashed.

He hammered her back with a series of blows meant to knock the weapon from her hand, but she kept hold of it. He almost had her against the wall when she dropped suddenly, hitting the mat flat on her back before rolling away from him and bouncing to her feet.

"Nice move," he said admiringly.

She grinned as she brushed back the strands of damp hair clinging to her flushed face. "I know."

Aiden laughed before going at her again. They sparred for nearly half an hour more before Vicky stepped back and planted the tip of her sword on the mat. They were both breathing heavily, and Aiden felt a little more in control of himself. He would spend hours more down here, working himself into a state of exhaustion. Hopefully he would be able to get at least an hour of sleep before rising to do it all over again tomorrow.

He wouldn't leave Ronan's mansion until it was time to meet with Maggie; he didn't trust himself enough to risk being around people. He hated the idea of Maggie being out there unguarded, but he wouldn't be able to stay away from her if he saw her. Declan had agreed to check on her occasionally and to keep his distance.

He'd much prefer someone watching her 24/7, but she'd be irate if she ever discovered he'd done that to her. Her fury would be worth it to make sure she was safe, but with no direct threat to her life anymore, he couldn't justify spying on her or having someone else do so.

"How about we eat and get back to it?" Vicky inquired.

"You're not tired yet?"

"Oh, I am, but no one ever comes at me as fiercely as you just did, and I need that."

"I'm sorry."

"I'm no delicate flower, Aiden Michael Byrne," Vicky retorted. "Don't apologize to me. I'm glad someone has finally stopped taking it easy on me, and yes, I realize you're still holding back a little, but nowhere near as much as you usually do."

"Hmm," he grunted and returned his swords to the wall. "Maybe we'll try something else after feeding."

"Sounds good to me," Vicky replied and returned her weapons too.

She walked beside him to the swinging, metal doors leading into the room where the blood was stored. Pushing open one of the doors, Aiden stepped into the room and walked over to the industrial refrigerator set against the back wall. He removed two bags from within and handed one to Vicky. Once she finished with hers, Vicky threw the bag away and waited for him as he consumed three more before finally feeling somewhat sated.

Opening one of the doors, they stepped back into the gym as Ronan and his mate, Kadence, entered. Walking next to Kadence was her brother, Nathan. Seeing him, Vicky stiffened, and a deer in the headlights look came over her face. Ronan said something and Nathan nodded.

"What is *he* doing here?" Vicky hissed.

Aiden frowned at her. "Nathan?"

"Yes, Nathan."

"He *is* Kadence's brother."

"He's also a hunter who slaughters our kind," she retorted.

"Not anymore. Ronan has an alliance with the hunters. I don't trust them yet—"

"Neither do I."

"I'm sure most here don't trust them, but fighting against Joseph together is better for all of us."

"Hmm," she grunted. "I have to go."

Aiden blinked at her abrupt words. He'd grown up in a houseful of women, so he knew about mood swings, but this was a bit much, even for Vicky who could be as temperamental as a grizzly bear some days.

"I thought you wanted to continue training?" he asked.

"I forgot I have something else to do. I'll see you later."

Before he could reply, Vicky stalked away from him. Instead of heading straight for the door, she walked to the wall and followed it all the way around the room. She kept her gaze resolutely forward, her shoulders back and her chin raised as she approached the door. Uneasiness churned in Aiden's gut when Nathan turned to watch her slip out of the gym.

"Shit," he breathed when he recalled asking Vicky if she'd met someone, her brusque reply, and the fact he'd sensed she'd lied to him.

He hoped he was wrong, it would be a rocky road for Vicky if she became entangled with a hunter, or worse, if he was her mate, but he couldn't deny he sensed something between the two of them.

CHAPTER FORTY-TWO

"So what do you think, Blue?" Maggie inquired as she sprinkled a couple of flakes into the bowl for him.

Blue's only response was a flick of his tail as he gulped his flakes. She took that as a sign he liked her plan. It was an acceptable plan; she only hoped Aiden would see it that way too.

Over the past four days, she'd come to realize how lonely her life was and how much she missed having him in it. Like a plant without the sun, she felt like she was shriveling inside without him, and if she kept scratching at her arms, she'd have no skin left.

Her arms looked like she'd brawled with a briar patch and lost, badly. She'd started wrapping her skin in white bandages to curb her itching, but it didn't help during those rare times she slept. The bandages had originally only encompassed her forearms, but they'd spread up to her biceps yesterday. If this kept up, she'd have to mummify herself.

The last time she'd slept for more than an hour at a time was in Aiden's arms. She'd almost called him a few dozen times a day, but each time she picked up the phone, she put it down before she dialed. She had to use this time away from him to sort through things.

She couldn't up and quit her job. She refused to leave them shorthanded, it could risk someone's life, and her coworkers had become a family to her, especially Roger. Besides, if for some reason things didn't work out with Aiden, she couldn't burn her bridges. She would need her career to fall back on, and if she couldn't get her old position back, she would at least get good references for her next job.

She also wouldn't leave Roger that way; she didn't plan to leave him at all as he'd always be a part of her life, no matter what. But she wasn't about to leave him high and dry with an unprepared partner.

A two-week notice would give her more time to get to know Aiden better while she was still human too. Perhaps, in that time, they'd discover they were better apart than together. With the way she'd felt these past four days, she doubted that would happen, but she wasn't willing to take the chance it would.

She'd considered continuing to work as a paramedic after turning, but decided it would be better to take some time away. She couldn't stand the idea of accidentally hurting someone if their blood proved too strong a temptation for her.

Besides, it would probably be best if she and Aiden spent some time together, adjusting to their new lives after she became a vampire. She wouldn't let him support her, she'd figure out some way to contribute to their relationship, but she was sure there would be plenty for her to learn about controlling herself and vampirism.

So, when she met Aiden today, she'd tell him she would give her notice at work. He'd have to be willing to give her those two weeks, if he wasn't, then it was a good sign their relationship wouldn't work, and she'd walk away. He might even have to give her longer than two weeks. They'd hired one new person, but they were still one staff member down after Walt and Glenn's deaths.

She resisted scratching her skin at the possibility Aiden wouldn't give her those two weeks. She wouldn't ask him to keep his distance during that time. No, she hoped he'd come stay with her. She would love to crawl into his arms and inhale his scent again. Just imagining it made the constriction in her chest ease and her skin stopped itching. Yes, he would understand. He had to.

Maggie glanced at the clock. It was only twelve, but she couldn't stay in this apartment anymore. It shouldn't take her more than half an hour to get to the hotel. She'd wait there for Aiden, and hopefully, he would come early too. Thankfully, it was her day off as she meant to spend most of it in bed with him.

Smiling at the pleasant notion, Maggie turned away from Blue. She picked her coat up from her bed as her phone rang. When she'd returned to work, she'd discovered that while her wallet and keys had survived the attack, her phone hadn't. She still had the phone she'd purchased from the convenience store. She'd planned to keep it anyway, in case Aiden called her, but now she used it for everyone else as she hadn't had time to replace her old one. It was on her ever-growing list of things to do over the next two weeks as she prepared for her new life.

She lifted the phone from her nightstand. When she saw the caller was her boss Pablo, she almost ignored it. She couldn't be called into work today of all days, but her conscience tugged at her. How many had covered for her while she'd been with Aiden?

Maggie answered the phone. "Hello."

"Maggie, it's Pablo."

She almost replied with... Yes, I know, caller ID is this nifty new invention... but something about his tone stopped her. A ball of dread formed in her stomach. "What is it?"

"It's..." He exhaled loudly. "It's Roger."

The break in his voice had her sinking onto her bed. "What happened?"

"It looks like he had a stroke. They've rushed him to Mass General. I'm heading over now."

"I'll meet you there."

Maggie didn't wait to hear his reply. She leapt off her bed, slipped her phone into her pocket, and slid on her coat. She didn't remember leaving her apartment, but she suddenly found herself taking the steps two at a time toward the first floor. Her feet barely hit the ground as she raced down the last flight and out the doors.

Plunging onto the sidewalk, she ran toward the closest T station. She fumbled to remove the phone from her pocket as she dodged the people on the sidewalk. She succeeded in pulling her phone free to call Aiden as she hit the steps to the T station and plunged down.

She was about to hit send when a woman, rushing up the stairs, bashed her purse into Maggie's ribs. Maggie stumbled to the side, her ankle twisted on the stairs and gave out. The phone toppled from her fingers; the cool metal railing slid against her palm when she grabbed it to keep from plummeting down the concrete stairs to the bottom.

"Are you okay?" a man inquired as he gripped her elbow to help steady her.

"Yes, yes, I'm fine. Thank you," Maggie said as she tested her ankle. It was sore but unbroken. "I... I dropped my phone."

"Here," the man bent and scooped it up. "It wasn't as lucky as you."

Maggie took the shattered pieces from him. "No, it wasn't."

It was only twelve o'clock when Aiden arrived at the bar, but he'd been unable to stay away. He sat on one of the stools and touched the inner pocket of his coat to reassure himself the tickets were still there. Earlier, he'd recalled Maggie's words about attending opening day with A.J., and he'd stopped on his way here to purchase tickets for them to go to the game.

Removing his coat, he draped it over the stool beside him. He ordered a Crown on the rocks as he settled in to wait. Outside, Declan, Brian, and Killean remained in the car in case Maggie didn't arrive, or she only came to tell him goodbye.

They would be necessary to take him down if either of those things happened.

Maggie paced back and forth in the waiting room outside of the OR. Half the ambulance company was crowded into the room, and more people spilled into the hallway or had wandered to the cafeteria. Police and firefighters had also arrived to give their support. As gruff and stubborn as Roger was, he was also well-liked.

People talked in hushed whispers, or not at all. One group had arrived with coffee and donuts over an hour ago. The coffee was gone, the donuts barely touched.

Roger's ex-wife had also come. Divorced years ago, they'd never had children together, but Roger talked highly of her, and Maggie knew they still exchanged calls and Christmas cards. The woman had remarried, and Maggie assumed her husband was the man sitting next to her, holding one hand while she chewed the nails of her other hand.

Maggie glanced at the clock on the wall and gulped. It was

322   BRENDA K DAVIES

already two o'clock. She had to call Aiden. She turned to Officer Harding to ask if she could borrow his phone when a doctor emerged through the swinging doors.

Maggie froze as the doctor walked over to speak with Pablo and the ex-wife for a minute. Their grave expressions made Maggie's stomach churn. Then, the doctor slipped away again. The ex-wife had paled visibly, and Pablo looked like he was losing a battle against food poisoning.

"What did he say?" Maggie asked tremulously.

"It was definitely a stroke," Pablo said as he ran a hand through his shaggy black hair. "They're doing the best they can, but it seems a fair amount of time passed between when he had the stroke and when I found him."

Maggie started at his words; she hadn't known Pablo was the one to discover Roger. Then, she recalled Roger telling her yesterday he planned to get in some bowling practice today. He and Pablo were on the same team, the 7/10 Splints.

Tears burned her eyes as she thought of poor Pablo finding his friend in such a way. They slid free when she realized Roger had most likely been lying there for a while, waiting for someone to come. She couldn't stand to think about how scared he must have been.

Maggie covered her mouth with her hand and choked on a sob. She wiped away her tears. She refused to cry. Not here. Roger would be so mad at her for that. Unable to remain standing, she sank onto a chair.

"You must be Maggie."

Maggie lifted her head and blinked Roger's ex into focus. He'd told her the woman's name, but for the life of her, she couldn't remember it right now. "Yes," she croaked.

The woman squeezed her knee, and Maggie realized she'd sat next to her. There was an almost surreal air about the woman's hand. Maggie knew it was touching *her* knee, yet she felt as if she were outside of her body, watching it.

"Roger has told me so much about you. He thinks very highly of you," the woman said.

"I think very highly of him too. I wouldn't be here if it weren't for him."

"You're like..." The woman's voice broke, and a tear slid free. "You're like a daughter to him."

Maggie didn't shy away when the woman leaned over to hug her.

And he's like a father to me.

AT THREE THIRTY, the doctor re-emerged to tell them they'd done everything they could, but they'd been unable to save Roger. Maggie wanted to curl into a ball and cry, but she bit her tongue. If she fell apart now, she'd never be able to pick herself up enough to leave the hospital.

Around the room, she heard the tears of some of the others.

AT THREE O'CLOCK, Brian came to sit beside him. At three thirty, Killean joined him. Amber liquid splashed in his glass as Aiden spun it between his hands. He'd been so certain Maggie would come. A small piece of him had feared she wouldn't, but deep down, he'd believed she cared for him too.

Lifting his glass, Aiden downed the rest of its contents in one swallow. Outwardly, he remained amazingly controlled considering the madness steadily building within him. On the bar, he stared at the phone he'd set before him, but the screen remained blank. She hadn't tried to call or text him.

He picked his phone up and dialed her number. No one answered, and he didn't leave a message. He called again a half an hour later, again his only greeting was a computerized voice telling him to leave a message. Had she gotten rid of her phone? Was this her way of telling him to fuck off?

He understood why she'd decided a no call, no show, was the best way to say goodbye. After everything she'd seen him do while they were together, she was probably afraid he would attack her if she said goodbye in person. But, he would give anything to hear her voice one more time.

He called again, and when the computer answered, his hand clenched on the phone. It shattered with an audible crack. Electronic bits slipped from his palm and clattered onto the bar. His head bowed, and he immediately regretted the destruction of his phone, but there was nothing he could do to fix it.

"We should go," Brian stated as he swiped the broken pieces into his hand and placed them in his pocket.

"One more hour," Aiden grated through his teeth.

At five o'clock, Aiden set his glass down, rose, and picked up his coat. "I'm going to her place."

"Aiden—"

"I won't go after her, Brian," he interjected. "I have to see."

"See what?" Killean asked gruffly.

"I don't know. That she's okay. That this is her choice. See *her* for the final time."

CHAPTER FORTY-THREE

IT WAS ALMOST four thirty before Maggie borrowed Pablo's phone and made her way outside to call Aiden. Feeling as if she were walking through a haze, she realized she'd left her coat inside only when the wind bit through her clothes and froze her cheeks.

He might be annoyed with her for not contacting him sooner, but she hoped Aiden would be able to meet her here. She needed to see him and hug him as Roger's death had only solidified her decision to join him. She didn't want to become a vampire because she was afraid of dying one day too, but because, for once, she wanted to jump in with both feet and truly *live* with Aiden.

If the relationship blew up in her face, then so be it. She would deal with the aftermath just as she'd dealt with every other curveball life had thrown her over the years.

Aiden didn't answer, and she hung up on the computerized voice mail. She shivered when the wind beat her hair against her cheeks, but she couldn't bring herself to go back inside yet.

326 BRENDA K DAVIES

If Aiden was waiting for her, wouldn't he have answered his phone?

Oh yeah, Maggie, you're so irresistible he's sitting by his phone hoping it rings. She hated the bitter thought, but once it took root, she couldn't shake it. Had he moved on already?

The hell he has!

She redialed Aiden's number, determined to get to the bottom of this. Then, she remembered she wasn't calling from a number he knew. If he were anything like her, he'd ignore it unless someone left a message. When the computer picked up, she waited until the beep.

"It's Maggie," she said. "Something's happened. I can't—"

"Maggie." She turned to find Pablo standing behind her, holding her coat open for her. "You must be freezing."

"I am." She stepped into her coat, and Pablo pulled it on as she finished her voice mail. "My phone's broken, but I'll call you again later."

She hung up and handed Pablo's phone back to him. "Thank you."

"Anytime. Some of us are going to O'Shanighans to toast Roger. Do you want to come?"

"I'd love to, but there's something I have to do."

He cupped his hands to blow into them as he stomped his feet back and forth. His black eyes were bright against his bloodshot whites. "Do you have someone to take you home?"

"I took the T here; I'll ride it home."

"You're not in the condition to deal with that right now. Come on, I'll take you home."

"No, I'll be all right. Go and be with the others."

"Roger would be pissed at me if I didn't see you safely home. Come on, let's get out of here. Hospitals give me the creeps."

Maggie gave him a wan smile and took his arm when he offered it to her. They didn't go back inside but walked around the building to the garage behind it. When he opened the door for her, she slid inside, and he closed the door. She rested her head against the window when Pablo settled behind the wheel.

"I'm going to miss him," she murmured.

"We all are. He was the kind of asshole you couldn't help but love."

She snorted with laughter as he pulled out of the parking spot. "That he was."

AIDEN WATCHED the red Ford slide into a parking spot across the street from the passenger seat of Declan's car. He smelled Maggie before he saw her inside the car. His hand fell on the handle, but he kept himself restrained from flinging it open and going to her. A man in his late thirties or early forties climbed out from behind the wheel of the car.

Maggie was already stepping out of the vehicle when the man arrived at her side. The wind whipped her hair forward, blocking Aiden's view of her face. Behind him, he felt Brian and Killean leaning closer. Beside him, Declan hunched over the wheel.

The man said something to Maggie and took her arm as he led her toward her door. Something malevolent swirled within Aiden as they stopped outside her building and the man hugged her. When she embraced him back, red filled Aiden's vision as the need for blood and death burst over him.

She'd made her choice, and it was another man.

A snarl erupted from him as all control and any sense of reason vanished. He was about to open the door when something smashed against his temple. Aiden spun on his attacker. His fangs sliced into his bottom lip as he lunged for Brian. Brother-in-law or not, Aiden would tear his throat out.

Brian recoiled from his attack as something else bashed Aiden in the head. Stars burst in front of his eyes, a ringing sounded in his ears, and pain lanced like lightning across his fractured skull. The blow staggered him but didn't stop him as his fingers curled around Brian's throat. When a third blow hit him, part of his skull caved in, and the world went black.

"Have you seen the man I was here with the other night?" Maggie asked one of the bartenders at the hotel when he walked over to speak with her. He'd served her and Aiden often enough she hoped he remembered them.

It was almost seven, she was beyond late, but by the time she'd gotten showered, changed, and felt emotionally capable of handling the T to make the trip here, it had been after six. Now, she was one of the few patrons in the bar, and she was acutely aware Aiden wasn't one of them. Fresh tears pricked her eyes, but she fought them back. If she started crying again now, she would never stop.

"He left a couple of hours ago," the bartender replied.

"But he was here?" she asked.

"He was."

"Okay, good."

She sat and bought a drink in the hope Aiden would return soon. At ten, she gave up hope. When the bartender returned to her, she paid him. "If he happens to return, could you let him know I went home?"

"Will do," the man replied, but he barely acknowledged

her, and she doubted he would remember to tell Aiden if he came back.

On her way home, Maggie stopped at a store to buy a new phone. She called Aiden again and left a voice mail with her new number, but by the time she returned to her apartment building, he hadn't called, and he wasn't waiting outside for her.

Holding her breath, she turned into her hallway with the hope of finding Aiden there, waiting outside her door, but her hallway was empty. He didn't know the code to the building, but she knew that wouldn't stop a vampire from entering the building, and especially not him. Besides, Mrs. Mackey would probably let him in and bake him an entire batch of cookies.

Maggie unlocked her door and entered her apartment. Slumping onto her couch, she gazed around the small space that no longer felt like her home. Her grief for Roger swelled within her and tears slid down her cheeks as she waited for Aiden to come.

THE RINGING of his phone roused Stefan from sleep. He glanced at Isabelle to make sure she hadn't been disturbed. Then, he threw back his blankets and rose from the bed. He padded out to where he'd left his phone charging in the living room.

A chill of foreboding slid down his spine when he saw Brian's number on the caller ID. Things were still a little strained between them, but they'd been working on establishing a new friendship. However, it was too late at night for this to be a friendly call. Answering the phone, he brought it to his ear.

"What happened?" he asked as he walked over to pull back

the edge of a curtain. He scanned the snow-covered field and the other homes, but nothing unusual stirred and none of the alarms were sounding.

"Aiden," Brian said.

Stefan's hand clenched on the curtain. "Is he dead?"

Brian hesitated before replying, "No, but he might be better off if he was."

CHAPTER FORTY-FOUR

MAGGIE TOSSED her rose onto Roger's grave and stepped away as the first shovelful of dirt hit the coffin. She cringed. It made no sense, but somehow, the thud of that dirt made Roger's death more final. She recalled feeling the same way at A.J.'s funeral too.

Turning, she strode through the headstones with the rest of the mourners as she made her way to Pablo's car and climbed into the back seat. She'd rode to the cemetery with him and his wife. Despite the fact she'd given her notice yesterday, Pablo had offered her a ride, but she should have known he would understand her decision to leave her position.

Aiden had never arrived at her apartment, never answered her messages, and she'd given up expecting him to do so, but she couldn't stay here anymore. She'd lived in Boston her entire life; she'd never considered leaving. Now, she couldn't wait to get away.

She'd anticipated jumping into life and starting to live it with Aiden. Now, she would jump in and start living it without him. She'd travel the country and do things she'd never dreamed of doing. She'd been so determined to have security, she'd never realized she'd put herself in a little box. It was time to get out of that box. When she was done exploring, maybe she'd come back to Boston, but she wasn't making any long-term plans, at least not for a while. And she wouldn't look for Aiden anymore.

The idea of never seeing Aiden again caused her to scratch at her skin. She felt torn between her grief for Roger and her burgeoning hatred toward the vampire who had walked into her life and tossed it upside down.

Why had he said those things to her about matehood and being with her forever if it had all been lies? Why had he played such a game with her? Was he somewhere watching her now and taking pleasure in her suffering? Did Roger's death bring him more joy over her misery?

Those thoughts ran through her mind, but none of them felt *right* to her. She didn't think he'd been lying to her or playing with her, but she didn't know why he hadn't contacted her or answered her messages.

She didn't think something had happened to him. A part of her believed she would have *known* if he'd died. Had he somehow broken his phone too and wasn't getting her calls and messages?

She'd tried calling him a couple more times, but she'd only received his voice mail. Even if he had broken his phone and never received her texts or calls, he knew where she lived. At least he knew where she lived for now. She would be moving soon. She hadn't given her notice to Mrs. Mackey yet, but she would soon.

"Are you coming to the bar with us, Maggie?" Pablo inquired.

She lifted her head and blinked when she realized he'd

already driven out of the cemetery and was in Brookline. "Ah, yes, yes, of course."

The idea of sitting alone in her apartment again wasn't something she could face. She'd been so entrenched in her melancholy she hadn't taken the time to celebrate Roger's life, to laugh and drink and reminisce with others about him. She intended to do that today.

Straightening her shoulders, she scratched at her arms as she determined not to let memories of Aiden intrude. Today was about Roger. She'd wasted enough time grieving a relationship that never was.

Maggie spent the next two weeks packing her things and planning her trip. Every spare minute she had, she devoted to searching for her mother's real identity. She'd told Aiden the past was best left to the past, and at the time she'd meant it, but that had been then, and now she wanted answers to something. She had no answers for what happened to Aiden, but she had a small chance of finding answers for this.

Never before had she considered learning her mother's story. She'd assumed, if the police hadn't been able to uncover her family, she'd never be able to do it. And honestly, she hadn't wanted to know.

What if knowing made things worse? What if her mother had fled a situation almost as bad as what she'd stumbled into while in Boston? Learning her heritage had always seemed like a pointless waste of time, but it had become the best distraction she had from memories of Aiden.

Inevitably, he would creep in again, and a sense of loss so extreme would fill her that some days she had to force herself out of bed. Going to work didn't help. It was only a constant reminder Roger was also gone.

Before, she'd thought she would miss working on the ambulance, but she was glad to be done. Yesterday, her coworkers bought her a cake for her last shift, and they took her out last night to celebrate. Next week, the day after she ran the marathon, she would leave Boston. She had too many people counting on her not to participate in the race, but she couldn't wait for it to be over.

She slid the packing tape over her last box and set the roll on top of it. Glancing around her tiny apartment, she expected to feel a sense of loss, but she felt none. She had no more room in her for more losses.

Most of her things would go to the Salvation Army, and she'd already scheduled for them to come the Saturday before the marathon to pick up those things. She'd have to sleep on an air mattress for a couple of days afterward, but she was all right with that. She'd experienced worse sleeping accommodations in her life.

She could have held off packing everything so soon, but she crammed doing as many things as she could into her every waking minute. She was certain she would sink into a pit of despair if she stopped for even a second. At the very least, she'd scratch at herself like a flea-infested cat if something didn't occupy her hands.

The scratching thing was getting on her last frayed nerve, but she couldn't stop it. The second she wasn't doing something, she found herself unconsciously scratching.

That was why she had to keep moving now. She removed her coat from the hook by the door. With her packing done, she couldn't put it off anymore; she had to go.

∾

ONCE SHE DECIDED TO TRAVEL, Maggie cashed in her small retirement plan at work. She'd taken a hit on it, but she'd had no other choice. The two hundred dollars in her savings account wouldn't take her far out of Boston, especially since she hadn't owned a car.

With the retirement money, she'd bought herself a decent used car and still had eight thousand left for her trip. She planned to travel the country, see the redwoods, the deserts, the Pacific Ocean, and any other thing that caught her attention. It would be her, Blue, her plants—though she'd given many of them to her neighbor—and the open road.

It didn't make her feel as happy or free as she'd hoped, but she was looking forward to it.

Maggie pulled her car onto a dirt road. The springs and struts creaked as she eased it over the ruts and icy puddles. All around her, the jagged peaks of the White Mountains rose high into the air. The lonely, stark appearance of the snow caps matched her mood.

After half a mile, she spotted a small white trailer set on a large expanse of open land. Maggie pulled in behind a rusting pickup and parked the car. Her heart raced, and sweat coated her palms as she stared at the trailer.

Yesterday, she'd stumbled across a recent article from a New Hampshire newspaper. The report announced plans for a twenty-fifth high school reunion. With the article was a picture of the celebrating class on the first day of their senior year. Maggie glanced over the eager, teenage faces in the photo and froze when her gaze fell on one of the women.

If she hadn't known better, she would have sworn she was staring at a photo of herself. The names listed below the teens revealed she was instead looking at a picture of Mindy Shea. Maggie searched the internet for more about Mindy Shea, but there'd been nothing beyond that photo. So, she'd started

336 BRENDA K DAVIES

looking for Sheas in the newspaper's distribution area and came across a Marsha Shea. She'd uncovered this address for Marsha in Ossipee, New Hampshire.

Shea. It could be her mother's last name and possibly *hers.* She could have a last name beyond the Doe given to her at birth.

She probably should have called Marsha before showing up on her doorstep. It would have been the sensible, polite thing to do, but something more than her car had driven her here. If she'd called and been told to stay away, she didn't know if she would have been able to. She wanted some answers to *something* in her life, and Marsha may have them.

This may have been the first impulsive thing she'd ever done, and she didn't care if it blew up in her face. Nothing could be worse than these last couple of weeks. She'd played it safe for more years than she could count, afraid of getting her heart trampled, but playing it safe hadn't kept her protected from loss. Plus, she'd decided that playing it safe was boring.

"Strap on your helmet. It's time to start living, Maggie," she said aloud.

Shutting the car off, she opened the door and climbed out. The crispness of the air robbed her breath from her, and she pulled her coat closer as she walked toward the trailer. Most of the bushes and plants surrounding the sun porch didn't have leaves, but they were all neatly trimmed.

A fenced-in area blocked off a patch of land to the left of the trailer. Maggie suspected it became a garden in the spring. Behind the garden was a chicken coop, with a dozen or so chickens huddled together for warmth. Surrounded by woods, Maggie couldn't see any neighbors nearby.

Snow still covered the lawn, but the slate walkway was clear beneath her feet. Maggie pushed her anxiety aside as she climbed the steps to the sunporch and rang the bell beside the storm door. The inner door of the trailer opened, and a woman emerged. The woman took one step before freezing.

"Mindy," the woman breathed and staggered toward Maggie.

A stab of guilt pierced her. "No, my name is Magdalene. I'm Maggie."

The woman gawked at her before shaking her head. "You look... like... like... a ghost." The woman's eyes continued to survey Maggie as she pushed open the storm door. "Can I help you with something?"

"I... uh... I think I might be your granddaughter."

Tears spilled down Marsha's unlined cheeks. Maggie guessed her to be around sixty, yet she barely looked older than forty-five. Her auburn hair had streaks of white running through it, but it remained more red than gray. Unlike Maggie's eyes, and those of her mother, Marsha's were the color of the sky, but there were more similarities in their looks than there were differences.

It hit her that her mother might have also chosen to name her Magdalene to continue the M name tradition.

"Looking at you, honey, I think you may be too," Marsha said, and before Maggie knew what the woman intended, she found herself clasped against a pair of ample breasts as Marsha held her close and sobbed.

CHAPTER FORTY-FIVE

MAGGIE PERCHED on the edge of the green sofa as she took in the trailer. It was small, but warm and homey like her apartment had been before boxes filled it. Pictures lined the wall across from her. They revealed the progression of her mother's life from a baby, to a pigtailed six-year-old, to a beautiful teen dressed as Dorothy in the Wizard of Oz. Then, Maggie realized a lot of the photos were of her mother dressed as some character in one play or another over the years.

Her mother had been so beautiful and happy. So completely different than the woman who sat in the institute now.

Glass figurines of dragons, fairies, unicorns, and other mythical creatures filled the curio cabinet. A basket of yarn and a half-completed blanket lay on the seat of the green recliner across from her. It was what she'd always pictured a grandmother's home to be like—those few times she'd allowed herself to dream of such a thing as a child.

A small orange cat leapt into her lap and purred when Maggie ran her hand over its back. A dalmatian slept on the floor by the stove and, judging by the scent filling the home, chocolate chip cookies were baking in the oven.

Maggie didn't know what she'd expected to find here, but it hadn't been this. She'd assumed her mother had fled a horrendous home life and that was why no one had reported her missing. She didn't see any signs of misery here. Instead, she saw pictures of a loved girl whose mother stood hugging her in more than a couple of the photos.

"Here you go, hon."

Maggie blinked and tore her attention away from the pictures. She accepted the mug of steaming, vanilla-scented coffee Marsha handed her. "Thank you."

Marsha settled onto the recliner and set her coffee down on the table beside her. Folding her hands, Marsha twisted them in her lap as she leaned forward. "Your mother, is she... is she...?"

"She's alive," Maggie said.

"Oh, thank God," Marsha breathed and dropped her head into her hands.

Maggie couldn't give this woman any false hope. "She's not well."

Marsha lifted her head and folded her hands in her lap again. "Is she dying? Did she send you because she needs a kidney transplant or something? I'll do it. I'll give it if I can."

Maggie almost choked on her tears. Why had her mother left this place? This woman? Was Maggie missing something here? But she didn't sense anything cruel or manipulative about Marsha. All she sensed was a woman desperate to hear about the daughter she hadn't seen in twenty-five years.

"She didn't send me," Maggie said. "And what's wrong with her isn't so easily fixed."

Marsha took a deep breath. "Go ahead, honey. Tell me what happened."

Maggie focused on the cat as she told her grandmother about what happened to her mother. She hated being the one to reveal this to her, but she couldn't not tell her. Marsha had a right to know what became of her daughter. She kept the reality of vampires from her, but she did tell Marsha that Mindy believed a vampire raped her.

Tears streamed down Marsha's face when Maggie finished speaking. "My poor baby," Marsha murmured and pressed her hand to her heart. "My poor, beautiful baby."

Maggie didn't know what to say, so she continued to pet the cat as Marsha absorbed Maggie's words.

"And what of you, honey?" Marsha asked after a few minutes. "Who took care of you all these years?"

When the cat jumped from her lap, Maggie felt unreasonably abandoned by the animal. "I was a ward of the state. I mostly took care of myself."

Fresh tears streamed down Marsha's cheeks. "That's not right."

"That's life, and it wasn't bad. I learned a lot." Maggie lifted her mug to sip at her coffee. "My mother doesn't want to see me, I bring back too many bad memories, but maybe, she would like to see you."

"Probably not, but I would like to see her."

"Why didn't you report her missing?" Maggie blurted. Perhaps it was a scab better left alone, but she had to know something of what happened here. Something of why no one ever claimed her mother, or *her*.

Marsha lifted her mug before setting it down again. "I didn't report her missing because she chose to leave." More tears pooled in her eyes, and she dabbed them away with a handkerchief. "I was only seventeen when I had your mom. Her father left me a year after she was born; he died a year later in a motorcycle accident. I tried to do my best with Mindy, to give her everything I could, but it wasn't enough. Mindy always had big dreams."

Marsha waved a hand at the pictures of Mindy dressed in different costumes. "From the time she was a child, she was in every play the school and town put on that called for someone of her age. She was the most talented and beautiful in every production, and I don't say that because I'm her mom, *every*one said it. Mindy was going places, they all agreed. We'd see her star on the Walk of Fame one day.

"When she turned fifteen, the two of us started fighting more than before, just as many teenage daughters do with their mothers. She was ashamed of me, of this place, of the little we had, and she wanted more. During that time, she worked, and she saved every dime she earned.

"April fourth, the day she turned eighteen, we got into our last argument. She meant to quit school and go to New York *that* day. I pleaded with her to graduate, and when pleading didn't work, I threatened her, but what could I do? What good were my threats? She was eighteen. I couldn't stop her.

"So, she packed her things as I screamed at her, and then I cried. Her last words to me were, 'I hope never to see you again.' My last words to her were..." Marsha's voice broke on a sob. She wiped her eyes with her handkerchief again.

Back in control, Marsha continued. "My last words to her were, 'If you leave, don't come back.' I didn't mean it, but I couldn't think of anything else to say to stop her from going. It didn't work. Mindy never looked back at me as she walked out the door for New York City. I only knew she took the bus because I followed her to the station. It was the last time I saw her."

Maggie swallowed the lump in her throat as Marsha's sorrow beat against her. What had her mother been thinking to throw this away? But then, Maggie realized Mindy had been like so many other stubborn teens with big dreams. An act of violence shattered all those dreams before her mother ever had a chance to live them.

"The bus must have stopped in Boston," Maggie murmured. "The police found her on April fifth."

"The bus did stop in Boston," Marsha confirmed. "I checked the schedule. And Mindy would often talk about visiting Boston too. She dreamed about seeing all the cities, so she probably decided to get off the bus to look around."

It had been the worst decision of her mother's life, but if she hadn't left here and stopped in Boston, then Maggie wouldn't be sitting here now.

"When is your birthday, hon?" Marsha asked her.

"December nineteenth," Maggie whispered, her voice choked with emotion.

Marsha leaned forward and rested her hand on Maggie's knee. "We all make choices. Some of them we regret for the rest of our lives. Others lead us somewhere better, but they are all our choices and we must *own* them. What happened between your mother and me was *our* fault. What happened to Mindy in Boston was the fault of a despicable man, but none of it, *none* of it is your fault."

Tears of gratitude and relief pooled in Maggie's eyes. She'd half expected this woman to hate her too. What had happened to her mother wasn't Maggie's fault, but she was the result of the brutal act that shattered Mindy. Marsha had given birth to Mindy, she'd raised and loved her, but Maggie was a stranger.

"I hoped, *every* day, I hoped she would call me again and let me have the chance to tell her I hadn't meant it and she could come home anytime. I never changed my number, never moved, in case she should try to contact me again. I tried to find her when the web started becoming popular, but I'm not much for computers. I'm glad you are," she said as she patted

Maggie's knee. "I always hoped to turn on my TV and find her staring back at me on some show or movie, but I never saw her again."

"Because of her rape and mental status, my mother's face was kept off the news after she killed the nurse, but missing people posters were originally passed around to try locating her family. I'm amazed no one from town saw her."

Marsha waved her hand and sat back. "The world was a much smaller place twenty-five years ago."

"It was."

"Why don't you tell me about you? What do you do? Are you married? Do I have great-grandchildren?" she asked excitedly and Maggie smiled.

"No husband and no children. Maybe one day." She ignored the twinge in her heart as thoughts of Aiden once again intruded. She was here, with her grandmother, and she refused to let his memory ruin it. Still, she found herself scratching at her arm as she told Marsha about her life.

Later, Marsha broke out photo albums and treated Maggie to more pictures of Mindy as she progressed through her life. By the time Maggie left, she had plans to return. Instead of heading south right away, as she'd originally intended, she would come here to spend some time with Marsha and get to know her better. She already liked her grandmother more than she'd allowed herself to hope she would.

She had no mother, but she may end up with a grandma. Maybe her journey would end here, and she would stay. Backing out of the driveway, she headed down the mountains. Maybe she'd trade in city life for snow-capped mountains and rural life.

She'd either go insane or discover she loved it. Either way, she had no concrete plans for her future and nothing holding her back.

The tears sliding down her face surprised her. She hadn't realized she was crying until she felt one drip onto her hand. She'd been so determined to leave everything behind, but the minute she did, there would be no chance of seeing Aiden again.

You haven't seen him in two weeks anyway, you idiot. He's moving on, and so are you.

Maggie kept that thought firmly in my mind as the setting sun kissed the mountain peaks.

CHAPTER FORTY-SIX

EXHAUSTION CLUNG to her as she trudged up the steps to her apartment. Due to an accident on the highway, it had taken her almost four hours to get home. It was only nine, but it felt like she'd been up for three days straight, and her back felt like she'd lifted over fifty patients today.

Stepping off the final stair, she turned the corner and froze. Her heart lurched in excitement when she spotted the man leaning against the wall beside her door. She forgot all about the unhappiness of these past two weeks as she prepared to race forward and throw herself into his arms.

Then, the man lifted his head and a set of emerald instead of leaf-green eyes met hers. With a sinking heart, she absorbed more of the differences between him and Aiden. This man's nose was different than Aiden's, his hair longer and straight instead of curly. His sweater stretched over his broad chest and clung to his thick biceps and forearms, but Aiden was more thickly muscled.

No matter the differences between them, she couldn't deny she was staring at a member of Aiden's family. After what

Aiden had told her about his siblings, she suspected she knew which one it was too.

The question was, why was he here?

She hadn't told anyone about what had happened with her foray into the vampire world, and she never planned to. He couldn't be here because he'd heard rumors along the vampire grapevine that she'd talked and he'd come to silence her. Whatever had brought this vamp to her door, she suspected it wasn't good.

She touched the stake tucked into the inner pocket of her coat. Looking at him, she highly doubted she'd get the chance to use it against him, but she'd make him regret attacking her if he tried to do so.

Pulling her keys from her pocket, she threw her shoulders back. She stood in the presence of another powerful vampire, but she refused to be intimidated by him.

His emotionless gaze raked her from head to toe. "Maggie?" he inquired.

"Ethan, I assume," she said as she strode forward.

"Aiden told you about me?"

"He did." She slid the key into the deadbolt, half expecting him to grab her, but he didn't try to stop her. "What are you doing here?"

"Can we talk?"

"We are talking," she replied as she unlocked the deadbolt and pushed her door open.

"Privately."

She stepped into her apartment and stood in the doorway, keeping it partially closed to block his view inside. She didn't care if he saw her things, she needed a minute to calm her acute disappointment that Aiden hadn't been waiting for her. No matter how often she told herself she was done with him, a burst of excitement had slammed into her when she first saw Ethan, before she realized he wasn't the vamp she loved.

Shit!

She'd been trying to deny it, but she couldn't anymore. Maybe they hadn't known each other for long, but she loved Aiden, and he'd crushed her heart.

Aiden had walked out of her life, so why did she have to be reminded of him by being forced to deal with his brother? Was Ethan here because she'd been wrong and something *had* happened to Aiden? But why wouldn't Ethan come to tell her that sooner? Surely Abby or Vicky would have informed him she existed and Aiden believed her to be his mate. Wouldn't they?

Her skin itched all over, her blood felt like sludge pumping through her veins as she took a deep breath and focused on Ethan again.

"I won't take much of your time," he said, "and I won't hurt you."

"I'm not afraid of you," she retorted.

She threw the door open to prove her point and walked into her kitchen to put some space between them. Shrugging out of her coat, she placed it on the counter. "You might as well come in," she called as she started removing things from her pockets. She wasn't much for purses as she had a habit of forgetting them, so her pockets were always stuffed.

Stepping inside, Ethan closed the door behind him. The click of it settling into place held an oddly final note. She didn't think he'd attack her, but she was terrified to find out why he'd come.

His gaze ran over the boxes stacked neatly in her living room before coming back to her. "You're moving?"

"Nope, I like keeping my things in boxes. Cuts back on dusting, and it's more feng shui that way."

He lifted a black eyebrow at her sarcasm. She removed her stake, placed it on the counter, and rested her hand on top of it. "Is that for me?" he inquired.

"Not unless you want it to be, but you don't go through what I've gone through without becoming more prepared for the things that go bump in the night. I have some pepper spray too. Though, I'm not sure how well it will work on you supernatural folk."

"I imagine it would burn like a bitch. I'd prefer not to find out. Are you moving because of what happened to you with the Savages? Do you feel unsafe here?"

"No."

"Then why are you going?"

"I'm sorry, but what business is that of yours?"

Annoyance flashed through his eyes. "Where do you plan to go? Are you moving in with someone else?"

"Not your concern. I must say, as delightful as this impromptu visit is, could you tell me what *you're* doing here so it can end?"

Ethan sighed and stepped toward her. "I'm here about Aiden."

There went her heart getting all bent out of shape again as his name brought forth memories of their brief time together and the way he'd held her. Unwilling to let Ethan see the sadness in her eyes, she looked away. No matter what, she wouldn't let him go back to Aiden and tell him she missed him.

"What about Aiden?" she demanded and hoped Ethan wouldn't realize her voice had changed.

"I know, you made your choice to move on from him and lead your life—"

Maggie's gaze shot back to him. "What are you talking about?"

"When you didn't go to the hotel, Aiden realized you'd made your choice."

"First of all, I *did* go to the hotel. I arrived later than planned, but I went. Second, I tried calling Aiden to explain why I was late, and I left him messages. I never heard back from him. I tried calling him again after, but he never responded."

Something in Ethan's demeanor changed, he went from looking at her like she was about to kick his nuts into his throat, to almost hopeful. He took a quick step toward her before stopping. "He tried to call you."

"He had the number for a burner phone I was using at the time. The day we were supposed to meet, I had an accident with it, and it broke. I called from a friend's phone and left him a message explaining that. I've texted him from my new phone and nada. Since I'm not one for stalking, I got the hint real quick."

"I don't have his number for that phone. I can't check the messages."

"What does it matter if you could check his messages or not? Aiden is perfectly capable of doing that himself. I've *seen* him do it."

"Aiden also broke his phone that day, and he... well, he hasn't exactly been himself lately."

"What does that mean?"

"Why were you late? Why didn't you meet him on time?"

Maggie slapped her hand on the counter. "What is this, the Spanish Inquisition? What does it matter? Something happened that day..." Her voice trailed off as she recalled the horrible phone call from Pablo. Fresh grief for Roger washed through her. She refused to cry in front of Ethan. Unable to continue speaking, she clamped her mouth shut and suppressed her tears until she felt more composed.

"I was late because I was late," she said more calmly. "It's none of your concern *why*. If Aiden couldn't wait for me or contact me to ask *why* I was late, then he can fuck off, and so can you! Now, I've had a long day, and until I saw you, it was a pleasant one, so if you don't mind—"

"Who was the man you were with?"

"Excuse me?" she blurted. "*What* man?"

"The man who drove you here the day you were supposed to meet Aiden. The man you embraced when he brought you here."

Maggie froze as fury burned away her sorrow. "Have you been spying on me?"

"Aiden came here that day; he saw you with a man."

"Did he now?" she murmured, her voice deceptively calm considering she wanted to stab something. "Let me guess; he jumped to conclusions instead of talking to *me* about it."

"He hasn't exactly been in the mood to talk."

"What a coincidence, neither am I. It's time for you to leave."

"If he'd approached you that day, he would have killed the man."

"I'm allowed to have friends," Maggie hissed from between her teeth.

"So the man was only a friend?"

"It's none of your goddamn business who he is!"

"But it is."

"And why is that?"

"Because my brother's life is on the line."

Her antagonism deflated faster than a popped balloon. "Aiden's life?" she breathed.

"Yes."

"Why? What are you talking about?"

"When you didn't make it to the hotel on time, and Aiden saw you with that man, he assumed you made your choice. He believes that man is who you want to be with and he... well, he snapped. If Brian, Declan, and Killean hadn't been there to take him down, there's no telling what he might have done."

Hundreds of imaginary spiders crept over her skin as a hollow pit opened in her belly. "Pablo is my boss, and he's my friend. Aiden should have come to me himself. I would have explained what happened."

"He couldn't come to you, not then, and not now."

Those spiders were now tap dancing along her spine. "What's happened to him?"

"Vicky revealed to me that Aiden never told you a vampire can't live without their mate, that they either kill themselves or go insane."

"They what?" she breathed, suddenly needing to sit but unable to find the strength to cross over to the table and pull out a chair.

Ethan walked forward to rest his hands on the counter as he studied her with a look that bordered on pleading. "A vampire without their mate is a broken shell. They can't survive without the other."

"I see," she murmured.

"Aiden wanted you to make your decision about joining him without the additional pressure of that knowledge. However, *I* am telling you because I'm trying to save my brother, if it isn't too late, and if you're willing to help him."

"Tell me what is going on."

"When a vampire encounters their mate, they feel instantly drawn to them. They can maintain control better if the relationship doesn't progress too far into the bonding, but from what I understand, your relationship progressed pretty far."

Maggie held his gaze as he revealed his knowledge of intimate details about *her* life. "He said I had to become a vampire to complete the bond."

"True, but the sharing of blood and sex escalates a vampire's need to forge the bond."

"Another thing he didn't tell me."

"He kept it from you because he had your best interests at heart. He was putting your needs ahead of his."

"So what do you want from me? Why are you here?"

"Aiden would kill me if he knew I was here, and I'm not just saying that, but I refuse to let him go without a fight."

"Go where?" she croaked.

"It's either death or insanity, he might even become a Savage without you. Right now, he's too far gone to care what happens to him, but I know that before this happened, he would have chosen death over becoming a Savage."

"Too far gone?" she croaked.

"Yes, but I'm hoping you can save him."

Ethan's gaze fell on her arm when she absently scratched at it. Her itching pulled the sleeve of her baggy sweater back to reveal the bandages beneath. They were still mostly white, but some of the wrappings were stained pink with her blood. At least, she'd stopped tearing at her hands as badly, but only because she couldn't keep them hidden like she could her arms.

Ethan gripped her wrist tenderly. "May I?" he asked and gestured at her arm.

"Yeah, whatever."

He pulled her sleeve up to inspect her arm before turning his attention to her other arm. More, pink-stained bandages covered that arm. She saw a flicker of concern cross his face before he pulled her sleeve gently into place and squeezed her hand.

"I don't know why, but I can't stop," she admitted.

"Did this start when you separated from Aiden?"

"The night he left to kill Carha I felt itchy, but it's becoming worse with every passing day."

"Humans can love us," he said kindly. "Many of them feel an instantaneous attraction too. My mother did to my father, my wife did to me, but it's not the same as what a vampire feels for their mate. Vicky and Abby informed me you have some vampire DNA in you."

She wasn't surprised they'd talked about her. She'd seen how close the siblings were with each other. "I do."

"You feel the bond to Aiden too. Not as intensely as a full vampire would, but it's there, and not having Aiden near has distressed you."

"My skin feels like I'm a twenty-four-year-old shoved into my ten-year-old sized body."

Ethan squeezed her wrist before releasing her. "It's worse for Aiden."

"Is he one of those *things*?" The idea of Aiden being anything like those monsters who had attacked them and killed Walt and Glenn made her skin itch far more than it ever had before. "Is that why you're here?"

"I'm not sure what he is now, but he's more like one of them now than he is one of us."

Maggie gulped. She'd seen Aiden lose control, seen him pulverize other vampires, but this sounded so much worse. *No, not my Aiden. I won't allow it.*

"Where is he? Will you take me to him?"

Ethan smiled and rested his hand on hers. "Yes."

CHAPTER FORTY-SEVEN

MAGGIE LEANED back to survey the squat, concrete building. A handful of windows faced her. Behind one of the glass planes, a light revealed the bars covering the window. Blue, concrete walls were visible beyond the bars. When Ethan pressed a button, a buzzer sounded on the other side. A clammy sweat coated her body as she gazed at the metal door before her with a sinking suspicion.

Maggie had no idea where they were as Ethan blindfolded her as soon as they'd left her apartment and settled into his car. The lessening of blowing horns and passing cars as he drove alerted her when they left the city, but they'd traveled for at least an hour before arriving here, where he'd removed her blindfold.

A high, barbed wire fence surrounded the property; the red lights on top of it indicated it was electrified. Beyond the fencing, she saw only trees. There were no other buildings and no distant lights.

She focused her attention on the simple, concrete building again. *It can't be.*

The door suddenly pushed open, and Vicky's head popped out. Like a fish flopping on dry land, her mouth opened and closed when she spotted Maggie. Then she turned her attention to Ethan before glaring at Maggie.

"What did you do, Ethan?" Vicky demanded.

"What is this place?" Maggie ignored Vicky to inquire.

"An old, county prison. It closed about fifteen years ago. Ronan recently purchased it to use as a prison for any Savages they could catch and interrogate," Ethan replied, apparently more than willing to ignore Vicky's continued, alternating glares too. "He had it modified to hold vampires, added security measures should one break out, and established a place he could also imprison purebreds, should it become necessary."

Maggie's eyes flew back to him. "This is a prison for vampires?"

"Yes."

"And Aiden is *here*?"

"Yes."

She gritted her teeth as she glanced between the siblings. "You allowed him to be *locked* up?"

"We had no choice," Ethan murmured.

"No thanks to you," Vicky retorted, and Maggie shot her a fierce look.

"Easy, Vicky," Ethan replied.

"Aiden wouldn't be here if she truly cared, and where's her new boyfriend?"

"*Her* is standing right here!" Maggie snapped. "And he's barefoot and cooking dinner in my kitchen, do you have a problem with that?"

Ethan shot his hand out to hold his sister back when Vicky stepped toward her. "Enough!" he barked. "This was all a big misunderstanding."

"There was no misunderstanding," Maggie snorted. "Your

brother assumed something he shouldn't have, and instead of talking to me about it, he jumped to the wrong conclusions." Her eyes slid back to Vicky. "It seems to be a shitty family trait."

Vicky glared at her again, but when Vicky's eyes swung back to Ethan, Maggie saw a flash of guilt in them. "A misunderstanding?" Vicky asked.

"Yes," Ethan replied. "I'm taking her to see him."

"He's going to lose his mind when he realizes you did exactly what he didn't want us to do."

"Or maybe he'll regain his mind," Ethan replied.

"Oh, I hope so," Vicky breathed.

Ethan nudged Vicky aside, and with a hand on the small of Maggie's back, he led her inside the old prison. Maggie glowered at Vicky as she walked past, but Vicky didn't return the look. Instead, she tugged at the ends of her disheveled hair.

"Is it really a misunderstanding?" Vicky asked her with a round-eyed stare that would have made Puss in Boots jealous.

Maggie's anger melted. She'd liked Vicky before, and she didn't blame Vicky for being protective of her brother. "It seems so," Maggie murmured.

Vicky wiped the tears from her eyes and pushed open a gated door to reveal the entranceway of the prison. Maggie entered and stopped next to the glassed-in reception desk on her left. No one sat in the square room. When she peeked inside, she saw a computer and numerous video monitors. The screens displayed changing video feed from the land surrounding the prison. She also saw herself, Vicky, and Ethan and looked up to find a camera pointed directly at her.

Vicky pressed a button and pushed open another solid, thick steel door when a buzzer sounded. The hair on Maggie's nape rose when they stepped inside, and the door clanged shut behind them. Overhead, caged lights protected the single bulb within those cages. The lights shone down on the dingy, gray tile floor.

Her sneaker caught and squeaked on one of the tiles as they made their way toward the row of concrete walls making up the cells. Arms hung out of the steel bars on the front of one of the cells; the hands clasped together as if in boredom. She almost ran toward the arms before realizing those fingers didn't belong to Aiden.

The man in the cell sniffed the air as they approached him. "Fresh meat," he purred in a voice distorted by his fangs.

When it sank in she was locked in a prison with vampires, she almost turned and bolted. *I can't run. Aiden is here somewhere, and I will at least talk to him.*

"It's okay," Ethan murmured when her step faltered. "He can't get out."

The prisoner's red eyes surveyed her when they walked by him. His lips pulled back in a leering grin. "Ripe for the fucking, fresh meat," the Savage purred.

Maggie didn't give him the satisfaction of responding in any way, and neither did the others as they left the prisoner behind. Maggie searched for Aiden, but he wasn't in any of the remaining, empty cells. Turning a corner, Vicky stopped before another solid, steel door.

"I was just down there talking with Aiden. Of course, I don't look in the window when I'm down there," Vicky said.

What an odd thing to say. Before Maggie could question her on it though, Vicky continued speaking.

"He doesn't..." Vicky's voice hitched. "He doesn't say much, but I think he listens."

Those words caused the hair on Maggie's nape to rise. She *thinks* he listens.

Vicky slid a key into the lock, and it clicked open. The

hinges squeaked as she pushed the door inward before turning to Maggie. "Don't be afraid."

"I'm not," Maggie replied.

She had to force herself not to wipe her palms on her jeans as she gazed down the long corridor ahead of her. When she felt sweat spreading beneath her arm pits, she shrugged out of her coat and held it out to Vicky.

"Will you hold this for me?" she asked.

"Of course," Vicky said and took it from her.

"Watch out, there might be stakes in it," Ethan cautioned.

Vicky's mouth pursed and she moved the coat away from her to hold it like it was a live grenade.

"Only one, and it's in the inner pocket," Maggie said before turning her attention back to the gloomy corridor. The only light illuminating the hall came from behind her, but it was enough to reveal that here, instead of concrete walls and bars, there were only what she could describe as steel cages.

What had happened to Aiden since she'd last seen him? What would she find down there? What if Ethan was wrong and she couldn't save him?

That was the most terrifying thought she'd ever had.

Ethan reached inside and flipped a switch. A row of dim, caged bulbs dangling over the middle of the corridor lit up the concrete floor and cages. Two of the bulbs flickered annoyingly.

"He's locked up and restrained. The cell is built specifically for purebreds, so he won't be able to hurt you," Ethan said.

"He would never! Aiden wouldn't..." The expressions on Ethan and Vicky's faces caused the rest of Maggie's protests to fade away.

"Come," Ethan prodded. "Vicky, I think you'd better stay here. He's going to be enraged, and it's better if he only focuses that on one of us. You should probably get the others too, in case something goes wrong."

"Okay. Good luck," she said to Maggie.

Unable to reply, Maggie gave a brisk nod and followed Ethan into the hall. Vicky didn't close the door behind them. When Maggie glanced back, she saw Vicky was gone. Focusing forward again, she tried not to dwell on the ominous, oppressive air encompassing this hall as she put one foot in front of the other.

Their steps weren't loud, and she knew it wasn't true, but she felt like their feet were louder than gunshots on the concrete. The bulbs cast their shadows over the steel doors in eerie patterns that danced and swayed and had her half expecting the laughter of trolls to sound from the bowels of this place. The potent scent of mildew filled the corridor, and with the dampness in the air, she guessed they were somewhere near water, most likely the ocean.

She couldn't help but feel as if this might be the path to hell. And Aiden was trapped within it.

The small, square windows in the doors they passed revealed the empty cells beyond. Needing a moment to steady herself, Maggie feigned curiosity as she stopped to peer into one of those windows. A simple cot was set against the right wall. A sink, toilet, and a shower head were the only other things in the cell.

"Ronan had the cells updated with the shower," Ethan said from behind her.

"How thoughtful," she muttered and stepped away from the door.

The further they walked down the hall, the more the scent of sweat and cloves mingled with the mildew. *Aiden.* The aroma of him and the prospect of seeing him strengthened her.

The door opening drew Aiden's attention toward the open window of his cell. His chains rattled as he emerged from the back corner. When the chains shackling his wrists and ankles pulled taut, he leaned forward until his face came within an inch of the window.

He didn't know how much time he'd spent trying to rip free of his manacles, but through the fog of insanity coating his mind, he recalled breaking his wrists and ankles so often that he'd lost count. Still, the bonds didn't give and he'd been unable to slip free of them.

His lips skimmed back when he heard footsteps approaching. His fangs snapped as his blood boiled. *Kill. Destroy. Die! Die! Die!* The mantra had looped through his head for days, weeks, months. He had no idea how long he'd been here, but he knew *why* he was here.

Insanity slithered through his brain like an insidious, parasitic worm. It urged him to do things he would never have done before, to kill himself, or to burn the world. The few moments of clarity he received were so full of anguish that he shied away from them to retreat into his haze of madness once more. Through it all, he remembered Maggie with her arms around another.

His Maggie. No, not his, not anymore. She'd chosen another.

Die! Die! Die! Often, he plotted to kill his jailers and break free of here. At other times, he tried to will himself into the peaceful oblivion of eternal sleep. Breaking free or dying had proven impossible, so far. He would succeed in one or the other soon.

Craning his head, he listened to the footfalls coming toward him. Two of his captors were approaching. It didn't matter how many there were; he'd murder them all if that was what it took to escape this place.

Today. He would break out today, and his destruction of everything he could get his hands on would start with those who had imprisoned him. At least then, they would be able to

364 BRENDA K DAVIES

feel a fraction of the pain ravaging him. Saliva filled his mouth as he contemplated sinking his fangs into numerous throats and draining his victims dry. They'd given him blood in here, but he needed to hear shrieks of pain. Those screams would ease him; they had to.

Every day, every second of every minute, his cravings for blood and death consumed him. Nothing kept them at bay anymore. Sometimes, he'd surface enough to question if he were losing his mind or becoming a Savage. Then, he'd realize it didn't matter; the madness would turn him Savage.

The one thing he wouldn't do when he was free of here was go near Maggie; he couldn't. More animal than man now, he still retained enough of a thread to his old self to know he could never harm her, though she had been the one to destroy him.

Some of his jailers were his siblings. Maybe if they hadn't already turned on him, he wouldn't go after them, but they'd betrayed him by locking him within this pit. He would stay away from the rest of his family too. They were the past, and he had a much different future.

Stepping away from the window, the chains shackling his wrists and ankles rattled as he paced his cell. He craned his head to see who they would send to him now with one of those disgusting blood bags. He needed a vein, a *real* one.

Then, the smell hit him. Sweet as butterscotch and far more enticing than any blood bag, it floated on the air to ensnare him. *Maggie!*

Aiden's fangs burst free, he lunged at the door, but the shackles yanked him back. The chains rattled but held firm when he jerked against them, and an overwhelming hunger seared his veins. *She* was the only thing that would finally ease his hunger.

Have to have her!

He stopped pulling at his chains as horror descended to

shove aside the madness enshrouding him. *His* Magdalene was here, and he was... he was... a monster.

Aiden recoiled from the door and slid into the shadows at the back of his cell. She couldn't see him like this!

It wasn't that he was filthy, he'd done nothing but plot death and ride the waves of lunacy since coming here, but he'd washed often. Animals didn't tolerate the stench of their filth. He ran a hand over his face. He may have showered often, but he hadn't shaved. A beard covered his face now, probably making him appear wilder than he was. His eyes were red; he didn't need a mirror to know that, he could feel it. He'd lost all control of the demon part of him when he lost her.

She'd dealt with enough insanity with her mother; she couldn't see it in him too. She deserved better than this, better than him. He'd let her go to live her life with another man; why had she come here?

A fresh stab of agony pierced his heart as he recalled seeing her embracing another man. He couldn't hate her for her decision. He wanted only happiness for her, no matter whose arms she found it in. Bringing her here, making her feel guilty, or intimidating her was not what he wanted for her. He'd made that clear at some point. He couldn't recall when he'd told his imprisoners not to get involved, but he was certain he *had*.

One of his jailers must have brought her here, either to try to help him or to torment him more than they already did by keeping him locked away.

"Get her out of here," Aiden said before they reached his door.

"Aiden, listen—"

"Get her out of here, *now!*" he bellowed, cutting off Ethan's words. He'd tear his brother's heart out for bringing her here.

Ethan turned as if to stop her, but Maggie stepped into view of the window. Even in the shadows surrounding her,

Aiden could see the unusual shade of her eyes and the loveliness of her features. His fangs pierced his lips when he bit back a choked sound. He stretched a hand toward her before jerking it back to his side.

"Get her out of here," he hissed again.

Maggie went to grab the window, but Ethan seized her hands before she could. "Don't touch her!" Aiden shouted, and Ethan released her.

"Aiden," Maggie said. Ethan held out an arm to keep her from coming any closer. "Where are you?"

Maggie searched the shadows at the back, left-hand corner of the cell. It was where his voice had come from, but she couldn't see him.

"Aiden?" she croaked. "Please let me see you."

"Get her out of here, Ethan," Aiden commanded.

"Let her speak," Ethan replied.

"I don't want her here! Not like this."

Ethan hesitated before turning toward her. "Maybe this was a mistake."

"No!" Maggie protested. "No. I'm not leaving until I see you, Aiden. Not until we get a chance to talk."

"You want to see me?" Aiden snarled.

The tone of his voice caused those spiders to start dancing across her skin again, but she lifted her chin and stepped closer. "Yes. You have things wrong. I—"

Maggie broke off from telling him she'd gone to meet him at the hotel when he partially emerged from the shadows. She flinched away from what the light revealed before she could stop herself. But even after everything she'd seen with the Savages, she'd never seen anything half as frightening as Aiden.

No hint of green remained in the ruby eyes blazing at her. Blood trickled from his lower lip and stuck in the hairs of the black beard covering half his face. Thick, steel cuffs encircled his wrists and ankles; they jingled when he moved.

Satan himself would have gotten out of Aiden's way if he saw him on the street.

"Do I scare you, Magdalene?" he purred in a taunting tone she didn't recognize.

There was no point in lying to him; he knew the truth. "Yes."

Aiden stopped a few feet away from the door. Despite the dampness of the cool air, he wore no clothes. She suddenly understood why Vicky said she didn't look in the window when she spoke with him.

Maggie bit back a cry of despair and fury when she saw the blood trickling from beneath the cuffs on his wrists and ankles. He'd fought against his bonds so much that he'd torn his skin worse than she'd shredded hers.

His struggles and pain had been for nothing. There would be no breaking the chains binding him. The links of the chains were easily larger than both her wrists put together and led inside the wall where she assumed they were bolted. Those chains were attached to the bands on his ankles and wrists and were at least three inches thick and five inches wide.

"Why did you do this to him?" she demanded and spun on Ethan.

Sorrow radiated from his eyes as he bowed his head. "We had no other choice."

Maggie wanted to punch him, but instead, she focused on Aiden again. "Aiden," she breathed as tears pricked her eyes.

For a fraction of a second, she swore she saw a flash of green in his eyes. Then, the red became brighter, and he returned to the shadows.

"You should be scared," he growled.

"No, I shouldn't," she argued. "You won't hurt me."

"Get her out of here, Ethan, and when I get out of this cell, I will *kill* you for bringing her here. I set her free. Let her go."

"No, Aiden, wait!" Maggie protested. She tried to grasp the window again, but Ethan pushed her hands down once more.

"Don't get any closer to him," Ethan cautioned at the same time Aiden shouted, "Don't touch her!"

Maggie stomped her foot as she gazed back and forth between the infuriating men. "I came here to talk to him, and that's what I'm going to do!" she declared.

She jerked her hands away from Ethan. Before she could touch the window, Ethan grasped her shoulder and pulled her back. "Stop it!" Maggie protested.

"GET YOUR FUCKING HANDS OFF HER!" Aiden roared so loudly the walls around them shook.

Maggie yanked her shoulder away from Ethan at the same time Aiden rushed at them with the force of a Mac truck. Before he could reach the door, the chains reached their end and yanked him back. Startled by the sudden rush, Maggie staggered away from the door before she could stop herself.

Aiden lunged against the chains again, his fangs snapping as his thickly corded muscles strained against his bonds. Veins bulged from his flesh; sweat beaded his forehead and shoulders as he hunched forward to pull more forcefully on the chains.

Maggie's eyes widened when Aiden's skin took on a reddish-black hue. She recalled thinking she'd seen the same thing when they'd been in the ambulance. Then, she'd believed she'd imagined it, but she couldn't deny the color seeping steadily across his flesh.

Metal screeched forebodingly.

Aiden lunged again, his muscles bulging as Ethan gripped her shoulder again and pulled her back a step. The second Ethan's hand touched her, Aiden howled.

"What's happening to him?" Maggie breathed. "Why is his skin turning that color?"

"That's what happens when a purebred is enraged," Ethan replied. "And there is almost no stopping them once it does. We have to go."

"No! I came to help him!"

"In this state, he may kill you, and then there will be *no* helping him!" Resting his hand on the small of her back, Ethan nudged her toward the door, but she stood her ground.

"Don't touch her!" Aiden bellowed.

Metal broke with a pop. One of the chains on Aiden's wrists wrenched free of the wall. Maggie threw up her hands and staggered away from the door when the broken end of the chain smashed against it.

"Shit!" Ethan hissed.

Lowering her hands, Maggie gawked at Aiden as he tore the cuff from his wrist before turning to grip the remaining chain binding his wrist to the wall with both hands. The color of his skin deepened as he yanked it from the wall. Then, he bent to tear off one of the cuffs around his ankles.

"Go!" Ethan shouted and pushed her toward the door at the end of the hall.

Despite that she'd come here to help him, fear propelled her toward the door. When she looked back to find Aiden's hands wrapping around the edges of the window, her step faltered. She watched in disbelief as the steel door bowed from Aiden pulling it toward him.

CHAPTER FORTY-EIGHT

"Vicky, get the others!" Ethan shouted as he hurried her faster down the hall.

Maggie's heart beat so fast she half feared it would explode. Her fight-or-flight instinct screamed *flight* at the top of its lungs, yet she knew she couldn't leave Aiden. Not like this.

She loved him, and she wouldn't give him up without a fight. The bulbs overhead danced and swayed from the vibrations rattling the walls as Aiden tore his cell apart. Ahead of them, Vicky and Brian appeared in the doorway. A black-haired man she didn't recognize and Saxon stood behind them.

"What the...?"

The black-haired man's question trailed off as his gaze went toward Aiden's cell. She couldn't hear her footfalls or breaths over the wrenching sound of twisting metal. Something crashed behind them, and the floor lurched beneath her feet.

Ethan grabbed her elbow and swung her up to clasp her against his chest. He started running. Over his shoulder, Maggie saw the ruined door of Aiden's cell falling into the middle of the hall. The door of the cell across from Aiden's was now bent inward, and she assumed Aiden had thrown his door into the other one.

Maggie gasped when Aiden stepped out of his cage and into the hall with his hands fisted, his legs braced apart, and his red eyes latched onto her. There was no denying the demon DNA coursing through him as, from head to toe, his skin pulsed with that reddish-black color and the veins in his arms bulged. She wouldn't be at all surprised if a set of horns sprouted from his head.

He'd kill them all, she knew, but she might be able to stop this. If Aiden was this crazed because Ethan had touched her, it meant he still cared for her, still wanted her even if he'd told Ethan to take her out of here. She might be able to reach him, somehow.

The others all stepped out of the way when Ethan carried her through the door and set her down. Maggie took two steps forward and spun back. Ethan was pulling the door closed when she ducked under his arm and ran back into the corridor with Aiden.

"Stefan, stop her!" Vicky yelled.

She realized that Stefan must be the black-haired man she didn't know, and she recalled Aiden saying he had a brother-in-law named Stefan.

A hand skimmed her back, seeking to pull her from the hall.

No! Maggie screamed inwardly. She threw herself forward, knowing she might be diving toward her death, but it was too late to stop her plunge.

Before the hand could get a firm hold on her and yank her back, another hand swung out of the shadows and knocked the first one away. Arms encircled her and spun her away. Aiden's scent filled her nose when she found herself clasped against his broad chest.

Behind her, the slamming of the door echoed in her ears and reverberated down the hall. For a minute, Maggie didn't breathe, and she couldn't bring herself to open her eyes as she remained unmoving in his arms.

Then she was set down so abruptly that she staggered to the side. She came up against a forearm as a wall of muscle pinned her into a cage made of flesh and bone. The cool metal door pressed against her back.

Chest heaving, Maggie tilted her head up to take in the ruby eyes blazing down at her. If she hadn't seen him in his cell, she never would have recognized Aiden now.

He'd planted his hands on either side of her head, keeping the door closed as the others banged and shoved against it. The door opened a couple of inches, pushing her forward a step before Aiden rammed it closed again. He didn't look at the door as his attention remained riveted on her.

Blood trickled down his forearms from the abrasions the cuffs had created on his wrists. It slid past her eyes and dripped onto the floor. Still, he stared unblinkingly at her. Maggie gulped, but she didn't dare move. Movement might set off his predatory instincts; if she tried to run, he would take her down.

"Maggie!" Vicky shouted. "Maggie, are you okay?"

Aiden's arms vibrated with tension as his gaze fell to her mouth before drifting to her neck. The red of his eyes intensified.

"Maggie!" Ethan shouted.

"I'm... I'm fine!" she called back as Aiden's eyes returned to hers. "Leave us be!"

Maggie bit her lip as she waited for them to continue trying to get in, but she heard nothing, and no one shoved on the door. Aiden continued to stare at her until Maggie wondered if he didn't recognize her. Then, he removed one arm from the door to stroke her cheek with his knuckles.

"Maggie," he breathed.

"Yes, it's... it's me."

"Why did you come here?" he demanded in a voice she barely recognized.

"For you."

Before he could reply, she slid her hand around the back of his head and rose onto her toes. She might be about to kiss a live wire, might be about to pay the price for doing something so stupid, but she sensed he needed contact with her if she were going to get through to him.

When she ran her tongue over his mouth, she licked away the trickles of blood beading his lower lip. He remained unyielding against her as she tasted him. The longer he remained unmoving, the more apprehensive she became that she'd come too late, he was too far gone, and he would kill her. However, while she lived, she wouldn't give up on him.

"I came for you," she whispered against his mouth.

She felt it when something within him broke and he lost control. Wrapping his arm around her waist, he lifted her against his chest. Maggie draped her arms over his shoulders as he gripped her hair and pulled her head back to deepen her kiss.

His beard abraded her skin, and she shoved her apprehension aside when his fangs pricked her bottom lip. She didn't try to fight him. He needed her, and she trusted him to keep her safe. When his fangs pricked her lip again, and he consumed more of her blood, he shuddered against her.

"Maggie," he breathed.

A part of him believed he'd hallucinated her outside his cell, but as the scent of her engulfed him and the heat of her body warmed his, he became increasingly convinced she was real. Then, her blood hit his tongue, and some of his madness ebbed. Only Maggie could taste so good.

"I came for you." Her words replayed in his mind as her fingers dug into his shoulders and she ground against his swelling cock. The rare times he'd slept since coming here, dreams of her had haunted him, and he'd woken with an aching need his hand failed to satisfy. Now that need tripled until his dick throbbed painfully.

He broke the kiss and lifted his head to look down at her. Heavy lidded, her eyes were dazed with passion, her mouth swollen from his kiss and stained a deeper red from her blood and his. He'd never seen anything as beautiful or amazing as her.

Aiden's eye flashed from red to green and back again as he struggled to regain complete control. She cupped his cheeks in her hands and drew him down for another kiss. His hands twisted in her sweater, and material shredded as he ripped the front of it open from her neck to her belly button.

Surprise crossed his face, and he pulled his hands away from her as he stepped back. Maggie held onto him. She was certain she could bring him back from the edge, but if she let go of him now and allowed him to retreat, she feared she'd lose him forever.

And she also held on for herself too. For the first time in weeks, she didn't feel like shredding her skin off, she felt at ease, and she almost sobbed with the joy of it.

"No," she said when he dropped his hands to her waist and started to pull her away from him.

"Can't. Too out of control," he grated.

She sensed his mounting confusion. "No, you're not." She ran her lips over his cheek and down to his neck. "I trust you."

When her hands slid over his shoulder blades, his muscles flexed beneath her touch, and his hands tightened on her waist. He could pull her off him, but he didn't. Her fingertips traced his shoulders before she ran them down his chest to his waist.

"I trust you," she murmured as she ran her tongue over his ear and slid her hand down between their bodies to grip his erection.

His cock was stiff and hot in her hand, yet soft against her palm. She ran a finger over the thick vein on the side of it before running her thumb over his silken head to spread the bead of precum forming there. The familiar feel of him created a pleasant ache between her thighs and she grew increasingly wet for him.

His head fell to her shoulder; he inhaled a ragged breath as he gazed at her belly. He'd torn the front of her sweater open, but she still wore her bra, and the sleeves remained on her arms. Unable to resist touching her, he glided his knuckles over her stomach before flattening his hand on her hip. His fangs scraped her neck, over her vein, but he didn't sink them into her.

"I need you too, so badly," she breathed.

He lifted her off him so fast she didn't register the movement until she was on her feet. Her breath caught, but she didn't have time to process what was going on before he was undoing her jeans and pushing them down her legs. Maggie kicked off her sneakers as he tugged her jeans off and tossed them aside.

His eyes were still a volatile shade of red when they met hers again, but the fury had ebbed from him. There would be no going back after this, no changing her mind, no keeping her mortality. She'd known that when she walked out of her apartment with Ethan.

She started to pull off the remains of her ruined sweater, but he seized her hips and lifted her again.

Maggie slid her legs around his waist and went to rest her hands on his shoulders. Before she could touch him, he snatched her wrists and pinned them against the wall over her

head. When she jerked against his hold, his hand only tightened on her.

She recalled him saying he hadn't allowed the women he'd
had sex with to touch him. Was he too far gone to accept her
touch now? Would he treat her the same way as all those
women before her? Could they ever repair the damage wrought
between them?

Her throat clogged at the possibility even as he sank his
shaft inside her. Maggie's head fell back as the exquisite sensation of him filling her again took control and pushed her
worries away. She'd almost forgotten how *right* it felt when they
joined together.

She would give anything to touch him, but he kept her
restrained as he pulled his hips back before impaling her again.
Aiden's forehead fell to her chest as his body took control of
hers. His fangs grazed the swell of her breast, above her bra.

The ravenous fire licking over his veins scorched his body.
Maggie could put those flames out, yet still, he hesitated to
drink from her. He'd been denied her too long, and she was *his*
mate. She was also his to protect, and right now, he was the
biggest threat to her. He was barely maintaining his control as
he listened to the blood racing through her veins.

"It's okay, Aiden," she whispered when his fangs scored her
skin again. Power emanated from him, the reddish-black hue of
his skin lessened but remained present. While that color
stayed, she sensed he wouldn't be in complete control. "Take
my blood."

He switched her wrists into one hand. His other hand fell
to her waist and snaked around it to drive her down onto his
shaft, taking her harder than he ever had before. The feel of
his body against her, the heat of him, the friction of his body
inside of hers pushed her closer and closer to the brink. When
his next thrust rubbed her clit, Maggie cried out. Then, his

fangs sank into her breast, and she nearly screamed as he drew her blood from her. Her back bowed at the same time her body came apart and waves of pleasure crashed through her.

Aiden growled against her breast when her orgasm caused the muscles of her sheath to clench around his cock, pushing him closer to spilling his seed. Her blood sliding down his throat extinguished the flames torching his veins as he greedily consumed it.

Small tremors still racked her when Maggie jerked her wrists against his hold again. "Let me go."

No matter what their relationship became now, she refused to be like the other women he'd been with before her. Aiden hesitated long enough she feared they wouldn't be able to get back what they'd had. Then his grip eased, and he let her go. Maggie's hands fell to his shoulders before cradling his head to her breast.

She nuzzled his temple and forehead as his body enveloped hers. His fangs retracted from her chest, and his hand entangled in her hair as he pulled her head back to gaze at her. More of the color had faded from his flesh, but she'd hoped to see his beautiful leaf-green eyes again; they remained red.

Aiden held her gaze as he continued to thrust into her. When he drove into her again, his body tensed and he came with a low groan. His head fell into the hollow of her shoulder, and he inhaled his scent on her skin as he ran his tongue over her collarbone. He felt more in control, but being inside her and feeding on her hadn't been enough to calm him completely.

"Maggie," he whispered hoarsely.

She ran her hands over his body, hoping to soothe him further, but the color was creeping back into areas where it had already faded. She'd expected him to be more relaxed now, or at least be able to talk with her. Instead, he seemed to be spiraling away again. "Aiden, what is it?"

"It's been too long. I can't control myself; it's too late."

"No." She clasped his cheeks and pulled his head out of her shoulder so she could look at him. "No, it is *not*."

"I need the bond to be completed, Maggie. I have to change you."

"Then do it. I didn't come here thinking I would walk away still human. I didn't go to the hotel that day thinking I wouldn't one day become a vampire."

"You went to the hotel?"

"Yes. So many things went wrong that day. We can discuss it later. Right now, all that matters is we're together again, and I want to be with you."

He drew her close to kiss her forehead. Tenuous at best, his control was good enough for him to know he couldn't change her here. It was bad enough he'd taken her in this foul place; he wouldn't change her here too.

"I will not allow it to happen here." Lifting her off him, he set her on the ground and brushed her hair back from her face. Clasping her cheeks, he kissed her tenderly.

"Are you stable enough for it to happen somewhere else?"

"Yes. Get dressed."

Normally, she would have bristled over his clipped command, but she knew it was because he was having a difficult time restraining himself.

Aiden watched Maggie reclaim her jeans and sneakers. The torn sweater flapped around her as she worked. He couldn't tear his gaze away from her. After so much time without her, it was difficult for him to believe she was real. He was terrified she'd vanish if he looked away and he would wake to find this had all been a dream.

When she finished dressing and stepped close to him, he

pulled her tattered sweater together to shield her from the others. He didn't care about his nudity, but he didn't want her exposed to those beyond this door. She clasped the pieces together as he swung her into his arms and held her against his chest. Resting her head on his shoulder, she kissed his neck.

"I can't believe you're here," he said.

"Believe it."

"I'm completely in love with you, Magdalene Doe."

She blinked back her tears. "I'm in love with you too, Aiden Byrne. Also, my name is Magdalene *Shea*."

"What?"

She smiled against his throat. "Something else we can discuss later, but I found my grandmother. I have a grandma."

Aiden held her closer when he heard the happiness in her voice. "I can't wait to meet her."

Lifting his hand, he banged on the door. The others had gone quiet, but he knew they were still out there. "Let us out," he commanded.

There was a minute of silence, then Vicky called out, "Maggie?"

"I'm all right, but I'd really like to get out of here."

After another hesitation, the key turned in the lock and the door swung inward to reveal the others. Aiden's lips skimmed back when he spotted Ethan. He forced his gaze away from Ethan before he put Maggie down and attacked his brother to ease some of his pent-up bloodlust.

Vicky and Abby stood next to each other, wearing identical looks of concern as they kept their gazes focused on Maggie. Brian positioned himself protectively in front of Abby; his red eyes warned Aiden to stay away from her. Saxon leaned against a wall with his arms over his chest, but despite his casual posture, Aiden knew Saxon was prepared to take him down.

"Your skin—" Vicky started.

"I'm handling it," he grated from between his teeth as Maggie rubbed his neck. "I need blood and somewhere we can be alone."

"There's a cottage out back. The guards used it for breaks and naps. We've been crashing there," Saxon replied as he walked over to unlock the back door. "There are blood bags in the fridge and extra clothes in the bedroom closet."

"Good. Don't bother us," Aiden said.

CHAPTER FORTY-NINE

THE WHITE COTTAGE was cute and old. The black shutters on the front sagged on their hinges and the lopsided slant of the windows made Maggie smile. The door creaked when Aiden swung it open before ducking to carry her through the doorway. In the murky radiance of the moon spilling through the windows, Maggie saw a sofa and a chair in the living room before Aiden carried her through a small dining room and into a kitchen that made her kitchen look huge.

With reluctance, Aiden set her down. He walked over, opened the fridge, and removed one of the blood bags to drink it. After Maggie's blood, the taste was bitter on his lips, but he consumed it all.

"How exactly does this work?" Maggie asked. "I know you said before, if I lost enough blood and was given the blood of a vampire, I'd change. Is that it?"

Aiden finished the blood, wiped his mouth, and tossed the bag into the trash. "I have to drain you to the point where you would never survive the loss before giving you my blood," he said.

He risked glancing at her to see how she would react to his words. He'd expected to see terror on her face; there was none.

"And then I'll become a vampire?" she asked.

"Yes," he said and drank another bag of blood.

"Is the transition painful?"

"I'm told it's excruciating, but the pain fades quickly. Pathways will open between our minds during the exchange, and once the bond is complete, we'll be able to communicate mentally."

"No more misunderstandings," she said with a smile.

"No more misunderstandings."

"If you're going to take my blood, then why are you drinking so much now?" Maggie perched on the edge of the table and kicked off her sneakers as she watched him.

"This blood isn't for me," he said and threw another bag away. "To complete the transition, a newly turned vampire has to feed soon after. I'm drinking this so you can feed on me. If you choose, after you turn, you'll only ever have to feed on me to survive."

Maggie's clothes suddenly felt too confining as his words caused her skin to tingle and her body to quicken with desire. She licked her lips in anticipation of feeding on him again.

Aiden's head turned slowly toward her; his nostrils flared as the scent of her arousal hit him. Maggie slid off the table, unbuttoned her jeans and tugged them off with her underwear. She removed the remains of her sweater before unclasping her bra and tossing it aside to stand before him with her nipples thrusting proudly forward.

Closing the door on the fridge, Aiden's dick stiffened as he stalked toward her. Then his gaze fell on the white gauze covering her arms from her wrists to her armpits. A red haze clouded his vision when he saw the pink of her blood staining those bandages.

"What the fuck happened?" he demanded as he tenderly clasped her wrists and drew them forward to inspect her arms. Carefully, he unraveled a bandage to reveal her raw flesh before removing the other to reveal the same torn flesh. "Who did this to you?"

His fangs slurred his words, and his hands shook as they held her.

"I did it," Maggie said.

"Why?" Aiden demanded.

"Ever since we've parted, my skin has felt too tight or like it's *wrong* somehow. I don't know how to explain it."

"You're part vampire," he murmured. "Your body craved mine."

"It still does," she replied with a sultry smile.

Lifting her, he set her on the table and drew her hips toward the edge before spreading her legs apart and stepping between them.

"I'm going to cherish you every one of our days together," he murmured as he sank into her.

"I have no doubt," she sighed as she turned her head to offer him her vein. He didn't refuse it.

Every muscle in her body ached, her bones felt like someone had taken a sledgehammer to them, but the discomfort was receding. Maggie blinked as she woke from the agony comprising her world for what seemed like forever, but she suspected it might be the same night.

She remembered being with Aiden in the kitchen, remembered the feeling of him inside her as he drank from her and the intensity of the orgasm rocking her even as her body weakened. He'd pressed his bleeding wrist to her mouth afterward and carried her in here to place her on the bed while she consumed his blood.

Fresh hunger surged through her as she recalled the delicious taste of it. Once, as a child, she'd gone to a fair and eaten cotton candy and fried dough. It was the first and only times she'd ever had either, but she still recalled how delicious they'd been. Aiden's blood was better than both those things combined.

Her stomach rumbled as her gums tingled. Curious, Maggie prodded a canine with her tongue and jerked when it lengthened into a fang. Then, she prodded it again and almost laughed when the fang extended further. She'd never experienced such a thing before, yet somehow, it felt right.

Aiden's hand rested on her shoulder. Rolling over, she discovered him lying beside her on the bed, his head propped on his hand as he stared at her. Uneasiness etched his face and radiated from his ruby-colored eyes. Against the white of the sheets and bedspread, the black and red hue of his skin was starkly pronounced. The colors had deepened and once more covered his entire body. If she hadn't woken, if something had gone wrong with her change, the rampage he would have gone on would have made King Kong cower.

"Maggie," he breathed.

"That's me," she murmured and smiled at him.

Rising, she ignored the twinges in her body as she kissed him. She rested her hands on his chest and pushed him back on the bed to straddle his waist. Particles of air caressed her flesh, and she realized her body felt electrified in a way she'd never experienced before.

She'd touched him often since meeting him, yet she felt like this was the first time she'd truly *experienced* him as her fingers memorized his muscles. The clove scent of his blood was different, sweeter somehow, and she realized it was because of her blood within him. His blood must have altered her scent too.

Her fangs retracted when she bent to lick the salty flesh of his chest. Hardening against her, his shaft brushed her belly and then her breasts while she worked her way down to his stomach. Her tongue dipped into his belly button as his hand ran over her hair.

When she traveled lower, her nipples brushed over his cock before her hand encircled it. She ran her tongue over the head of his shaft as she took him into her mouth. She licked and sucked him as he guided her over him with a hand on the back of her head. A thrill of power went through her when his hips rose and fell in rhythm to her motions.

Releasing him, she made her way back up his body. Grasping his shaft, she guided it inside her and moaned as every cell in her body came alive in a way she'd never experienced. It was as if her cells lacked something before, but now they were full and letting her experience all the things she'd missed.

"Oh," she breathed when she felt the pulse of blood in Aiden's cock as she rode him.

Aiden ravenously watched as Maggie's head fell back and her body arched forward. He'd never seen anything so glorious as her as she ran her hands between her breasts and cried out when she caressed her pert nipples.

"It's all so...." Her gaze fell on him, and a flash of red ran through her eyes.

Aiden growled with his need to complete their bond and have her drink his blood. Her smile revealed her fangs as she lowered herself toward him. "It's all so what?" he demanded.

"So *right*," she whispered and ran her tongue over his throat.

His fingers tore into the sheets when her fangs scraped his skin. "You have to feed."

"Will I hurt you?" she inquired.

"No. You'll know what to do."

"I hope so."

When her fangs pierced his skin, Aiden jerked and shredded the sheets in his grasp. He released the tattered remains to clutch the back of her head when he felt his blood leaving his body. It was the first time another vampire had ever fed from him, and it was *Maggie*.

Wrapping his other arm around her waist, he rolled to pin her beneath him. Her fingers dug into his back when he sank his fangs into her shoulder.

Tears of joy spilled down Maggie's cheeks as something mystical strengthened between them until it bound them together. Thoughts and emotions tumbled so rapidly through her mind that it took her some time to realize they weren't just hers, but also Aiden's. He was a part of her, and she was a part of him.

She clung to him as his blood filled and sated her for the first time in her life. She'd never realized how starved for blood she'd been, until now.

Aiden cradled her head as the pathway between them opened, and her mind mingled with his. *Complete.* The anger, emptiness, and misery he'd battled receded as the peace Maggie gave him returned. He retracted his fangs as she continued to feed on him, her happiness swelling and growing within him.

Releasing her bite, Maggie grinned when she opened her eyes to meet Aiden's leaf-green ones. She'd worried she'd never see their beautiful spring hue again, but there it was. The colors were also fading from his flesh as he regained control. He was back, and he was *hers*.

When she ran her hands over his back, she was so lost in the new sensations, that she didn't at first realize something was different about him. When she did, she had to touch him a few more times to make sure. "Aiden, your scars; I think they're gone."

"That's because you've healed me," he said as he kissed her again.

CHAPTER FIFTY

"I was preparing to leave my apartment at twelve to meet you that day," Maggie said as she gazed at the woods fifty feet away from the back patio. The leaf buds on the trees were no bigger than a dot but clearly visible to her. However, she never would have seen them yesterday. She inhaled the warm air redolent with the ripe smell of the frost melting from the dirt. It was the first day that felt like spring as the sun warmed the earth and her.

They'd decided they would have to get dressed and out of bed if they were going to get any talking done today. It had taken almost a day for them to reluctantly separate and dig some clothes out of the closet. Thankfully, though she knew some of the others were still around—she could *hear* and *smell* them—they had left the two of them alone.

"Amazing," she murmured as a breeze stirred the branches. "I can see and hear so much now. There are scents I can't describe."

"It will take some getting used to," Aiden said and placed his hand over hers. "But you'll get there."

She smiled as she turned her hand over to squeeze his. The wicker chair she sat in faced his. "I have no doubt."

"So you were preparing to leave at twelve," he prompted.

"Oh, yes," she said as she recalled what they'd been talking about. "Anyway, I was leaving at twelve. I knew I'd be early, but I couldn't wait anymore."

"I was already there."

That didn't surprise her. "This bond, I feel it now, and it is so strong; how did you ever let me go?"

"Because I love you too much to cage you if you preferred to be free of me. You had to make your own choices and be happy, even if what made you happy wasn't me."

"But it is you, it always has been! You knew, when you let me go, there was a possibility you might lose control if I didn't come back?"

"Yes."

Maggie believed she'd loved him before, but now her love for him grew stronger. He'd sacrificed himself for her, and she had no doubt he would do it again.

"Ethan told me a mate cannot live without the other."

"True," he said. "Which is another reason I let you go. If I wasn't what you wanted, I wasn't going to force you to tie your existence to me."

"You are what I want, you always have been. I needed time to figure that out because I was afraid of losing everything I've worked for. I grew up with nothing, Aiden, to risk it all terrified me."

"I know, but I promise you, Maggie, I *will* give you a future filled with love and security."

"I believe you," she said. "That's why I was planning to go to the hotel. I was about to walk out the door when my boss, Pablo, called me."

Maggie turned her head away from him, and he felt her sorrow through their bond.

"Did Pablo make you go to work that day?" he asked.

"No." She took a deep breath and turned to face him. "Roger had a stroke. He was in the hospital. I tried to call you as I was running down the stairs to the T, but someone bumped me and I dropped my phone. It broke."

Aiden went completely still as tears shimmered in her eyes. A sick feeling formed in the pit of his stomach while he watched her.

"I meant to call you a couple of times from the hospital, but I kept getting distracted. Then, the doctor came out to tell us that Roger didn't survive."

He knew how much Roger had meant to her, how much she cared for the man, and Roger for her. She'd had so few people she loved in her life and who loved her. She'd lost another, and he hadn't been there for her when he should have been. "Maggie, I'm so sorry."

She pulled her hand away from his to wipe the tears from her face. "I called you from outside the hospital and left a voice mail, but you never picked up, and you never called back."

Aiden closed his eyes as the sick feeling grew to become a tsunami of self-loathing. "I broke my phone," he admitted.

"Ethan told me. He also told me you saw me hug someone, that was Pablo. He gave me a ride home from the hospital. He hugged me because he's my friend, he was Roger's friend, and—"

"Don't," Aiden said and reclaimed her hand. "Pablo is your friend. I understand. I couldn't understand it that day because I'd already slipped too far away to think about anything reasonably."

"You should have told me what became of a mated vampire without their mate."

"No, I shouldn't have. You had to return to me because it was what you wanted and not because you felt guilted into it."

Maggie sighed, she wanted to argue with him further about it, but he was right. She'd needed the time to work through her life and how she felt for him. If he'd told her, she would have resented feeling pressured.

"Thank you for that," she murmured and kissed him briefly. If she kissed him for any longer than a second or two, they would end up back in bed. No matter how tempting that was, they had to sort all this out.

"Once I felt emotionally stable enough to leave my place, I went to the hotel," she said. "The bartender told me you'd left, but I sat and waited, hoping you'd come back. When you didn't, I went home and waited for you to come, but you never did."

"They knocked me out and brought me here that night," Aiden said. "I probably would have killed someone if they hadn't. I was an idiot and lost control; it shouldn't have happened."

"You never hid from me that you were walking a tightrope. That one misstep could push you over the edge."

"It still *never* should have happened. I hurt you when I didn't come for you."

"You did, and I hurt you too, but neither of us meant to do it. Things went so wrong that day."

"They did," he agreed. He grasped her wrists and pulled her arms toward him. His blood and her transition had healed her scratches, but he still recalled the ugly red gouges on her skin. "I let you down. It *won't* happen again."

"It's not like I don't know you can be a bit of an ass, Nosferatu," she teased as she took her wrists from him and rested her hand on his freshly shaven cheek. She'd missed seeing his face. "Do you think you could still lose control? Do you still crave blood, death, sex, and pain as badly as you did?"

She held her breath, petrified of his answer. She could feel the intensity of the bond between them, but what if she wasn't enough for him? What if what she'd seen from him yesterday was only the beginning and it was only a matter of time before she lost him?

"No," he said and reached across to pull her into his lap. "Like the scars on my back, our bond has healed me. It's curbed my more malevolent nature and tamed the demon part of me. However, I will destroy anything threatening you or those I love, but I won't slip into that madness again, and I no longer worry about losing control and becoming a Savage, not with you in my life."

Maggie curled up in his arms and rested her head on his chest. "Good."

"I'm going to quit working with Ronan and the others."

She lifted her head to gawk at him. "That's what you've been training for, why would you give it up?"

"I did it to keep myself in control. I *needed* the blood, death, and violence to remain stable; I don't anymore."

"Aiden—"

"I'll still help them whenever it's necessary. There is a big battle looming on the horizon between Savages and vampires. I won't turn my back on it, but I don't want you to be a part of this life."

"I can handle it."

"I know you can, but for now, I want to be with my family and *you*. Those things are my focus. I want time to enjoy our relationship. I've also shut my family out a lot recently. It's time I go home."

"And afterward?"

"We'll decide our future together. If we decide I should

return to working with Ronan and the others, so be it. If not, then we'll figure out our next step."

"Okay, but I don't want you thinking you *have* to give it up for me."

"I don't," he said, and she felt the truth of that through their bond. "I don't think we should be gone for long though; I'm concerned about Vicky."

"Why?"

"She pretends everything is okay, but it's not."

"We'll be here for her," Maggie said decisively. "I'd still like to run the marathon."

"You're going to cheat the humans?" he teased, and she laughed.

"I'll hold myself back, but I can't let my coworkers down. The race is next week. Will I be able to be around people by then?"

"You should be fine, and if you run into any trouble, I'll be there to get you through it."

He recalled the baseball tickets he'd bought for her, but he didn't bring them up. If the date hadn't passed already—he wasn't sure what day it was now—the game would be soon, and he didn't think she would be up for that. There was no reason to disappoint her over something he couldn't change. He would take her to lots of other games this year.

"So, are you going to tell me about Grandma?" he asked.

The smile that lit her face warmed his heart.

"She's wonderful," Maggie breathed and explained to him how she'd discovered Marsha, their meeting, and everything else that occurred since they'd last seen each other.

They talked for over an hour before footsteps drew Aiden's attention away from her. He looked over his shoulder to find the others standing in the doorway leading to the kitchen of the cottage.

"We heard you talking and hoped you were up for some company," Abby said.

He was enjoying this time alone with Maggie, but the hope in Abby's eyes kept him from turning her away.

"Of course," Maggie said as she sat up in his arms.

They filtered onto the patio, spreading out around it.

"Watch out for the stake," Vicky said to Maggie and winked as she handed her coat back to her.

Maggie laughed and settled the coat on her lap. "Thank you."

Vicky and Abby settled onto the other two chairs. Brian rested his hands on the back of Abby's chair while Stefan leaned against the corner of the house. Saxon walked to the edge of the patio to survey the woods before turning to Aiden. Ethan remained in the doorway.

"I assume you told Ronan those cells and chains won't hold a purebred," Aiden said to Saxon.

"I did," Saxon replied. "He's going to work on modifying them, but it's difficult to judge how strong a purebred can get, especially if someone threatens their mate."

"I wasn't threatened," Maggie protested.

"At that moment, in Aiden's mind, you were," Saxon replied.

"Yes," Aiden agreed as he recalled the strength of his fury and the colossal power thrumming through his body when he'd given himself over to the demon seeking to rule him. He'd never experienced anything like that before, and he hoped never to feel it again. If he did, it meant there might be a genuine threat to Maggie's life.

Aiden met Ethan's eyes over Maggie's head. "I have to speak with my brother," he said as he kissed Maggie's temple.

"Aiden—"

"It will be okay," he murmured.

"Just remember, I wouldn't be here if it wasn't for him," she whispered in his ear before rising from his arms.

Aiden stood and started toward the doorway. Ethan strode ahead of him through the rooms and out the front door of the small cottage. Stepping outside, Aiden's jaw clenched when he spotted the single story, concrete building where he'd been imprisoned. He'd been in there once before his confinement, when he'd helped to interrogate the Savage who told them about Carha. He hoped to never see the place again.

He couldn't fault the others for what they'd done, he would have done the same, or he would have destroyed the vampire, but he *loathed* seeing the reminder of what he'd become. He clearly recalled the madness whispering incessantly through his mind.

He'd let everyone down, especially Maggie, and he would do everything he could to make it up to her. Every day for the rest of their lives together, she would know only security and love.

"You shouldn't have gone to her," Aiden said. "I don't remember a lot of what happened, but I know I made it clear to the others she was to be left alone."

"They told me you wanted her left alone, and I didn't go to her until it became clear she might be the only one who could save you. I was right."

Aiden gritted his teeth when he recognized the older, wiser brother tone that sometimes crept into Ethan's voice. It didn't happen often, but it was there now. Ethan was older, possibly wiser, but he had to know he wouldn't win a fight between the two of them, not anymore. Ethan had the advantage of age on him, but Aiden had spent countless hours training to kill with some of the most lethal vampires on the planet. He'd also been killing and occasionally feeding on Savages. He'd honed himself into a killing machine; Ethan had become a dad.

"If I hadn't gone to her, you would have died. *We* would have had to kill you or make the decision to have someone else do it," Ethan said.

"I know, but—"

"She was in pain too. I saw the bandages and her blood. I know what her heritage is, and though she didn't know why she couldn't stop hurting herself, the vampire part of her was suffering without you."

Aiden couldn't stop himself from wincing at the reminder of Maggie's physical and emotional pain. "You still shouldn't have gone to her. What happened that day was a *big* misunderstanding, but what if she really had chosen someone else over me?"

"Then I would have left her alone, but she needed to know."

Aiden rounded on him. "You still went against what I instructed with *my* mate."

"Yes, but what would you have done if I was the one rotting in a cage with only death as my ultimate end? Would you have stood by and watched me spiral further into madness if there was a chance you could prevent it?"

Aiden studied his older brother as he pondered this, but he knew the answer. He wanted to choke Ethan, to brawl with him as they'd done when they were younger, but he would only be fighting a choice he would have made himself.

"No," he admitted. "I would have gone to Emma too."

"I didn't do it because I thought you were wrong and I knew best." Ethan smiled when Aiden glanced sharply at him. "I know that's what you're thinking. I did it because I love you and I couldn't stand by and watch you die without a fight. I would have left Maggie alone if she'd told me to get out of her place, that she was with another and wanted nothing to do with you. I swear I would have. She didn't say that though, and listening to her, I knew she loved you too."

"What if I'd killed her or forced the change on her when you brought her here?"

"If you do recall, I was trying to get her out of there to prevent that from happening when you tore your cell apart. I've felt the rage that takes over when someone threatens a mate; I know we can push the boundaries of the rules placed on us, but I never saw that coming. I also didn't realize how fast she was and that she would be able to dodge me to get at you."

"She's been training for the Boston Marathon, and her father was a vampire."

"I know, but I still underestimated her; it won't happen again. She wanted you almost as badly as you wanted her. She saw what you did to that cell and still trusted you not to hurt her. Even with you as out of control as you were, I also believed you wouldn't hurt her."

"I'm glad one of us did," Aiden muttered as he gazed at the back wall of the prison.

"It was bad for you after you reached maturity, far worse than you let on, wasn't it?"

"Yes."

"What did you crave the most?"

Aiden released a snort of humorless laughter. "What didn't I crave? I wanted blood, pain, death, and sex all the same." Aiden's jaw clenched as he recalled the compulsions that had ruled him every day for years. When he felt his temper rising, he searched out Maggie's mind with his. The brief touch with her calmed him again.

"Apparently, according to Declan, it happens to some," he murmured and then realized Declan wasn't with them. "Where is Declan? He was in the car with us."

"Saxon said he couldn't be here. I don't know why."

"He couldn't handle being so close to a vampire without their mate."

"If you say so," Ethan replied.

"I should punch you."

"You should, but you won't. You owe me one."

"Hmm," Aiden grunted.

"Your mate is a feisty one. She didn't care I was a purebred vampire standing in her apartment."

"She invited you in?"

"She did."

"She shut the door in my face."

Ethan laughed and grasped his shoulder. "I like her."

"Good, because she's family now."

"She is," Ethan agreed.

CHAPTER FIFTY-ONE

MAGGIE STOOD IN THE SHADOWS, unwilling to go any closer as her grandma cautiously approached Mindy's chair. Aiden stood behind her, his hand on her shoulder. Marsha pulled a chair over from a table and sat across from her daughter.

For a minute, no one spoke. Then, Marsha leaned closer and rested her hand on Mindy's knee. "Mindy," she whispered.

Standing more than fifty feet away, outside the door of the large room with the TV droning, conversations carrying on, and almost two dozen other patients gathered within, Maggie heard her grandmother.

"Mindy, do you remember me?" Marsha asked.

Mindy's eyes shifted to Marsha before sliding away. Then, they came back again. Maggie's heart leapt when she saw the spark of recognition in those eyes. "Momma," Mindy breathed.

Tears spilled down Marsha's cheeks, and she choked on a sob. "Yes, baby girl, it's me."

"Momma," Mindy smiled before her gaze went back to the window.

Mindy didn't speak again, but the smile didn't leave her

face while Marsha sat and talked with her. As Maggie suggested, Marsha didn't tell her daughter how she'd finally discovered her, or mention Maggie at all. It was for the best, especially if it kept that smile on her mother's lips.

~

MAGGIE'S LUNGS BURNED, her legs felt like rubber, but she pushed herself onward. Even with all her training, even with her new, supernatural strength that she'd kept in check throughout the entire course, she *loathed* Heartbreak Hill.

Then, she was at the top and coming down. Air rushed back into her lungs, her legs didn't wobble quite so bad, and some of her ex-coworkers laughed. She exchanged high-fives with them. It didn't matter they still had miles to go. After successfully climbing the hill, they knew they would all make it.

Maggie focused on the road while she matched her pace to those around her. Soon after changing, Aiden noticed she was faster and stronger than the average turned vamp, but not as strong as a purebred.

They'd been on a run together and she'd nearly beaten him. Afterward, he'd had her lift things that other changed vamps wouldn't be able to lift so soon after turning. He'd shouted his joy when she succeeded in one thing after another.

Then, he'd approached Ronan about his decision to pause his training. Ronan hadn't argued with Aiden's choice to walk away, for now, but while they remained in Massachusetts, Ronan asked if he could run her through a series of physical, mental, and endurance tests. All those tests confirmed what Aiden already suspected; she was not the normal, changed vamp, but then she hadn't been the average human either.

The crowds cheered as they reached Kenmore Square. A

fresh burst of adrenaline hit Maggie, and Aiden's mind brushed against hers. It took everything she had to maintain her restraint when they turned onto Boylston street and the finish line came into view. She wanted to unleash her power and race toward that beckoning end.

Crossing over the painted Finish Line section of road, Maggie released a whoop of joy and laughed as she hugged her team members, all of whom were wearing pins to honor the memory of Roger. She was hugging Pablo when she spotted Aiden over his shoulder. She slapped Pablo on his shoulders, and he set her down before turning to hug someone else.

Aiden swung her up into his arms. "How did you get over here?" she inquired breathlessly. Family members and friends were supposed to be waiting for them at a designated meeting area.

"I'm irresistible," he replied and winked at her.

She laughed. "That you are, but from now on, no compelling the police."

"I can't make any promises."

Like the rest of her supernatural abilities, her ability to compel a person was stronger than it should have been, but she hated using it. After the test where she'd used her compulsion on a human, she'd put her foot down and informed Ronan she wouldn't do it again. He'd frowned at her, and she got the feeling he didn't often hear no from anyone, but he hadn't asked her to do it again.

"I'm proud of you," Aiden said.

Setting her down, he walked her over to the others who had come to watch the race. Abby, Brian, and Vicky were at the front of the pack, waving American flags. Ethan and Stefan had returned home before coming back with their mates, Isabelle and Emma. Ian and his wife Paige had arrived last night.

They'd all left their children behind, claiming some much-needed grown-up time, but Maggie had a feeling they wanted a chance to interrogate her without interruption. They'd also all been happy to assure her there were plenty of others eagerly waiting to meet her.

That knowledge wasn't as off-putting to her as it would have been a month ago. She was excited to embrace her new life with Aiden, willing to let down her guard and allow more people and vampires into her life. She was looking forward to finally experiencing a life filled with love and family. She was also relieved to discover that she liked everyone she'd met. They were warm and open and excited to have her in their lives.

"I never realized how much fun this could be!" Vicky gushed. "All the excitement, the competition, the beer! I'm going to have to check out one of those ball games next. I feel like I've been missing out!"

"*You* want to go to a baseball game?" Maggie inquired.

"Oh, I don't care what balls are involved, just as long as I get to cheer for them."

Maggie blinked at her. "I don't know how to respond to that."

"No one does," Aiden muttered, and Vicky laughed.

Maggie grinned when she saw her grandmother pushing her way through the crowd. For the first time in her life, she had a relative at something to cheer for *her*. She hugged Marsha as she fought against crying. Today was not a day for tears. It was a day for celebration.

Later, they would meet up with her teammates to celebrate their success, the money they'd raised, and Roger. Tomorrow, she and Aiden were leaving for New Hampshire where they would spend a week with her grandma before going to Maine to meet the rest of his family.

A month ago, the only family Maggie had was Roger. She missed him every day, but as she gazed around, she realized how much her family had grown in such a short time. Tilting her head back, she grinned at Aiden and leaned against his side.

I love you, Nosferatu, she whispered into his mind.

You're my savior and my love, Magdalene Byrne.

She rose on her toes to kiss him. "Byrne? Are we married then?" she murmured in his ear so no one else could hear her.

"We're more than that, but I'll gladly marry you to make it official."

"Do I get a ring?" she teased.

"Two of them."

She laughed, but when she stepped away from him, she saw how serious he was. She opened her mouth to say more, but he went down to his knee and pulled out a ring box. Lifting the lid, he revealed the beautiful sapphire ring, surrounded by small diamonds, within. Maggie's hand flew to her mouth as she gawked at it.

"Will you marry me?" he asked her.

Tears streamed down her face as she nodded, unable to speak, and the others cheered. Rising, he slid the gorgeous ring on her finger and embraced her. She laughed as he spun her around before setting her down, clasping her face, and kissing her.

That night, they also celebrated their engagement as they stood surrounded by friends and family. Maggie had never dared to dream of having so much love in her life, but then, before she met Aiden, she'd barely known love at all. Even though she wished A.J. and Roger could have been here to see this, she'd never been happier.

Aiden embraced Maggie against his chest while he danced with her in the shadows of the bar. He'd been so certain he'd never find her in time to save himself, but as he held her close, he had no concerns the darkness would call to him again. He couldn't wait to introduce her to the rest of his family.

"Aiden," she murmured.

"Yes?"

"I've decided you aren't the devil, but I'd gladly go through Hell for you."

It took him a second to recall the conversation they'd had in the car when he'd first taken her from her apartment to the hotel.

"You ever hear the saying the devil you know is better than the devil you don't?" she'd asked.

"And I'm the devil?" he'd replied.

"I haven't decided."

"Let me know when you do."

"I will."

He smiled as he kissed her neck. "There's no need for you to do that. You've already rescued me from Hell."

～

Read on for a sneak peek from *Consumed*, Book 8 in the series. Or purchase now and continue reading:
brendakdavies.com/Cnwb

Vicky and Nathan's story is told in *Bound by Vengeance*, The Alliance, Book 2. Find out what happens when Vicky delves deeper into the world of the hunters! It's available now:
brendakdavies.com/BBVwb

～

Visit the Erica Stevens/Brenda K. Davies Book Club on Facebook for exclusive giveaways and all things book related. Come join the fun:
brendakdavies.com/ESBKDBookClub

Stay in touch on updates and new releases from the author by joining the mailing list! Mailing list for Brenda K. Davies Updates:
brendakdavies.com/ESBKDNews

SNEAK PEEK
CONSUMED, VAMPIRE AWAKENINGS BOOK 8

Mike pushed open the door to the small, smoky, dimly lit bar and stepped inside with Doug and Jack following him. The scents of stale alcohol and cigarettes choked the air, but beneath it he scented the nearby ocean and lemon polish. The door closed on the howling wind. It might be early June, but this far north in Canada, the storm rolling off the sea brought colder air with it.

Stomping his feet, Mike clasped his hands and blew into them as he surveyed the vampire bar they'd entered. The small town on the coast of Labrador had a population of only a couple thousand, but it had attracted a fair number of vampires.

Whether that was due to the shorter daylight hours, which attracted Savages, or the fact vampires were fleeing the growing Savage problem in the States, Mike didn't know. Unfortunately, the three of them couldn't detect a Savage by their scent like a pureblood vamp could, so he didn't know if they'd just walked into a room full of killers or not.

He did know most of the patrons were vampires, as like knew like.

"Guess we won't be settling into this area," Jack muttered.

"I don't think they're killers," Doug murmured.

"What makes you say that?" Jack asked.

"The humans are still alive," Mike answered as he surveyed the fifteen vampires and the handful of humans seated amongst the scarred wood tables.

Jack's hazel eyes narrowed on him in annoyance; strands of his light brown hair had fallen into one of his eyes, but he didn't push it away before he huffed out a breath and stalked over to the bar. Doug chuckled while he ran a hand through his short, dark blond hair. His ocean-blue eyes twinkled with amusement as he watched Jack slide onto a barstool and order a beer.

"I take it we're staying for a drink," Doug said.

"I guess we are," Mike replied.

Their boots thudded on the wood floor, and the planks bowed beneath Mike's weight as they strolled over to join Jack. Like Jack, they settled onto stools where they could watch the patrons behind them in the mirror lining the wall behind the bar. Liquor bottles filled the shelves and reflected in the glass, but Mike still had a clear view of the patrons.

The bartender placed a beer in front of Jack before turning wary eyes on them. Mike nodded to her, but her blue eyes revealed no warmth and a smile didn't curve her mouth. Glancing around the bar again, Mike realized most of the occupants had stopped talking and focused on them. He didn't sense hostility from them, but more distrust. Mike didn't blame them for being uneasy; he didn't trust them either.

"What can I get you?" the bartender asked. Her clipped New York accent was out of place in this northern land.

"I'll take a Crown and ginger and an ashtray," Mike said.

"Scotch on the rocks," Doug said.

"You got it." The woman pushed an ashtray toward Mike and turned to fill their order.

Mike pulled out the pack of cigarettes he'd tucked into the inner pocket of his coat. He undid the packaging and tapped one free. It had been a few months since he last smoked, but he'd purchased the pack at the border last week.

Now seemed as good a time as any to light one as most of the patrons held a cigarette or had a pack before them, and he knew well how smokers congregated to talk. *When in Rome.* He removed his silver Zippo from the pocket of his jeans, flipped the top open, and lit the cigarette. He inhaled a drag as the bartender returned with their drinks.

"What brings you to these parts?" she asked, her gaze on Mike.

"We're doing some traveling," he replied, "and exploring the area."

"Planning to move north?"

"Maybe, if we find something we like."

Mike didn't want to move, but with the growing Savage problem, he and his friends weren't taking any chances. After some careful consideration, they'd all decided it would be best if they had a safe place to retreat to if it became necessary.

The past two times they'd moved, they had to search out a property before leaving, but this time they would have one ready and waiting. There were too many children to protect now for them not to have a backup place.

And they sought a property more remote than their compound in Maine. They could have searched online or hired a realtor to help them, but they wanted to keep their trail as small as possible should something go wrong and they were forced to flee. Mike also preferred to see the land, surrounding towns, and the residents instead of relying on Internet searches and real estate agent phone calls.

So far, the three of them had found numerous tracts of land for sale, but they were hoping to find something with houses, or at the very least one home, already on it. Building new houses would take more time than they were willing to spend to get their emergency retreat ready.

Unfortunately, they hadn't found anything that would work yet. Mike wasn't ready to give up. They'd all prefer to stay near the coast, but they might have to forego that or perhaps find a lake or pond. David wouldn't be happy about boating around a pond, but he would have to suck it up.

The bartender leaned closer in such a way that she revealed more of her breasts in her low-cut, black top. He didn't know if she was trying to distract him with her cleavage or if her interest in him had taken a turn toward the sexual.

Either way, he wasn't interested.

Maybe, if it was thirty years ago and he was still in college, or twenty years ago when he'd only been looking for a good time, or ten years ago when boredom propelled him from woman to woman and new thrill to new thrill. But over the past few years, apathy had taken its toll and extended into every area of his life.

At fifty-two, he was too young to be bored with immortality. No, not bored with immortality—bored with the way he'd been living his life. The only problem was, he didn't know how to change it. But this bartender sure wasn't the change he was looking for, he decided as he flicked his ashes and inhaled another drag of his cigarette.

"I might not be able to help you find a place, but I could help you find something else you might like," she purred.

From the corner of his eye, Mike saw Jack roll his eyes, and Doug smirked before sipping his drink.

Unwilling to offend the woman—they might be able to get some useful information out of her about this place and the area—Mike smiled back at her. "What's your name?" he inquired.

He didn't want to lead her on either and felt asking her name was a neutral question.

"LeNae," she replied, and smiled to reveal her white teeth. With her dirty-blonde hair and pale blue eyes, she was pretty and had an alluring figure, but he felt no interest in her.

"Nice to meet you, LeNae. I'm Mike, this is Doug, and that's Jack."

Doug's wholesome face broke into the grin that had disarmed more people over the years than any military truce. LeNae smiled back at him. Jack remained stone-faced before turning his full attention to his beer, finishing it off, and pushing the bottle across the bar toward her.

"Would you like another?" LeNae asked.

"Yes," Jack replied, and leaning back on his stool, he turned to survey the occupants of the bar.

Most of the customers had gone back to drinking, but a few still watched them. Mike braced himself as he waited for Jack to say something to annoy someone, it was what he did after all, but he turned back around.

LeNae returned with his beer and set it before him.

"How long have you lived here?" Jack asked her.

"A few months," she replied.

"Why did you come here?"

"The same reason most everyone else in this place did."

"Which is?"

"Things are getting a little ugly down south, and we all know it." Her gaze traveled over them. "Isn't that what brought you here too?"

"It is," Doug said, "but it's a little strange to see so many vamps in such a remote location."

The bracelets on LeNae's wrist jangled when she set her

hand on the bar. "Remote might be the only thing keeping us all alive and out of harm's way... until that doesn't work anymore."

Mike hoped she was wrong and the problem with the Savages would soon be handled, but he wasn't willing to take any chances either, and neither was the rest of his family.

"Everyone in this bar is okay?" he asked her.

"Depends on your definition of okay, but no one is a killer, and we don't tolerate them here either." LeNae gave each of them a pointed look.

Mike stubbed out his cigarette before raising his hands; Doug gave her his winning smile again, and Jack drank his beer.

"I wouldn't either," Mike assured her.

"None of us would," Doug said.

LeNae's attention shifted to Doug. Mike didn't mind; he'd met his fair share of fickle women over the years, and she'd have better luck with Doug anyway. Doug wasn't burned-out like he was or as cynical as Jack.

His burn-out wasn't helped by the fact two of his best friends, and an increasing number of what he considered his nieces and nephews, had met their mates, fallen in love, and settled down. Watching how happy they all were with each other, Mike sometimes found himself longing for someone he could spend an eternity with too.

He cursed himself for being an idiot. He would either find his mate one day or he wouldn't, but getting bogged down by his desire for it to happen wouldn't help anyone, especially not him. Besides, he could always discover his mate only to have her reject him and ruin his life. In that case, single was the far better option.

~

Download *Consumed* and continue reading:
brendakdavies.com/Cnwb

**Stay in touch on updates, sales, and new releases
by joining to the mailing list:**
brendakdavies.com/ESBKDNews

**Visit the Erica Stevens/Brenda K. Davies Book
Club on Facebook for exclusive giveaways and all
things book related. Come join the fun**:
brendakdavies.com/ESBKDBookClub

FIND THE AUTHOR

Brenda K. Davies Mailing List:
brendakdavies.com/News

Facebook: brendakdavies.com/BKDfb

Brenda K. Davies Book Club:
brendakdavies.com/BKDBooks

Instagram: brendakdavies.com/BKDInsta
Twitter: brendakdavies.com/BKDTweet
Website: www.brendakdavies.com

Books written under the pen name
Brenda K. Davies

The Vampire Awakenings Series
Awakened (Book 1)

Destined (Book 2)

Untamed (Book 3)

Enraptured (Book 4)

Undone (Book 5)

Fractured (Book 6)

Ravaged (Book 7)

Consumed (Book 8)

Unforeseen (Book 9)

Forsaken (Book 10)

Relentless (Book 11)

Legacy (Book 12)

The Alliance Series
Eternally Bound (Book 1)

Bound by Vengeance (Book 2)

Bound by Darkness (Book 3)

Bound by Passion (Book 4)

Bound by Torment (Book 5)

Bound by Danger (Book 6)

Bound by Deception (Book 7)

Bound by Fate (Book 8)

Bound by Blood (Book 9)

Bound by Love (Book 10)

The Road to Hell Series

Good Intentions (Book 1)

Carved (Book 2)

The Road (Book 3)

Into Hell (Book 4)

Hell on Earth Series

Hell on Earth (Book 1)

Into the Abyss (Book 2)

Kiss of Death (Book 3)

Edge of the Darkness (Book 4)

The Shadow Realms

Shadows of Fire (Book 1)

Shadows of Discovery (Book 2)

Shadows of Betrayal (Book 3)

Shadows of Fury (Book 4)

Shadows of Destiny (Book 5)

Shadows of Light (Book 6)

Wicked Curses (Book 7)

Sinful Curses (Book 8)

Gilded Curses (Book 9)

Whispers of Ruin (Book 10)

Secrets of Ruin (Book 11)

Tempest of Shadows

A Tempest of Shadows (Book 1)

A Tempest of Thieves (Book 2)

A Tempest of Revelations (Book 3)

Coming Winter 2024/2025

Historical Romance

A Stolen Heart

Books written under the pen name

Erica Stevens

The Coven Series

Nightmares (Book 1)

The Maze (Book 2)

Dream Walker (Book 3)

The Captive Series

Captured (Book 1)

Renegade (Book 2)

Refugee (Book 3)

Salvation (Book 4)

Redemption (Book 5)

Vengeance (Book 6)

Unbound (Book 7)

Broken (Book 8 - Prequel)

The Kindred Series

Kindred (Book 1)

Ashes (Book 2)

Kindled (Book 3)

Inferno (Book 4)

Phoenix Rising (Book 5)

The Fire & Ice Series

Frost Burn (Book 1)

Arctic Fire (Book 2)

Scorched Ice (Book 3)

The Ravening Series

The Ravening (Book 1)

Taken Over (Book 2)

Reclamation (Book 3)

The Survivor Chronicles

The Upheaval (Book 1)

The Divide (Book 2)

The Forsaken (Book 3)

The Risen (Book 4)

ABOUT THE AUTHOR

Brenda K. Davies is the USA Today Bestselling author of the Vampire Awakening Series, Alliance Series, Road to Hell Series, Hell on Earth Series, The Shadow Realms Series, A Tempest of Shadows Series, and historical romantic fiction. She also writes under the pen name, Erica Stevens. When not out with friends and family, she can be found at home with her husband, son, and pets.